Jules Festu

Practical Lessons on the Comparative Construction of the Verb in the French and English Languages

SALZWASSER
VERLAG

Jules Festu

Practical Lessons on the Comparative Construction of the Verb in the French and English Languages

Reprint of the original, first published in 1863.

1st Edition 2022 | ISBN: 978-3-37500-159-9

Verlag (Publisher): Salzwasser Verlag GmbH, Zeilweg 44, 60439 Frankfurt, Deutschland
Vertretungsberechtigt (Authorized to represent): E. Roepke, Zeilweg 44, 60439 Frankfurt, Deutschland
Druck (Print): Books on Demand GmbH, In de Tarpen 42, 22848 Norderstedt, Deutschland

PRACTICAL LESSONS

ON THE

COMPARATIVE CONSTRUCTION OF THE VERB.

PRACTICAL LESSONS

ON THE

COMPARATIVE CONSTRUCTION OF THE VERB

IN THE

FRENCH AND ENGLISH LANGUAGES.

BY

JULES FESTU

LONDON

1863.

PREFACE.

SINCE the introduction of Competitive Examinations, and the adoption of Free Trade on the Continent, the teaching of French, in these countries, has been making rapid strides in the right direction. The old classic system, by translation from the French, no longer preponderates to the same extent, and translating from English into French now begins to take the lead, and will sooner or later predominate. Everybody learning French would like to speak and write it. This desideratum has been so strongly felt in England, that in the leading public schools, not only one, but two and sometimes three French masters are to be found. Materials for translating English into French have been published, but no book which could initiate the student into the Construction of French, as compared with English, has as yet been brought out. Our grammars, excellent though they may be, fall short of what is now required. The transition from their exercises to regular composition is not gradual enough, because their Syntax only treats of the Concord instead of the Construction. Now, Syntax is one thing and Construction another. The one simply teaches the concordance of words in their various accidents; whereas, Construction shows how to shape, build, and cement those words together in the rendering of our thoughts. The present book, therefore, is not intended to supersede any Grammar, but to occupy the intermediate ground between Grammar and Composition, treating especially on the Construction. To proceed from the known to the unknown,—to teach progressively,—to show how to express the reciprocal peculiarities of both languages, and to elucidate the comparative structure belonging to the genius of each,—has been the constant aim of the Author; his deep conviction being, that such process is the surest and most effectual way of becoming master of the idiom the student desires to learn. If a Frenchman wants to learn English, let him turn French into English; if an Englishman wants to learn French, let him turn English into French.

The first difficulties an English student has to overcome are difficulties of his own, *i.e.*, how to render the structure and the deficiencies of his own tongue intelligibly into another language, and then how to convey his thoughts in the ways and forms of the foreign idiom. If he has not been taught it, how can he possibly be expected to render the following sentences and the like:—*She* RECEIVED *company once a week. She* RECEIVED *a blow on her temple. She* RECEIVED *me very coolly. As soon as she* RECEIVED *the letter, she unsealed it. She said that, from the information she* RECEIVED, *she did such a thing.* Examples in which we see the word RECEIVED capable of being translated by *recevait, reçut, a reçu, eut reçu, avait reçu,* according to the usage of the Tenses in the French Language.

If he has to express his English Participial Construction, which may correspond to any Tense of our Verb, or be rendered by Nouns or Infinitives, is he, with Grammarians of considerable ability, to appeal to Cobbett's opinion, who will tell him, "The Present Participle is of much more frequent use in English than in French. Nothing can more characterize the two languages. Not the least resemblance is there between them in this respect." As if Cobbett, who shirked the point at issue, could possibly be an authority as to the proper rendering of the English Participial Construction into French!

Difficulties exist in every language, and they must be faced, and faced boldly. Conjurors, with methods, systems, and panaceas, like "French without a Master," "French in Six Months," &c., daily profess to remove these difficulties. But these devices, intended to gull the uneducated as by magic, are mere quackeries. They appear and disappear, succeed and supersede one another, with a rapidity which sufficiently bears testimony to their inefficiency; and this because they are not the living, the spoken, and classic forms of the language, but strings of *Avez-vous*, jumbled and tagged together. They bewilder the understanding, but do not store it with ideas—contracting the mind instead of expanding it. But what else could be expected from books which drone into a student's head sentences like the following: *Have you the horse which I have? No: I have not the horse which you have, but I have the horse which your sister has.* And yet this is the kind of logic which is heard daily repeated in many of our schools,—the kind of French too frequently taught in these countries.

The illustrations of the rules of the book now offered to the public have been taken from our best classics; and, throughout the exercises, the examples, though of a familiar yet not of a trite parlance, are the purest forms of the conversational language. The colloquial idiom has been preferred to the rhetorical and studied language of composition, it being of far greater importance to foreigners for the common purposes of life.

The Author hopes that the performance may prove useful. During the long and toilsome time of its compilation, he has had no other object in view than to elevate the teaching of the French language. If ability has failed him, and if his expectations should be frustrated, the book, if not the best that could be written, still claims to be the only one that has yet appeared on the Comparative Construction of English and French. He has opened a new way—a broader way;—let men of greater power smooth and level it, for it is the only one which will effectually lead the student to a knowledge of French.

3, Clarence Place,
Dec., 1863.

CONTENTS.

LISTE

DES AUTEURS ET DES OUVRAGES CONSULTÉS ET CITÉS.

ACADÉMIE.—Son Dictionnaire.

ARNOLD'S First French Book.

AUVRAY.—La Clef des Participes.

BOISTE.—Principes de Grammaire.

BURNOUF.—Grammaire Latine.

CHARENTE'S French Course.

COBBETT.—Le Maître d'Anglais.

CONTANSEAU.—Practical Dictionary. French Grammar.

CULLEN.—L'Anglais Parlé.

D'AMBLY.—Grammaire Française.

DARBOIS.—Dictionnaire des Dictionnaires.

DES CARRIÈRES.—French Grammar.

DELILLE.—French Grammar.

DEVEREUX.—Dictionnaire Français-Anglais.

DOUVILLE.—French Grammar.

DUBUC.—French Grammar.

ENCYCLOPÉDIE MÉTHODIQUE.—Grammaire et Littérature.

FLEMING AND TIBBINS.—Grand Dictionnaire. Stepping-Stone.

FLEMING.—Difficultés de la Langue Anglaise.

FRAEDERSDORFF'S First German Book, and BECKER'S Grammar.

GASC'S Materials for French Composition. Second French-Book.

HALLARD'S French Grammar.

JOBERT's French Questioning.
LAVEAUX.—Dictionnaire des Difficultés.
MANESCA's French Course.
MERLET's French Grammar.
MULLIGAN.—Structure of the English Language.
NOEL ET CHAPSAL.—Grammaire Française.
SADLER.—Grammaire Pratique.
SAIGEY.—Nouvelle Grammaire Allemande.
SOULICE ET SARDOU.—Petit Dictionnaire des Difficultés.
SIRET.—Eléments de la Langue Anglaise.
SPIERS.—Grammaire Raisonnée.
SMITH AND HAMILTON.—English and French Dictionary.
TIBBINS.—The Learner's First Book.
WILSON (REV. JAMES).—French and English Dictionary.
WHEATCROFT.—Grammaire Anglaise.
WOLSKI's French Grammar.

PRACTICAL LESSONS

ON

THE STRUCTURE OF THE VERB.

ON THE INFINITIVE CONSTRUCTION.

I.—An Infinitive may either be the Nominative, or the Predicate or Attribute, of a Proposition.

Aller du connu à l'inconnu est le meilleur mode d'instruction. The best mode of instruction is to proceed from the known to the unknown.

II.—The Present Participle, used in English either as Nominative or Predicate, is translated in French by the Infinitive.

Enseigner est une chose que peu de personnes sachent faire. Teaching is a thing which few persons can do.

Qu'est-ce que dormir et veiller, si ce n'est vivre et mourir ? What is sleeping and waking but living and dying ?

TURN INTO FRENCH.

Sitting-down-to-dinner,[1] *eating*, *drinking*, and *behaving* like-other-people,[2] appeared to him disagreeable ceremonies.[3] That-is-no[4] *dancing*, it is only *fluttering-about*.[5] It is[6] not safe *walking* in frosty weather. It is bad *striving*[7] against wind and tide. It is *behaving* ill.

It is *being* very-cowardly-to[8] insult him in his misfortune. It is *working* too much. It was *acting* without reflection. It was *destroying* a fine work. It would be *doing*[9] them an actual[10] service. This would be *taking-up*-your-time-for-nothing.[11]

But reflecting that this would be *abusing* the generosity of the lady, I relinquished that thought. It is *being* incredulous, never-to-trust-anything-but-what-one-sees.[12] It is easier *ordering*[13] than *executing*. It is like-*standing*,[14] like-*sleeping*[15] over a volcano.

My wife observed[16] that *rising* too early would hurt[17] her daughter's eyes.[18] *Buying* is one thing, and *selling*[19] another. It is not *selling*, it is *giving-things-away*.[20]

1. Se mettre à table.—2. Tout le monde.—3. Cérémonial.—4. Ce n'est pas là.—5. Se trémousser.—6. Fait—7. Lutter.—8. Bien lâche que de—9. Rendre.—10. Véritable.—11. Abuser de vos moments.—12. Que de ne jamais s'en rapporter qu'à ce qu'on voit.—13. Commander.—14. Se placer.—15. C'est dormir.—16. Me fit observer.—17. Fatiguer.—18. La vue.—19. Vendre en est.—20. Donner.

III.—The Present Participle, used in English as the Objective either of a Verb or of a Preposition, is translated by the Infinitive in French.

La vraie dignité ne consiste pas à posséder des honneurs, mais à les mériter. Dignity does not consist in possessing honours, but in deserving them.

À donner et à prendre, on peut aisément se méprendre. In giving and taking, there may be mistaking.

Après avoir longtemps tournoyé, il retrouva son chemin. After turning and winding about for a long time, he found his way again.

En is an exception; it always requires the Present Participle.

Qu'espérez-vous en entretenant son erreur? What do you hope from keeping him in his mistake?

TURN INTO FRENCH.

Fire has the property of *calcining*, of *dissolving* all bodies. There is a time for *weeping*, a time for *laughing*, a time for *talking*, and a time for *holding* one's tongue.

The multitude have-neither[1] the talent of *judging*, nor that of *doubting*. The-weak-minded[2] and superstitious avoid *being* thirteen at table. What-avails[3] *talking* so much? There is nothing I hate (*Subj.*) so much as *paying* visits.

The wheels of this carriage want[4] *greasing*. The trees wanted *pruning*. This plant wants *watering*. This knife wants *sharpening*.

What do you purpose *doing* to-morrow? We renounce *going* there for-the-present,[5] since they have declined-*having*-anything-to-do-with-it.[6] She-is-for-ever-*harping-upon*[7] the same thing. Do you call that *backing*[8] your friends? He regrets *having* accepted.

After describing several circles in the air, the bird pounced-upon[9] his prey. The rays, *after having* deviated towards this body, converge, and meet[10] in different focuses.

What has she gained *by*[11] *taking* it? He began *by raising* new taxes, and ended *by ruining* the country. He began *by complaining*, and ended-*with*[12] *asking* money.

He went out *without shutting* the door. I shall not start *without bidding*-you-good-bye,[13] nor *without having seen* your father. The soldiers attacked the enemy *without having*-got-the-order.[14] How many people,[15] *instead of helping*[16] the poor, are-satisfied[17] *with pitying* them!

How-noble-it-is[18] for a prince to forgive his enemies, *instead of avenging* himself on them! *Instead of reproaching* your friends, hasten[19] to help them. *Instead of complaining* of the shortness of life, make a good use of it.

We also intend[20] *going*. He is employed on the wharf *in sawing* wood. She takes a delight-*in-dressing-up*[21] her child. I-congratulate-you-*on*[22] *having succeeded*. She denied *having been* there.

She was far *from being* displeased-*at*[23] *seeing* the affairs embroiled. He will excuse you *for*-not[24] *coming*. There is no such-thing-as-*keeping*-them-within-doors.[25] That child is sick *from having* eaten all kinds of trash.[26] He made-himself[27] sick *with*[28] *eating.* He killed himself *with drinking.* He deferred[29] *vindicating* his rights. I am-very-desirous[30] *of seeing* or *hearing* him. He is-fond-*of*[31] *domineering.* He says he prefers *being* a farmer.[32] I do not recollect *having given* you the errand.[33]

1. N'a ni.—2. Ceux qui ont l'esprit faible.—3. à quoi sert de.—4. Avoir besoin de.—5. à présent.—6. Refusé de s'en mêler.— 7. Elle ne fait que rebattre.—8. Soutenir.—9. Fondit sur.—10. Se réunir.—11. à.—12. Finit par.—13. Vous avoir dit adieu.—14. En avoir reçu l'ordre.—15. Gens.—16. Secourir.—17. Se contenter.—18. Qu'il est beau.—19. S'empresser de.—20. Se proposer.—21. à parer.—22. Je vous félicite de.—23. Fâchée de.—24. De n'être pas.—25. Moyen de les retenir à la maison.—26. Vilenies.—27. Se rendre.—28. à force de.—29. Attendre pour.—30. Désirer beaucoup.—31. Aimer à.—32. Cultivateur.—33. Commission.

IV.—The Infinitive may refer to a Present, a Past, or a Future time.

Je l'entends, je l'ai entendu, je l'entendrai chanter. I hear, I heard, I shall hear him sing.

Je croyais pouvoir payer. I thought I could pay.

J'avais cru pouvoir payer. I had thought I could have paid.

J'aurais cru pouvoir payer. I should have thought I could have paid.

TURN INTO FRENCH.

After *reading,* I write. After *reading,* I wrote. After *reading,* I shall write. I think I *shall gain* my lawsuit. I thought I *should gain* my lawsuit. I had thought I *should have gained* my lawsuit.

I see him *come.* I saw him *come.* I shall see him *come.* I thought I *heard* the voice of an angel. I thought I *heard* him sing. I hope I *shall be able* to take them.

V.—The Compound of the Infinitive is formed by means of *avoir* or *être,* according to the nature of the verb.

Les plus sévères l'excuseront d'avoir eu pitié d'un homme qu'elle voyait malheureux. The most rigid will excuse her for pitying a man whom she saw miserable.

Il ne pardonnera jamais à B. d'avoir entraîné le peuple à prendre les armes. He will never forgive B.'s influencing the people to take up arms.

Comment peuvent-ils venir sans être vus? How can they come without being seen?

TURN INTO FRENCH.

After I *have walked*,[1] I read. I wish *I-may-have-been-deceived*[2] on your account. He is flushed-*with-running*.[3] After I *had taken supper*, I wanted[4] to go out, but he detained me.

After *having spoken*[5] a few words, he remained silent. I dislike *being* followed. We cannot approve-of-*your-doing*-it.[6] After *having* done, he went away. I deem myself happy in-being-so-fortunate-as[7] to please him. After *hunting*, we shall repair[8] to your country-house.

I pity her *to be obliged* to go out in-such-weather.[9] Not content with[10] *betraying* him, you slander him. He disclaims[11] *having had*-any-share-whatever-in[12] the work. I esteem myself peculiarly[13] happy in[14] *having been able to render him* such-a[15] service. I am sorry *for involving*[16] you in-so-much-trouble.[17]

1. Se promener.—2. Avoir été trompé.—3. Tout rouge d'avoir couru. —4. Vouloir.—5. Dit.—6. Vous approuver de l'avoir fait.—7. D'avoir pu.—8. Se rendre.—9. Par un temps pareil.—10. De.—11. Nier.—12. Pris la moindre part à.—13. Très.—14. De.—15. Ce.—16. Attirer.—17. Tous ces embarras.

VI.—The latter of two Verbs is generally put in the Infinitive, if both Verbs have the same Nominative.

J'ai failli mourir de rire. I thought I should have died with laughing.

Les crimes des habitants de la terre étaient montés

à un tel excès que Dieu se repentit d'avoir fait l'homme. The crimes of the inhabitants of the earth had arisen to such a pitch that it repented the Lord he had made man.

I said generally, because there are cases when the repetition of the same personal pronoun as Nominative is a more forcible construction.

Je promets que je ne vous abandonnerai jamais. I promise I shall never forsake you.

Je crois que j'irai faire une promenade à cheval ce matin. I think I shall take a ride this morning.

Quand il a vu qu'il était trop faible, il s'est joint à un tel. When he saw he was too weak, he joined with such a one.

TURN INTO FRENCH.

Oh! I wish[1] *I had* confessed my fault at-once,[2] and *that I had* not calumniated poor William. I wish *I were asleep.* I fear *I am* intruding.[3] I wish *I had* his signature to a cheque[4] for five hundred pounds. I wish *I could* oblige you.

I thought *I should have found* you at-home.[5] I did not think[6] *I would be obliged* to start so soon. I promised your sister *I would go.* I am confident *I sent back* your umbrella.

He will-put-you-off[7] a long time before *he pays* you. He expects[8] *he shall be back* in time. He says *he heard* everything.[9] He complained that *he could not get*[10] a bottle of Port. Cato, before *he killed himself,* read the treatise of Plato on the immortality of the soul. He pretended he *could* render himself invisible.

Did she not look-as-if-*she-would-apologize*?[11] She does not look as if *she were pleased.* Does she pare[12] her nails before *she washes* her hands? She will go and see you before *she starts* from this town. Will she go to Lyons before *she repairs*[13] to Paris? She started before *she had terminated* the business. She promised *she would reward* him.

One[14] should think before *one acts.*

Does it look *as if it were-going-to-be-fine?*[15] It will not-be-long[16] *before it rains.* It looks *as if it were going to be bad weather, to be cold, to be stormy.*[17] The weather looks *as if it-were-going-to-be-fine, to-be-cold, to-be-rainy.*[18] Does not the weather look *as if it were going to rain?* It looks *as if it were going to rain.* Does it lighten before *it thunders?* The child wishes *it had* a piece of sugar.

We wish *we could* assist you. We think *we cannot* pay them so-soon.[19] We presume *we may* call[20] to-day or to-morrow. We are afraid *we have made* many mistakes in our exercise. We thought *we should inform*[21] you of that news. You should think before *you act.* Do you brush your coat before *you put it on?* Did you reflect before *you acted?*

Do they say *they saw* us at-the-watering-place?[22] Yes, at Vichy. They cannot do it; they wish *they-could.*[23] They pretend *they have not* acted-contrary[24] to the laws. They should think twice before *they speak.* They expected *they-would-be-better-received*[25] by their friends. They must consider[26] before *they give*-you-an-answer.[27]

1. Oh! que je voudrais.—2. Tout d'abord.—3. Importun.—4. Bon.—5. Chez vous.—6. Compter.—7. Vous traînera.—8. Compter.—9. Tout.—10. Se procurer.—11. Avoir l'air de vouloir faire des excuses.—12. Se faire.—13. Se rendre.—14. On.—15. Vouloir faire beau temps.—16. Ne pas tarder.—17. De l'orage.—18. Vouloir se mettre au beau, au froid, à la pluie.—19. De sitôt.—20. Passer.—21. Faire part.—22. Aux eaux.—23. Le pouvoir.—24. Contrevenu.—25. Etre mieux accueillis.—26. Réfléchir.—27. Vous rendre réponse.

VII.—The latter of two Verbs can also be put in the Infinitive, if the Objective to which it relates can be turned into a Nominative.

Il me faut aller le trouver, i.e., *Il faut que j'aille, &c.* I must go and find him.

Il me pria de m'asseoir. He begged I would sit down.

Je suis fâché de le voir ainsi prodiguer son argent. I am sorry to see that he throws away his money.

TURN INTO FRENCH.

My father forbade *me* to-keep-company[1] with that bad boy.[2] I exhort *you* to summon your courage. I ordered[3] *my servant* to go to your house. Sir, allow *us* to go out. My mother requests *you* to forgive my brother.

Tell *him* to sit down. Desire *her* to[4] come. Invite *me* to dinner. He bade[5] *him* go for[6] the physician. I wrote to my *friend* to intrust me with his affairs. It suits[7] *you* indeed-to[8] speak in this manner. Paul allows *us* to read.

I pray you-have-*me*-excused.[9] Allow *me* to absent myself for half an hour.

1. Fréquenter.—2. Sujet.—3. Commander.—4. Priez-la de.—5. Ordonner à.—6. Chercher.—7. Convenir.—8. Bien de.—9. De m'excuser.

VIII.—The Verb which follows a Verb of Motion is put in the Infinitive Mood in French, and the Conjunction *And* is not expressed.

Je dois aller faire une visite à Mademoiselle B. I am to go and pay a visit to Miss B.

Je suis bien tenté d'aller prendre l'air à la campagne. I have great inclination to go and take the country air.

Nous voudrions bien aussi aller nous promener. We should also like to go and take a walk.

TURN INTO FRENCH.

Come *and see* the queerest[1] animal you ever saw (*Subj.*). He came *and complained* to me of your ways-of-doing.[2] They came *and awoke* me at five o'clock. Pull the bell that they may come *and open* the door to us. Go *and tell* the servant to-let[3] nobody in.

You ought to go *and pay* him a visit. Run *and tell* him to wait for me. He came *and told* us that he could not come. The old rogue proposed that they should go (*Subj.*) *and rob* some travellers who were going from Rochester to London. Ask-him-to[4] come *and speak* to me. Who will come *and walk* with me?

Do you think it-worth-while[5] to go *and speak* to her? Go *and fetch* your book. Come *and take* a walk. I have a room at-your-service.[6] Please[7] to walk up *and see* it.

If you will not believe me, go *and-see*-it-yourself.[8] It-would-be-a-great-accommodation-to-me,[9] if you could go *and fetch* it. What I desire is to go *and see* her. Go *and ask-after*[10] the lady's health. He went *and dared* him even-in his-house.[11] He came *and disclosed*[12] to them all he knew of the plot. I forgot[13] he was[14] to come *and fetch* me.

1. Drôle.—2. Procédés.—3. Laisser entrer.—4. Priez-le de.—5. Qu'il vaille la peine.—6. à vous offrir.—7. Veuillez.—8. Allez-y voir.—9. Cela m'arrangerait bien.—10. S'informer de.—11. Jusque chez lui.—12. Révéler.—13. Ai oublié.—14. Devoir.

IX.—It is in the genius of the language to admit of two, three, and sometimes four Infinitives, one after another.

C'est faiblesse, c'est vanité, c'est ignorance grossière de son propre intérêt que d'espérer de pouvoir cacher ses fautes en affectant de les soutenir avec hauteur et fierté. It is a weakness, a vanity, a gross ignorance of his own interest, when a man expects to be able to conceal his faults by affecting to defend them with haughtiness and arrogance.

Qu'ai-je affaire d'aller me tuer à travailler pour des gens dont je ne me soucie point? Why should I work myself to death for persons I am not at all concerned about?

Nous devons nous appliquer à faire cesser nos desirs plutôt qu'à les satisfaire. We must take care that our desires should cease rather than they should be satisfied.

Il faut faire examiner votre malle avant de pouvoir la faire transporter à l'hôtel. You must get your trunk examined before it can be removed to the hotel.

When three or four Infinitives, one after another, are dissonant, their number should be lessened by using another Mood. Thus, instead of saying, *Je crois pouvoir m'attendre à le voir arriver;* it were better to say, *Je crois que je puis m'attendre à le voir arriver.* I think I may hope to see him arrive yet.

TURN INTO FRENCH.

I have sometimes wished *that I could see* him. He did not like *to see* the-boy-*running.*[1] I should like *to see* the-ship-*sinking.*[2] The child would like the-ass-*to-bray.*[3] I fear *I shall let*-the-opportunity-*escape*[4] of seeing you.

I wish I *could share* mine with you. I wanted to *get up* to *make* them *believe*[5] I was desirous of *accompanying* them. I wish to *speak* to him, and-*entreat*-him[6] to *come* and *see* me.

Must-I *go*[7] and *tell* him to *come* and *put* up the curtains? I am afraid I *shall be obliged to-summon*[8] him. I think I *can go for him.* I wish I *were able to-join*-in[9] the conversation. She thinks she *can go* and *take* a walk. She-thought[10] she *heard* something *move.*[11] I would not advise you to *attempt*[13] *depreciating* such a poet.

1. Courir l'enfant.—2. Couler le navire.—3. Entendre braire l'âne.—4. Laisser échapper l'occasion.—5. Accroire.—6. Pour le prier de.—7. Me faut-il.—8. Faire assigner.—9. Me joindre à.—10. Il lui a semblé.—11. Remuer.—13. De vouloir.

X.—After *Voir, entendre, écouter, sentir,* the Present or the Past Participle, used in English, is translated by the Infinitive.

Je voyais se dessiner sur la muraille l'ombre des gens qui allaient et qui venaient. I saw delineated on the wall the shadows of people who were going and coming.

J'ai entendu raconter des choses qui tiennent du prodige. I have heard some things related which sound miraculous.

Je vois luire dans le sable quelque chose qui ressemble à de l'or. I see in the sand something glittering like gold.

Il sentait la force lui revenir. He felt returning health and vigour.

TURN INTO FRENCH.

Do you see the swallows *skimming*[1] over the surface of the lake, the rays of the sun *dispersing* the mist, the sea *breaking* on the beach, the sheep *grazing* in the meadows?

I have seen little William from-next-door[2] *loitering* about-in[3] our garden, near the apricot tree. I heard him *calling* you. I hear the bell *ringing*. He saw them *dying*, one-after-another.[4] Do you hear the lambs *bleating?*

Have you seen the horses *sold?* Have you seen the river *crossed* by a good swimmer? Will you buy the duet we heard *sung?* Do you pity the poor wretch whom we have heard *sentenced?* I heard them *blamed* by their masters. I must pay my taxes, if I-do-not-want[5] my furniture[6] *seized.*

In-proportion-as[7] you felt the wind *rising* and the waves *swelling*,[8] did you not feel your heart beat? I felt my heart *rending*.[9] Have you heard drunkards sing? I heard them *coming*, *bawling*, *laughing*, and *singing*. Towards the middle of autumn, the-swallows-are seen[10] *assembling*, *fluttering*, and *holding* a sort of council.

I heard him *groaning* all night. One might hear serpents *hissing*. The water is seen *springing-up*[11] on all sides. I perceived a constant[12] *passing* and *repassing* of men. I felt myself gradually *drooping*. The Dutch fleet had been seen *sailing-up*[13] the Thames.

We[14] heard the winds and the waves *roaring*.[15] I hear a *whispering*.[16]

1. Raser.—2. D'à côté.—3. Dans.—4. Les uns après les autres.—5. Vouloir voir.—6. Meubles.—7. à mesure que.—8. Se soulever.—9. Se déchirer.—10. On voit les hirondelles.—11. Sourdre.—12. Sans cesse.—13. Remonter.—14. On.—15. Rugir.—16. Chuchoter ou parler bas.

XI.—After *Comment, que, où, pourquoi, à quoi bon,* the Infinitive has the Verb it depends upon left out.

Un lièvre en son gîte songeait, (car que faire en un gîte, à moins que l'on ne songe?) A hare in her form was musing (for what else but muse could she do there?)

A quoi bon se mettre en colère? discutons de sang-froid. What signifies getting into passion? let us reason coolly.

Comment donc lui faire entendre raison? How shall we make him listen to reason?

The English language sometimes, but seldom, admits of the same construction.

Que faire de ces livres? What to do with these books?

TURN INTO FRENCH.

What *can we** do? Why *do you* stop?[1] Why *do you* tell me such a thing? How *can we* suppose that? Where *shall we* find another man like him? What *shall I* imagine?

What *shall I* contrive?[2] How *is* this to be explained? Where *will you* find roses without thorns? What-*is*-to-be-done-to[3] bring down his pride? How *can one* pass over-such-abuse?[4] Why *do you* score[5] one pound more[6] to me?

How *can we* get out of this, and-not[7] be seen? Why *do you* come back, sir? If he lose the stage, how *is he* to go back? How *could they* have-carried-on[8] a war at-such-a-great-distance?[9] Why *do you* constrain[10] yourself?

To whom *shall we* trust? What-*is*-the-use-of[11] telling stories? What use *is* it to-give-yourself-up-to[12] melancholy?

1. S'arrêter.—2. Inventer.—3. Comment s'y prendre pour.—4. De pareilles impertinences.—5. Me mettre.—6. De plus.—7. Sans.—8. Soutenir.—9. Si loin.—10. Se gêner.—11. à quoi bon.—12. S'abandonner à.

XII.—Sometimes the Infinitive, preceded by *De*, has also the verb it depends upon left out; in which case it

* The words in italics are not to be translated in this exercise.

may be resolved by a tense of the Indicative corresponding to that of the preceding verb.

Grenouilles aussitôt de sauter, i.e., *s'empressent de, se hâtènt de.* The frogs immediately leaped into the water.

Eux de chercher, eux de combattre, i.e., *s'empressèrent de.* Away they sought, away they fought.

As this form of the Infinitive is a little antiquated, I shall merely give a French exercise.

TURN INTO ENGLISH.

Ainsi parla le loup, et les flatteurs *d'applaudir*, et la cour *d'admirer!* Le bruit cesse, on se retire: rats en campagne aussitôt; et le citadin *de dire:* achevons tout notre rôt. Grenouilles *de rentrer* dans leurs grottes profondes.

Serviteur, dit-il, et *de courir.* Il y tombe (*i.e.*, dans le filet) en danger de mourir; et mon chat *de crier*; et le rat *d'accourir.*

L'autre aussitôt *de s'excuser.* Le fanfaron aussitôt *d'esquiver.* Aussitôt les ennemis *de s'enfuir* et *de jeter* les armes. Il y avait deux cents litières au siège d'Orange, et *de rire.* Alors hurlements *de cesser*, larmes comiques *de tarir.*

XIII.—To express wonder, indignation, or any vivid feeling of the soul, the Infinitive, in Exclamatory or Interrogative propositions, often begins a sentence, the Verb of the leading proposition being left out.

Vous, tenir ce langage! You use such language!

Moi, souffrir un pareil affront! Non, jamais. I put up with such an affront! No, never.

Moi, vaincue! I conquered!

I, THOU, HE, and THEY are then to be translated by *moi, toi, lui, eux.*

TURN INTO FRENCH.

To-*exercise-sway-over*[1] men, and *give* them laws; these-are[2] the cares of authority, not-its[3] pleasures!

He *love* my mistress! I *betray* her! I *have* not written to you! I *deceive* the best of my friends! He *write* French! Why,[4] let him learn English first. What, *eat* another's[5] grass! What a dreadful crime!

We *commit* a mean-action![6] Whom do you take us for? What! you *let* yourself be beaten that way![7] They *put up* with an affront like-this![8] They *work!* they are too fine ladies for that.

They *yield* the place to you! Surely you do not think of it. *To steal* the fruit himself, and-then-to-lay-it-to-poor William's-charge![9] I a slave! I *born* to command! Alas! it is only too true.

1. Commander à.—2. Ce sont là.—3. Ce n'en est pas le.—4. Mais.—5. D'autrui.—6. Bassesse.—7. De la sorte.—8. Comme celui-là.—9. Et puis en accuser le pauvre Guillaume.

XIV.—The passive Infinitive of the English is rendered in French by the active voice, and is generally preceded by the preposition *à*.

Comment fallait-il l'abriter? How was it to be sheltered?

C'est un homme à noyer, à pendre. He is fit or deserves to be drowned, to be hanged.

However, instances of a similar construction are to be met with in English, as:

Cette maison est-elle à louer ou à vendre? Is this house to let or to sell?

TURN INTO FRENCH.

The thing is *to be done.* It is *to be remarked.* He is *to be feared.* She is *to be blamed.*

Beautiful *to be seen.* Useful *to be known.* Fruits *fit-or-ready-to-be-pulled.*[1] That meat is not fit *to be eaten.* This poor wretch is *to be pitied.*

The advice is not *to be despised.* This is an event much *to be dreaded.* It is *to be hoped* that we shall soon have fine weather. It is much *to be wished* that this weather should (*Subj.*) end. It is not *to be supposed* that he will (*Subj.*) come.

There is money *to-be-made.*[2] What remains *to be said.* I know of a house *to be sold.* What is the treatment *to be followed?* Such an opinion cannot *be advocated.*[3] From all this may *be elicited*[4] the following[5] truth. In what part[6] of the book is[7] that engraving *to be placed?*

1. Bons à cueillir.—2. à gagner.—3. Se soutenir.—4. Déduire.—5. Que voici.—6. Endroit.—7. Devra-t-on.

XV.—The French Infinitive, still preceded by *à,* is used to translate the English Present Participle after the verb *To be,* when the latter describes a thing a-doing or continuing.

Elle est à s'ajuster pour aller au bal. She is dressing to go to a ball.

Le vicaire de M. Yorick était à fumer sa pipe auprès du feu de la cuisine. Mr. Yorick's curate was smoking a pipe by the kitchen fire.

Il y a une demi-heure qu'ils sont à jouer. They have been playing this half-hour.

TURN INTO FRENCH.

He is always *playing* instead of studying. Make no noise while she is *sleeping.* We were two days *pumping*-up the water.

Is your sister *dressing?* No, sir; she is *dressing-her-hair.*[1] She is *reading,* is-she-not?[2] You were *listening* at the door, were you not? They are *taking-stock,*[3] are they not?

My shoes are *being mended.* Call us, even-if-we-are[4] *taking tea.* Who can be *ringing?* Either-he[5] is *talking*, or he is on a journey. They are *dancing.*

1. Se coiffer.—2. N'est-ce-pas.—3. Faire l'inventaire.—4. Quand même nous serions.—5. Il.

XVI.—*Must have,* implying supposition, inference, and referring to the Past, is generally rendered by the Past Indefinite, and sometimes by the Pluperfect of *Devoir,* and the English Past Participle is turned into an Infinitive in French.

J'ai dû me tromper ; il a dû en être ainsi. I must have been mistaken ; it must have been so.

Il n'a pas seulement fait allusion à ce sujet ; cependant il a dû y penser. He never once adverted to the circumstance, though he must have thought of it.

Il avait dû recevoir les lettres. He must have received the letters.

Un tel langage a dû blesser son amour-propre. Such language must have been grating to his feelings.

TURN INTO FRENCH.

She *must have been* very handsome. We *must have told* it to you. You *must have perceived*[1] it. They *must have been busy-about-it.*[2] He *must have got out* by the window.

Somebody *must have accompanied* her. You *must have been delighted*-to[3] see her again. He *must have escaped* without your perceiving it (*Subj.*). Somebody *must have come, must have written, must have known.*

She *must have been* very ill, since her physicians gave-her-over.[4] You *must have been* very much frightened.

The writing *must have been dictated* by a feeling of envy. It *must have been* of great service[5] to you. That *must have disappointed* him a-great-deal. Every plant *must have grown* in some place[6] or other. Something *must*[7] *have happened* to him.

1. S'en apercevoir.—2. S'en occuper.—3. Enchanté de.—4. L'ont abandonnée.—5. Utilité.—6. Endroit.—7. Il a dû.

XVII.—*Ought to have* and *Should have*, alluding to the Past, and followed by a Past Participle, are expressed by the Compound Conditional or the Pluperfect of the Subjunctive of *Devoir*, if these expressions are dependent on words or verbs requiring that Mood, and the English Participle is turned into an Infinitive in French.

Quoique je n'eusse dû en rien dire, cependant je n'ai pu m'empêcher de parler. Though I ought not to have said anything about it, yet I could not help speaking.

N'aurait-elle pas dû s'y prendre mieux qu'elle n'a fait? Should she not have managed the thing better than she has done? *J'aurais dû avoir égard à leur position.* I should have had some regard for their position.

TURN INTO FRENCH.

You *ought* not *to have said* that. He *ought to have kept silent.* How *ought* she *to have managed* the thing? She *ought to have managed* the thing as I did.

You *ought* not *to have left* your little sister in the street; the cart *might have knocked*[1] her *down.* He *should have asked* me. *Should* you not *have sent* for[2] the physician?

Thou didst not work as thou *shouldst have done.* I beg your pardon, I *ought* not *to have kept-you*[3] waiting so long. Whatever[4] your intentions may be, you *should have* acted differently. This, to-be-sure,[5] was what he *ought to have done.* You *should have written* to me, since you knew where I lived. You *ought* to *have paid* me two francs more,[6] two francs less. You *ought* not *to have invited* him without asking[7] me.

These gentlemen *ought* not *to have promised* what they could not give. We[8] *should have been warned* of what has happened. She *should* never *have separated* from him. You *ought to have run* after her, and *have asked* her what she meant.[9]

Your brother *should* not *have interrupted* me. You *ought to have been*-sorry.[10] You *ought to have given*-them-*in-charge*.[11] They *ought to have given* me some intimation.[12] She *ought to have taken*-care.[13] The goods *ought to have been forwarded*[14] sooner. You *ought to have informed* me of it. *Ought* they not *to have paid* the first purchase before[15] making the second? You should have *called-him-to-account*[16] sooner.

1. Renverser.—2. Chercher.—3. Vous faire.—4. Quelles que.—5. Sans doute.—6. De plus.—7. Inviter.—8. On.—9. Vouloir dire.—10. En être fâché.—11. Les faire arrêter.—12. Avis.—13. Y prendre garde.—14. Expédier.—15. Avant d'en.—16. En demander compte.

XVIII.—*May* and *Can have* are translated by the Past Indefinite or the Subjunctive of *Pouvoir*, changing still the Past Participle into an Infinitive in French.

À quoi peut-on s'attendre d'un tel évaporé? What can be expected from such a flighty youth?

Si c'est une chose qui puisse se faire, je vous en aurai obligation. If it is a thing that can be managed, I shall be obliged to you.

Son revenu peut se monter à deux millions. His revenue may be computed at two millions.

Cela peut se faire en sûreté de conscience. That can be done with a safe conscience.

C'est le plus beau tapis qu'il soit possible d'avoir, mais on peut se le procurer ailleurs à meilleur marché. That carpet is the finest that can be had, but the article may be had much cheaper elsewhere.

TURN INTO FRENCH.

I do-not-know[1] what cause[2] you *may have given* her to hate you. You *may have been told* this or that, but do not believe it.[3] *May* he *have come* during your absence? It[4] *may be said* that-that-was[5] the iron age.

Who *can have spread* this false news? Who-but-he[6] *can have done* it? What-*can-have-kept*-you-out-so-late?[7] What *can* I *have done* with[8] my cigar-box? It *cannot be said* that the boy is[9] spoiled, for his parents overlook-nothing[10] in him. What greater[11] piece of injustice *can be imagined?* (Translate—What can one imagine of.)

The transport with which he was again beheld by his almost broken-hearted[12] parents, *may be* more easily *conceived* than described. (Translate—It is easier to conceive than to describe the transport with which.) I cannot conceive how such-imprudent-words[13] *can have escaped* me. What *can have made* you so sick? Such-*may-have*[14] *been* the case.[15]

On my return to my country, if a Jew *can be said* to have a country. I know not what *can have estranged*[16] him from me. Where *can* he *have imbibed*-such-an[17] opinion?

1. Ignore.—2. Sujet.—3. Y.—4. On.—5. Que c'était alors.—6. Quel autre que lui.—7. Qui est-ce qui a pu vous retarder?—8. De.—9. Soit. —10. Ne passer rien à.—11. Plus inique.—12. Désolés.—13. Un propos si indiscret.—14. Il a pu.—15. Ainsi.—16. Indisposer contre.—17. Puiser cette.

XIX.—*Might* or *Could have* is expressed by the Compound Conditional of *Pouvoir*, or one of the Compound Tenses of the Subjunctive, the Past Participle being still resolved by the Infinitive in French.

Vous auriez bien pu vous dispenser de me rapporter cet impertinent entretien. You might have dispensed with repeating that impertinent conversation to me.

Je ne conçois pas que vous ayez pu faire tant de cas de si peu de chose. I cannot conceive how you could have thought so highly of so poor a performance.

On a commis des maladresses, mais je ne vois guère comment on aurait pu les éviter. Blunders were committed, but I scarcely see how they could have been avoided.

TURN INTO FRENCH.

Had-he-addressed-me-in-becoming-language,[1] I *might have listened* to him. I *might*, perhaps, *have granted* it to your entreaty,[2] but I refuse it to your threats. We *might have remained* there a long time. That advocate suppressed the circumstances which *might have been-hurtful*[3] to his cause.

It *might have rained* very hard. I *could have told* you that a-month-ago.[4] *Could* you not *have done* it at much less expense?[5] The letter *might have been* addressed to her. Had the river been deep, he *might have been drowned.* I recovered[6] sooner than *might have been expected.*[7]

You *might have done* still better. You *could have written* your exercise, if you had been willing. We *might have had* more details. *Could* he not *have saved* them all? This cloth *could have been* pressed-down.[8] With a little foresight, the evil *might-have-been*[9] *avoided.*

1. S'il se fût servi à mon égard d'un langage convenable.—2. Prières.—3. Nuire.—4. Il y a un mois.—5. Frais.—6. Se rétablir.—7. S'y attendre.—8. Fouler.—9. On aurait pu.

XX.—*Would have,* expressive of Will or Choice, and followed by a Past Participle, is resolved by the Compound Conditional, or a Compound Tense of the Subjunctive of *Vouloir,* and the Past Participle is turned into an Infinitive in French.

Il aurait bien voulu épouser ma sœur, mais elle n'en a pas voulu. He would fain have married my sister, but she would not have him.

Si j'avais été que de lui, je ne crois pas que j'eusse voulu le faire. Had I been he, I do not think I would have done it.

If *Would have* expresses mere Contingency, it is to be translated by the regular Compound Conditional.

Tout autre que lui ne s'en serait pas si bien tiré. No other than he would have extricated himself so well.

TURN INTO FRENCH.

I *would have spoken*, but I did not know what to say. She *would have answered*, but she got-confused.[1] He *would have done* it, but she prevented[2] him. She *would have torn out* his eyes.

The plebeians *would fain*[3] *have enacted*[4] a law to abolish the custom. I *would fain have told* him so. He *would fain have eaten* dry bread. He *would fain have persuaded*[5] me that he *would have built*[6] a house, but-he-wanted-means.[7]

He engaged himself more than he *would have wished.*

1. S'embarrasser.—2. Empêcher.—3. Bien.—4. Faire.—5. Faire accroire.—6. Faire bâtir.—7. Mais les moyens lui manquaient.

XXI.—*Have* and *Get*, followed by an Objective, and subsequently by a Past Participle, are translated by *Faire*, and the Past Participle is changed into an Infinitive.

Si le porteur d'une lettre de change n'en fait point faire l'acceptation à temps, il n'a point de garantie sur le tireur. If the bearer of a bill of exchange does not get it accepted in time, he has no further claim on the drawer.

The Objective in French must not be placed between the two Verbs. If it is a Pronoun, it must precede *Faire* (except in the Imperative affirmative); if a Substantive, it must follow the Verb in the Infinitive.

Faites tordre le cou à cette oie, faites-le lui tordre. Have that goose's neck wrung off, have it wrung off.

J'ai fait relier ces deux tomes en un seul; je les ai fait relier pour un franc. I got those two volumes bound in one ; I got them bound for a franc.

TURN INTO FRENCH.

He *has had* his passport *signed.*[1] *Have* a pair-of-trousers[2] *made* for me. Waiter, *get* these boots *soled*[3] and *mended,* and please[4] tell the chambermaid *to have* a few shirts *washed* for me. Where could I *get* this penknife *sharpened?* Had-you-not-better[5] *get* my shoes *cleaned* and *blackened?*[6] He *will-get*[7] his account *paid.* When can you *get* it *done?* I cannot *have* it *done* before next week.

Have you *had* your gown *dyed?* Yes, I have. (Translate —I have made it to dye.) What-colour[8] have you *got* it *dyed?* Black,[9] grey, green or blue? Have you *had* it *dyed* a-deep-or-a-light-colour?[10]

She has *had* her likeness *taken.* Will you see *to have* the dinner *brought in?* See and-*let-us-have*[11] supper. Will-the-gentleman-*get*-his-dinner-*served-up*-in-his-own-room?[12] Why do you not *get* your *hair cut?* I am going to *get* it *cut.* Where are you going to *get* your hair *cut?*

His creditors have *had* his coach *seized,* and have *had* him *arrested.* How will you *get* your drawing-room *fitted-up?*[13] Could you *get* this five franc piece *changed* and this bill *discounted* for me? Have you taken-care[14] *to have* the horses well *shod?*

You should *have* that bad tooth *drawn.* I am going to *get* it *drawn.* She ought *to have* her tooth *stuffed.*[15] I will *have* this letter *conveyed*[16] to her. Do-you-want[17] to get in and see the exhibition? Can you *get* me *in?*[18] I *will have* a coat *made* by your tailor. I *have had* a coat *made* by your tailor. I *will get* a pair of boots *made* for you. I want to get my money before I *get* anything *made.*

1. Viser.—2. Pantalon.—3. Ressemeler.—4. Veuillez.—5. Ne feriez-vous pas bien.—6. Cirer.—7. Se faire.—8. Comment.—9. En noir.—10. D'une couleur foncée ou claire.—11. à nous faire.—12. Monsieur se fera-t-il servir chez lui?—13. Arranger.—14. Eu soin de.—15. Plomber.—16. Parvenir.—17. Voudriez-vous.—18. Entrer.

XXII.—*Faire*, in the sense of *to order, to cause to be done, to bespeak, to oblige, to force, to put upon one*, may be joined to the Infinitive of any Verb, and is said of what is the near or distant cause of anything; of what gives place to, or occasions such a thing.

Faites circuler la bouteille. Pass the bottle.

Il fit venir son commis dans son cabinet. He ordered his clerk to come into his study.

La pauvreté fait faire bien des choses. Poverty drives one to strange extremities.

TURN INTO FRENCH.

He *ordered* my companions *to be disarmed*. *Order* the cab *to-be-driven*[1] into the yard. *Order* the coachman *to pull up*.[2] They *were-ordered*-into-custody.[3] She *had-ordered*[4] a fire in her bed-room. He *ordered* a coat, a waistcoat, and trousers *to-be-made* for me.

I *caused* myself *to be initiated* into-the[5] mysteries of Ceres. He *caused* her head *to be cut off*. We *caused* him *to be shot*. You *caused* me *to be scolded*. He *caused* the fields *to-be-enclosed*.[6] They *caused* all the bells in France *to be melted*. He *caused* (has caused) all the trees of the road *to-be-cut-down*.[7] He *caused* him *to be put to death*. She *caused* him *to do it*. We have *caused* a ditch to-*be-dug*.[8]

Have you much work for-them-*to-do*?[9] *Have* her *in*.[10] *Have* him *out*.[11] *Have* them *into*[12] the yard. *Bid*-them[13] *come in*. *See* him *up*.[14] *Show* the young lady *down*.[15] *Show* her *into*[16] the dining room. *Bring out* the dogs. *Bring* the prisoner *in*. Tell the cook *to-send-up*[17] dinner. This *brought*-a-blush-upon-her-cheeks.[18] He will *bring-you-again*[19] into his favour.[20] This *brought*-him-into-disrepute.[21] A gentle shower *causes* mushrooms *to-spring-up*.[22] *Show* the gentleman *in, up*.

1. Rentrer.—2. Arrêter.—3. Faire conduire en prison.—4. Laisser l'ordre de faire du.—5. Aux.—6. Enceindre de fossés.—7. Abattre.—8. Creuser.—9. à leur faire faire.—10. Entrer.—11. Sortir.—12. Des-

cendre dans.—13. Qu'on les fasse.—14. Monter.—15. Descendre.—16. Entrer dans.—17. De faire monter.—18. Faire monter le rouge au visage.—19. Faire rentrer.—20. Bonnes grâces.—21. Le faire tomber en discrédit.—22. Venir.

XXIII.—If the Infinitive that is dependent on *Faire* has no direct Objective, *Faire* ought to be preceded by *le, la, les;* but if it has one, by *lui* or *leur*, or by a Noun in the Dative, *i.e.*, preceded by *à*.

Cette pluie fera lever vos plantes, elle LES *fera lever.* This rain will fetch up your plants, it will fetch them up.

J'ai fait avoir à votre ami un bon emploi. I have procured a good situation for your friend. *Je lui ai fait avoir un bon emploi.* I have procured him a good situation. *Je le lui ai fait avoir.* I have procured it for him.

TURN INTO FRENCH.

They-should-be[1] *made* to rise early. She *ordered him* to be put to death. They *made her* renounce[2] her pretensions. He wishes to *make them* enjoy[3] their rights. How shall we *make him* pass? He could not *make her* hear. Could he not *induce*[4] *her* to come? I had much-to-do[5] to *get him* to come.

The height of the trees and the thickness of the foliage (pl.), soon *made them* lose sight of the mountain over which they bent[6] their steps.

These imprudent measures of the minister *made the king* lose the love of his subjects. I *make him* believe[7] what I like. Could he not *make her* see her fault? Could you not *procure*[8] a pension *for her?*

I *had* a house built *by him.* I had a house built *for him.* What profession are you going to *make him* follow? *Make your pupils* learn these lessons; *make them* learn them by heart. *Make them* feel that private-interest[9] happens[10] always to be the common interest.

She-*was-taught*[11] reading, writing, and singing. The lightning which flashed-across[12] the horizon *made him* see that his safety[13] was on land.

The wind *blows*[14] *the dust*; it *blows it* about. They *made the air* ring[15] with shouts of-joy.[16] I will *make them* speak. Do not *make your sister* cry. The child tires my-patience out,[17] I cannot *make him* sleep. I *shall make her* rise at-an[18] early hour. *Make your horse* walk a little. He is in-a[19] bad humour, because I *made him*[20] write his exercise. I *will make* that *shocking*[21] *liar* tell the truth. A short sleep *made him* for a while forget his misery.

1. Il faut les.—2. Renoncer.—3. Jouir de.—4. Faire.—5. Bien de la peine à.—6. Diriger.—7. Accroire.—8. Faire avoir.—9. L'intérêt des particuliers.—10. Se trouver.—11. On lui fit apprendre.—12. Sillonner. 13. Sûreté.—14. Faire voler.—15. Retentir.—16. D'allégresse.—17. M'impatiente.—18. De.—19. De.—20. Faire.—21. Impitoyable.

XXIV.—The English Past Participle referring to the Objective of a Reflective Verb, is translated by the Infinitive in French.

Le froid se faisait déjà sentir. The cold was already felt.

Je me sentis tout-à-coup saisir d'un mouvement de crainte qui m'arrêta. I found myself, all of a sudden, seized with an emotion of fear, which arrested my steps.

TURN INTO FRENCH.

He makes *himself understood* and *listened to.* Can you speak French? I speak it just enough to make *myself understood.* Dumb-as-she-is,[1] she knows how to make *herself understood.*

A[2] tyrant makes *himself feared.* She is a woman who sings well, plays upon several instruments, and makes *herself beloved.* The mule, when defending himself, felt *himself stabbed.*[3]

1. Toute muette qu'elle est.—2. Le.—3. Percer de coups.

XXV.—*To have just*, or *To be just*, noting an action which has just taken place, is translated by *Je viens de, je venais de, que je vienne de, que je vinsse de,* or by *ne faire que de,* and the English Participle is turned into an Infinitive in French.

Quelle heure croyez-vous qu'il soit? Six heures viennent de sonner. What o'clock do you think it is? It struck six just now.

Ces fleurs sont tout aussi fraîches que si l'on ne faisait que de les cueillir. These flowers are every whit as fresh as if they had been just gathered.

TURN INTO FRENCH.

I am very glad that you *have just given* her a long lesson to learn. I *have just lost* the two children I so dearly loved. I *saw her-go-by-just-now.*[1] Do you think she *has just stept*[2] into the next room? It *was just* one o'clock.

What[3] *has just* happened? What[4] *have you just seen* and *heard*? The cow has *just calved.* That house *has just failed.*[5] The sun *is just set.*[6] The moon *is just up.* You *were just born* when your father died. Who *has just arrived?* Is-your-master-at-home?[7] No, Sir, he *is just gone out.* I beg your pardon, he *is just back.* I *have just said* that the proposition, *having just been explained,* needs not to be repeated. *What has* that man *just done?* He *is just*[8] *gone out.*

He *has just started.* I *have but just left* him. The mail post *is but just arrived. Have* you *just come* here? I *am just up.* I *was just gone out.* You had *but just left* him. You *had but just spoken* to me. I *had just arrived* in France when war was declared. The candle *is just gone-out.*[9] The first number[10] *has just been published.*[11]

1. Venir de la voir passer.—2. Passer.—3. Qu'est-ce qui.—4. Qu'est-ce que.—5. Faire faillite.—6. Se coucher.—7. Monsieur est-il chez lui?—8. Ne faire que de.—9. S'éteindre.—10. Livraison.—11. Paraître.

XXVI.—*De* is indispensable after *Ne faire que,* because if omitted, *Ne faire que* would denote merely the repetition of an action.

C'est une âme basse ; il n'a fait que valeter toute sa vie. He is a grovelling soul; he has done nothing but cringe all his life.

Il ne fait que tracasser tout le long du jour. He does nothing but bustle about the whole day in the house.

On ne fait que bavarder. There is nothing going on but gossiping.

TURN INTO FRENCH.

He *does nothing but* laugh. She *does nothing but* cry. He *does nothing but* fiddle.[1] She *does nothing but* trifle.[2] It *does nothing but* snow. It *does nothing but* rain.

He *does nothing but* sleep. They *do nothing but* complain. He *does nothing but* go out. He *does nothing but* boast.[3] Thou *dost nothing but* buzz-about.[4] They *did nothing but* make-game-of-him.[5] They *do nothing but* whisper.[6]

1.—Niaiser.—2. Vétiller.—3. Se vanter.—4. Bourdonner ça et là.—5. Le persifler.—6. Chuchoter.

XXVII.—*To* before an Infinitive of Purpose, is translated by *Pour.*

Il se mit une perruque et des lunettes pour se vieillir. He put on a wig and spectacles to make himself look older.

Elle lui donna un couteau pour jouer avec. She gave him a knife to play with.

Although, in this last example, the two languages offer a similarity of construction, still the Prepositions *in, on, with,* &c., affixed to the English Verbs in the first paragraph of the following exercise are not to be rendered.

TURN INTO FRENCH.

He had a brush *to brush* his clothes *with.* Do you know a good place[1] *to swim in?* Is the water deep enough *to dive in?* Those poor people[2] have no wood *to warm themselves with.* Have they no bed *to sleep in?* They have nothing *to feed on.*[3] Is there any ice *to skate on?* He wishes he had some friends *to talk-with.*[4] What is the-fittest age *to marry at?* Have you a rope *to skip with?*

The English sent a picked-body-of-men[5] *to occupy* the defile and *stop* the enemy. He sent somebody *to inform* me. He did it *to make* me uneasy.[6] He had neither horse nor carriage *to convey*[7] him.

Are you going to the fish-market *to buy* fish? Are you going to Belfast *to buy* linen? Will you go to the bank *to receive* your money.

I am sufficiently your friend not *to flatter* you, and too frank *to deceive* you. How-many-men[8] think they have genius enough *to govern* the state, though they have not sense[9] enough *to manage*[10] their own business. I esteem science too much, not *to blush* at (*of*) my own ignorance. He is too weak *to carry* such heavy burdens.

1. Endroit.—2. Gens.—3. Se nourrir.—4. Causer.—5. Corps d'élite. —6. De la peine.—7. Porter.—8. Que d'hommes.—9. Bon sens.— 10. Bien administrer.

XXVIII.—*To* before an Infinitive of Purpose is rendered by a relative Clause, either in the Indicative or the Subjunctive, as the case may require.

J'aurais besoin d'un homme qui s'enquît soigneusement de ses mœurs et m'en rendît un compte fidèle. I have occasion for a man to inquire carefully about his reputation, and bring me a faithful account of it.

The English language sometimes admits of the French construction.

J'ai besoin d'un domestique affectionné qui épouse mes intérêts et qui mette toute son attention à conserver mon bien. I have occasion for an affectionate servant, who will espouse my interest, and employ his whole attention in husbanding my estate.

TURN INTO FRENCH.

Would any one fancy-himself[1] in Toledo? Not a guitar to enliven[2] this dreary night, not a breath of air *to cool it!* He is melancholy; he wants[3] somebody *to stir* him *up.*[4] I am looking out for a horse *to match*[5] the one I have; I do not see anything *to please* me.

Have I said anything *to displease* you? What have I done *to displease* you? If you are so easily-huffed,[6] you will meet with much *to displease* you in life. The beauty and fertility of France are not the only things *to excite* admiration. Eastern[7] princes have always people *to fan* them when-at-meals.[8]

You will have a variety-of[9] commentators *to explain* difficult passages to you. You will find people enough *to serve* you. There was no labour *to fatigue*[10] his body or depress[11] his spirit. Is there anything *to oppose* itself to-my-doing-it?[12] He-could-hardly-find[13] any one *to do* it for him. If you wish for spectacles *to suit*[14] your sight, do not take that number.[15]

I am looking out for a clue[16] *to guide*[17] me out of this labyrinth. If I could find a clue *to guide* me through this endless maze.[18] Youth is naturally fiery, and requires some shackles[19] *to-keep*-it-within-bounds.[20] Give-me[21] a description of her person *to-make*[22] her contemptible to me.

1. Se croire.—2. Egayer.—3. Il lui faudrait.—4. Le réveiller un peu.—5. Assortir.—6. Susceptible.—7. De l'Asie.—8. Quand ils dînent.—9. Assez de.—10. Pouvoir fatiguer.—11. Abattre.—12. à ce que je le fasse.—13. C'est à peine s'il trouverait.—14. Aller.—15. Numéro-là. 16. Fil.—17. Diriger dans.—18. Immense dédale.—19. Entrâve.—20. Retenir.—21. Fais-moi.—22. Rendre.

XXIX.—English Infinitives, with an Objective before them, are rendered by the Indicative or the Subjunctive, as the case may be.

On dirait que vous êtes fou. One would suppose you to be mad.

Qui croyez-vous que c'est ? Whom do you fancy it to be ?

Personne au temps de Shakspeare ne soupçonna que cet acteur populaire fût le poéte du genre humain. Nobody in Shakspeare's time ever suspected that popular actor to be the poet of the human race.

There is another construction which consists in omitting the verb *To be* in French.

Je le tiens pour honnête homme, pour homme d'honneur. I hold him to be an honest man, a man of honour.

TURN INTO FRENCH WITH THE INDICATIVE.

I know *him to be* wise. I believe *him to be* learned. I know *him to be*[1] a thief. I suppose *him to be* an honest man. He has-proved-*himself*[2] *to be* a coward. We acknowledge *it to be* true. I warrant *the watch to be* good.

This curiosity of the king caused-*us-to-be*[3] presented to him. He avers[4] *it to be* a fact. You must prove *it to be* true. I believe *her to be* a virtuous woman. The Pope declared *the triumph* of the Holy See *to be* inevitable. He declared *it to be* the will of God. I expect[5] *you to have finished* your task against[6] night.

1. Que c'est.—2. Il a montré qu'il.—3. Fit qu'on nous.—4. Affirme.—5. Compter.—6. Avant qu'il soit.

TURN INTO FRENCH WITH THE SUBJUNCTIVE.

Somebody knocks ; whom do you suppose *it to be ?* I do not suppose *it to be* her. You want *me to go* with you, do you not ? Only[1] suppose *yourself to be* at Paris. Will you have *me belie*[2] my heart? I like *people* always *to act* in an open[3] manner. Do you think *it to be* honest to-act-in-that-way?[4]

Mr. B. wishing *me to see* his lawyer before beginning the prosecution,[5] I shall call on him to-morrow. Mr. B. wishing *me to see* his lawyer, I have already had several interviews with him. Allow[6] *me to* tell you what has happened. I will never allow *you to do* any-such-thing.[7]

What-do-you-desire[8] *me to do?* I require[9] *you to pay* attention to what you are told. At what o'clock do you wish *me to come* to-morrow? I require[10] *you to be* at my house at seven o'clock. Do-you-like[11] *me to retire?* He intends *you to do* it.

I forbade *you to do* such a thing. If you can induce-*him*[12] *to do* so. I order *you to do* it without-further-delay.[13] She would wish[14] *him to return* early. I scarcely-expect[15] *him to-come*-now.[16] God permits *it*[17] *to be* done.[18] We should like very much the-weather-to-be-fine[19] to-morrow. She allowed[20] *me to tell* her the truth.

I want *you to-boil*[21] these eggs hard. I want *him to-put-down*-the-head[22] of the carriage. He will not suffer his *compassion*[23] *to be abused.* He cannot bear *to-be-disturbed.*[24] Hand me a good *knife to carve*[25] the turkey. You would-not-choose[26] *him to come up.* I believe[27] *it to be* unfit.[28]

I would-not-have[29] you write. Masters wish *their servants to obey,* and not *to-murmur.*[30] Do you wish *the room to be furnished* or *unfurnished?*[31]

1. Seulement.—2. Trahir.—3. Franche.—4. D'en user de la sorte.—5. Poursuite.—6. Souffrir.—7. Une chose semblable.—8. Que vous plaît-il.—9. Demander.—10. Exiger.—11. Vous plaît-il.—12. Obtenir de lui qu'il.—13. Sans plus tarder.—14. Désirer.—15. Ne plus espérer.—16. Pouvoir venir.—17. Que cela.—18. Se faire.—19. Faire beau temps.—20. Souffrir.—21. Faire durcir.—22. Baisser la capote.—23. De sa pitié.—24. Déranger.—25. Découper.—26. Vouloir.—27. Ne pas croire.—28. Convenable.—29. N'être pas d'avis.—30. Raisonner.—31. Ou non.

XXX.—In indeterminate Propositions, Passive Verbs, followed by an Infinitive, are rendered by, *On dit que, on présume que, on croit que, on suppose que,* and the

English Nominative becomes as it were the Nominative of the Infinitive, which in French must be translated by a Personal Mood.

On dit que, on croit que César est ou a été le plus grand général de l'antiquité. Cæsar is said to be, or is said to have been the greatest general of antiquity.

On dit que les ours lèchent leurs petits pour achever de les former. Bears are said to lick their cubs into shape.

TURN INTO FRENCH.

The red *squirrel* is said *to drive*[1] the gray squirrel out-of-the[2] woods where he lives.[3] *She* was supposed *to be* the author of that novel. *The French* and *the English* are thought *to have committed* a signal fault in[4] not marching on Sebastapol, after the battle of the Alma.

The first *bayonets* are said *to have been made*[5] at Bayonne. *He* was supposed *to have made* a compact[6] with the devil. *He* is reported[7] *to have lost* fifteen pounds. *He* was not expected[8] *to survive* long. *He* is said *to be* a good swordsman;[9] but *he* is said *to have been* very imprudent in the matter.

She is said *to be* as pretty as her sister. *Paris* is now said *to contain* above[10] one million souls. The *dog* is said *to be* the only animal who knows his master. That *castle* is said *to have been built*[11] four-hundred-years-ago.[12] The *navigation* was expected *to be* long. *You* are expected *to be* at your post by six o'clock to-morrow. *He* is expected[13] *to leave* on Monday. The *attendance* is expected *to-be*-large.[14] *It* is believed *to be* he who spoke. *He* is said *to be* an honest man. When swallows fly low, *it* is thought *to be* a sign of rain. The *merchant* is thought not *to have left* a shilling.

Cæsar is-said[15] *to have dictated* to several secretaries at-once.[16] Certain *poisons* are-said[17] *to-curdle*[18] the blood in the veins. The *house* is said *to-be-haunted*-by-ghosts.[19] *The planets*[20] were formerly believed *to have* an-influence-in-the-fortune-of-men.[21] The *enemy* was said *to have ravaged*[22] all the country.[23]

1. Chasser.—2. Des.—3. Qu'il habite.—4. De.—5. Fabriquées.—6. Pacte.—7. Dit.—8. S'attendre.—9. Tireur.—10. Plus de.—11. Construire.—12. Il y a quatre cents ans.—13. Présume.—14. Qu'il y aura beaucoup de monde.—15. On prétend que.—16. En même temps.—17. On a prétendu.—18. Figer.—19. Fréquentée par des revenants.—20. Astres.—21. De l'influence sur la destinée.—22. Désolé.—23. Province.

XXXI.—When English Adjectives or Participles are preceded by *So, such,* or other words of an intensive meaning, and followed by *As,* connecting them with an Infinitive, this Infinitive is often resolved in French by a verbal clause, though sometimes an Infinitive construction may also be used.

On construit certaines voûtes de manière à ce qu'elles ont beaucoup d'écho. Certain vaults are so constructed as to give loud echoes.

Il est tellement pauvre qu'il lui faut mendier. He is so poor as to be obliged to beg.

Le salaire devra être suffisant pour permettre à l'heureux candidat de vivre respectablement. The salary must be such as to allow the successful candidate to live respectably.

TURN INTO FRENCH.

The weather-is-so-warm[1] *as to dissolve*[2] the snow on the mountains. He is so wise *as* not *to confide* in[3] men whom he does not know. He is no such fool[4] *as* not *to know*[5] what he does. They were quite-intoxicated-so-much-so[6] *as* not *to be able* (Translate—that they have not been able) to walk. She is so peevish[7] *as to be hated* by all her servants. He is so low-spirited[8] *as to be unable* to speak. The heat had been so strong *as to dry-up*[9] the rivulet. They are so much alike *as to-be*-easily-confounded.[10] He is such a simpleton *as to believe* everything she says. He-ordered-matters-so[11] *as to be*[12] alone with her.

1. La chaleur est si forte.—2. Fondre.—3. à des.—4. Sot.—5. Savoir bien.—6. Ivres au point.—7. Acariâtre.—8. Triste.—9. Dessécher. —10. Qu'on s'y méprend facilement.—11. Arranger tellement les choses.—12. Se trouver.

XXXII.—After an Impersonal Construction with *for me to, for thee to, for him to, for her to, for us to, &c.*, the English Infinitive is translated by the Subjunctive.

Trouvez-vous bon que j'aille le voir? Je trouve bon que vous le fassiez, car il est grand temps que vous agissiez. Do you think it advisable for me to go and see him? I think it advisable for you to do so, as it is high time for you to act.

TURN INTO FRENCH.

Is it proper[1] *for me to act?* It is not proper[2] *for him to go* now. Is it suitable *for her to receive* his note, *read it*, and answer it? It is not proper *for her to do* so. What is proper *for us to do?* It is fit *for a man to know* his own faculties, abilities, and weaknesses.

It is lucky *for you to-have-come*[3] before the rain began. Is it necessary *for me to be* there? It is time *for thee to be* off. Is-it-reasonable *for thee to waste* thy time so? It is impossible *for me to understand* him. It is impossible *for you to stay.*

When will it be time *for him to come?* It will be time *for him to come* at seven o'clock. Is-it-not-better[4] *for him to start* when you will? It is time *for you to read, translate,* and *write* your exercise.

It is natural *for man to pretend* that his will should be law. It is impossible *for you to succeed;* he is too strong *for you to pretend* to resist him. It is useless *for you to undertake* this business. It is useless *for you to speak* about it. It was-not-sufficient[5] *for you to know* the essential of the matter, it was still necessary *for me to-inform*-you-of-the-particulars.[6]

Would it not be better *for me to go* and speak to him? What-occasion is-there[7] *for you to go* thither? It is better *for you to remain* here. There is no occasion[8] *for you to say* that. It is useless *for her to do* this work. It is useless *for me to undertake* the matter. Is it useful *for me to go to* her house?

1. Convenable.—2. Convenir.—3. Rentrer.—4. Valoir mieux.—5. Ne pas suffire.—6. Instruire des détails.—7. Qu'est-il besoin.—8. Nécessaire.

XXXIII.—An Infinitive Nominative to *Est* may be used with or without *Ce* before it, if the Predicate or Attribute is a Noun.

La sottise de la plupart des mères est de croire leurs enfants très-jolis. The weakness of the greater part of mothers is to believe their children very pretty.

Laisser dire le monde, et toujours bien faire; c'est une maxime qui, étant observée, assure notre repos et établit enfin notre réputation. To let the world talk, and always act well, is a maxim which, being properly observed, secures our repose, and at last establishes our reputation.

TURN INTO FRENCH.

To hate *is* a torment; to love *is* a want of the soul. To be too much dissatisfied with oneself *is* weakness; to be too well satisfied with oneself *is* folly.

To relieve the unfortunate *is* the duty of the rich. To govern the French *is* more difficult than you think. The first step towards wisdom *is* to know that we are ignorant.

It-is-a-most-heinous-impiety[1] to despise Him who is able to destroy us. My highest ambition *is* to be of service to you. The-readiest-way-to-be-cheated[2] *is* to think oneself more cunning than other people. The shortest way to arrive at glory *is* to endeavour to be such-as-we-wish[3] to appear. To bear an evil which we cannot prevent *is* patience; to expose ourselves for the good that may result from it *is* courage. To have real friends, and to be satisfied with one's lot, *is* an existence to-be-envied.[4]

1. C'est de toutes les impiétés la plus détestable.—2. Le vrai moyen d'être trompé.—3. Tel qu'on veut.—4. Digne d'envie.

XXXIV.—Should *C'est* and the Predicate come first, *De* or *Que de* separate the Predicate from the Infinitive Nominative.

C'est la sagesse des Orientaux de chercher des remèdes contre la tristesse avec autant de soin que contre les maladies les plus dangereuses. It is the wisdom of the Orientals to seek remedies against melancholy as against the most dangerous distempers.

C'est outrer les ouvriers que de les faire travailler si longtemps sans relâche. It is over-harassing workmen to make them work so long without cessation.

TURN INTO FRENCH.

It is a paradox (*de*) *to say* that poverty is preferable to wealth. It is a strange desire which-men-have[1] *to seek* for power and *lose* their liberty. It is a grand,[2] a glorious action *to deliver* one's country. It is a disgrace for a soldier *to have run away* from a battle.[3] The first step toward repentance is *to-humble-oneself.*[4]

It is a rarity[5] (*que de*) *to see* you. It is loss of time *to-debate*-about[6] such trifles. It is a kind of shame *to be* unfortunate. It is a great-mortification[7] *to-be-reduced*[8] to beggary after being in affluence.

It is great wisdom *to know* one's own[9] ignorance. It is a misfortune *to have met-with*-such-an-accident.[10] It is misery[11] *to live* with such people. It is death[12] *to have* to do with such a man. It is death-to-me[13] *to be obliged* to speak to him. *Not to hinder* a crime, when in our power,[14] is-in-some-measure[15] to participate in it. It is a grievous-condition[16] *to-be-hurried*-by[17] one's passions.

1. Qu'ont les hommes.—2. Belle.—3. Combat.—4. Faire acte d'humilité.—5. Nouveauté.—6. Disputer.—7. Etrange réduction.—8. D'être obligé.—9. Propre.—10. Si mal rencontré.—11. Un martyre que d'avoir.—12. Une mort.—13. Ma mort.—14. Quand on le peut.—15. C'est en quelque sorte.—16. Etrange misère.—17. Se laisser emporter à.

XXXV.—When both the Nominative and the Predicate are Infinitives, *Ce* is used before *Est.*

Vouloir c'est pouvoir. Where there is a will, there is a way.

C'est s'aimer bien peu que de se donner la peine de haïr quelqu'un. He has little affection for himself who takes the trouble of hating another.

Except, however, in some negative or colloquial sayings, as—

Accuser n'est pas prouver. Accusing is not proving.

TURN INTO FRENCH.

To hope *is* to enjoy. To be idle *is* to be vicious. It *is* not living to be always ill. To reveal a secret *is* to violate a sacred deposit. To suffer so-infamous[1] a usurper to-fill-the-throne[2] *was*-a-disgrace-to[3] the nation.

It *is* like-a[4] wise man so to live. To be satisfied with one's lot *is* to be happy. To love nobody *is* not to enjoy the pleasures of friendship. To despise riches *is* to secure one's liberty. Not to know how to-conquer[5] one's passion *is* to condemn oneself to a hard slavery.

To-get-into-a-passion[6] *is* to punish oneself for the faults of another. To live in expectation and anxiety *is* not to live. Acting[7] so *is* abusing his kindness.

Not to be listened to *is* no reason for being silent. Not-to-go-forward[8] *is* to-go-backward.[9] To be able to perform[10] grand things *is* being very rich at home.[11]

1. Si monstreux.—2. Sur le trône.—3. Déshonorer.—4. Agir en.—5. Maîtriser.—6. Se mettre en colère.—7. Que d'en agir.—8. Ne pas avancer.—9. Reculer.—10. Faire.—11. Chez soi.

XXXVI.—After several Infinitives, the Verb *être* is put in the singular, if the Noun which follows is in the singular.

Boire, manger, dormir, c'est le partage de la brute; penser avec liberté, sentir avec délicatesse, agir avec courage, c'est le partage de l'homme. To eat, drink, and sleep is the lot of the brute; to think with freedom, feel with delicacy, and act with spirit, is the heritage of man.

But the Verb is put in the plural, if the Noun which follows is plural.

Se voir dans un pays étranger sans argent, sans connaissances, ce sont d'étranges extrémités. To see oneself in a strange country, without money or acquaintances, is a sad extremity.

Promettre et tenir sont deux, i.e., *choses.* It is one thing to promise, another to fulfil.

TURN INTO FRENCH.

Speaking well and *writing* well *are* two different things. *Playing* well and *singing* well *are* two different things. *Reading* too much and *reading* too little *are* two faults.

To-*turn*[1] English into French *is* the only way to learn French. To *turn* French into English *is* the system of those who do not know the French construction.

Saying and *doing are* two different things. *To be rich* and *to have been rich are* not the same thing.

1. Traduire.

XXXVII.—According as the construction sounds best, we use the Infinitive or Relative clauses in incidental Propositions.

Il marcha contre les ennemis qu'il savait avoir passé la rivière, rather than *qu'il savait qui avaient passé la rivière.* He marched against the enemies whom he knew had crossed the river.

D'où vous vient cet ennui qu'on voit qui vous dévore? rather than *qu'on voit vous dévorer?* Whence comes the weariness which we see preys upon you?

TURN INTO FRENCH.

He did-a-good-turn[1] to all those whom he knew *had loved* his son. He consulted those he thought *had* more experience than himself.

The plurality of gods is an idea which-we-cannot-conceive[2] *to have been adopted* by sensible[3] men.

1. Faire du bien.—2. Qu'on ne peut s'imaginer qui.—3. Sensés.

XXXVIII.—Verbs which require the Preposition *À* before the Infinitive which follows them :—

S'abaisser, to stoop.
Aboutir, to end, to come out,
S'accorder, to agree, to coincide.
S'acharner, to be intent, bent, or set upon.
Accoutumer, to accustom.
S'aguerrir, to inure oneself.
Aider, to help.
Aimer, to like, to be fond of.
S'amuser, to amuse oneself.
Animer, to animate, to incite.
S'appliquer, to apply oneself.
Apprendre, to learn, to teach.
S'apprêter, to get ready.
Aspirer, to aspire, to aim.
Assigner, to assign, to summon.
Assujettir, to subject.
S'attacher, to apply oneself, to strive.
S'attendre, to expect.
Autoriser, to authorize.
Avoir, to have.
Balancer, to hesitate.
Borner, to limit, to confine.
Chercher, to try, to attempt.
Commencer, to begin.
Se complaire, to take delight.
Concourir, to concur.
Condamner, to condemn.
Condescendre, to condescend.
Consentir, to consent.
Consister, to consist.
Conspirer, to conspire, to concur.
Consumer, to consume, to waste.

Contraindre, to compel.
Contribuer, to contribute.
Demander, to ask.
Destiner, to destine.
Se déterminer, to resolve upon.
Disposer, to dispose, to prepare.
Se disposer, to prepare.
Se divertir, to divert oneself.
Donner, to give.
Employer, to employ, to use.
S'empresser, to be eager.
Encourager, to encourage.
Engager, to engage, to invite.
Enhardir, to embolden.
Enseigner, to teach.
S'entendre, to be skilful, to be a judge, to know (how to).
S'étudier, to make it one's study.
Exceller, to excel.
Exciter, to excite.
S'exercer, to exercise oneself.
Exhorter, to exhort.
Exposer, to expose, to endanger.
Se fatiguer, to get tired with.
Gagner, to gain.
Habituer, to accustom.
Haïr, to hate.
Se hasarder, to venture.
Hésiter, to hesitate.
Instruire, to instruct, to teach.
Intéresser, to interest.
Inviter, to invite.
Se mettre, to begin, to set about.
Montrer, to show, to teach.
S'obstiner, to persist.
S'offrir, to offer, to propose oneself.
Parvenir, to succeed.
Passer, to spend.
Pencher, to incline, to be inclined.
Perdre, to lose.
Persévérer, to persevere.
Persister, to persist.
Se plaire, to take delight.
Prendre plaisir, to find pleasure, to delight.
Se plier, to bend, to bow, to comply.
Préparer, to prepare.
Provoquer, to provoke.
Réduire, to reduce.
Renoncer, to renounce.
Répugner, to be repugnant.
Se résigner, to be resigned.
Résoudre, to resolve.
Réussir, to succeed.
Servir, to serve.
Songer, to dream, to think, to mean, to purpose.
Suffire, to suffice. This verb may govern *pour*, and, when used impersonally, it governs *de*.
Tendre, to tend.
Tenir, to be anxious.
Travailler, to work, to labour.
Viser, to aim.

XXXIX.—Verbs which require the Preposition *De* before the Infinitive which follows them :—

S'abstenir, to abstain.
Accuser, to accuse.
Achever, to complete, to finish.
Affecter, to affect.
S'affliger, to grieve, to mourn.
S'agir, to be in question, to be the matter, to be at stake.
Ambitionner, to be ambitious, to aspire.
S'applaudir, to applaud oneself.
Appréhender, to be apprehensive, to fear.
Avertir, to warn.
S'aviser, to think, to take it into one's head.
Blâmer, to blame.
Brûler, to burn, to be anxious.
Cesser, to cease.
Se charger, to undertake, to take charge.

er, to commission.
r, to choose.
nder, to command.
er, to conjure, to entreat.
ller, to advise.
tenter, to be contented.
nir, to agree.
dre, to fear.
gner, to disdain, to scorn.
dre, to forbid.
, to defy.
écher, to make haste.
outumer, to disaccustom.
érer, to despair.
oler, to be grieved.
er, to detest.
oir, to owe it to oneself.
er, to defer, to delay.
to tell, to bid
tinuer, to discontinue.
venir, to disown, to deny.
ser, to dispense, to exempt.
per, to exculpate.
der, to dissuade.
r, to doubt.
, to write.
cher, to prevent.
er, to be enraged.
prendre, to undertake.
er, to try.
ner, to wonder.
tonné, to be astonished.
, to avoid.
ser, to apologize.
pter, to exempt.
re, to feign.
ter, to congratulate.
to finish.
tter, to flatter oneself.
ir, to shudder.
ir garde, to beware, to forr.
der, to beware, to forbear.
, to moan, to lament.
rifier, to glory, to boast.
ler, to scold.
ter, to make haste.
ter, to impute.
igner, to be indignant.

S'ingérer, to intermeddle.
Inspirer, to inspire.
Jurer, to swear.
Méditer, to contemplate, to project.
Se mêler, to concern oneself.
Menacer, to threaten.
Mériter, to deserve.
Négliger, to neglect.
Nier, to deny.
Offrir, to offer.
Omettre, to omit.
Ordonner, to order.
Oublier, to forget.
Pardonner, to forgive.
Parler, to speak.
Permettre, to permit.
Persuader, to persuade.
Se piquer, to pride oneself.
Se plaindre, to complain.
Prescrire, to prescribe.
Presser, to press.
Se presser, to hasten.
Présumer, to presume.
Prier, to pray.
Promettre, to promise.
Proposer, to propose.
Se proposer, to purpose.
Protester, to protest.
Punir, to punish.
Se rassasier, Etre rassasié, to be sated.
Rebuter, to discourage.
Recommander, to recommend.
Refuser, to refuse.
Regretter, to regret.
Avoir regret, to regret.
Se réjouir, to rejoice.
Remercier, to thank.
Se repentir, to repent.
Reprocher, to reproach.
Se ressouvenir, to remember.
Rire, to laugh.
Risquer, to risk, to venture.
Rougir, to redden, to blush.
Seoir, to be becoming.
Sommer, to summon.
Souffrir, to suffer.
Soupçonner, to suspect.
Se souvenir, to remember.

Suffire, to suffice.
Suggérer, to suggest.
Supplier, to beseech.
Prendre à tâche, to make it a point.
Tenter, to attempt, to endeavour.
Trembler, to tremble.
Se trouver bien, to derive benefit.
Se trouver mal, to fare ill.
Se vanter, to boast.

XL.—Verbs which require no Preposition before the Infinitive which follows them :—

Aimer mieux, to like better, to prefer, to have rather.
Aller, to go.
Compter, to purpose, to intend.
Croire, to believe, to think.
Daigner, to deign.
Devoir, to owe, to be obliged; should, ought, must.
Entendre, to hear.
Envoyer, to send.
Faire, to make, to cause, to get.
Falloir, must.
S'imaginer, to fancy.
Oser, to dare.
Paraître, to appear.
Pouvoir, to be able ; can, may.
Préférer, to prefer.
Prétendre, to mean, to intend.
Savoir, to know how to.
Sembler, to seem.
Sentir, to feel.
Venir, to come.
Voir, to see.
Vouloir, to will, to wish, to want.

XLI.—Finally, the following Verbs offer a peculiarity of their own in the use of the different Prepositions they require before the Infinitive which follows them :—

Convier à is to invite, to send an invitation to one: *Je l'ai convié à dîner.* I invited him or requested his company to dinner. *Convier de* is to beg, to entreat one to do a thing. *On l'a convié de s'y trouver.* He was invited to be there.

Coûter may be followed by *à*, *de*, or *pour*. *Il en coûte à bâtir.* Building is expensive. *La gloire coûte à acquérir.* Glory is dear to purchase. *Que coûte-t-il de souhaiter?* Nothing so easy as wishing. *Je vis qu'il lui en coûtait pour obéir.* I perceived with how much reluctance she obeyed.

Prétendre, in the sense of to aspire, to lay claim, to sue, requires *à*. *Il ne prétend à rien moins qu'à me chasser de ma place.* All his aim is to get me out of my place.

In the sense of *to mean, to intend,* it requires no Preposition. *J'ai prétendu badiner.* I did not say it in earnest; I only meant to jest.

Tarder, to defer, to delay, requires *à* when the object of the action is without. *On a trop tardé à envoyer ce secours.* They delayed too long in sending that assistance. *Il ne tarda guère à le châtier.* He did not long put off his punishment.

Il me tarde, il lui tarde, &c., require *de* before the Infinitive. *Il nous tardait bien d'en être défaits.* We thought it long till we were rid of them.

Appartenir, impersonally used, takes *de*: *Il appartient aux pères de corriger leurs enfants.* It becomes a father, it is the duty of a father, to chastise his children.

Désirer, with the Preposition *de,* expresses a desire, the accomplishment of which is uncertain, difficult, or independent of one's will. *Je désire de réussir.* I wish I could succeed. *Je désire d'en être débarrassé.* I wish I were rid of him.

When, on the contrary, *Désirer* expresses a desire, the fulfilment of which is almost certain or easy, and more or less dependent on one's will, it requires no Preposition. *Je désire le voir, l'entendre; amenez-le-moi.* I wish to see him, to hear him; bring him to me. *Venez, elle désire vous parler.* Come, she wishes to speak to you.

Espérer sometimes requires *de* before an Infinitive,

especially if the Verb by which it is immediately followed is also in the Infinitive. *Peut-on espérer de vous revoir?* May we hope to have the pleasure of seeing you again?

Laisser à in an affirmative, *laisser de* in a negative phrase. *Je laisse à penser la vie que firent ces deux amis.* You may easily imagine what a life of it these two friends lead. *Il ne faut pas laisser d'aller son chemin.* We must jog along for all that.

Penser either takes *à* or *de*, or no Preposition before the Infinitive. *À quoi pensez-vous de faire cela?* What do you mean by that? *Il pensait à me surprendre*, or *me surprendre.* He thought to surprise me, or to take me by surprise.

In the sense of *to be like to, to be on the point of*, &c., the Preposition is generally omitted. *J'ai pensé être tué.* I had like to have been killed.

Résoudre generally takes *de* and sometimes *à*. *Se résoudre* always takes *à*. *Il a résolu d'aller à Paris.* He has decided on going to Paris. *On ne saurait le résoudre à faire cette démarche.* He cannot be brought to take that step. *Il ne pouvait se résoudre à le prendre.* He could not be prevailed upon to take it.

Souhaiter is used with or without *de* before an Infinitive, when the action is confined to the Nominative. *Je souhaiterais de pouvoir, je souhaiterais pouvoir vous obliger.* I wish I could oblige you.

Suffire takes *à* before Nouns, *pour* before Verbs. *Cette somme ne peut pas suffire à tous les besoins.* That sum cannot answer all occasions. *Cette rente ne lui suffit pas pour vivre.* The rent is not sufficient for him to live upon.

Il suffit, impersonal, takes *de* before Nouns or Verbs. *Il suffit d'être malheureux pour être injuste.* Misfortune is sufficient to make one unjust.

Valoir mieux, followed by two Verbs in the Infinitive, takes *que de* before the second Infinitive. *Il y a beaucoup d'occasions où il vaut mieux se taire que de parler.* There are a great many occasions when it is better to be silent than to speak.

Aimer mieux, followed by two Infinitives, with *que de* before the second, implies a preference of WILL. *Elle a mieux aimé rester fille que de faire le mariage qu'on lui proposait.* She had rather remain single than to make the match which was proposed to her.

When *que* alone is placed between the two Infinitives following *aimer mieux*, it indicates a preference of TASTE. *J'aime mieux quitter que disputer.* I rather choose to give up than to dispute. *J'aime mieux lire que jouer.* I am fonder of reading than playing.

Il vaut sometimes admits of the same construction. *Il vaut autant lui donner que lui prêter.* One had as well give him as lend him.

Commencer à indicates tendency to an end, to an object in view, that will have further development. *Ses nuits sont plus calmes, il commence à dormir un peu,* His nights are quieter, he enjoys some sleep.

Commencer de implies that an action is begun with the probability of its being continued, though it might accidently be interrupted. It does not involve an object in view. *Je commençais de dormir, quand ce bruit m'éveilla*, I was hardly over or asleep when this noise awoke me.

Continuer à indicates an intention, an object in view. *Continuez à bien vivre*, continue to live virtuously or to do well.

Continuer de means not to discontinue doing a thing though there might be intervals of suspension. *Il fallut donc continuer de me contraindre, et d'exercer mon emploi d'échanson.* I was then obliged to persist in my dissimulation, and continue to exercise the post of cup-bearer.

Contraindre à, is said where there is tendency to an action or an object in view. *On contraignit les soldats à marcher, à s'avancer, à se battre.* The soldiers were compelled or forced to walk, to advance, to fight.

Contraindre de, where there is cessation of action: *On le contraignit de se taire, de rester, de s'enfuir, de se tenir en repos.* He was compelled to keep silence, to stay, to run away, to keep quiet.

It nearly always takes *de* in the passive: *La ville fut contrainte de se rendre.* The town was compelled to surrender.

Demander à—if the action of the two verbs is done by the same agent: *Philoclès demanda au roi à se retirer.* Philocles asked the king's leave to retire.

Demander de—in the contrary case, *Je vous demande de m'écouter*, I beg you would listen to me.

Obliger à supposes the operation of some outward cause, duty, or obligation. *L'équité nous oblige à restituer ce qui ne nous appartient pas.* Equity makes it our bounden duty to restore that which does not belong to us. *La loi nous oblige à payer.* The law compels us to pay.

Obliger de supposes an obligation within ourselves: *Je me trouvai mal, je fus obligée de m'arrêter.* I felt unwell, and I was obliged to stop. *Obliger,* by doing a service, requires *de;* but *obliger,* in the sense of *porter, exciter, engager,* takes *à.*

Vous m'obligerez beaucoup de faire cela. You will oblige me greatly by doing it. *Quelle raison vous oblige à faire ce que vous faites?* What induces you to act in this manner?

Distinguer d'avec supposes an opposition, a contrast between two beings or things of different qualities, *distinguer la vertu d'avec le vice, la fausse monnaie d'avec la bonne, l'ami d'avec le flatteur.* To make a distinction between virtue and vice, between false money and good, between a friend and a flatterer.

Distinguer de implies a shade, *distinguer la sensation du sentiment, la douceur de la bonté, la piété de la dévotion.* To discriminate sensation from feeling, mildness from goodness, piety from devotion.

S'efforcer, in its literal sense, takes either *à* or *de.* *Ne vous efforcez pas à parler.* Do not overstrain yourself with speaking. *S'efforcer de soulever un fardeau.* To strive to lift up a burden.

Figuratively, it generally requires *de: Je m'efforce de gagner votre amitié.* I endeavour to gain your friendship. *Il s'efforçait de paraître calme.* He endeavoured to appear cool.

Faillir à indicates that the action passes from the agent to another. *Il a failli à être tué.* He was very near being killed. *J'ai failli à le battre.* I was even ready to beat him.

Faillir de implies that the action is confined to the subject. *Il a failli de se contredire, de tomber.* He well nigh contradicted himself, he well nigh fell, or he was nigh falling. *J'ai bien failli de l'oublier.* I had very nearly forgotten it.

Faillir is also used without a Preposition. *Nous faillîmes être assassinés.* We were well nigh being assassinated. *J'ai failli mourir.* I was very near dying.

Manquer de, before an Infinitive signifies *to fail, to forget, to neglect, to miss,* and is generally used negatively. *Ne manquez pas de vous y trouver.* Do not fail to be there.

Manquer de signifies also *to be all but* or *very near to. J'ai manqué de tomber.* I almost fell down,. I was very near falling.

Manquer à signifies to fail in one's duties, one's word or promise. *Manquer à son devoir, à ses amis, à ses engagements.* To fail in one's duties, to one's friends, to one's engagements.

Contraindre, forcer, take *à* or *de* in the Active, but but these verbs have nearly always *de* in the Passive. *On le contraignit de faire* or *à faire cela.* He was obliged to do it.

Consentir à when we freely assent to a thing: *Je consens à vous suivre, à partir.* I am ready to follow you, to start. *Consentir de* when we do not prohibit, prevent, or oppose a thing. *Je consens de le voir, de l'entendre.* I do not object to see him, to hear him.

ON THE ACTIVE PARTICIPIAL CONSTRUCTION.

XLII.—Whether alone, or followed by an indirect Objective, the Verbal Adjective agrees like an Adjective, because it describes the state, the nature or quality of the Noun to which it refers.

Ma femme, vous savez que je n'ai pas l'âme endurante, et que j'ai le bras assez bon. You know, wife, that I am not over-patient, and that my hand is not very light.

Sur l'animal bêlant à ces mots, il s'abat. So saying, he stooped on the bleating creature (*i.e.*, an animal which bleats).

Pleurante après son char, voulez-vous qu'on me voie? Would you have me be seen bathed in tears behind her chariot wheels?

Le drap noir est salissant quand il est neuf. Black cloth soils everything when new.

Le blanc est une couleur salissante. White is a colour that soon soils, *i.e.*, is easily soiled.

From the above examples, we may deduce that Passivity is the characteristic of the Verbal Adjective; Activity is that of the Present Participle.

TURN INTO FRENCH.

The meeting lasted long, and an *important* question was agitated.[1] This lady pleases me, though she has a[2] *forbidding* face. These two venerable[3] men were an *affecting* sight[4] to-this-assembly-of-so-many-nations.[5] This young lady has *engaging* manners.

Why-return-him[6] so *biting* an answer? I have known very *obliging* people. The most regular beauties are not always the most *fascinating*.[7] Those ladies are *tiresome*[8] and *fatiguing*. I found her *dying*. The field was strewn[9] with dead and *dying*. I found her *shivering*[10] all over with cold. The dogs returned *panting* from the hunt. That child is the *living* image of his father.

That man is *quite-enough-to-kill-one*.[11] That conversation is *tiresome*.[12] The mistress of the house is extremely *kind*.[13] These are all *conclusive*[14] reasons. Cabs are not-so-*liable-to-overturn*[15] as Irish cars. She is a very *bustling*[16] woman. An *overwhelming* misfortune. *Troublesome*[17] visits.

Your most humble and *obedient* servant (*f.*). An *interesting* work. This young man has a *good*[18] countenance. *Quivering* limbs. *Palpitating* entrails. Those sovereigns are *of-the-full-weight*.[19] The garrison went out of the place under a *pelting*[20] rain, drums (*sing.*) *beating*, matches lighted, colours flying.[21] This manufacturer has twenty looms *going*.[22]

The-maid-put-in[23] her *smiling* face. The thing being rather unusual, not to say *startling*.[24] The atmosphere was hot and *sultry*.[25] I-called-at-his-house[26] and-found-no[27] *living* creature at home. I hate *slandering* women.

1. Il s'agita.—2. La.—3. Si vénérables.—4. Spectacle.—5. à tant de peuples assemblés.—6. à quoi bon lui faire.—7. Piquant.—8. Ennuyant. —9. Jonché.—10. Trembloter*.—11. Tuer.—12. Tuer.—13. Prévenant.—14. Conclure.—15. Moins versant.—16. Allant.—17. Accablant. —18. Intéressant.—19. Trébuchant.—20. Battant.—21. Enseignes déployées.—22. Battant.—23. La jeune fille montra.—24. Saisissant.—25. Étouffant.—26. J'ai été chez lui.—27. Et je n'y ai.

XLIII.—With or without an Objective, the Present Participle is invariable, if it expresses an action done either by the Nominative or the Objective.

N'osant vous porter les excuses qu'il m'a faites, il

* The Present Participle, or the Verbal Adjective, is to be formed from the Infinitive given in the Notes.

m'a prié de les recevoir en votre nom, et de vous les faire agréer. Being ashamed to excuse himself to you, he begged me to receive his apology in your name, and to prevail upon you to accept it.

Puis j'aperçus un peu plus loin, Fabricius dans la pauvreté, Scipion mourant dans l'exil, Epictète écrivant dans les chaînes, Sénèque et Thraséas les veines ouvertes, et regardant d'un œil tranquille leur sang couler. Then I perceived a little further, Fabricius in poverty, Scipio dying in exile, Epictetus writing when in chains, Seneca and Thraseas with their veins opened, looking calmly at their blood flowing.

TURN INTO FRENCH.

A moment after, Fidèle was at their feet *barking, howling, crying,*[1] and *devouring*[2] them with his caresses. I wanted to drown myself; but *hearing*[3] you lived here, I said to myself, since there are some good white people, I-need-not[4] die yet. The few rats that did remain, *afraid*-of[5] leaving their hole, did not eat half-their-fill.[6] His wife *growing* uglier every day, became shrewish[7] and unbearable.

Having[8] to start to-morrow morning early, had-we-not-better[9] go to bed? *Having* to see the minister, I shall give him your petition. *Happening*-yesterday-to-be[10] in that neighbourhood, I paid[11] her a short visit. *Being*[12] to see her no more, he embraced her with tears in his eyes. We found her *struggling*-for-life.[13] I come to denounce to you a culprit whom his uncle caught *climbing* a tree, and *plundering* the finest fruit of your garden.

I caught him *reading* the letter which he said he had not received. I found my sister *playing* at her piano. We surprised him *picking*[14] the lock. We met them *walking* arm-in-arm.[15]

We saw two men *shooting* on your estate,[16] and *running* away on our approach. *Fearing* lest you should not be happy, I offer you my services. *Fearing* lest you should come, I wrote you to stay. *Fearing* lest you should not have seen him, I directed to him the first letter you wrote me.

The roaring of the wind in the pines *preventing* him from making himself understood, he went-up-to-the[17] shepherd. We perceived the fire-men *running* to the fire. Never *studying*, never *knowing* your lessons, do you expect you will-improve?[18] *Smoking*, *drinking*, and *keeping*-such-late-hours[19] as you do, how can you expect to be in good health?

The sublimest object in the universe is a good man *struggling*-with[20] adversity. What a week I would have had to spend, had she always been about me, *weeping* and *urging*[21] me to turn an informer,[22] a Lord Howard! Greece *having* been swallowed-up[23] by a deluge, new inhabitants came to people it.

Being alone, my brother cannot go-out-of-way.[24] The town *having* been taken and delivered up to plunder, the soldiers made an immense booty. The town *having* refused to surrender, but *having* been taken by storm, all the inhabitants were put-to-the-sword.[25]

The babes *girdling*[26] one another in their innocent arms. All profits *issuing*-from-the-stock[27] shall be divided into equal shares.[28] Either-of-them[29] *believing*-he-could[30] deceive the other. So[31] they went out and made the sepulchre sure,[32] *sealing* the stone, and *setting*-a-watch.[33] Women *talking-scandal*[34] at a tea-table, have a natural eloquence. I, thou, he, or they, *knowing* their intentions, &c.

1. Gémir.—2. Accabler de.—3. Savoir.—4. Il ne faut pas.—5. Ne pas oser.—6. Le quart de son soûl.—7. Acariâtre.—8. Devoir.—9. Ne ferions-nous pas bien de.—10. Se trouver hier.—11. Faire.—12. Devoir.—13. Lutter contre la mort.—14. Crocheter.—15. Bras dessus bras dessous.—16. Terre.—17. Monta vers ce.—18. Faire des progrès.—19. Rentrer aussi tard.—20. Lutter contre.—21. Forcer à.—22. Délateur.—23. Abîmée.—24. S'absenter.—25. Passés au fil de l'épée.—26. S'enlacer.—27. Provenir du capital.—28. Parties.—29. Chacun.—30. S'imaginer.—31. Donc.—32. Assurer.—33. Mettre des gardes.—34. Médire.

XLIV.—However, the English Participle, referring to the Nominative, the Predicate, or the Objective, is more frequently translated in French by a Relative Clause than by a Participial Construction.

Je n'espère plus bonne issue d'une affaire qui traîne tant. I can hope for no good from so lingering a business.

Il nous faut non un homme qui pérore, mais un homme qui agisse. We want not a talking, but an acting man.

Vous verrez à Paris un homme qui a de quoi vivre jusqu'au jour du jugement, qui travaille sans cesse et court risque d'accourcir ses jours pour amasser, dit-il, de quoi vivre. You shall see at Paris a man who has enough to live upon up to the day of judgment, working night and day, and venturing his life to get, as he will tell you, a subsistence.

TURN INTO FRENCH.

We hear the child *making* a great noise. We heard the child *making* a great noise. We shall hear the child *making* a great noise. The vapours *arising* from the Thames are unhealthy. They are idle-fellows[1] *basking* in-the[2] sun. We heard some one *talking* with great[3] volubility. He is a mountebank *amusing* the rabble.

He said to those *standing*[4] around him that he hardly believed the news *spreading*-about.[5] I should not be displeased[6] to see a letter written by a Spaniard *travelling* in France. It is the blind *leading* the blind. I found him *rummaging*-about[7] my drawers.

We found her *drawing* water from[8] a well. Do you like to ride a *stumbling*[9] horse? Do you see those pretty lambs *sporting* by the side of their mother? There is not one in[10] a thousand *possessing* the like qualities. There is something *exciting* to the imagination. There is a fawn *following* its dam,[11] a sole *frying*, a lioness *defending* her young, a *bubbling*[12] spring, a rivulet *gliding*-through[13] the meadow.

There are too many lamps *burning*. Do you hear cats *fighting* on the roof of the house? I saw you *gathering up* coffee on the wharf. He embarked in a vessel *sailing* to Madagascar. I saw a kite *bearing* off a partridge. He has an uncle now[14] *living*.

Every *thinking* man. They thought they saw[15] a boat *lurking*-at[16] that place. Plucking off faded roses, and tying *drooping* pinks. The nations *inhabiting* this country. A man was seen *making*-towards[17] the house. She shall-be-a-pattern[18] to all the princesses *living* with her. That book is no-longer-to-be-met-with;[19] I have the only *remaining* copy.

Speaking of the things *pertaining*-to[20] the kingdom of God. I saw something *swimming*-in[21] the water.

Peasants discovered[22] *drinking, dancing*.

1. Fainéants.—2. Au.—3. Beaucoup de.—4. Se trouver.—5. Se répandre.—6. Fâché de.—7. Fureter.—8. à.—9. Broncher.—10. Sur.—11. Mère.—12. Bouillonner.—13. Fuir dans.—14. Encore.—15. Y voir.—16. Louvoyer près de.—17. Se diriger.—18. Servir de modèle.—19. On ne trouve plus.—20. Regarder.—21. Flotter sur.—22. On voit.

XLV.—The Present Participle, with *En* expressed or understood, is called Gerundive. This Gerundive differs from the Present Participle in so far that it can never refer to the Objective. It represents the Nominative in action, and performing two things at the same time.

Il tremblait en l'écoutant. He trembled as she spoke.

Ne buvez pas en mangeant. Do not drink while you eat.

Les feuilles du laurier décrépitent en brûlant. The leaves of the laurel crackle when burning.

Pourquoi allez-vous branlant la tête et vous tortillant comme des imbéciles, dit une oie à ses oisons? i.e., *en branlant, en tortillant.* Why do you go nodding and waddling like fools, said a goose one day to her goslings?

But we must not say, *Je l'ai vu en mourant maudire ses assassins*, because it would convey that it was the speaker who was seen dying, instead of the person spoken of, who, when dying, was heard cursing his murderers.

TURN INTO FRENCH.

I saw your sister *as I was going* to school. I saw your sister *going* to school. I perceived you *as I was working.* I perceived you *working* diligently.

I met her *as I was going* to the railway. I met her *going* to the railway. I met him *as I was going* to the country. I met him *going* to the country. We met them *as we were going* to the play. We met them *going* to the play.

I saw your brother *as I came* here. I saw him *crossing*[1] the street. I saw him *speaking* to his son. I saw him *as I was speaking* to his son.

He came-up-to[2] her *with a smile.* He gave-himself-a-slash[3] in the chin *while shaving.* I have cut my chin *in shaving.* When milk is stale,[4] it turns *in boiling.* Broth thickens *in boiling.*[5] It[6] came to nothing *in cooking.*

Do you still dream *when sleeping?* Those fruit turn red *when ripening.* Among animals, some[7] feed *whilst they walk*, others *whilst they crawl;* others take their food *as they fly*, and others *as they swim.*

He ran like a madman, *upsetting*[8] all that opposed his passage. He-fell-down[9] *in climbing-up*[10] a tree. Dick came[11] *running in.* The water comes[12] *gushing-out*[13] of the rock. You will-go-through[14] this town *on your way* to Paris. He spoiled[15] four cravats *in putting* them on.

The man went away *saying* it-required-no[16] answer. My girls came *running* to me for[17] a shilling. I am-not-wrong[18] *in surmising*[19] you to be a midshipman.[20] He-was-seized[21] with a cramp *in swimming.* You disoblige me greatly *in not accepting.* *In attempting*[22] to arrange matters,[23] he has embroiled them the-more.[24] The water freezes *in falling*, or *as it falls.* Many a truth has-been-said[25] *in jest.* He went away *muttering.*

I said to the mountebank,[26] *assuming*-the-patron,[27] Well,[28] friend, I shall answer your purpose. *In hurrying*[29] a little, will she arrive in time?

1. Traverser.—2. Aborder.—3. Se faire une taillade.—4. Vieux.—5. Cuire.—6. Cela.—7. Les uns.—8. Culbuter.—9. Il a tombé.—10. Vouloir monter.—11. Entrer.—12. Sortir.—13. Bouillonner.—14. Traverser.—15. Abîmer.—16. Qu'il n'y avait pas de.—17. Me demander.—18. Ne pas se tromper.—19. Conjecturer.—20. Aspirant de marine.—21. Il lui prit.—22. Vouloir.—23. Choses.—24. Davantage.—25. On a souvent dit.—26. Saltimbanque.—27. Trancher du protecteur.—28. Allez.—29. Se presser.

XLVI.—On, signifying *at the moment of, after,* and denoting the time when an action took place, is oftener translated by a Participial Construction, with or without *En,* than by an Infinitive Construction.

En considérant, ayant considéré, ou *après avoir considéré cette question.* On considering the question.

TURN INTO FRENCH.

On seeing this, *on hearing* this. What direction did he take *on starting?* *On seeing* the man, did she burst-out[1] laughing? *On leaving* me, did you go to her house? Who or what is that fop, to make-such-a-fuss[2] *on entering* a ball-room? *On coming*-home,[3] did you find them waiting for you?

Jugurtha exclaimed, *on leaving* Rome, Oh, venal city! thou wouldst sell thyself if-there-were[4] anybody rich enough to buy thee! Can any-one[5] *on his entrance* into the world be-fully-secured[6] he[7] shall not be deceived? *On glancing*-over[8] the article, my eye fell-on[9] the obnoxious[10] passage. That woman fainted away *on hearing* of the death of her husband. *On hearing* that news, she felt-a-dreadful[11] shivering. *Upon hearing*[12] these things, they rejoiced greatly.

1. Eclater de.—2. Faire tant d'embarras.—3. Rentrer.—4. S'il y avait.—5. On.—6. Etre sûr.—7. On.—8. Parcourir.—9. Tomber par hasard.—10. Répréhensible.—11. Il lui prit un horrible.—12. Apprendre.

XLVII.—By, denoting the manner, the instrumental cause of an action, the way of doing something, is translated by *En*.

Les conquérants en poussant leurs conquêtes et en subjuguant leurs ennemis s'en font toujours de nouveaux. Oh, qu'ils s'entendent mal en gloire, d'en espérer une solide en ravageant la terre et en répandant le sang humain! Conquerors, by extending their conquests and subjugating their enemies, always bring fresh ones on themselves. Oh, what a wrong notion they have of glory, since they expect to obtain it by ravaging the earth and by shedding human blood!

TURN INTO FRENCH.

We move[1] *by walking, running,* or *turning*;[2] animals move *by creeping, swimming,* or *flying*.

He has misrepresented[3] the fact *by changing, by suppressing*[4] several leading circumstances. You will oblige me *by doing* that. Those grovelling men rose *by cringing*.[5]

Beware-how[6] you commit yourself *by promising* what you cannot perform.[7] A work is often improved[8] *by being-abridged*.[9] Chemists decompose bodies *by making* them act upon-one-another.[10] He put-himself-out-of-the-road[11] *by leading*-us-astray.[12]

By sitting-a-little-closer,[13] you will all find room on this bench. People[14] often deceive themselves *by judging* from[15] appearances, because imagination always deceives us *by showing* us everything[16] better or worse than-it-is.[17]

By remaining some days at his country-house, I am afraid I-would-be-troublesome-to-him.[18] I got an abatement *by taking* the whole web. Some grow-richer[19] *by giving* than others *by receiving*.

Do-not-betray[20] your ignorance *by talking* of what you do not know. He thought he would do-her-a-great-compliment[21] *by inviting* her to dance. Throughout-most-part-of[22] Europe, the men salute *by taking off* their hats (*sing.*) and *bowing*.[23]

1. Remuer.—2. Se retourner.—3. Dénaturer.—4. Taire.—5. Ramper. 6. Prendre garde de.—7. Tenir.—8. Améliorer.—9. Raccourcir.—10. Les uns sur les autres.—11. Se dérouter.—12. Dérouter.—13. Se gêner un peu.—14. On.—15. Sur.—16. Les choses.—17. Qu'elles ne sont.—18. De le gêner.—19. S'enrichir.—20. N'allez pas montrer.—21. Lui faire bien de l'honneur.—22. Dans presque toute.—23. S'incliner.

XLVIII.—The Present Participle can be preceded by two sorts of *En*—the first a Preposition, the second a Pronoun.

Je n'osais vous parler de cela, mais vous me mettez à l'aise en m'en parlant le premier. I dared not speak to you about it, but you have relieved me by being the first to mention it.

This construction, however, should be sparingly used, as it is not very harmonious, and should be avoided if the Present Participle should commence with *En* or *Em*, as *en en emportant, en en allant chercher d'autres. En en cherchant d'autres.*

TURN INTO FRENCH.

He attempted to exculpate himself *by throwing*[1] the blame (of it) on his companions. In cutting bread, did you not cut your finger? *In* cutting *some*, did you not cut it? *When* coming *from it*, did you meet with him?

1. Rejeter.

XLIX.—The Pronoun *En* ought never to be put before a Present Participle if governed by the Infinitive which follows, as,

Je vous ai remis mon fils en voulant faire un bon peintre. It should be, *voulant en faire.* I placed my son into your hands, as I wish to make a good painter of him.

TURN INTO FRENCH.

He sends, sent, or will send his son to Cambridge, wishing *to make* a good mathematician *of him.* As-I-am[1] *to make* an engineer of him, he must thoroughly[2] know mathematics.

1. Devant.—2. à fond.

L.—*Tout,* before a Present Participle, has an intensive force variously rendered in English.

Jasant tout en allant. Chatting as they went.

Elle travaillait tout en parlant. Her talking did not prevent her working.

Tout en sentant vivement le reproche, il répondit avec sang-froid et modération. Keenly as he felt the reproach, he replied with coolness and moderation.

TURN INTO FRENCH.

Even while asserting-the-truth-of-your-remark[1] I did not think the step[2] to be proper. *At-the-same-that-he*[3] *complained* that the dinner was bad, he went-on-eating-as-much-as-any-four-would have-done.[4] A father loves his children, *even while he hates* their faults.

Even while sweeping the stairs, she stopped and stood-motionless,[5] forgetting her broom and the whole universe. The-evening-before,[6] *even while drinking* with the carriers, *while smoking, while singing* stupid songs, he spent[7] the evening observing the stranger, watching[8] him like a cat, and studying him like a mathematician.

All-in-a joke,[9] he told her unpleasant truths. *Much as I esteem her,* I am far from admiring her conduct in this matter. *Severely as I appear* to judge of her conduct, I nevertheless respect her.

Greatly[10] *as I love her,* I feel it-my-duty[11] not to yield to her entreaties. *Highly*[12] *as I esteem her,* I will not intrust her with my secret. She read the newspaper *while she waited.* We are-very-fond-of-speculating[13] *as we walk-*through[14] the streets.

Even while speaking to me, he stole money from me. *All in a joke,* he related his misfortunes to me. They were gossiping[15] *over-a-bottle-of-wine.*[16] *Though jesting,* I give you, I gave you, I shall give you a serious advice.

1. Convenir de la vérité de ce que vous dites.—2. Démarche.—3. Tout en se.—4. Manger comme quatre.—5. Rester immobile.—6. La veille.—7. Passer à.—8. Guetter.—9. Plaisanter.—10. Beaucoup.—11. Qu'il est de mon devoir.—12. Infiniment.—13. Aimer beaucoup à faire des spéculations.—14. Aller par.—15. Causer.—16. Tout en buvant.

LI.—With *Aller*, the Present Participle denotes that a thing is going on better and better, worse and worse, more and more, less and less.

Elle ne guérissait pas, mais plutôt allait en empirant. She was nothing better, but rather grew worse.

TURN INTO FRENCH.

Two lines *continue*[1] *widening.*[2] These mountains *stretch themselves* (go stretching). The river *winds-about.*[3] Mankind *goes on improving.*[4] They complained that their fatigues *had-been-going*[5] *on increasing,*[6] and the means of bearing up with them *decreasing.*

The evil will *go on increasing.* At-that-spot,[7] the bed of the river, the road *begins*[8] *to-narrow.*[9]

After the 21st of December, the days *go on increasing;* and after the 21st of June, the days *go on decreasing.* They *go on* skipping and dancing. His excesses *went on increasing.* He *went about tippling*-at-his-tenants'-houses.[10]

1. Aller.—2. S'écarter.—3. Aller en serpentant.—4. Se perfectionner. —5. Eussent été.—6. Croître.—7. Dans cet endroit.—8. Aller.—9. S'étrécir.—10. Se griser chez ses fermiers.

LII.—Verbal clauses resolved by a Participial Construction.

Les recors, étant allés pour exécuter ses meubles, trouvèrent maison nette. The bailiffs who went to distrain his goods, found everything had been cleared off.

En le prenant sur ce ton-là, vous m'intéressez à vous servir. Since you talk in that style, I am interested in your behalf.

Celui-là était la vraie lumière qui éclaire tout homme venant au monde. That was the true light which lighteth every man that cometh into the world.

TURN INTO FRENCH.

I cannot have the pleasure of dining with you, *since I have* business which will detain me in town. We saw it plainly[1] *as-we-approached*[2] the town. You met-with[3] a great loss *when you lost* your father.

I shall read his letter *when-I-take-a-walk.*[4] The canons, *as they enter* the choir, bow-down-to[5] the altar.

The carts, *as-they-went-off,*[6] peeled-the-bark-off[7] that tree. *As* that machine *was rising,* the rope broke.[8] *As I have* an opportunity to serve him, I will not fail-in-doing-so.[9]

As he has no money, he cannot pay you. *As she got* up, she-fell-in[10] a swoon. I had but two hundred pounds *when I set-up.*[11] *As* my father *was in* the country, I could not go-out-of-the-way.[12] *As* my brothers *were* at the theatre, I could not go out. *As he is* unwell, he cannot go out. *As I am not able* to receive his visit to-day, I shall invite him for Sunday next.

As he passed, he threw the parcel to me, and I caught[13] it in my hat. *As we were afraid* to wake you, we spoke quite low. *As-I-have*[14] to start to-morrow, I came to bid-you good-bye.[15] *As you are* here for a long time, and *have* nothing to do, you may as well come and see me. *As I have promised* to-be-there,[16] I must keep my word.

Marius, *though-he-had-been*[17] six times a consul, was nevertheless obliged to beg publicly for his life. Do you live in Paris? No; we are here only-*temporarily*.[18] We sat listening[19] to the rain *as it pattered*[20] on the boat. I cannot go with you, *as I have* something to do. *When I entered* the room, I bowed to her. I am sure that *if you work* diligently[21] you will soon beat[22] your schoolfellows. Bourbon, *who led* the foremost[23] of the enemy's troops, found him in this position.

1. Distinctement.—2. Approcher de.—3. Faire.—4. Se promener.—5. Faire une inclination devant.—6. Passer.—7. Ecorcher l'écorce de.—8. Se casser.—9. Y manquer.—10. Il lui prit.—11. Commencer.—12. S'absenter.—13. Recevoir.—14. Devoir.—15. Faire ses adieux.—16. De m'y trouver.—17. Ayant été.—18. Qu'en passant.—19. Ecouter le bruit.—20. Tomber.—21. Assidûment.—22. Surpasser.—23. La tête.

LIII.—The Participle and Verb may also, when the actions are of nearly equal importance, be translated by two Verbs with *And*, or One of the Verbs is resolved by a Participial Construction.

Ils s'avancèrent ET *écrasèrent*, ou *Ils s'avancèrent en écrasant tout ce qui se trouvait devant eux*. They advanced and mowed down everything before them.

Elle flatte Ménélas, en lui disant qu'il possède toutes les qualités de l'esprit et du corps. She compliments Menelaus, and says he wanted no accomplishment either of mind or body.

TURN INTO FRENCH.

The next day, I was horrified by seeing the ink-bottle had struck *and split*[1] on the wall of the newly-painted[2] drawing-room. They exclaimed, *and drew* their swords. They returned to the citadel, *and declared* it to be their determination to fight to the last gasp.

As soon as the queen entered the House of Commons, all the members rose up *and cried*: Long live the queen! Mentor *pushes Telemachus, and* precipitates him into the sea. He *arose*[3] *and* rebuked the winds and the sea. The knife *fell down and* cut his wrist.

As soon as Cæsar entered the Senate, all the conspirators threw themselves upon him *and stabbed* him.

1. Se briser.—2. Fraîchement décoré.—3. Se Lever.

ON THE ABSOLUTE PARTICIPIAL CONSTRUCTION.

LIV.—The Passive Participle, with *Étant* or *Ayant été*, sometimes expressed, but generally understood in French, forms an isolated and independent Proposition, which seems neither to be governed nor to govern anything.

César étant mort, l'armée ayant été détruite, ou *César mort, l'armée détruite.* Cæsar being dead, the army having been destroyed.

LV.—Sometimes the English Present Participle is expressed in French by the Past Participle.

Le pauvre paysan, sur sa bêche appuyé, peut se croire un moment seigneur de son village. The poor peasant, leaning on his spade, may for a while dream he is the lord of his village.

TURN INTO FRENCH.

She was *sitting* with her head *leaning* on her hands. Turenne was found *sleeping* on a gun carriage in the dead of winter. My little boy, *riding* on his pony, was following us.

The ceremony *being**-*over*,[1] we bent-our-steps[2] each to our

* From this paragraph the Present Participles are not to be translated.

home. This resolution *being taken*, we finished[3] our supper. This *being done*, he got up, and I helped him to dress. *Having become* the mistress of her actions, she dismissed some servants.

The shepherd *being struck*, the sheep are scattered.[4] The bargain *being done*, and the supper *over*, we went to bed. But *having become* a mother, she feared no more the shame of a refusal.

We slept soundly *being-done-up*[5] with the fatigues of the previous-day.[6] We sat up all night, *being frightened at* the state we had seen him in.

Spring *being come*, they-threatened-to[7] destroy a rising[8] town which refused to obey them.

The battle *being lost*, the town *being taken*, the soldiers committed[9] every sort of cruelty. Carthage *having become* rich sooner than Rome, was also the sooner corrupted.

1. Finir.—2. S'en retourner.—3. Achever.—4. Dispersés.—4. Epuisés. —6. La veille.—7. Ils menaçaient de.—8. Naissante.—9. Se permirent.

ON THE ENGLISH PARTICIPIAL CONSTRUCTION.

INDICATIVE PRESENT.

LVI.—The English Participial Construction is the Present Participle preceded by MY, THY, HIS, HER, OUR, YOUR, THEIR, expressed or understood, or by a Genitive Construction.

Ces fleurs passent presque au moment où elles s'épanouissent. There is scarce an instant between these flowers blooming and their fading.

TURN INTO FRENCH.

You will-be-amused-*at-my*[1] *making* such a proposal. She laughs *at*[2] *my not being able* to speak French. He is offended *at-my-not-going*[3] to see him. Such circumstances account *for his insisting*-on-immediate-payment.[4] The advantage which that house has over the other is-*in-its*[5] *being* better *situated*. That distemper proceeds from-the-juices[6] *being* vitiated.

I cannot account-*for-his*[7] *favouring* this party. This comes *of*[8] *judging* by-the-eye[9] without consulting the reason. Many articles improve[10] *on being kept.*[11] They quiz him, *without his perceiving* it (translate—and he does not). *Our borrowing* (translate—we borrow) words from[12] other nations is now[13] a-wantonness,[14] not a necessity. He is-offended-*at*[15] *my not going* to see him.

I am surprised *at-her-not*[16] *coming, at her not writing.* What-is-the-reason-of[17] *your coming* so late? *It being* my intention to go and see you, I-shall-let-you[18] know when

1. Aller rire de ce que je.—2. De.—3. De ce que je.—4. Vouloir être payé à l'instant.—5. C'est qu'elle.—6. De ce que les sucs.—7. M'expliquer comment il.—8. De ce qu'on.—9. Sur le témoignage des yeux.—10. Se bonifier lorsqu'on.—11. Les garder.—12. Aux.—13. Aujourd'hui.—14. Par licence.—15. S'offenser de ce que.—16. De ce qu'elle.—17. Pourquoi.—18. Je vous ferai.

IMPERFECT.

Salluste loue Pompée de ce qu'il courait, sautait et portait un fardeau aussi bien qu'homme de son temps. Sallust praises Pompey for his running, his leaping, and his carrying a burden as well as any man of his time.

TURN INTO FRENCH.

This arose-from[1] *her imagining* she was pretty. *His leaning*[2] towards the side of authority was once or twice remarked (translate—one remarked that). A blackbird perched upon a tree was jeering a hare *at-his*[3] *being* under the talons of a kite, and *at his making* great lamentations. He gently reproached her *with*[4] *expressing* herself in a language which she did not know.[5]

He was displeased-*with-your*[6] *doubting* his ability.[7] We[8] may recollect *their imputing* the miscarriage[9] of the plans to the inability[10] of the general. This arose *from her inuring*[11] herself to fatigue, and *from her living* alone. Did you observe *their whispering?*[12] He was-angry-at[13] so many bars[14] *being-thrown*[15] in-his-way.[16]

He was-ignorant[17] of *our being* so near. We were ignorant *of your keeping*[18] so many servants. I appeared to be persuaded *of his being*-in-the-right.[19]

We drank Lady Franklin's health at the old gentleman's table, and,[20] *it being* his daughter's birth-day, her's too.

1. Provenir de ce que.—2. Pencher.—3. De ce qu'il.—4. De ce qu'elle. —5. Comprendre.—6. Blessé de ce que vous.—7. Capacité.—8. On.—9. Echec.—10. Incapacité.—11. S'endurcir à.—12. Se parler à l'oreille. —13. S'irriter de ce qu'on.—14. Obstacles.—15. Opposer.—16. Lui. —17. Ne pas savoir.—18. Avoir.—19. Avoir raison.—20. Et comme.

PAST DEFINITE.

La proposition qu'il me fit d'entrer dans les affaires. His proposal for my engaging in business.

L'esprit de faction et de mécontentement éclatèrent avec une animosité d'autant plus grande qu'ils avaient été longtemps comprimés. Faction and discontent, from being long repressed, burst forth with fiercer animosity.

TURN INTO FRENCH.

It-was-*his*[1] *reprobating* their proceedings[2] that made-him-insist-upon[3] *being-tried.* Since the-time-*of-his*[5] *resigning*-the[6] office of regent. We-may[7] recollect *of their inventing* an instrument. From[8] the time *of his quitting*[9] the House of Commons. They escaped the-penalty-*by*[10] *pleading* ignorance of the law.

We may recollect *his obliging* the troops to march. *His giving* a-public-audience[11] to the envoy excited violent suspicions. What-do-you-think-*of-his*[12] *sitting down* in that very chair, and of *his crying*[13] like a child?

I will not relate the-distress-occasioned-by[14] *my being-desired*[15] to carve a fowl, or help-to[16] various dishes that stood[17] near me.

1. C'est parcequ'il.—2. Conduite.—3. Qu'il insista pour qu'il.—4. Etre mis en jugement.—5. L'époque où il.—6. Se démettre de la. —7. On doit *ou* on peut.—8. Depuis.—9. Se retirer.—10. à la peine

parcequ'ils.—11. L'audience publique qu'il.—12. Croiriez-vous qu'il.—13. Se mettre à pleurer.—14. L'embarras que j'éprouvai quand on.—15. Prier.—16. Servir de.—17. Se trouver.

PAST INDEFINITE.

Il a fait soixante milles à cheval en un jour, que pensez-vous de cela? What do you think of his riding sixty miles in one day?

Elle s'est mise dans une colère épouvantable contre lui parcequ'il a osé lui dire la vérité. She got into a mighty rage with him for his daring to tell her the truth.

TURN INTO FRENCH.

He grumbles-at[1] his brother's *having* a larger share than himself. It-is-pleasing-to-them-as-a-reward-*for-their*[2] *being* good. Do you recollect *being shown* a hammer at the first inquest? This was the-only-reason[3] of Brown's *intrusting* the goods to him.

He owns[4] *having found* it. Do you remember[5] *his passing*-sly-remarks-about[6] her? Do you remember *my telling* you of it? She complains *of being insulted.* I feel myself quite another-man[7] since *taking* that resolution.[8] He complains *of having been overtaxed.* She complains *of her having been kept-in*[9] unjustly. *His succeeding* is no reason for *your succeeding* (*Subj.*). *My-saying*-so[10] is no reason for *her repeating* it (*Subj.*).

1. Murmurer de ce que.—2. Cela leur est agréable en recompense de ce qu'elles.—3. Par ce seul motif.—4. Avouer que.—5. Se souvenir.—6. Faire de malignes remarques sur.—7. Autre.—8. Parti.—9. Retenir.—10. Si je l'ai dit.

PAST ANTERIOR.

Après qu'il eut examiné mon compte, il me paya tout de suite. On his looking over my account, he paid me at once.

TURN INTO FRENCH.

On his[1] *receiving* the money, he spent it. *On his obtaining* the situation, he tendered-his-resignation.[2] *On his*[3] *being asked* the reason, he did not know what[4] to answer. *After their crossing* the river, and *their receiving* the order from their general, they attacked the enemy at once. *After their checking*[5] the account, I found another mistake.

1. Dès qu'il.—2. Se démettre.—3. Lorsqu'on lui.—4. Que.—5. Vérifier.

PLUPERFECT.

On avait remarqué qu'il s'était tenu en embuscade dans les environs. His lurking about the place had been noticed.

TURN INTO FRENCH.

I knew *of his having written* to his father. Did you know *of his having set out* for France? There-was-a-report-*of-his*[1] *having left*[2] her a considerable legacy. I was not aware *of their exchanging* horses. She complained *of his buying* it. He greatly complained *at having been prevented* from ——.

This arose from *B.'s imbibing*-their-errors,[3] *from his incurring* the queen's displeasure, *from-his-ingratiating*-himself-with[4] your uncle, from the *king's imposing* too rigid[5] laws upon them. This arose *from imbuing-them*[6] with bad principles. This arose *from B.'s ordering-out*-his-troops-early.[7]

The horses could be of no service, from the servant's *having neglected* to have them shod.

1. Le bruit courut qu'il lui.—2. Fait.—3. Donner dans leurs erreurs.—4. S'insinuer dans les bonnes grâces de.—5. Sévères.—6. Inculquer à.—7. Mettre les troupes en mouvement de bonne heure.

FUTURE.

Il ne lui arrivera aucun mal tant qu'il sera sous ma garde. No evil shall befall him while in my keeping.

TURN INTO FRENCH.

You may be sure *of their paying* you well for[1] your compliance. You will be able to distinguish-the-king-*by-his*[2] *remaining* covered. Be assured *of my ever remaining*[3] your dutiful son. Who will vouch *for your being* more reasonable for the future? You may depend *upon hearing*-from-me.[4] You may[5] depend *upon his dispensing* with your services.
I depend *upon his writing.*

1. De.—2. Reconnaître le roi à ce qu'il.—3. Demeurer.—4. Recevoir de mes nouvelles.—5. Soyez sûr qu'il.

CONDITIONAL.

Quant aux expressions grotesques dont il se serait servi, mon opinion est qu'elles ne le sont pas. As to his using ludicrous expressions, my opinion is that they are not so.

TURN INTO FRENCH.

I was in hopes *of his coming.* In the event-*of-his*[1] *being* asked for the key. Their support was-made-conditional-*upon-her*[2] *quitting* the wretched man. We depended-*upon*[3] *his lending* the money.

1. Le cas qu'on.—2. Ne lui fut accordé qu'à la condition qu'elle.—3. Compter.

SUBJUNCTIVE PRESENT.

Il est impossible que vous soyez utile à quoi que ce soit. There is no possibility of your doing any service.

TURN INTO FRENCH.

I see no[1] inconvenience in[2] *your doing* that. I find-no-fault-with[3] *your going* there. What occasion is there *for your doing* it? We are not offended-with-a[4] dog *for having* a-better[4] nose than his master. I despair[6] of ever *seeing*-him-do-good.[7]

I dislike *your appearing* in the business. I consent *to her doing* it. I rejoice[8] *at their falling*-within-our-subject.[9] She doubts *his returning*. He insists[10] upon everything *coming from*, and *depending on*[11] him. What likelihood is there *of his ever making* a fortune? What probability is there *of his being* still alive?

I insist *upon your going*. I do not care-much-about[12] that man. I do not care *for his coming*. I am not astonished *at your seeing* it. I remember without *your telling* me. She will-not-hear[13] *of his going*. There is no-necessity[14] *for your interfering*. You will not oppose[15] *his marrying* your sister. Do you doubt *my being* sincere? I do-not-approve[16] of *your associating with* such people.

1. Nul.—2. à ce que.—3. Ne pas trouver à redire que.—4. Choqués de ce qu'un.—5. Plus de.—6. Je n'espère pas qu'il.—7. Faire quelque chose de bon.—8. Etre charmé que.—9. Rentrer dans notre sujet.—10. Prétendre.—11. De.—12. Se soucier de.—13. Ne pas vouloir.—14. Inutile. —15. S'opposer à ce que.—16. Ne pas trouver bon *ou* trouver mauvais.

PAST SUBJUNCTIVE.

Je suis fâché qu'on vous ait fait attendre si longtemps.

I am sorry at your having been kept waiting so long.

TURN INTO FRENCH.

I wonder-*at*[1] *your having had* the courage to undertake so difficult a task.[2] Nothing seems to denote *his being attacked* by[3] that disease. He is indignant *at your having broken*[4] your word. I am astonished *at his leaving* so comfortable[5] a situation.

I wonder *at-his-extricating-himself*-so-well-out-of-the-scrape.[6] I wonder at your father's *growing*-so-fond-of[7] her. I cannot think of-*his-gambling*.[8] I regret *your-spending*-so-much-labour[9] for nothing. I regret *her labouring*-under-such-a-mistake.[10] You are-found-fault-with[11] *for having* done so.

I am indignant *at-your-having-been-disrespectful*[12] to your mother. I wonder *at your not having provided*-against-such-an[13] accident. I disapprove much *of his having gone*[14] without my leave. I understand[15] *his not having been* satisfied with your conduct. You do-not-deny[16] your *having been* sorry for it, but I deny *having been* sorry for it. I am not at all surprised at *his having* got-into[17] so many difficulties.

1. Admirer que.—2. Chose.—3. De.—4. Manquer à.—5. Bonne.—6. Se tirer si bien d'affaire.—7. S'éprendre d'une telle passion pour.—8. Devenir si joueur.—9. Se donner tant de peine pour.—10. Etre tombé dans une telle méprise.—11. On trouve à redire que.—12. Manquer.—13. Prévoir cet.—14. Partir.—15. Concevoir.—16. Ne pas désavouer.—17. S'attirer.

IMPERFECT SUBJUNCTIVE.

La nation commençait à perdre l'espoir qu'Elisabeth se mariât. The nation began to despair of Elizabeth's marrying.

TURN INTO FRENCH.

You desire your son to amass riches by intrigue; I[1] should prefer *his living* in an honourable poverty. Our masters insisted[2] *on our being* attentive, and wondered *at our making-wrong-answers*[3] to dry questions that we did not understand at all. We wondered *at their entertaining*[4] such hopes. There was no further reason[5] for the regent's *producing* proofs.

Doubts-had-been-entertained-*of*[6] *their being able* to reach the fort. They-were-astonished-*at*[7] *our returning* so late. I could-perceive-no indication-of[8] the house *being inhabited.* There would be no harm *in-your-keeping-away-for*[9] a week or two. They were allowed to fight-out[10] their quarrel without anybody *interfering*[11] on either side.

We could not account-for[12] *his enduring* her insolence. They opposed *his enforcing*-the-law.[13] The Venetian would-have-insisted-on[14] the Englishman's *getting*[15] into the carriage. They had been adverse-*to-his*[16] *managing*[17] the concern. Great-objection-was-taken-against-*his-directing*[18] the concern.[19] She insisted upon the landlord's *leaving*-the-room.[20]

1. Moi, je.—2. Exiger.—3. Répondre mal.—4. Avoir.—5. Motif.—6. On avait douté que.—7. On a été étonné que.—8. Ne voir aucun indice que.—9. Faire une absence de.—10. Démêler.—11. S'y intéresser.—12. Comprendre qu'il.—13. Faire exécuter la loi.—14. Aurait voulu que.—15. Monter.—16. Opposés à ce qu'il.—17. Diriger.—18. On s'opposa fortement à ce qu'il dirigeât.—19. L'établissement.—20. Sortir.

PLUPERFECT SUBJUNCTIVE.

Notre examinateur ne s'étonna-t-il pas que nous eussions mal répondu à des questions que nous ne comprenions pas? Was not our examiner surprised at our not having answered those questions which we did not understand?

TURN INTO FRENCH.

My father approved *of-my-having-helped*[1] those unfortunate-wretches.[2] He denied *having entered* into any[3] league. I approved *of her having taken* precautions. I was surprised at *her having arrived* so soon. I was not aware *of your having returned.*[4]

The day passed without *our being-aware*-of-it.[5] Should-you-have-acted[6] thus without[7] *being*-ordered?[8] They were-displeased-with[9] *our having done* so without leave.

1. Secourir.—2. Infortunés.—3. Aucune.—4. Revenir.—5. S'en apercevoir.—6. Deviez-vous agir.—7. Sans qu'on.—8. Avoir reçu l'ordre.—9. Trouver mauvais que.

INFINITIVE MOOD.

Je puis leur pardonner de m'avoir trompé, mais je ne puis leur pardonner de l'avoir trompée. Their having deceived me, I can forgive; but I cannot forgive their deceiving her.

TURN INTO FRENCH.

Perhaps *my*[1] *being* here prevents *her coming.* They hamper[2] our souls, and hinder *their-flying-upwards.*[3] We cannot approve *of your doing it.* What hinders you *from having* the same right? I do not recollect *my having* given you the order. The pew opener suggested-the-propriety-of[4] *his retiring* into the vestry.

That novel is hardly worth[5] *reading.* He insisted upon

addressing[6] the meeting. It was[7] *the keeping*[8] of bad company that injured[9] his reputation.

1. Peut-être est-ce moi qui.—2. Embarrasser.—3. De s'élever vers le ciel.—4. L'engagea à.—5. Ne pas valoir.—6. S'adresser à.—7. C'est pour.—8. Fréquenter.—9. Qu'il a ruiné.

LVII.—English Participial Construction resolved by Nouns or by Infinitives.

Je ne fis point un mystère de ma sortie de l'archevêché. I made no mystery of my leaving the archbishop's service.

Il y a de quoi établer tant de chevaux, tant de bœufs. There is stabling for so many horses, so many oxen.

Doutez-vous de ma solvabilité? Do you doubt my being able to pay?

La persévérance seule le fera. Nothing but keeping on will do it.

TURN INTO FRENCH.

The-settling[1] of the throne, laws, religion, authority, power. *The-affecting*-of[2] liberality and magnificence breaks[3] the merchant. *Your-slighting*[4] him will-take[5] ten thousand subjects from your power.[6] It has cost so much for *the sawing* of that block of marble.

At *the opening* of the book, he lighted[7] upon such a chapter. I shall acquaint[8] him with *your-setting-out*[9] I cannot-put-up-with[10] *his shufflings.*[11] *The-transporting*-of-earth-from-one-place-to-another[12] is very expensive. *Seeing*-the[13] world improves[14] a young man. The street is quite encumbered by *the-pulling-down*[15] of those houses.

The wavering-testimony[16] of the witnesses made[17] their depositions suspected. *The-tossing*[18] of the ship was so violent that it made her quite sick.

The-lowering[19] of the wall has thrown[20] more light upon the house. *The-falling*[21] of the mercury in the barometer. *The barking* of this dog has hindered me from sleeping. He forgets *eating*[22] and *drinking.*

The-sinking[23] of the ground in that place is considerable. There is a good deal of waste[24] in *the-refining*[25] of sugar. *The-bedding*[26] of this establishment is periodically purified by a chemical process. On *his coming*-to[27] the throne. On *the rising* of the curtain.

The fifth of May was fixed for *the-meeting*[28] of Parliament. Is that the cause of *their being*-poor?[29] *Their singing* was much admired. He gives all his time *to studying. Reading* is bad-for-your[30] eyes. Lay-by[31] your *reading*, and come and take a walk. *His having-been-educated*[32] was of great use to him.

The first thing they-gave-themselves-unto[33] was *the tilling of* the earth. She is gone *a-hunting. His-dealings*[34] are-somewhat-of-kin[35] to the butcher's. *The lading* of ships. *His indulging*[36] in pleasantry lost[37] him many friends. Is *the learning* of French difficult?

This is a scheme of *his devising*.[38] *Their meaning*[39] is plain.[40] *Proceedings*-had-been-taken-by-Sam-for-the-recovery[41] of his son. I persuaded her to give me a *sitting* or two.

Bullying[42] won't-do.[43] The sun has an-influence-in[44] *whitening* cloth. *His layings-out*[45] exceed *his comings-in*.[46] The invention of *printing* dates from the 15th century. *The ripening*[47] of the fruit depends on the sun. *The reading* of such authors has[48] depraved his taste. It-must-be-no-easy-matter-to find[49] his match for *fencing, boxing*,[50] *running*. Let not *my being-here*[51] hinder you from doing what you please. Do you understand *gardening*?

1. L'affermissement.—2. Les prétentions à.—3. Ruiner.—4. Mépris pour.—5. Enlever.—6. Empire.—7. Tomber.—8. Informer.—9. Départ.—10. Ne pas s'accommoder de.—11. Faux-fuyants.—12. Le transport des terres.—13. La fréquentation du.—14. Fait bien.—15. Cet abatis.—16. La vacillation.—17. Rendre.—18. L'agitation.—19. L'abaissement.—20. Donné.—21. L'abaissement.—22. Le manger.—23. L'affaissement.—24. Déchet.—25. L'affinage.—26. La literie.—27. Avènement à.—28. L'ouverture.—29. Pauvreté.—30. Fait mal aux.—31. Quitter.—32. Instruction.—33. à laquelle ils s'adonnèrent.—34. Ses occupations.—35. Se rapprocher assez de.—36. l'enchant à.—37. Faire perdre.—38. Invention.—39. Intention.—40. Evident.—41. Faire des démarches pour ravoir.—42. Fanfaronnades.—43. N'être pas de saison.—44. La propriété de.—45. Dépenses.—46. Revenus.—47. Maturité.—48. Lui a.—49. On trouverait difficilement.—50. Au pugilat.—51. Présence.

ON THE PASSIVE PARTICIPIAL CONSTRUCTION.

LVIII.—A Past Participle, used without an Auxiliary, takes the Gender and Number of the word to which it relates.

Que de machines imaginées et construites par le génie de l'homme pour économiser le travail! How many machines for saving labour has the ingenuity of man devised and constructed!

LIX.—Conjugated with *Etre*, the Past Participle agrees with the Nominative, whether the latter be placed before or after the Verb.

Cette affaire a été rompue et renouée plusieurs fois. The matter has been off and on several times.

L'identité du prévenu avec l'homme signalé à la police n'a pas encore été bien constatée, bien reconnue, bien prouvée. The identity of the accused with the man denounced to the police has not been as yet well established, well acknowledged, well proved.

TURN INTO FRENCH.

Your shoe-strings are *untied.* The strings[1] of your bonnet are *untied.* This skirt[2] is not *sewed;* it is only *basted.*[3] She is *occupied* in sewing.

She was *broken* on the wheel, *burnt,* and *buried* in the Place-de-Grève. She is well *inclined*[4] towards you; what-if[5] you proposed-for[6] her? She is *engaged*[7] to Mr. Such-a-one. The previous[8] question was *put*[9] and *carried.*[10]

Whole streets in Paris have been *levelled*-with-the-ground.[11] When she is *married*, will-she-be-*better-off*?[12] I do not think your conduct will be *approved* of (*Subj.*). The Christian religion has been *sealed* by the blood of the martyrs. I do not think the play was *performed* (*Subj.*) before the end of the month. His hopes (*f.*) have been *deceived.*

Ladies, are-you-willing[13] to stop when you are *tired?* Are you (*f.*) *used*[14] to getting up early? Is your lady *disposed* to come to the concert? Has your niece *got-cured*[15] of her illness? The table must be *covered* with a white tablecloth. The half of your apples *got-spoiled.*[16] The army was quite *dispirited*[17] by such a succession of defeats.[18]

1. Brides (*f.*).—2. Jupe.—3. Bâtir.—4. Disposer.—5. Et si.—6. Demander en mariage.—7. Promettre.—8. Préalable.—9. Proposer.—10. Adopter.—11. Raser de fond en comble.—12. Etre plus avancée.—13. Disposer.—14. Accoutumer.—15. Guérir.—16. Gâter.—17. Démoraliser.—18. Revers.

LX.—With any other Verb than *Avoir*, the Past Participle agrees with the Nominative.

La condition où elle se voit réduite est déplorable. The situation to which she sees herself reduced is deplorable.

TURN INTO FRENCH.

She gave-herself-up-for-*lost.*[1] *She* remained *caught*[2] by her gown. *She* looked very *excited.*[3] *She* seems *afflicted. She* seems to be much-*altered.*[4] *We* feel ourselves *overwhelmed.*

They feel *tired.* Those *ladies* remained *surprised, confused, dismayed.*[5] *She* reigned *beloved* of her subjects.

The *deputies* started, *charged* with[6] their instructions. The *gate* had lain-wide[7] *open. She* seemed quite *dispirited.* Did *she* not believe herself *trifled-with*[8] by him, *outraged*, and *deserted?* Her *energies*[9] seemed to be *annihilated.*

1. Se croire perdu.—2. Accrocher.—3. Agiter.—4. Bien changer.—5. Déconcerter.—6. De.—7. Rester toute.—8. Bafouer.—9. Facultés.

LXI.—The Past Participle of Intransitive Verbs, conjugated with *Etre*, agrees with its Nominative.

Comment êtes-vous devenus si intimes? How came you and he to be so confidential?

Je crois que votre sœur serait partie plus tôt si elle avait su que vous ne vinssiez pas. I think your sister would have started sooner, had she known you were not coming.

TURN INTO FRENCH.

The letter *reached*[1] me at seven o'clock. Those are the latest news that *have reached* (*Subj.*) us. Does your mother still keep her room? No; she *came down* to-day for the first time. I do not think my sister *will-be-back*[2] (*Subj.*) before six o'clock. Let-us-resume[3] the discourse where we *left-off.*[4] The young-birds[5] *are-hatched.*[6] My flowers *are-blown.*[7] His ewes *died* of the rot.[8] A dozen of men *came* to ask-for money.

Had you *been born* when she *was born?* She *departed*-this-life-in[9] the twentieth year of her age. They *went-off*[10] quicker than they *came.* She *is* not yet quite *recovered*[11] from her fright. They *became* rich by keeping boarders. What *is become of* all our years? They *have passed-away*, they are lost.

Will you breakfast before your sister *is back* (*Subj.*) from the market? When she *is back* what will she do? I do not think those ladies *have agreed*[12] (*Subj.*) to go to Paris. This poor woman *died* this morning. Did they *succeed-in*[13] finding a better situation? Is it not a-pity[14] that the young ladies *are-out*[15] (*Subj.*)? *Are* they *gone* to the ball?

1. Parvenir.—2. Revenir.—3. Reprendre.—4. Rester.—5. Petits.—6. Eclore.—7. Eclore.—8. Clavelée.—9. Décéder à.—10. S'en retourner.—11. Revenir.—12. Convenir.—13. Parvenir à.—14. Dommage.—15. Sortir.

LXII.—Conjugated with *Avoir*, the Past Participle agrees with the Objective, *i.e.*, with the *Régime direct*,

or *Accusative*, when it is preceded by it, but remains invariable when the Objective is placed after the Participle, or when there is none either before or after it.

Il rejeta sur les autres les fautes qu'il avait commises. He laid his own faults against others.

Quelques propositions qu'on lui ait faites, il n'a pas voulu y mordre. Whatever proposals could be made, he would not close with them.

On a demandé bien des fois sa main, ou *Elle a eu bien des demandes en mariage.* She had a great many offers.

TURN INTO FRENCH.

I *saw* her seated. I *thought* her dead and buried. The young girl who was *found* dead. The letters I *received* opened.

The losses the little vessel *had sustained.*[1] I *sent-for*[2] them, *paid*, and *dismissed*[3] them. I have put my mark on (to) the piece of linen I *bought.* I want another pen; the one[4] you *gave* me yesterday is lost.

The seeds I *sowed* are beginning to-come-up.[5] It is a thing I often *told* them. I *knew*[6] them directly by their voice. The pains you *have taken* are lost. Whatever faults he has *committed* (*Subj.*), I will forgive him. I shall never forgive myself for the folly I *have committed.* You *have persuaded* them of it.

Has this merchant *been indemnified* for the losses he has endured? He must be indemnified for the losses he *has sustained.* I am not yet recovered from the fright I *was-in.*[7] The inquiries I *made*-about[8] his conduct are not very satisfactory. She is not such as you *described* her to us. What lesson *have* you *learnt?*

What[9] misfortunes we *have experienced!*[10] What trouble you *have taken!* What sorrows he *endured!*[11] What evils she *has caused!* So many buckets of water I *drew* for her at the well! Such a heat I *bore-with*[12] in turning the spit in her stead! I *found* her in-a-state-of-distraction.[13]

What* patience the martyrs *have displayed.*[14] The tortures which the prisoners *endured.* The religion which our fathers *practised.* The rewards which our friends *offered* us. The horses which my brothers *bought.* The books which your sister *lent* me.

These are the three most delightful hours I *spent*[15] (*Subj.*) in my life. He is one of the gravest men I ever *saw* (*Subj.*). It is the last letter he wrote (*Subj.*). How great soever may be the actions he *has done,* let him be prudent. We shall not seal this letter until-you[16] *have read* it (*Subj.*). There are few nations whose ferocity can (*Subj.*) be compared to that of the Greeks and Trojans, such as Homer *described*[17] them to us. What offence *has* he *done?*

They have *answered* our expectation.[18] He *drew*[19] us a picture of his misfortune. *Have* you *heard* the report[20] of my gun? I *received* my letter after you *received* yours. *Has* she neither *been able* nor *willing* to do it? They *have spread* false news. We *have lost*[21] the train.[22]

The false hope which *had seduced* us. I thank you for the kindness you *have shown*[23] me. I shall suffer for a long time from the fall I *had.*[24] The step[25] she *has taken*[26] is very rash and inconsiderate.[27]

1. Souffrir.—2. Mander.—3. Congédier.—4. Celle que.—5. à pousser. —6. Reconnaître à.—7. Avoir.—8. Prendre sur.—9. Que de.—10. Eprouver.—11. Eprouver.—12. Souffrir.—13. Tout bouleversée.—14. Montrer. —15. Passer.—16. Que vous.—17. Dépeindre.—18. Attente.—19. Faire. —20. Détonation.—21. Manquer.—22. Convoi.—23. Avoir.—24. Faire. —25. Démarche.—26. Faire.—27. Indiscrète.

LXIII.—The Noun which follows the Interrogative Adverb, *Combien de,* is considered as the Objective of the Past Participle, *i.e.,* the Participle agrees with it; but when this Noun is replaced by *En,* the Past Participle remains invariable.

Combien de phrases avez-vous apprises? Combien

* In this paragraph invert the Nominative.

en avez-vous appris? How many sentences have you learned? How many have you learned?

Combien de visites avez-vous faites? Combien en avez-vous fait? How many visits have you paid? How many have you paid?

TURN INTO FRENCH.

How many shots *did* you *fire?*[1] I *fired* six. How many visits *have* you *received?* I *received* several. How many ladies *have* you *seen?* How many *have* I *seen?* How many enemies *has* not this prince *conquered?*[2] How many *has* he *conquered?*

How many letters *have* you *received?* How many glasses of wine *have* you *drunk?* How many of them *did* you *buy?* How much *did* he *offer* for[3] your table? How much *did* he *offer* for it?

How many books *have* you *read?* How many *have* you *read?* How many games[4] *have* you *played?*[5] We *have played* several.

1. Tirer.—2. Vaincre.—3. De.—4. Parties.—5. Faire.

LXIV.—Conjugated with *Avoir*, the Past Participle of Intransitive Verbs is invariable.

Combien a-t-il péri de personnes? How many lives were lost?

La justice et la modération de nos ennemis nous ont plus nui que leur valeur. The justice and moderation of our enemies have hurt us more than their valour.

Remark.—Sometimes Intransitive Verbs are used Transitively, in which case they follow the rule of Transitive Verbs, *i.e.*, agree with the Objective if it precedes them.

Je ne regretterai pas la peine que m'ont coûtée mes*

* The Past Participle of *coûter* is variable, when it signifies to cause, to give, to occasion.

expériences. I shall not regret the trouble my experiments cost me.

Qui l'a fleurie de la sorte? Who has decked her in that way?

LXV.—The Past Participle of Intransitive Verbs, preceded by *Que,* meaning DURING WHICH, remains invariable.

Les années qu'a duré sa magistrature. The years during which his time of office lasted, during which he was in office.

TURN INTO FRENCH.

We *slept* soundly.[1] We *breakfasted, dined,* and *supped* earlier than-usual.[2] She *smiled* at me. She *has run-about*[3] all day on[4] that business. That plant *has grown* much.

On-that-very-spot[5] other men *felt,* and *thought,* and *suffered* like himself. Do you regret the sums that this horse *cost* you?

The French language, which M. Nodier *spoke* and wrote so well. The dangers to which I *have been exposed.*[6] The pains[7] which his education *cost* me. He found again the two children he *had* so long *mourned-for.*[8] The trouble which this affair *has cost* me has quite upset[9] me. She *appeared* pleased to see me.

The five minutes I ran have quite put-me-*out-of-breath.*[10] The days this chimney *smoked* have been rainy. The ten hours I *slept* consecutively[11] quite recovered me. The nights she *coughed.* All the time she *suffered.* Who could reckon all the evils which war made me commit, during the span of sixty years which I *lived?* Your answer did not *please* them.

1. Profondément.—2. Que d'ordinaire.—3. Courir.—4. Pour.—5. Dans les mêmes lieux.—6. Courir.—7. Soins.—8. Pleurer.—9. Bouleverser.—10. Essouffler.—11. De suite.

LXVI.—The Past Participle of Reflective Verbs is variable when the Objective Pronoun which precedes means MYSELF, HIMSELF, HERSELF, OURSELVES, &c.

Ainsi se sont perdues tant de jeunes personnes. That's the way in which so many young persons have been lost.

Vos sœurs se sont méprises sur mes intentions. Your sisters have mistaken my intentions.

The Past Participle of Reflective Verbs is invariable when the Objective Pronoun means TO MYSELF, TO HIMSELF, TO HERSELF, TO OURSELVES, &c., and is not preceded by any other Objective.

Ils se sont dit quelques paroles désobligeantes. There passed some hard words between them.

Ils se sont juré une amitié éternelle. They have vowed one another an eternal friendship.

La foi que deux époux se sont jurée. The fidelity which husband and wife have plighted to one another.

C'est de tant de droits que ses prédécesseurs s'étaient arrogés, presque le seul qui lui reste. This is the only right left him out of so many which his predecessors had arrogated.

In the last two examples, the Participles agree, not with *Se*, but with the Objective *Que*.

LXVII.—The Past Participle of *Se plaire, se déplaire, se complaire, se rire, se sourire, se nuire, s'entre-nuire, se parler, se succéder, &c.*, is invariable.

Elle s'est nui dans mon esprit. She lost in my estimation.

Ces arbres ne se sont pas plu dans ce terrain. Those trees did not thrive in that ground.

LXVIII.—The Past Participle of Impersonal Verbs is invariable.

Il s'est fait de grandes traites de blé. A vast quantity of corn has been exported.

Il lui est venu des cloches aux mains à force de travailler. His hands are all over with blisters from hard work.

Que de démarches il nous a fallu faire! How many steps we had to take!

TURN INTO FRENCH.

How many times *has* she *sat* in this arm-chair? After *warming themselves*, they *undressed* and *went to bed.* *Did* your mother *take-notice*[1] of it? She *did* not *complain* of it to me. *Did* she *get-tired*[2] at the ball? No, but she *caught-a-cold.*[3] *Have* those pupils *complained* that an injustice was done (*Subj.*) to them?

The half of the goods *have-been-sold*[4] at cost price. This woman *happened*-to-be[5] innocent. Where *did* your daughters *go-to?*[6] When *did* those young men *present themselves?* The days we spent[7] together *have-passed-away*[8] very rapidly. Those workmen *have accustomed themselves* to idleness.

This water *has-cooled.*[9] *Has* not this matter *been-noised-abroad?*[10] The-affair[11] *was*[12] otherwise than you say.

The cat (*f.*) *scratched herself.* She *scratched* her[13] face with that pin. We *threw ourselves* into-each-other's-arms.[14] Those schoolboys *pelted*[15] snowballs at one another. She *trimmed-herself-out*[16] to go and see you. She *has-given-herself*-a-cut[17] and the blood runs-out-from it.[18] She *bit* her tongue. She *bit* it for having spoken too much. They *pinched one another.* She *has pinched* her finger. She *has built* herself a small retreat.

I *cut* my lip. I *cut* it when shaving. She *has-sprained-*her[19] ankle. She *sprained* it when dancing. *Has* this child *washed* his hands? Yes, he *has* (washed them). *Did* he *blacken* his face? He *blackened* it. *Has* he *put*-his-shoulder-*out-of-joint?*[20] He *put* it *out of joint* when falling. *Has* this little boy *thrust-a-splinter*[21] into his finger? Yes, he *thrust* it when robbing[22] nests.

These two women *took-a-dislike*-to-one-another-at-first-sight,[23] though they *smiled* (*Subj.*) and *spoke* to one another as-if-nothing-had-been-the-matter.[24] They *have-injured*[25] one another. She *was-pleased*[26] in contradicting me. She *has laughed* at[27] my losses. They *have succeeded* from-father-to-son[28] in that office.[29] Events *had succeeded* with rapidity. Several errors *have-slipped*[30] into that work.

A dispute *had-arisen*.[31] A meeting[32] *was held* yesterday. She[33] *is forbidden* to drink wine. *It rained* a good deal yesterday. There *came* two gentlemen who wanted to speak to you. False news *was-spread*.[34] *Has*[35] a lady *come* to my house? There *was a-fall*[36] of snow. *Has* anything *fallen* out-of[37] the window?

A bottle *has fallen*. *Have*[38] several gentlemen *gone up* to your room?

1. S'apercevoir.—2. Se fatiguer.—3. S'enrhûmer.—4. Se vendre.—5. Se trouver.—6. S'en aller.—7. Passer.—8. S'écouler.—9. S'attiédir.—10. S'ébruiter.—11. La chose.—12. Se passer.—13. La.—14. Dans les bras l'un de l'autre.—15. Se jeter.—16. Se faire belle.—17. Se faire une coupure.—18. En découler.—19. Se fouler la.—20. Se démettre l'épaule.—21. S'enfoncer une écharde.—22. Dénicher.—23. Se déplaire au premier abord.—24. Comme si de rien n'était.—25. Se nuire.—26. Se plaire à.—27. De.—28. De père en fils.—29. Charge.—30. Se glisser.—31. S'élever.—32. Assemblée.—33. Il lui.—34. Se répandre.—35. Est-il.—36. Tomber.—37. Par.—38. Est-il monté.

LXIX.—The Past Participle of *Faire*, followed by a Verb in the Infinitive, is always invariable.

La fortune m'y conduisait pour me faire jouer de plus grands rôles que ceux qu'elle m'y avait déjà fait faire. Fortune conducted me thither, in order to make me act higher parts than those which I had hitherto performed.

TURN INTO FRENCH.

The snow which Providence *caused to fall*, has destroyed the insects, and *made* them *perish*. The music we heard together; the pictures she *has-shown*[1] me; the books she *made* me *understand*. This general *got*-himself-*drawn*-on[2] horseback, surrounded by his staff.[3] That lady *got* herself *drawn* holding her youngest child on her knee.

Have you *made* those boys *work?* I *made* them *work*. Have you *got* the room properly *swept?*[4] Have you *got* the table *mended?* Why did you *make* them *drink?* Did you *get a* gown *made?* Where did you *get* it *made?*

1. Faire voir.—2. Se faire peindre à.—3. Etat-major.—4. Comme il faut.

LXX.—Between the Relative *Que* and the Conjunction *que*, or between *que* and *qui*, the Past Participle is invariable.

Telle est la conséquence que j'ai prétendu que vous en tirassiez. Such is the conclusion, or inference, I intended you should draw.

Je n'ai pas reçu les marchandises que j'ai cru qui me viendraient de Paris. I have not received the goods which I expected would come from Paris.

TURN INTO FRENCH.

The answers I *foresaw* would-be-given[1] to you. The difficulties I *knew* you were-in[2] have-hastened[3] my departure. The situation which you *thought* I would-get[4] has been given to another. The letter I *thought* you were writing to me has not reached[5] me. The letter I *presumed* you should receive has not been post-paid.[6]

The lesson you *desired*[7] me to study was very difficult. The modern language which you *would have* me to learn was very useful to me. The letter which you *wished* me to write. The lesson I *intended* you to study is at the beginning of this book.

The horses I *wished* him to buy have been sold too dear.

1. Faire.—2. Aviez.—3. Accélérer.—4. Obtenir.—5. Parvenir.—6. Affranchir.—7. Vouloir.

LXXI.—The Past Participle preceded by *Le* referring to a Proposition, and meaning *it, so, that,* is invariable.

Tu avais promis à ma mère mourante de protéger ma sœur, l'as tu fait? You promised my dying mother to protect my sister, did you do so?

TURN INTO FRENCH.

However-comfortable[1] this house may be, it appears to me to be quite-different-from-what[2] I *had expected.*[3] This letter is more interesting than I *had thought.* The affair is less serious than I *had supposed.*[4] The business did-not-turn-out[5] as I *had-thought-it-would-have-done.*[6]

All men die sooner than they think, because old age comes on sooner than they *had expected.* The famine arrived as Joseph *had foretold.* This room is not so large as I (had) *thought.*

Did your sister believe it would rain? Yes, she *did* (believe it). Did your sister not believe that young lady was rich? Yes,[7] she *did.*

1. Quelque commode.—2. Toute autre que.—3. Espérer.—4. Penser.—5. Ne pas aller.—6. Se l'imaginer.—7. Si fait.

LXXII.—Preceded by *Le peu,* the Past Participle takes the gender and the number of the Noun which follows *le peu,* if that expression means *what little, the few, the little,* and implies quantity in a literal or figurative sense.

Je ne crois pas que j'eusse besoin de cet exemple d'Euripide pour justifier le peu de liberté que j'ai prise. I do not think I needed that example from Euripides to justify what little liberty I have taken.

TURN INTO FRENCH.

The little friendship he *has shown* me gave-me-heart.[1] *The few* friends I *found* have-been-of-great-service-to-me.[2] *The few* visits I *received* have been tiresome.[3] *What little* beer she *drank* quite-upset[4] her. *The few* lessons I *have taken* have-been-sufficient.[5] I shall not speak of *the little* skill[6] I *acquired* in the army.

The few potatoes I *have kept* will-do[7] me. *What little* ground I *have* myself *cultivated* and *sown*[8] has yielded far more than I anticipated. You may recover[9] by-additional-labour[10] *what few* weeks you *have lost.*

1. Encourager.—2. M'ont été très-utiles.—3. Ennuyeuses.—4. Rendre toute malade.—5. Suffire.—6. Capacité.—7. Suffire.—8. Ensemencer.—9. Rattraper.—10. Par un surcroît de travail.

LXXIII.—Should *Le peu* involve a negative sense, and denote want, absence, privation of the thing spoken of, the Past Participle remains invariable.

Le peu d'affection qu'il m'a témoigné m'a découragé. The little, *i.e.*, the want, the absence of affection, the heartlessness he has shown me discouraged me.

TURN INTO FRENCH.

The want of diligence and punctuality he *put* in the management[1] of the business, is the cause of its not-having-succeeded.[2] *The little* trouble he *took*,[3] is-a-proof-to-me-of[4] his indifference. *The little* instruction he *has got*,[5] makes him fall into a thousand mistakes. *The little* security I saw for my life in[6] returning to Naples, made me renounce it for ever.

1. Conduite.—2. Echouer.—3. Se donner.—4. Me prouve.—5. Avoir. —6. De.

LXXIV.—The Past Participle of *Devoir, Pouvoir,* and *Vouloir,* is invariable when the *Que* which precedes is the Objective, not of the Participle, but of an Infinitive expressed or understood.

Don André m'a rendu sans intérêt tous les services

qu'il a pu, i.e., *me rendre.* Don Andrew, in the most disinterested manner, did me all the service he could.

But we must always say, *Il m'a toujours payé toutes les sommes qu'il m'a dues.* He always paid me all the sums he owed me.

Il veut fortement les choses qu'il a une fois voulues. He is strongly bent upon the things which he once desired.

Because, in the two last examples, the *Que* which precedes is not the Objective of any Infinitive, but of the Participle.

TURN INTO FRENCH.

I have-done[1] him all the service that I *have been able.* This is the house I *did* not *want*[2] to buy. This is the young lady I *could* never bear, and whom I *did* not *want* to marry. He has obtained all the favours he *wished for.* I gave him all the advice I *could* give him. She has made all the apologies she *ought.*

She did not make all the efforts she *should-have-done.*[3] She made all the corrections she *wished.* He took[4] all the trouble[5] he *could.* He made all the excuses he *could.*

1. Rendre.—2. Vouloir.—3. Devoir.—4. Se donner.—5. Peine.

LXXV.—The Objective preceding a Past Participle, followed by an Infinitive, may be the Objective either of the Participle or of the Infinitive; in the first case it is Variable, in the second it is Invariable.

La fleur que j'ai vue s'ouvrir. The flower I saw blooming.

La fleur que j'ai vu cueillir. The flower I saw being culled.

Les personnes que j'avais engagées à vous voir sont

ici. The persons I prevailed upon to see you are here.

Voici les dames que vous avez tant desiré voir. These are the ladies you were so anxious to see.

Les offres de service que nous leur avons entendu faire. The offers of service which we heard being made to them.

Les offres de service que nous les avons entendus faire. The offers of service which I heard them make.

L'imprudence que j'ai eue de parler. My imprudence in speaking.

TURN INTO FRENCH.

Geography is a science which my sister and I *liked to cultivate.* The questions which they *thought* proper-*to*[1] *ask* you. The truth which they *neglected to follow.* The case[2] I *heard pleaded.* The difficulties which they *thought they-should*[3] explain to you. I am waiting for the nurse; I *sent* the lady's maid *for*[4] her. The wounded soldiers whom I *saw carried* to the field-hospital[5] died this morning.

The insurgents whom I *saw disarmed* have-been-shot.[6] Let-us-go-to[7] the brewery that you *promised to show* me. The difficulties she *had learnt to overcome.* The fable she *had begun to read.* The lesson I *forgot to explain.* The great actions she *has endeavoured-to-keep*[8] secret. Is the letter I *told* you *to copy* signed? You *let*[9] us *be expelled.* Why did you *let* her *be scolded?* The books which I *let fall.*

To get-on[10] in the study of science (*pl.*) we must never deviate from the road we *have begun to follow.* The lady whom you *left-off*[11] *visiting* is very witty.[12] The persons I *left off associating with.* The newspapers I *heard read.* The pears which I *forbade* you *to eat.*

Ladies, it is a science which we have *exhorted* you *to-study.*[13] The workmen whom I *obliged to work* did not come back. The difficulties you *gave* me *to-solve.*[14] The cases this barrister *had to plead.* The lesson I *gave* you *to learn.* I am waiting for the nurse, I *sent* her *for*[15] coffee.

The soldiers whom I *saw carrying* their officer to the field-hospital. The soldiers whom I *saw disarming* the insurgents behaved with bravery. The-thunderbolt[16] I *saw falling* or *lighting*. The flame I *saw rising up*. The cloud I *saw coming down*. The flowers I *saw budding*-up.[17] Is the letter I *have given* him *to copy* finished? Why did you *let* her *scold*? I approve-of[18] the resolution you *have taken* of *going* to the country.

The criminals that *have been condemned to die*. The soldiers that *have been compelled-to*[19] *leave* the town. The ladies whom I *invited to dine*. The young men I *invited*[20] *to come*. I am sorry for the opportunity I *let slip*.[21]

My sister has bought the flowers which you *have seen planted* again. Those are the consequences they *pretended-to-infer*[22] from it. That is the watch which I *saw* them *take*. That is the watch which I *saw being taken* from them.

Do you know the young lady I *engaged*[23] to dance? Do you remember the resolution you *had taken* to quit all bad company? How many men fall daily into the disorders they *had promised to shun!*

We are they whom you *pretended* not *to know*. I *left* them *talking* on business. Where did you meet-with[24] these children? Why *did* you *let* them *play-like-blackguards*[25] about the streets? Why *did* you *let* them be *beaten* by a bad boy? Why *did* you *let* them *fight?*[26]

1. Utiles de.—2. La cause.—3. Devoir.—4. Chercher par.—5. Ambulance.—6. Fusiller.—7. Allons voir.—8. Tâcher de rendre.—9. Laisser. 10. Avancer.—11. Cesser de.—12. Spirituelle.—13. à cultiver.—14. à traiter.—15. Chercher.—16. La foudre.—17. Naître.—18. Applaudir à. —19. Contraindre de.—20. Prier.—21. Echapper.—22. Tirer.—23. Inviter.—24. Trouvé.—25. Polissonner.—26. Se battre.

ON THE INDICATIVE CONSTRUCTION.

INDICATIVE PRESENT.

LXXVI.—The time during which a State or an Action has been continued, is expressed in French by the Present of the Indicative, or the Subjunctive, and not by the Perfect, as in English.

C'est une coutume qui dure depuis la Conquête. This has been the practice down from the Conquest.

Les pyramides d'Egypte subsistent depuis bien des siècles. The pyramids of Egypt have existed for many centuries.

Quoique l'on parle et que l'on écrive depuis six mille ans, il y a encore bien des choses qui n'ont pas été dites. Although people have spoken and written these six thousand years, there are still many things which have not yet been uttered.

TURN INTO FRENCH.

*Has** she *been* long *gone out?* She *has been out* these two hours. How long *has* her father *been dead?* We *have-been-walking*[1] these three hours. I *have been* here these three days. We *have* now *been living* these two years abroad.[2] Dinner *has been kept* for you this-hour.[3]

* Commence sentences of this kind by *Y avoir*, or *Voilà*, followed by the expression of time, as, *Y a-t-il longtemps qu'elle est sortie?* *Voilà*, ou *il y a deux heures qu'elle est sortie.*

I *have been waiting* for you three hours. Have-you?[4] The babbler *has been boring*[5] me this half-hour.

Chesterfield said in his old age—Trawley and I *have been dead* these two years, but we do not wish it to be known.[6] I *have been running*-about[7] that affair a long time. We *have been* at school an hour. We-*have-been*[8] *waiting* long enough for[9] you. I *have been looking* for you this hour. The poor man *has been-buried*[10] these eight days.

How long* *has* she *been* in service? *Have* you *been* long out-of[11] place? How long *have* you *resided* here? How long *have* they *been* absent? How long *have* you *been* acquainted-with-one-another?[12] Our friendship *has been* of-long-standing.[13]

What have you done since you *have been* here? Have you learned-a-Scotch-reel[14] since you *came* to Scotland? How long is it since you *came* from home? My niece *has been* ill since yesterday. He *has-been*-ailing[15] these some days back. That *has been running*-in-his[16] head for a long time.

He *has been confined*-to-his[17] bed for three months. I *have been* now six months *rambling-over*[18] Spain and Portugal. I *have been gazing*[19] an hour on the man without being able to recognize him. How long *has-he-held*[20] that post?

1. Se promener.—2. En pays étranger.—3. Il y a une heure que.—4. Vraiment.—5. Assommer.—6. Savoir.—7.—Trotter pour.—8. Il y a longtemps qu'on.—9. Après.—10. En terre.—11. Sans.—12. Se connaître.—13. Dater de loin.—14. Apprendre à danser une ronde écossaise.—15. Etre indisposé.—16. Trotter dans la.—17. Retenir au.—18. Parcourir.—19. Contempler.—20. Occuper.

LXXVII.—The French denote the time that is elapsed by the Past Indefinite, the English by what they call the Imperfect.

Y a-t-il longtemps que tu n'as vu la comtesse?

* Translate sentences of this kind by *Depuis combien de temps*, or simply by *Depuis*, as the case may be. *Depuis combien de temps sert-elle? Elle me sert depuis quinze ans avec un zèle tout particulier.* She has served me these fifteen years with a singular zeal.

À peu près six semaines. Is it long since you saw the countess? Some six weeks now.

The English say, Since you *saw*; the French, Since you *have seen*.

TURN INTO FRENCH.

How long is it since she *left*[1] this country? It is nearly a year since I *saw* her. It is more than a year since I *paid*[2] her a visit. How long is it since you *came* here? It is two years since I *came*. I *saw* him three days ago.[3] We *met* him in Paris six months ago.

Is it long since he *wrote* to you? I have not heard-from-him[4] this long while.

1. Partir de.—2. Rendre.—3. Il y a trois jours.—4. Recevoir de ses nouvelles.

LXXVIII.—To denote a State or an Action, the effects of which were still lasting at a time referred to, the French use the Imperfect, the English the Pluperfect.

Il y avait deux ans que cet ouvrage était en vente. The work had been on sale for two years.

Il y avait deux heures que nous écrivions. We had been writing for two hours.

But if, at the period alluded to, the Action was over, the Past Definite must be used instead of the Imperfect.

C'est alors qu'Alcandre et Septimius achevèrent leurs études à Athènes et se rendirent célèbres, l'un comme le plus habile dialecticien du Lycée, et l'autre comme le plus éloquent orateur de l'Académie. It was at that time that Alcander and Septimius had finished their studies at Athens and had become celebrated, the one as the most able logician of the Lyceum, the other as the most eloquent orator of the Academy.

TURN INTO FRENCH.

She was an-old-gentlewoman[1] who *had lived* more-than[2] twenty years in that family. How long *had* you *been playing* cards when I came in? He knew not how long since each house *had-been*[3] *built*. They *had been acquainted*[4] long ago. She *had been dead* a year.

Had she not *been* ill three months when she died? We *had been* in bed two hours when he came in. I *had* not *been* long at the inn when-somebody-came-in-and-asked-for-me.[5] I *had sought* for you three days when I saw you.

I *had been reading* the newspaper about an hour when he came in. He *had gone* scarcely two minutes before. He *had been waiting* for the last ten days. I knew[6] the house, and I knew[7] it *had been built* a very long time. I *had* not *seen* her for-three-months.[8] We *had been out*[9] for three hours. Mary *had-been*-a-close-prisoner[10] for sixteen years.

1. Une vieille personne.—2. Plus de.—3. Etait.—4. Se connaître.—5. Lorsqu'il vint quelqu'un me demander.—6. Connaître.—7. Savoir.—8. Il y avait trois mois que.—9. Sortir.—10. Etre détenue.

LXXIX.—*Y avoir* with the Future and the Conditional.

TURN INTO FRENCH.

At Christmas* your brother *will have been* six months at school. *Shall* we not *have been* six months here next-June?[1] I *shall have been* here a year. The work *will have been* on[2] sale two years by-to-morrow.[3] It *will be* two years to-morrow since the work was[4] published. We *shall have been writing* an hour.

Would you not *have been* a month in the country had-you-

* Translate: There will be six months at Christmas that your brother is, &c.

remained[5] three days longer? How long *will* it *be* since they have not spoken-to-one-another?[6]

1. Au mois de Juin prochain.—2. En.—3. Demain.—4. A été.—5. Si vous y étiez resté encore.—6. Se parler.

LXXX.—Although we can say *C'est*, ou *Ce fut moi qui parlai.* It was I who spoke. Yet, the genius of the language seems to prefer *C'est* to *Ce fut* as being the more precise of the two, especially if the assertion was particularly true at a time referred to, and is likewise so at the time of speaking.

C'est pendant la Révolution que les Français se montrèrent le plus redoutables. It WAS during the French Revolution that the French showed themselves most formidable.

The rule is the same for general truths, *i.e*, truths that exist independent of all times.

J'avoue que les histoires sont remplies de guerres de religion; mais qu'on y prenne bien garde, ce n'est pas la multiplicité des religions qui produit ces guerres, c'est l'esprit d'intolérance. I confess histories are full of religious wars; but, let us take care, it WAS not the diversity of religions that OCCASIONED these wars, it WAS the spirit of intolerance.

TURN INTO FRENCH.

Amyot *was* one of the first who polished[1] our language. It *was* Boileau who first taught the art of always speaking properly.[2] It *was* either Fox or Pitt who said that. It *was* Cardinal Mazarin who introduced in France a-taste-for[3] operas. It *was* with[4] James the First that series of misfortunes commenced which gave[5] the House of Stuart the title of unfortunate. *Was* it the Phœnicians who invented navigation?

I proved to you that God *was* good. St. Augustine described the nature of God as a circle whose centre *was* everywhere, but whose circumference *was* nowhere.

Galileo proved that the earth *revolved* round the sun. I demonstrated to you that the earth *was* round. The-matter-in-question-was-to-know[6] if the sufferings of the damned *were* eternal.

I remember[7] having heard you say that she *was* an angel. *Was* it not you who said it? It *was* I. It *was* he. It *was* she. It *was* they. Your physician *was* the first who taught (*Subj.*) the doctrine, and the last who practised it (*Subj.*). It *was* flattery that set-forth[8] the doctrine that kings hold their crown from-God-alone.[9] It *was* I who advanced the money for him.

1. Défricher.—2. Convenablement.—3. Le goût des.—4. à.—5. A fait donner.—6. Il s'agissait de savoir.—7. Se rappeler.—8. Faire avancer. —9. Que de Dieu.

LXXXI.—Often in vivid and rapid narrations the Present is used instead of the Past to enliven the style.

Le monarque des dieux leur envoie une grue,
Qui les croque, qui les tue,
Qui les gobe à son plaisir.

The sovereign of the gods sent them a crane, who crunched, killed, and gulped them down at pleasure.

TURN INTO FRENCH.

The shepherd *came, caught* and *caged* them. At the given signal, the horsemen of Gaul *drew* their swords, *spurred-on*[1] their horses, and *fell*[2] upon the enemy.

Alexander, frantic,[3] *ran* on all sides, *punished*[4] the one, *exhorted* the other, and *revived* the combat which had already begun to-flag.[5] In an instant all *were* on foot, they *seized* their swords and carabines, *advanced* to the place where I was with Domingo.

1. Presser.—2. Fondre.—3. Furieux.—4. Châtier.—5. Se ralentir.

LXXXII.—The Present or the Past Indefinite is sometimes idiomatically used instead of the Future.

On m'a dit que vous êtes ici pour un mois. I have been told, you will be here for a month.

Permettez-moi de faire cette seule observation, et j'ai fini. Allow me to make this one observation, and I shall have done.

TURN INTO FRENCH.

We *shall go* to the concert this evening. I *shall set off* to-morrow for Paris. Wait for me, I *shall be back* in an instant. Make haste, I *shall wait for* you down-stairs.[1] I *will be* with you in a minute. I *shall come* to you in a moment.

It *will* soon *be* a year since he died. *Will* you soon *have done?* I *shall have done* in a moment. As-soon-as-I-have[2] done, I *shall be* with you. I *will-be*-here-again[3] directly.

1. En bas.—2. Dès que j'aurai.—3. Etre de retour.

IMPERFECT.

LXXXIII.—The Imperfect corresponds to *Was* and any Present Participle. It denotes a thing being done, continuing, or progressing at the moment when another took place.

La mère criait et voletait autour de son nid, lorsqu'on emportait ses petits. The mother screamed and fluttered over her nest when they were carrying away her young ones.

LXXXIV.—The Characteristic of the Imperfect is to represent the action, the state or situation it describes, as being more or less permanent, or as being habitually done and repeated.

Au pied de la montagne, il y avait un ruisseau, sur le bord duquel était la chaumière du sage. At the foot of the mountain was a rivulet, on the banks of which stood the wise man's cottage.

Le vieux chêne qui avait ombragé sa chaumière était encore debout. The ancient oak which had shaded his cottage was still standing.

Les Pharisiens affectaient les premiers rangs dans les assemblées. The Pharisees sought the first place in public meetings.

TURN INTO FRENCH.

He *felt* his end *was-drawing*-nigh.[1] He *was-enjoying*-himself[2] after his day's work. He *was-enjoying*-himself-over-a-glass-of-wine.[3] They *were-footing*-it-away-cheerily[4] together. The dogs-*were-worrying*-each-other[5] with such inveteracy.[6]

I was walking up-and-down[7] the parlour. His hair *was getting*-gray.[8] He *was waiting* yesterday in the antechamber when we came in. They *were* perpetually *playing*-some-prank-upon-me.[9] He *was meditating* while we *were playing* on the flute.

Among the Romans, the candidates *were* clad in white. The Egyptian pyramids *were-intended*-for[10] the sepulture of the kings. They *made-away-with*[11] one-half of the provisions that[12] *were bought* for the family.

Louis XIV. *used-to-hum*[13] the prologues containing his panegyrics. Scipio *used to say* that he never *was* less alone than when he *was* quite alone. The ancients *used-to-have*-themselves-anointed-on[14] leaving the bath. Formerly he *used to ride* on horseback, but now he-seldom-does.[15] Every day he *used to loiter*-about[16] the streets.

He *was* my tutor when I *was* at college. I *looked* over[17] his shoulder as he *wrote*. Innocence and virtue *reigned* among men when the world *was* yet in its infancy.[18]

The house in which Epictetus *dwelt*, *was* without a door. Alexander *was* short of stature.[19] The clergy formerly *held*[20] the first rank[21] in the kingdom. Gentlemen and ecclesiastics *were* exempted-from-taxation[22] in the good old times. Those who *could* not fight in[23] person, such as old men, the-lame,[24] ecclesiastics, and ladies, *furnished* champions.

Napoleon *did* not *sleep* more than four hours. Peter the Great *rose* regularly at four in the morning; at five, they[25] *brought* him a light breakfast; he *dined* at eleven, but never *supped*, and *went* to bed early. In[26] the reign of Henry the Fourth, they *dined* at court at eleven,—a custom which *was*-still-prevalent-in[27] the commencement of the reign of Louis XIV.

George II., King of England, *went*-every-other-year[28] to his German dominions. The ancients *distributed* the night in four watches.[29] The Romans *had* the power-of-life-and-death[30] over their slaves. The ancients *observed* carefully[31] the flight of birds, to draw presages from it. He *passed* through their court regularly twice a day. The-common-forms[32] of society *appeared* to him either odious or ridiculous.

I *wore* spectacles formerly. He *was* nothing but skin and bone. We *were* at such a distance that we *could* not distinguish the cavalry from[33] the infantry. The ancient Romans *buried* their dead near the high roads.

1. Approcher.—2. Se délasser.—3. Se donner le plaisir d'un verre de vin.—4. Cheminer gaîment.—5. Se déchirer.—6. Acharnement.—7. De long en large.—8. Commencer à grisonner.—9. à me faire quelque niche.—10. Destiner à.—11. Détourner la.—12. Qu'on.—13. Chantonner.—14. Se faire oindre au.—15. Il y monte rarement.—16. Flâner dans.—17. Par dessus.—18. Adolescence.—19. Corps.—20. Etre.—21. Ordre.—22. N'être point taillables.—23. De leur.—24. Les estropiés. 25. On.—26. Sous.—27. Prévaloir encore au.—28. Aller visiter tous les deux ans.—29. Veilles.—30. Droit de vie et de mort.—31. Curieusement.—32. Les usages les plus simples.—33. D'avec.

PAST DEFINITE.

LXXXV.—The Imperfect, as we have seen, denotes habit or duration; the Past Definite merely records a fact or an action as having taken place in a Period of time in which we are no more, but does not, as the Imperfect, lay any stress on its duration or its repetition. It may or may not have been of long continuance; it may or may not have been repeated.

La malle fut retardée par le mauvais état des routes. The mail was delayed by the bad state of the roads.

Venise fut longtemps le centre du commerce et des richesses. Venice was long the mart of commerce and wealth.

In this last example, the span of time alluded to may have lasted centuries.

Il reçut un coup d'épée dans le cœur, et tomba roide mort un moment après. He received a thrust in his heart, and fell down stone dead in an instant.

Toutes les fois qu'il vint au café, nous fîmes une partie de piquet. Every time he came to the coffee house, we had a game at piquet together.

In this last example, the actions are represented as being occasional rather than habitual. A man may have gone many a time to a coffee house without being, for all that, what the French call an *habitué,* a regular customer, such as the Imperfect would describe him to be, thus—

Toutes les fois qu'il venait au café, nous faisions une partie de piquet. Whenever he came to the coffee house, we played a game at piquet together.

And in this example, the actions are represented as being habitual or customary.

But though an action may have been habitual, yet, if the mind obliterates the recurrence of this action, and simply records a fact which is no more, the Past Definite must be used. It is from this principle that VICTOR HUGO said—

À partir de cette heure bénie et sainte, où un baiser fiança ces deux âmes, Marius vint là tous les soirs. From that blessed and holy hour, when a kiss affianced these two souls, Marius came there every night.

LXXXVI.—The Characteristic of the Past Definite is to denote the Transition from one action to another, from one state to another.

Une tuile coula du toit, lui tomba sur la tête, et le tua. A tile slipped off the roof, fell on his head, and killed him.

Here remark the transition: The tile slips off, falls, and then kills him.

Il n'eut pas la paupière fermée qu'on mit le scellé chez lui. Scarcely were his eyes closed when all his effects were sealed up.

LXXXVII.—Both the Imperfect and the Past Definite may express Simultaneousness of States or Actions.

The Imperfect describes the states as co-existent, or represents one of the actions a-doing and progressing when the other happened.

Quand j'étais jeune, j'étais toujours bien portant. When I was young, I was always in good health.

Elle entra précisément comme le bal commençait. She dropped in as the ball began, *i.e.*, was beginning, it had actually begun.

The Past Definite represents the simultaneous actions it describes as Spontaneous Occurrences.

Dès qu'il la vit, il se sentit épris. As soon as he saw her, he fell in love with her.

Quand la Reine entra dans la Chambre des Communes, tous les membres se levèrent et crièrent : Vive la Reine ! When the Queen entered the House of Commons, all the members rose up and cried : Long live the Queen ! *i.e.*, rose up crying.

TURN INTO FRENCH.

Joan of Arc was the-avenger[1] of France. That age *was* barren in great men. A letter addressed to one of the conspirators *was intercepted.* A-fellow-named[2] Ernest *was chosen* for this singular negotiation. He *declined*-complying-with[3] his request. He *deferred*[4] answering.

He *was cut-off*-in-the-prime-of-life.[5] Why don't you leave the door open? Why, sir, you *scolded* me yesterday because it-was-left-open.[6] A door *flew-open,*[7] and there *rushed*-out[8] a shoal-of-boys.[9] The hawk *pounced*[10] upon its prey, and *bore*-it-*off*[11] in its clutches.[12] Cæsar *crushed* the Roman Republic, and *brought*-it-under[13] arbitrary power.

At the end of the American War, General Washington *bade* farewell to his companions in[14] arms; *presented* himself before the Congress, to which he *tendered*[15] his powers; and then *retired* into private life. He had scarce made-up-his-mind,[16] when he *sprung* from his chair, *brushed* his coat, *buttoned* it, *put* his hat *on*, and *sallied*-forth.[17]

The siege *lasted* so many months. After the death of Cromwell, England *remained* for a year in the confusion of anarchy. Such a pope *held-up*-the-papacy[18] so many years. Pompey *triumphed* thrice. A thousand times *did* he *repent* the past. The matter *was*-long-*debated.*[19] The meeting *lasted* long, and these-are[20] the questions which-*were-debated.*[21]

He *made* a false step, and *tumbled*-head-over-heels-downstairs.[22] The arrow *pierced* his buckler, and *nailed*-it-to-his[23] breast. So-saying,[24] he *put on* his spectacles, *opened* a register which lay[25] on the table, *turned over* some leaves, and *began* to-read-as-follows.[26] He *asserted*[27] it so often that we *believed* him.

We *read* that news a few days ago, but we *did* not *believe* it. We *went* a-shooting yesterday; we *fired* but two shots, and *killed* four partridges. The troops *stole* along-the[28] ditch, and *got*[29] in the place. The elephant *took* him with his trunk, and *tossed*-him-in[30] the air. In three courses he *shivered*[31] three lances.

The dog *snapped*-his[32] leg. I *saw* him ten days before-he-died,[33] and *observed*[34] he began to droop.[35] The Spaniards *expelled* the Moors from Spain.

The liberty of the Roman Republic *died*[36] under Tiberius. The ship *went off*, and we *lost sight of her* in a moment. The plague *swept away* many people. It was a long while before it got well, and she *had* a dreadful scar as-long-as-she-lived.[37]

1. La vengeresse.—2. Un sieur, un certain, *ou* un nommé.—3. Se refuser de se conformer à.—4. Différer de.—5. Moissonné au printemps de ses jours.—6. Elle l'était.—7. S'ouvrir brusquement.—8. S'en échapper.—9. Bande d'écoliers.—10. S'abattre.—11. L'enlever.—12. Serres.—13. Soumettre à.—14. De.—15. Remettre.—16. Prendre son parti.—17. Sortir brusquement.—18. Siéger.—19. On agita longtemps.—20. Voilà.—21. Qui s'y agitèrent.—22. Culbuter du haut en bas de l'escalier.—23. Le lui clouer sur la.—24. En achevant ces paroles.—25. Etre.—26. De lire en ces termes.—27. Affirmer.—28. Le long du.—29. Entrer.—30. Le jeter en.—31. Rompre.—32. Lui happer la.—33. Avant sa mort.—34. S'apercevoir.—35. S'affaiblir.—36. Expirer.—37. Toute sa vie.

LXXXVIII.—Imperfect and Past Definite contrasted.

TURN INTO FRENCH.

Before the Revolution, Paris *was divided* into wards.[1] In the beginning of the Revolution, Paris *was divided* into forty-eight sections. I *was* always at home. I *was* at home the-whole-of-yesterday.[2] He often *delivered*[3] speeches. The last speech he *delivered* was[4] admirable.

The kings of France, on their consecration,[5] *were-anointed*[6] with oil from the holy ampulla. Samuel *anointed* Saul. His mother *sold* apples. Esau *sold* his birthright[7] for a mess-of-pottage.[8] He *drank* his bottle of wine every day. He *drank* out[9] of his hand. The ancients frequently *put-away*[10] their wives. Napoleon *put away* Josephine.

He *shot* very well. He *shot* two brace of partridge. I *sang*, but I sing no more. She *sang* two pretty ballads. Formerly I *used to sleep* longer. My brother *slept* till eight o'clock. The slightest noise *awoke* him. The king, who was but dozing,[11] *awoke* a few minutes after. Whenever he came, he *brought* me something. Every time he came he *brought* me something. The classes *began* at seven o'clock every morning. When he *began*[12] speaking, everybody *kept-silent*[13] to hear him.

The athletæ *rubbed* themselves with oil before-they-entered-the-lists.[14] I *rubbed* his arm with oil. While she *wrote*, she *bedewed* her paper with her tears. He *wrote* on the 6th of April. She *fainted* every time she *was bled*. He *fainted* when they *bled* him. When we *went out*, we always *went* to see him. When he *went out*, he *met* me. He *lived* at-the-rate-of[15] ten thousand a-year. He *lived* and *died* amongst his brethren. The poor-sick-woman[16] *sunk*-apace.[17] The sun *sunk*[18] behind the hills. He *used to beat* them more cruelly than me. He *beat* them more cruelly than I. I *took-a-ride*[19] every morning in Hyde Park. I *took a ride* yesterday. In-the-evening[20] I *sat down* by the river-side. He *sat down* by me.

1. Quartiers.—2. Hier toute la journée.—3. Prononcer.—4. Est.—5. Sacre.—6. On oignait.—7. Droit de naissance.—8. Plat de lentilles.—9. Dans le creux.—10. Répudier.—11. Assoupi.—12. Commencer de.—13. Se taire.—14. Avant de lutter.—15. Sur le pied de.—16. La pauvre malade.—17. Baisser à vue d'œil.—18. S'abaisser.—19. Se promener à cheval.—20. Le soir.

PAST INDEFINITE.

LXXXIX.—The Past Indefinite, as its name implies, does not always determine the Period or space of time when a fact or an action took place.

Les hommes ont mieux aimé les ténèbres que la lumière, parce que leurs œuvres étaient mauvaises. Men loved darkness rather than light, because their deeds were evil.

D'anciens philosophes ont cru faussement que les insectes naissent de la corruption. Some ancient philosophers wrongly believed that insects were bred from corruption.

XC.—When no Specific Time is mentioned, we may, in some cases, indifferently use the Imperfect, the Past Definite, or the Past Indefinite.

César était, César fut, ou *César a été un grand homme.* Cæsar was a great man.

Still we could not, with equal propriety, say: *César vainquait Pompée, César vainquit Pompée, César a vaincu Pompée.* Cæsar conquered Pompey.

The last of these illustrations can alone stand independent, the two others must needs be determined by a context of time, as,

César vainquait Pompée tandis que les Romains demandaient aux Dieux la victoire pour ce dernier. Cæsar conquered Pompey whilst the Romans asked of the Gods victory for the latter.

La présomption de la noblesse, la faute qu'elle fit d'abandonner Rome et l'Italie, la célérité de l'ennemi qui la poursuivait furent cause que César vainquit Pompée. The presumption of the nobles, the fault they committed in their leaving Rome, the swiftness of the enemy pursuing them, were the causes why Cæsar conquered Pompey.

XCI.—Although, when the period of time is not mentioned, the Past Definite and the Past Indefinite can be used in the same phrase, yet they must not be used indiscriminately.

Le général assembla ses troupes et leur parla en ces termes : Nous avons traversé des pays immenses ; vous avez surmonté toutes sortes d'obstacles ; vous laisserez-vous abattre maintenant que vous tenez presque la victoire ? The general assembled his troops, and spoke to them as follows : We have crossed immense countries, you have overcome all sorts of obstacles, and would you flag now when victory is at hand ?

In the above or similar examples, the Past Definite describes the Past Actions as single and definite occurences that took place at some Past Time or other. The Past Indefinite merely unites the Past to the Present, as : *We have crossed, You have overcome,* but yet *You have still victory to gain,* all the actions are not over yet.

Besides, there is still a remarkable peculiarity between these two Tenses, which is, that the Past Definite can generally be resolved by the Historic Present, whereas, the Past Indefinite can seldom if ever be so.

Thus, we may say, *parle, assemble,* instead of *parla, assembla ;* but we could not say, *nous traversons, vous surmontez,* without mutilating the sense of the passage.

XCII.—To express a Past State, the effects of which are still lasting, the French can only use the Past Indefinite, and not sometimes the Perfect and sometimes the Imperfect as in English.

Les Septante ont interprété l'Ancien Testament. The Seventy have translated the Old Testament.

La soupape de sûreté a été une grande amélioration dans la machine à vapeur. The safety valve was a great improvement in the steam engine, *i.e.*, WAS and IS still a great improvement.

XCIII.—To record an event that occurred through the day, the French use the Imperfect, the Past Indefinite, or the Past Definite.

The Imperfect to express simultaneous actions.

Je vous parle bien éveillé :
J'étais bien éveillé ce matin, sur ma vie ;
Et bien éveillé même était l'autre Sosie
Quand il m'a si bien étrillé.

I talk to you broad awake; I was broad awake this morning upon my word; and broad awake too was that other Sosius when he curried my hide so heartily.

Should the actions not be simultaneous, the Past Indefinite is generally used.

J'ai vu ce matin la personne dont vous m'avez parlé hier. I have seen this morning the person you spoke to me of yesterday.

Gil-Blas, me dit-il, qui est ce grand escogriffe que j'ai vu tantôt avec toi? Gil-Blas, said he to me, who is that tall spunger in whose company I saw thee to-day?

Yet there are cases when the Past Definite is the only tense that can be used.

Ce matin nous nous sommes rendus chez le ministre

de l'intérieur; il n'y était pas, nous résolûmes de l'attendre. This morning we went to the Home Office; the minister was not at home; we determined to wait for him.

If we said, *Nous avons résolu,* it might convey that we are still waiting for him.

XCIV.—With reference to an event which took place *yesterday, last week, last year,* &c., the French use the Past Indefinite, the English cannot.

J'ai reçu une lettre le mois dernier. I received a letter last month.

Il a plu hier toute la journée. It rained the whole of yesterday.

XCV.—In the colloquial language, the Past Indefinite is often preferred to the Past Definite as being less stiff and pedantic.

Finally, the English Compound Perfect is translated by the Past Indefinite, or by *Venir de. J'ai parlé* ou *Je viens de parler.* I have been speaking. *Il a neigé* ou *Il vient de neiger.* It has been snowing.

TURN INTO FRENCH.

Napoleon *was* a great man. Charles XII. *lived* in the time of Peter the Great. Physicians *wore* wigs.

They *made* such a noise that my-head-is-still-aching-with-it.[1] Harvey *discovered* the circulation of the blood. Certain pagan philosophers *believed* the world to be eternal. I *drank* it at-one-draught;[2] that *made* me much-worse-than-I-was.[3] The physicians *held*-a-consultation-about[4] his illness.

He had a-mind[5] to travel, but his friends *dissuaded* him from it. I *came*[6] too late; I *missed* my man. The stage *dropped*[8] a passenger at the inn. He *lived* a hundred years. She *spent* three hours in adorning herself. He *died* a year after his wife to-a-day.[9] He *kept* us two hours doing nothing. Is it not as I *told* you?

The Saracens *occupied* Spain for several centuries. The Romans *vanquished* the most warlike nations in the world. That city *was overturned* by an earthquake. The shocks[10] *were* very violent. That bad-boy[11] *broke* two panes. My watch is stopped; I *forgot* to wind it up. I *heard* that song sung.

What-sort-of-a-passage[12] *had* they? Which regiment *fought*[13] best? For whom is that grave dug?[14] The man who *dug* it *did* not tell me. I *had* the honour to-see-her-home.[15] I *had* this cloth very cheap. I *sold* so many bales of cotton. I never *did* any business with that house. By-whose-instigation[16] *did* he *do* it? He *was* very *guarded*[17] in his expressions.[18] I never *saw* the painting, but I *have* seen the engraving. I not only *paid* him, but I *overpaid*[19] him.

God *created* the world: he *made* man after[20] his own image; he *formed* him out-of-the-dust-of-the-earth.[21] Christ *died* for him since he *died* for all! The fruits of the earth *were* the first food of man. The French Academy *was instituted*[22] to-promote-the-improvement[23] of the language.

My orange trees *have lost* half their blossoms;[24] your-trees[25] have still all theirs. Most legislators *have been* men of-limited-capacities,[26] whom chance *has-raised*-to-the-government-of-others.[27] The sun and rain *have-mildewed*[28] the corn. The rain *has* sufficiently *soaked*[29] the ground.

Is this the young man you *spoke* to me about this morning? She *died* this afternoon. I *was* very unwell this morning. I *was unwell* this morning when you *came;* I *was* in my bed. I *saw* your uncle this week. It *was*[30] very cold this month, this year. I *was engaged*[31] this afternoon when you called. I *had* a headache the-whole-day.[32] I *had* a headache when I went out this afternoon.

He *went out* this afternoon. We *had* much company this winter. We *spent* a very pleasant[33] evening. The-south-wind-*has-prevailed*[34] for a week. It has been raining all night. The meeting *was-held*[35] on Wednesday. It *blew* the whole of last night. I shall be obliged to undo all that I *did* yesterday. The patient *kept-up*[36] very well last-night.[37] I *had*-not-a-moment's-sleep[38] the whole night. The people whom we *met* yesterday. We *had* an argument[39] last week. The servant (*f.*) whom I *turned away* last month.

He *has been trotting about* all day. I *have been singing* all the morning. She *has been dancing* all night. We *have been writing* letters. He *has been examining* them. She *has been paying* visits. It *has been freezing.* I *have been taking a bath.* I *have been bathing.* I *have been visiting* my friend.

He *wrote* yesterday. Who *told* you that? Which of them *spoke* first? How much wine *did* he *drink?* He *drank* a bottle.

1. En avoir encore mal à la tête.—2. D'un seul trait.—3. Beaucoup plus malade.—4. Consulter sur.—5. Quelque envie.—6. Arriver.—7. La diligence.—8. Laisser en passant.—9. Jour pour jour.—10. Les secousses. 11. Polisson.—12. Quelle traversée.—13. Se battre.—14. Faite.—15. De l'accompagner jusque chez elle.—16. à l'instigation de qui.—17. Mesuré.—18. Paroles.—19. Surpayé.—20. à.—21. Du limon de la terre.—22. Etablie.—23. Pour travailler à la perfection.—24. Fleurs.—25. Les vôtres.—26. Bornés.—27. Mettre à la tête des autres.—28. Nieller.—29. Imbiber.—30. Faire.—31. Occupé.—32. Toute la journée.—33. Agréable.—34. Avoir le vent du midi.—35. Avoir lieu.—36. Se soutenir.—37. Cette nuit.—38. Ne pas fermer l'œil.—39. Discussion.

PAST ANTERIOR.

XCVI.—The Past Anterior, like the Past Definite, denotes the transition from one state to another, from one action to another. The thing or event it records is hardly over, but it is immediately followed by some other occurrence.

À peine eut-il achevé de parler qu'il expira. He had hardly done speaking when he expired.

J'eus à peine dit quatre mots qu'il me donna deux démentis. I had scarce spoken four words before he contradicted me twice.

With the conjunctive expressions *aussitôt que, dès*

que, d'abord que, as soon as; *après que,* after; *lorsque, quand,* when; *pas plus tôt que,* no sooner; *à peine,* scarcely; the English sometimes use their Imperfect but the French must have the Past Anterior to describe a fact or an action prior to another equally over.

Je ne l'eus pas plus tôt aperçue que je courus à elle. I no sooner caught sight of her than I ran up to her.

Quand il eut obtenu ce qu'il désirait, il repartit. As soon as he obtained what he wished, he went off again.

TURN INTO FRENCH.

Scarce *had* he *assumed*[1] the government of his estates. when[2] he thought of carrying war into Africa. As soon as he *had listened* to my complaints he made his own. As soon as she *had done,* she drove the flock into the sheep-fold which was at the other end of the house. After he *had filled* his pipe he went away.

As soon as I *had received* the parcel I forwarded it to him. The ambassador *had* scarcely *begun*[3] speaking when everybody was-silent.[4] When he *had finished* his discourse the king ordered him to withdraw. As soon as the late king's eyes *were closed* they-set-about[5] establishing a new administration (Translate—As soon as the late king had closed the eyes). As soon as I *had done* my work I carried it to him. He *had* no sooner *committed* the crime than he repented. When I *had heard* him through[6] I inquired-of[7] him what I could do for him? As-soon-as-he[8] *was intrusted* with the secret he revealed it to her. After I *was gone,* several gentlemen came to see me. When we *were seated,* the master explained our lessons to us. As soon as Cæsar *had crossed* the Rubicon, he had no longer to deliberate.

As soon as he *obtained* the situation, he gave in his resignation. The policemen soon *dispersed* the mob. The smoke soon *drove*[9] us from the room. When the young man *heard* that saying[10] he went away sorrowful,[11] for he had great possessions. We no sooner *perceived* him than we ran-up[12] to him.

1. Prendre.—2. Que.—3. Commencer de.—4. Se taire.—5. On pensa à.—6. D'un bout à l'autre.—7. Demander à.—8. Dès qu'on.—9. Chasser.—10. Paroles.—11. Tout triste.—12. Accourir à.

XCVII.—To describe an Action prior to another in a period of time still going on, as, This day, this week, *J'ai eu, tu as eu*, &c., followed by another Past Participle, is another form of the Past Anterior. It is used pretty much in the same way as the Past Indefinite, with this exception that it cannot be applied to a period of time entirely past.

Je n'ai pas eu plus tôt lâché cette parole que je m'en suis mordu la langue. I had hardly dropt the word, when I could have bit my tongue for it.

TURN INTO FRENCH.

When I *had learnt* this morning the news of your nomination, I ran to-acquaint[1] your friend with it. As soon as I *had finished* my letter, I sent it to-be-delivered.[2] As soon as I *had finished* it, I sent it. They-went-away[3] as-soon-as-they[4] *had read* your letter. They went away as soon as it *was read.* To-day after[5] I *had dined* I went out. When I *gave* him the-toast[6] I thought it was proper to tell him, I was Captain Shandy's servant. When the Lieutenant *had taken* his wine and toast he felt himself a-little-revived.[7]

1. En faire part à.—2. Porter.—3. On s'en est allé.—4. Dès qu'on.—5. Dès que.—6. La rôtie.—7. Un peu ranimé.

PLUPERFECT.

XCVIII.—The Pluperfect, like the Imperfect, denotes a state or an action, habit or custom, or something progressing and a-doing when something else took place.

L'oiseau s'était pris à la glu et ne pouvait se déprendre. The bird stuck to the bird-lime and could not get off.

Sur le bruit que cet homme était mort de poison, on a fait déterrer le corps pour le visiter. On the report being spread that the man died of poison, they took up the body to have it examined.

Dès que j'avais diné, j'allais me promener. As soon as I had dined, I went-a-walking.

Je n'avais pas encore mangé le premier morceau que l'hôte entra, suivi de l'homme qui l'avait accosté dans la rue. I had not yet swallowed the first morsel, when the landlord came in, followed by the man who had stopped him in the street.

But we could not say, *Je n'eus pas encore mangé le premier morceau que,* &c., because the Past Anterior, like the Past Definite, can only be said of things entirely elapsed.

TURN INTO FRENCH.

When my letter was sealed, I found I *had forgotten* to tell you to come by the first train. I *had come*-to-a-determination[1] when he came to solicit me. Some people-or-other[2] *had clothed* him with rags out of charity. She *had delayed*[3] creating him an earl. The fatigue I *had undergone*[4] threw me into a fever. The string I *had touched* ceased to vibrate. He has-redeemed[5] all the lands that *were-alienated*-by[6] his ancestors.

You *brought* birds hither and the hurricane has killed them. You *planted* this garden and it is now destroyed. You have forgotten that you *promised* to come yesterday. That prince, both a legislator and a warrior, polished[7] the nations he *subdued.*[8] The formidable empire which Alexander *conquered* did not last longer than his life, which was very short. The merchants brought back most[9] of the goods they *carried* to the fair. I have-laid-out[10] the money I *received* without-pocketing-a-farthing.[11] I strictly observed the-diet[12] *prescribed* to me.

I let-him-have-back[13] the house he *sold* me. I was told you *called upon* me a little while ago. He has rewarded those of his servants who *served* him well. Immediately[14] he took off his coat, and climbed the tree to which the bird *escaped.* I *promised* you money on-such-a[15] day; I come to redeem[16] my word; there it is. They have-always-felt obliged[17] to her for the share she *had* in their reconciliation. The person whom she *destined*[18] to be her husband. He *promised* me-a-visit,[19] but he disappointed[20] me.

Have you performed-the-charge[21] he *gave* you? The Sybarite complained that a-fold[22] in one of the rose leaves on which he lay-stretched,[23] *prevented* him from sleeping. They *left* the-print[24] of their footsteps in the snow. He left-off-at-the-point[25] where he *began.*

1. Pris mon parti.—2. Gens quelconques.—3. Différer de.—4. Endurer.—5. Retirer.—6. Hypothéquer.—7. Policer.—8. Conquérir.—9. La plupart.—10. Dépenser.—11. Je n'en ai rien emboursé.—12. Le régime. 13. Lui recéder.—14. à l'instant.—15. Tel.—16. Dégager.—17. Savoir toujours bon gré de.—18. Choisir.—19. Venir me voir.—20. Ne pas tenir parole.—21. Exécuter les ordres.—22. Le pli.—23. Etait couché. —24. L'empreinte.—25. En rester au point.

FUTURE.

XCIX.—Shall and will, involving futurity of state or action, are to be translated by the Future of the Infinitive which follows.

J'y passerai, sinon, vous y passerez. I shall call, but if I do not, you will.

Nous le ferons dans un temps ou dans un autre. We shall do it some time or other.

TURN INTO FRENCH.

I *shall-call*[1] upon you in the course of the week. *Will* you *come* as you promised? Of-course-I-will.[2] I *shall-credit*-the-sum-to-you.[3] I *shall guess* to-a-day.[4] This *will-not-admit*[5] of difficulty. How much *will* he *charge*-for[6] discount?

He *will-see*[7] you to the door. We *shall-have*-some-fun.[8] How *will*-he-*get*-his-living?[9] I *shall get*[10] him a situation. *Will*-she-*get-better*[11] of her illness? I *shall-go*-and-meet-her.[12] If you suffer[13] loss, I *will-make*-it-*good*[14] to you. He *will-dress*-your-hair.[15] I *shall take* one. I *will find* better and cheaper-ones.[16]

If you do it, you *will-smart*[17] for it. Do it and you *shall-be-whipped.*[18] He that liveth-by[19] the sword *shall die* by the sword. He *will do* it, and nobody *shall prevent* him. When *will* the meeting *take*-place?[20]

Shall we *see*[21] the play out?[22] *Shall* I *help*[23] you to a little wine? When *can* you let-me-have[24] my boots? But the world *will* not *live, think,* or[25] *love* as I do. If you continue drinking you *will-impair*[26] your health. The righteous *will-be-discriminated*[27] from the wicked. All the documents-connected-with[28] the negotiation *shall-be-laid*-before[29] the House.

1. Aller voir.—2. Bien entendu.—3. Porter cette somme à votre avoir.—4. à un jour près.—5. Souffrir.—6. Prendre de.—7. Accompagner.—8. S'amuser.—9. Gagner de quoi vivre.—10. Faire avoir.—11. Se rétablir.—12. Aller au-devant d'elle.—13. Eprouver une.—14. En tenir compte.—15. Coiffer.—16. De moins chères.—17. Cuire.—18. Avoir le fouet.—19. Se servir de.—20. Avoir lieu.—21. Voir jouer.—22. Jusqu'au bout.—23. Offrir.—24. Me donner.—25. Ni ne.—26. Ruiner.—27. Séparer.—28. Pièces rélatives à.—29. Communiquer à.

C.—When SHALL interrogative involves the acquiescence of the person spoken to, it is often translated by *Vouloir* and the Subjunctive.

Voulez-vous que mon domestique aille vous chercher une voiture? Shall my servant call a coach for you?

Sometimes it is expressed by the Future of the Infinitive which follows.

Vous servirai-je un autre morceau de volaille? Non, pas davantage. Shall I help you to another piece of of this fowl? No, not any more.

TURN INTO FRENCH.

Shall I *go* for him, or *shall* I *send* for him? *Shall* I *go* and call him? *Shall* I *help*[1] you to some fish? *Shall* I *open* the window? *Shall* I *believe* a man who so often deceived me? *Shall* I *read* aloud?[2] *Shall* I *read* it to you? Yes, read it to me. *Shall* he *go* and tell them you want them? *Shall* my servant *go* there? *Shall* I *apologise*[3] for you? *Shall*-I-*lay*-before-thee[4] the-occasion[5] of all their disorders? *Shall*-I-*put*-you-*up*-to[6] what has been done during your absence?

1. Servir.—2. à haute voix.—3. Faire des excuses.—4. Veux-tu que je te dise.—5. La cause.—6. Vous mettre au courant de.

CI.—WILL, signifying *Wish* or *Choice*, is also expressed by *Vouloir,* followed by a Noun, an Infinitive, or the Subjunctive.

Voulez-vous nous faire le plaisir de dîner avec nous? Will you give us the pleasure of your company at dinner?

Je ne suis pas sûr qu'il veuille acquiescer à ce qu'on souhaite de lui. I am not so certain that he will acquiesce in what is required of him.

TURN INTO FRENCH.

Will you have the goodness to wait for me till I am back? I can and I *will* do it. *Will* you keep-him-out-of-his-due?[1] They *will* have him to appear as-a[2] witness. I *will* have no person disturbed[3] for me. *Will* you hear-me-say[4] my lesson? *Will* you take[5] a turn in the garden?

If they *will* call I shall be glad to see them. The thing is too difficult, I *will* not so much as attempt it.

1. Faire tort de ce qui est dû.—2. Comme.—3. Se déranger.—4. Me faire répéter.—5. Faire.

CII.—SHALL and WILL are often translated by *Aller* when they denote a future at hand.

Avec ce vent-là, les chemins vont bientôt sécher. The roads will soon be dried with that wind.

Je vais vous raconter ma triste aventure. I shall tell you my fatal story.

Faites attention, ou vous allez casser ce verre. Mind, or you will break that glass.

TURN INTO FRENCH.

I *will* go with him. I *will* cut it into four. I *will* wait for you. That silkworm *will* die if you shut the box.

I *will* throw them to him. What-pleasure[1] we *shall* have! I *will* ask mamma. He *will* buy each-of-us[2] a pony. He *will* soon be the most unfortunate man in the world.

1. Que de plaisir.—2. à chacun de nous.

CIII.—WILL and WOULD, denoting habit, are translated, the first by the Present, the second by the Imperfect of the Infinitive which follows.

Avec le temps, les os cassés reprennent et deviennent fermes. Broken bones will in time knit and become sound.

Quand elle était montée à un certain point, elle se retournait et disait quelque chose. When she was wrought to a certain pitch, she would turn and say something.

La bonne mine fait faire plus de chemin à la cour que le bon esprit partout ailleurs. A good mien in a court will carry a man greater lengths than a good understanding in any other place.

TURN INTO FRENCH.

Damascus steel *will-cut*[1] iron. Men of ability *will* sometimes *give-themselves-up*[2] to drinking. She is so lazy that she *will stay* for hours together[3] without doing anything. The red squirrel is a-saucy-fellow,[4] and when on a tree he *will* often *chatter*-at[5] a dog or a boy that happens to go by.

Ducklings *will swim, dive,* and *dabble*[6] as well as ducks. The turkey-cocks are great cowards, and *will-run*-at[7] the sight of a cat. The buffalo is as large as an ox, but *will-run-away*-from[8] a man.

Some apples *will*-not-*keep*[9] in winter. Though rich he *would* not *despise* the poor. He had a dog that *would* not *growl,*[10] or[11] *snarl,* or *snap,*[12] or *bite;* but[13] *would bark, hunt,* and *guard* the house from[14] the thieves, and *would-go*[15] to Dick Grange, if-he[16] did but cry, "Dash! Dash!"

He *would* often *give* five guineas when five shillings would-have-done.[17] Sometimes he *would go out* to[18] supper; on such occasions I *would-attend*[19] him with a lantern.

He *would* not *run out* in the mud to splash his legs, and when he came in-doors[20] he *would rub* his feet on the mat and then *hang* his hat on a peg. Often he *would-creep*[21] into a corner or into an empty room and *cry* in secret when he had been called a thief. He then *would exclaim,* sobbing, "Oh! I wish I had not taken the cherries!"

When he had finished his own task he *would-join-in*[22] hers. The sound of her lute *would-come*-stealing-upon-the-stillness-of[23] her chamber.

1. Trancher.—2. S'adonner.—3. Entières.—4. Petit effronté.—5. Se moquer de.—6. Barboter.—7. Se sauver à.—8. Eviter.—9. Ne pas se garder.—10. Gronder.—11. Ni ne.—12. Happer.—13. Mais

qui.—14. Contre.—15. Venir.—16. Pour peu qu'il.—17. Suffire.—18. Pour aller.—19. Accompagner.—20. Rentrer.—21. Se cacher.—22. Aider à faire.—23. Pénétrer faiblement dans.

CIV.—In conjectural statements, the French often use the Future or the Conditional, instead of the Perfect or the Pluperfect used in English.

"Hé quoi!" lui répondis-je, "ce voleur met effrontément à dix pistoles un poisson que ne lui en aura coûté que quatre, et tu veux que je lui passe cet article-là?" "How," answered I, "shall that robber charge in his bill ten pistoles for a fish that did not cost four, and I pass over that article?"

Seigneur, si vous eussiez été ici, mon frère ne serait pas mort. Lord, if thou hadst been here, my brother had not died.

Je voyais clairement que si nous fussions restés à bord, nous serions tous venus heureusement à terre. I saw evidently that if we had kept on board, we had all got safe on shore.

TURN INTO FRENCH.

All I can do for you is-to-quarter-you-in[1] the barn, and it won't, I suppose, be the first time you *have slept* upon straw. The success of your affair depends upon the turn that *is given* to it. They *have been surprised* by the night (Translate—the night shall have surprised them), and they *have come* into the wood to wait for the day.

A father who *had married* his son without giving him the-management-of-his-estate,[2] had not used him differently-from-what-Mazarin-did.[3] I *were* a great knave to do it. It *were* a shame to speak of it.

The French ship Ressource was-shipwrecked[4] forty miles from Valparaiso; out-of[5] six hundred persons who were on board, five only *were saved*. It-is-reported[6] that the Sumpter *was seen* near Genoa, at a few leagues off the port. From the intelligence[7] we receive from Warsaw, a revolution *has-broken-out*[8] in Poland. I-am-apprehensive[9] he has not *understood* me.

What will be the-portion[10] of those who *have-derided*[11] God's word? The Lord will not hold him guiltless,[12] that *taketh* his name in vain. I *had dined* with you, but the rain prevented me.

1. C'est de vous mettre dans.—2. L'administration de son bien.—3. Autrement que Mazarin.—4. A naufragé.—5. De.—6. Dit-on.—7. Avis.—8. Eclater.—9. Je présume.—10. Le partage.—11. Se moquer.—12. Pour innocent.

CV.—After *Quand, lorsque,* when; *aussitôt que, dès que,* as soon as; *du moment que,* the moment that; *tant que,* as long as, as often; *tandis que, pendant que,* whilst; *toutes les fois que,* every time that, whenever; *quiconque,* whoever; *celui qui,* he who; *le premier qui,* the first that; the PRESENT is often translated by the FUTURE; the IMPERFECT, by the CONDITIONAL.

Quand vous aurez acheté une belle chose, il vous en faudra encore acheter dix pour que tout soit uniforme. When you have bought a fine thing, you will require to buy ten more to have everything to match.

Je lui ai dit qu'il aurait la récompense aussitôt qu'il aurait fini sa tâche. I told him he should have the reward as soon as he had accomplished his task.

Nous n'obtiendrons de lui que juste ce qu'il voudra. He will only let us have what he pleases.

Tant que je serai dans mon bon sens. So long as I keep in my right wits.

TURN INTO FRENCH.

I shall call upon you as soon as ever it-*is*-fine.[1] Come at any time you *like*. I shall go to your house as many times as you *like*. As long as he *is* ambitious.

After you *have-come*-to-such-a-place,[2] do not go straight-on,[3] but turn a little aside.[4] Is the canal deep? I will tell as soon as I *have dived*. Do not make any noise; after I *am gone*, do as you *please*. When you *have-reached*[5] the wood turn to the left. When, as soon as, the moment that you *are arrived*, come and see us.

As[6] you *study* and *learn* the French tongue, you will find more beauties in it. You shall be paid as you *work*. You will send me my money as-fast-as[7] you *receive* it. I shall work when I *am*[8] well and (*am*) strong. I will crawl-there-as[9] well as I *can*. Whatever I *earn* I will share with you. I will give you whatever you *ask*.

The minister will appoint whomsoever he *pleases*. When the law *is passed*, the public will be satisfied. Start all-of-you,[10] he who *comes in* first shall have the silver watch. You shall have all you *wish for*. When you *have done* so much for the public, what will you get by that? You will not have been there a fortnight before[11] you *make* acquaintances.

So long as you *behave* well, you shall be respected. I shall reward him according-as-he[12] *has served* me. Take either-of-these[13] coats which *suits*[14] you. So long as he *has* money enough.

He thought he should be quiet when the war *was* over. You promised to pay me in proportion as you *gained* money. I was to let him know your arrival as soon as you *came*. Have I not told you that whoever *arrived* first should have the prize?

I told you that everything should be done to please you, so long as you *behaved* and *learned* your lessons well. Have I not said to you that whoever *answered* best should have the premium? He said he would come as soon as he *had done*.

When you *have arrived* and[15] *rested*.[16] The less you *speak* of your own merit, the more I shall think of it. Come whenever it *suits* you. The sooner I *see* him the-better.[17] By-the-next-time[18] I *see* you. When once I *have acquainted* you with all the particulars, you will cease feeling-surprise.[19]

It is forty to-one[20] he *loses*. I will introduce[21] you to her whenever you *please*. So long as she *is* virtuous, she will be admired. Look-in-at[22] our garden when[23] you *pass* that way.

The next coat I *buy* shall be black. He shall be paid in proportion to what he *has done*. When his-turn-*is-served*,[24] he will care no more for us. Take such-as[25] *suit* you.

Stay as-long-as[26] you *can*. Come as early as you *can*. Bring as-many-more-as[27] you *can*. Be as indulgent as you *can*. Be as-little[28] indulgent as you *can*. Be back as-soon-as[29] you *can*.

1. Faire beau temps.—2. Arriver à tel endroit.—3. Tout droit.—4. à côté.—5. Arriver à.—6. à mesure que.—7. Au fur et à mesure que.—8. Se porter.—9. Se trainer comme.—10. Tous ensemble.—11. Que.—12. Suivant qu'il.—13. De ces.—14. Aller.—15. Et que.—16. Se reposer.—17. Mieux cela vaudra.—18. La première fois que.—19. D'être surpris.—20. Contre un.—21. Présenter.—22. Veuillez entrer dans.—23. La première fois que.—24. Obtenir ce qu'il désire.—25. Ceux qui.—26. Le plus longtemps que.—27. Le plus que.—28. Le moins.—29. Le plus tôt que.

CVI.—Shall and will are translated by the Subjunctive when dependent on verbs, words, or forms of speech expressing wonder or surprise, purpose or doubt.

Il n'y a pas d'apparence que cela ait aucune suite. It is not likely that it will be attended by any consequence.

TURN INTO FRENCH.

It is not probable that she *will answer*. I expect-that[1] she *will be* there. It is rather-hard[2] that she *will* not *have* me. Whether she *will* or not, it-is-nothing-to-me.[3] It is not possible that she *will consent*. It is not impossible that-she[4] *will come*. It is not probable that he *will do* it.

Provided he *shall go*. I must-absolutely-insist[5] that he *shall be rewarded* for his fidelity. He has ordered that dinner *shall be served up* at seven o'clock. Whether he *consent* or not, it-shall[6] be so. Do you expect she *will come?* Is it not feared we *shall be* cold? Are you not afraid that I *shall* not *give* it *back* to you?

Do you think it *will be* fine weather to-morrow? Do you think he *will have found* a house before the end of his lease? I will lend you my grammar provided you *will return*[7] it to me.

I expect[8] you *will do* all she requires. I do not hope you *will do* it. Do you think such conduct *will-do*?[9] I do expect you *will do* it.

1. S'attendre à ce que.—2. Un peu fort.—3. Cela m'est indifférent.—4. Qu'elle ne.—5. Entendre.—6. Il faut que.—7. Rendre.—8. Entendre.—9. Etre convenable.

CVII.—MAY and CAN, denoting physical or moral force or ability, or something eventual, probable, conjectural, or approximative, are translated by *Pouvoir*. These expressions have either a Present or a Future sense, and are in this respect subordinate to the rest of the passage.

Je ne puis m'empêcher de rire. I cannot help laughing.

Pourrai-je venir vous chercher demain? May I call for you to-morrow?

CAN, in the sense of *to know how*, or *understand*, is translated by *Savoir*.

Savez-vous parler Français? Can you speak French?

TURN INTO FRENCH.

Let us see which-of-us[1] *can* jump the highest? *Can* you leap over that wall? Say-what-you-will,[2] you *cannot* do it. Return as soon as you *can*. He will do all he *can* for her.

I shall-call-again[3] as soon as I *can*. *Can* the thing be done? *Can* you not come to-morrow?

Bears *can* stand[4] and walk on their hind legs. If a man *cannot* carry it, a horse *may*. He took[5] all the trouble he *could*. He made all the excuses he *could*.

May I come in? *May* I come next week? *May* I not see him? We *may* do what is-not-against[6] decency, propriety, or good-manners.[7] It *may* do as a pastime. An infant *may* destroy[8] life, but all the kings upon earth *cannot* restore it.

1. Qui d'entre nous.—2. Quoi que vous puissiez dire.—3. Repasser.—4. Se soutenir.—5. Se donner.—6. N'être pas contraire à la.—7. Bonnes mœurs.—8. Oter.

CVIII.—May and can, when preceded by words, verbs, or forms of speech governing the Subjunctive, are rendered in French by the Subjunctive of their own Infinitive, or that of the following Verb.

Si mince que soit un cheveu, il fait de l'ombre. However slender a hair may be, it produces a shade.

TURN INTO FRENCH.

It will be impossible that you *can*-have-any[1] hold upon him. I hope[2] he *may* succeed. I do not doubt but you *may* succeed. I am sorry you *cannot*-eat.[3] Send some one hither who *may* take[4] a message to him. None-but-a-bad-boy[5] *can* use such language. I have said nothing which *can* derogate[6] from his reputation.

Do you believe he *can*-afford[7] to spend a guinea a day? Write him a-word[8] that he *may* know what is-going-on.[9] Some say he was killed in a duel, others that he died of a fever, however-it[10] *may* be, he is certainly[11] dead. Whatever-he[12] *may* say to you do not believe it.

Whoever you *may* be, I am not afraid of you. To-whom-soever[13] you *may* speak, be civil. It is the-least-thing[14] you *can* do. We have no orators that[15] *can* be put in opposition[16] to Demosthenes or Cicero. Choose a friend whom you *may* esteem and who esteems you. I do not fear these-people[17] whatever they *may* be. Give me one, however-small[18] it *may* be. I-know-nobody[19] that *can* be compared to him. After that I-will-not[20] swear but there *may* be a communication between the moon and the earth. Whatever[21] your intentions *may* be.

However good his father *may* be. I do not know whether he be a Jew or a Christian, but whatever he *may* be, he looks-like[22] an honest man. I do not know who has done it, but whoever he *may* be, I will punish him. Whoever those ladies *may* be, I will not allow them to enter.

You *may* have possibly[23] written to me, but your letter never reached me. He *may* have been-there,[24] but I did not notice-him.[25] It *may* be so, but I do not believe it.[26] You *may*[27] not always fall into such good company. He *may* be dead now.

1. Avoir aucune.—2. Souhaiter.—3. Ne pas avoir faim.—4. Porter.—5. Il n'y a qu'un polisson qui.—6. Porter atteinte.—7. Avoir les moyens.—8. Un petit mot.—9. Se passer.—10. Quoiqu'il en.—11. Bien.—12. Quoi que ce soit qu'il.—13. à qui que ce soit que.—14. Le moins que.—15. Que l'on.—16. Opposer.—17. Ces gens-là.—18. Si petit que.—19. Je ne sache personne.—20. Je ne veux plus.—21. Quelles que.—22. Avoir l'air.—23. Il se peut que.—24. Qu'il y fût.—25. Prendre garde à lui.—26. Cela.—27. Il est possible que.

CONDITIONAL.

CIX.—When expressing a Future Contingent, *i.e.*, something which may or may not happen, SHOULD, COULD, WOULD, and MIGHT are translated by the Conditional of the Infinitive which follows, or by the Conditional of their own Infinitives.

Il résolut de se défendre jusqu'à la dernière extrêmité contre quiconque l'attaquerait. He resolved to fight it out against whomsoever would assail him.

Ne vous jouez pas à un homme si puissant; il vous écraserait. Avoid playing with a man of his power; he would crush you.

Vous voudriez nous indisposer contre eux. You would set us against them.

Ne pourriez-vous pas soulever ce sac? Could you not lift up that bag?

On le prendrait sur le fait, qu'il ne rougirait pas. Though he were taken in the fact, yet he would not blush.

The Conditional is also sometimes used instead of the Indicative, as a milder form, to avoid positiveness of expression.

L'archevêque voudrait avoir un jeune homme qui eût de la littérature et une bonne main pour mettre au net ses écrits. The archbishop wants a young man of letters, who writes a good hand, to make fair copies of his writings.

TURN INTO FRENCH.

It was determined[1] he *should remain* three years longer[2] at Paris. It was decided[3] he *should be put* to the torture. They were-contending[4] who *should-discover*[5] the most dutiful-attachment.[6] Why *should we shrink*-from[7] what we cannot shun?

Would you really[8] *have* the assurance to deny it? They assured him he *would obtain* nothing, on-which[9] he withdrew.

How many oysters *could* you *eat?* Why, I dare say I *could eat* four dozen. You *would* not *tell* him so to his face. I *would* not *do* it for all in-the[10] world. I *could stay* a whole day listening to him. I *could love* her well enough if she had but[11] money.

Any-one-except-me[12] *might approve* of his plan. *Might* she not *write* her letter while we are reading? The thing *might be done.*[13] I was-desirous-of[14] rendering him such services as his unfortunate condition[15] *might admit*-of.[16] He is so lean that one *might count* his ribs.

She *would upbraid* me with having ruined-her-fortunes.[17] He *would* never *forgive* your hurting-her-feelings.[18] If she hated me, I *should know* what passion to-deal-with.[19] What-mind[20] *would* not *revolt* against such injustice? He screamed-out[21] that he *would* never *consent*. Who *would* not *be impatient* at such delays?

Though-I-*should-have-seen*-it,[22] yet I *would* not *have believed* it. Though she *should die*, I *would* not *be sorry* for it. He *would see* me die, yet he *would* not *be concerned*[23] at it. Though he *should-enjoy*[24] all the gold in the world, he *would* want more.

1. Décider.—2. Encore.—3. Arrêter.—4. Se disputer.—5. Montrer.—6. De zèle.—7. Reculer.—8. Bien.—9. Là-dessus.—10. Au.—11. De.—12. Tout autre que moi.—13. Se faire.—14. Désirer.—15. Situation.—16. Permettre.—17. Causer sa perte.—18. Lui faire de la peine.—19. Combattre.—20. Quelle âme.—21. Crier d'une voix aiguë.—22. Je l'aurais vu que.—23. Touché.—24. Avoir.

CX.—Do not mistake *Quand, quand même, quand bien même, lors même*, meaning Though, although, if, if even, &c., implying condition, supposition, which must have the Conditional with *Quoique, bien que, encore que*, Though or although, which must have the Subjunctive.

Quand même il n'aurait pas été pressé, je doute qu'il se fût assis. Even though he had been in no hurry, I question whether he had sat down.

Je doute que vous trouvassiez un meilleur cheval quand vous chercheriez pendant six mois. I doubt whether you would find a better horse, though you were to seek six months for it.

Quoique j'aie l'aveu de votre père, ne vous imaginez pas que je veuille m'en prévaloir pour faire violence à vos sentiments. Although I have your father's consent, do not think that I intend to avail myself of it to do violence to your inclination.

Souvenez-vous que de tous les attributs de Dieu, bien qu'il soient égaux, sa miséricorde l'emporte. Remember that of all the attributes of God, although they are equal, yet his mercy prevails.

TURN INTO FRENCH WITH THE CONDITIONAL.

Though you *should do* it, you would not get anything by it. *Though* he *should-come*-in-the-shape[1] of a bag of money. I will follow you *if* you *walk* till-morning.[2] *Though* it *were* so, everyone has his fancy, *though* it *be* but-a-trifle.[3] *Even though* he *should come*. *Even though* this-*should-be-called*[4] a small advantage.

Though I *should* stay here fifty years, I shall not leave this place till I have dethroned the King of Poland.

Even if he *should have said* so, it was no reason for your repeating it. *Though* he *should see* me, I-do-not-care.[5] *Even though* he *should have done* that, what-does-it-signify?[6] *Even though* you *should* only *send* them next week, it would be time-enough.[7] I will do it *if* I-*should-die*-for-it.[8] *Although* he *would consent* to it, that could not be done. *Even were* he[9] *to-beg*[10] it of me himself, yet I would not do it.

1. M'apparaître sous la forme.—2. Jusqu'à demain.—3. Dans des choses de la moindre importance.—4. Regarder cela comme.—5. Je m'en moque.—6. Qu'est-ce que cela fait?—7. Encore temps.—8. Devoir m'en coûter la vie.—9. Il me le.—10. Demander.

TURN INTO FRENCH WITH THE SUBJUNCTIVE.

Though he *be* poor, he is an honest man. *Although* I *am* often alone, I never feel-dull.[1] *Though* I *have*-no-important-affair-on-hands,[2] yet I am continually employed. *Although* he *is* rich, he is-not-a-bit-the-better[3] for it. *Though* thou *hast* my forgiveness, thou shalt for-ever[4] have my contempt. His philosophy was adopted, *though* they *opposed* it at first.

I shall overtake him, *though* he *runs*. We should overtake him, *though* he *should run.* He has never learned French, *although* he[5] *has been taught* it five years. *Although* those boys *were idle,* yet they improved.[6] *Although* I *have* to complain of him, yet I continue to see him, and he continues writing to me.

Although he *set out* before me, I soon joined him. The church is therefore[7] one, *though* the members *be* many.[8] Some men pretend they are rich, *though* they *have* nothing. *Although* I *wish* it with the best of my heart, I cannot do it. The town is handsome enough, *though* its streets *are* narrow and ill-paved.

1. S'ennuyer.—2. N'être chargé d'aucune affaire importante.—3. N'en valoir pas mieux.—4. à jamais.—5. On.—6. Faire des progrès.—7. Donc.—8. Nombreux.

CXI.—SHOULD, COULD, WOULD, and MIGHT, dependent on verbs or words denoting purpose, doubt, wonder, or surprise, are translated by the Subjunctive of the Infinitive which follows, and sometimes by the Subjunctive of their own Infinitive.

Il serait à désirer que vous rentrassiez en vous-même. It were to be wished you would turn your thoughts within.

Votre mère est désireuse que vous remportiez des prix cette année. Your mother is desirous that you should gain prizes this year.

Je ne me serais jamais défié que vous dussiez m'abandonner au besoin. I could never have suspected that you could fail me in time of need.

Ces jumeaux se ressemblent tellement qu'il n'y a personne qui ne s'y méprenne. Those twins are so like, or so much alike, that anybody might mistake them.

La seule chose dont on s'étonne, c'est que nous ayons

pu l'endurer si longtemps. The only wonder is that we could have put up with it so long.

TURN INTO FRENCH.

The proposition is so absurd that I am-surprised[1] you *should make* it. That you *should have committed* a first fault is-conceivable,[2] but that you *should have committed* a second, nay, even[3] a third, astonishes me. Does she wish some fire *should be lighted* for her?

It-is-very-odd-that-you-should-think-one[4] *must*-blindly-*follow*[5] your advice (*pl.*). I am of opinion[6] that you *should write.* You won't-take-it-amiss[7] I *should*-write[8] to you.

He ordered that he *should be put* to death. He proposed that we *should go* to London. He does-not-deserve[9] that anything *should be done* for him. Can you imagine[10] that he *should have refused* such a thing? He complains that you *should have mentioned*[11] the business.

That you *should have dismissed*[12] him does-not-surprise-me,[13] but that you should recall[14] him is-beyond-my-comprehension.[15] Did-you-expect[16] I *should do* it? I am only sorry they *should do* it. Is-it-your-pleasure-that[17] we *should go* and fetch it?

Do nothing that *might* displease him. Have you found no one who *could* explain this passage to you? I wonder that they *could*[18] think of putting-off[19] such bare-faced[20] lies. It-never-came-into-my-head[21] that he *could* fail-in[22] his duty. Whatever I *might say,* he gave-me-to-understand[23] that-he-would-not-recede-from-his-resolution.[24] I am surprised that you *should-set*-so-little-value-on[25] it.

If I had known you *would come* so late. I did not think she *would come* so soon. I wish he *would settle*[26] in this land. It was not to be supposed that they[27] *would do* such a thing.

I wish he *should be* a sailor. I wish he *would-be*-a[28] sailor. Let us suppose he *would consent.* It-was-a-great-while[29] before he *could-resolve*-upon-it.[30] He entreated[31] that we *would* not *exact* any promise. I did not expect that he *would keep*[32] his word.

Did you think that Sylla, after having governed with the most capricious tyranny, *would lay-down*[33] the dictatorship?

It was not probable that they *would have sold* their horses. I wish he *would take* some trouble.

I wish you *would set off*. There is nothing but he *would do*[34] for her. He begs you *would deign*-to-listen-to-him.[35]

1. S'étonner que.—2. Se concevoir.—3. Même.—4. Je vous admire de vouloir qu'on.—5. Suivre aveuglément.—6. Avis.—7. Ne pas trouver mauvais que.—8. Prendre la liberté d'écrire.—9. N'être pas digne. —10. Concevoir.—11. Parler de.—12. Chasser.—13. Cela ne me surprend pas.—14. Faire revenir.—15. Voilà qui me passe.—16. Espérer. —17. Désirez-vous que.—18. Aient pu.—19. Débiter.—20. Effronté.—21. Il ne m'est jamais entré en pensée.—22. Manquer à.—23. Me faire juger.—24. Qu'il n'en démordrait point.—25. Faire si peu de cas de.—26. S'établir.—27. On.—28. Consentir à se faire.—29. Il se passa bien du temps.—30. Vouloir le faire.—31. Demander instamment.—32. Tenir.—33. Déposer.—34. Etre prêt à faire.—35. Daigner l'écouter.

CXII.—SHOULD, preceded by THAT in exclamatory sentences, is very often rendered by *Faut-il que,* when expressive of regret and bitter deception.

Faut-il que les hommes mettent dans leur bouche un ennemi qui leur dérobe leur cerveau! Oh! that men should put an enemy into their mouth to steal away their brains!

TURN INTO FRENCH.

That life *should* be but a dream! *Should* your friendship for an unfortunate stranger be so fatal to you! Oh, that I *should* have such a son! Oh, that you *should* be my child! That I *should* be so unfortunate! Why *should* man thus-feel-pain?[1] That Clarinda *should* betray me!

That I *should* be deprived of so dear a friend! That things *should*-have-come-to-such-a-pass-as-this![2] That he *should*-have-so-far-forgotten-himself![3] That I *should* be betrayed by the son of Achilles! That men *should* be foolish enough not to know how to distinguish real-blessings-from-false![4] That I *should*-be-debarred-the-sight[5] of my children!

1. Connaître ainsi la douleur.—2. En venir jusque là.—3. S'oublier à ce point.—4. Les vrais biens d'avec les faux.—5. Privé.

ON THE VARIOUS APPLICATIONS OF SI.

CXIII.—With *Si*, followed by a verb negatively used, *Pas* may be used or omitted; if omitted, it is an elegance of construction.

S'il ne paie pas, il faudra le faire actionner. If he does not pay, we must bring an action against him.

Ne pleure point, mon ami, si tu ne veux m'accabler de chagrin. Do not weep, my friend, or you will distress me with grief.

CXIV.—When *Si* means if, supposing, granting, and denotes condition, supposition of something which may or may not be realized, the French do not use the Future or the Conditional, but the Present or the Imperfect of the Indicative.

S'il m'arrive jamais de faire la moindre faute, il ne manque jamais de la relever. Should I happen to make the slightest slip, he is sure to take it up.

S'il vient demain avec nous, nous partirons de bonne heure. If he will come with us to-morrow, we shall start early.

S'il pleuvait, ne m'attendez pas. If it should rain, do not wait for me.

Si, meaning *whether*, can refer to the Past, the Present, the Future, or the Conditional.

Pourriez-vous me dire s'il a achevé son ouvrage? Could you tell me whether he has finished his work?

Je ne sais si cela est vrai. I do not know whether that is true.

Je doute si je viendrai à bout de cela. I doubt whether I shall bring it about.

Savez-vous s'il viendrait, si je l'invitais? Do you know whether he would come, were I to invite him?

TURN INTO FRENCH.

If they *do not make-it-up,*[1] they will ruin themselves with[2] lawsuits. If I *do not mistake,* you pretend to know everything. *Should* he *come* here now, he would be greatly astonished. If Mr. D. *should-meet*-with-such-a-loss,[3] I would not pity him. *Should* you *repeat* it, I would no longer have confidence in you. If anybody *should say* to you, have you been eating your father's cherries, what would you say? If you *could accommodate*-me-*with*[4] five hundred pounds, you would oblige me. If I *could not,* I would borrow the sum to-oblige-you.[5]

I doubt whether[6] he *will succeed,* whether he *can do* it. Do you know whether he *will come?* Tell me whether you *will go* there. The frog asked whether she *was* bigger than the ox. I do not know whether he *sleeps* or[7] *listens.* I do not know whether he *will repent.*

I did not know whether the king *would come.* I do not know whether he *would have come.* I do not know whether it *would not be* more advantageous. I do not know whether he *would repent,* whether he *would have repented.*

They deliberated whether they[8] *should*[9] *set out* immediately. I ask you whether you *will come?* Judge others[10] by yourself, and see whether you *would be* glad that anybody would behave so to you. Do you know whether he *will accept* your offers or not? Inquire[11] whether he *would have accepted* them. Have you ascertained[12] whether he *would come?* If this *be* true, he is guilty; now, this is true, therefore he is guilty.

1. S'accommoder.—2. En.—3. Faire une pareille perte.—4. Me prêter. —5. Pour vous rendre service.—6. Si.—7. Ou s'il.—8. On.—9. Falloir. —10. D'autrui.—11. S'informer.—12. S'assurer.

CXV.—*Si*, at the beginning of a sentence, can be repeated in the second clause, or replaced by *Que*, which requires the Subjunctive.

Si vous sortez et si vous le rencontrez dites-lui de venir. If you go out and chance to meet with him, tell him to come.

Si votre ami est ici, et qu'il veuille venir me voir, je serai enchanté de le recevoir. If your friend is here, and will call upon me, I shall be very glad to see him.

TURN INTO FRENCH.

If I were doing it; *if* you had done it for-my-sake.[1] *If* Rome formed projects of war; *if* she signed treaties of peace, it was with-a-view-to[2] satisfy her glory and her ambition.

If a proposition is-studied-and[3] *well conceived*. *If* he comes, and *should* I not *be* at home, send for me. *If* she loves me, and *wish* to persuade me to it, she must behave differently. *If* your brother were at court and *were* willing to-be-of-service-to-me.[4] *If* he should come back and *claim*-something-of you,[5] you would be greatly puzzled.

If you should call at my house, and I *was* not at home, please[6] to wait for me. *If* your friend has-offended-you[7] in his passion, and *if* he *be willing* to own his fault,[8] accept his apology. *If* you were going to France, and *if* you *would-take-charge*[9] of this small parcel for me, I would be very much obliged to you. *If* you consent and *come* with her.

If the Gauls had been as prudent as they were brave, and *had* all *united*[10] against Cæsar, they would not have been conquered. *If* Alexander had been able to master his passions, and *had* not *tarnished* his glory by his foolish pride, he would have been worthy to be considered-as-a-model[11] for all princes. *If* men were wise, and *would follow* the precepts of reason, they would be happy.

If you have a mind[12] to go out, and *want*[13] a coach, mine is at your service. *If* your uncle comes, and *if* you *are obliged* to go with him, do-not-stand-on-ceremony.[14] *If* you see them, and *find* they are ready to accept the offer, why-then,[15] make it.

1. Pour l'amour de moi.—2. Dans le dessein de.—3. Si l'on étudie et que.—4. Me servir.—5. Vous faire une réclamation.—6. Veuillez.—7. Vous blesser.—8. Torts.—9. Vouloir bien se charger.—10. Se réunir.—11. Servir de modèle.—12. Envie.—13. Avoir besoin.—14. Ne vous gênez pas.—15. Eh bien alors.

CXVI.—The Subjunctive Mood is used in the subordinate clause depending on *Si*, whenever doubt arises in the speaker's mind as to the existence of a thing, the actuality of a fact, or of an event.

Si j'avais su que vous dussiez venir, j'aurais fait préparer quelque chose de plus. Had I known that you were coming, I would have got something additional prepared.

But if there is no doubt as to the actuality of the thing asserted, the Indicative must be used.

Cette somme est à votre disposition, si vous croyez qu'elle peut vous être de quelque utilité. You are welcome to the sum, if you think it would be of use to you.

Si j'avais su que c'était un trompeur, je ne me serais pas fié à lui. Had I known him to be a deceitful man, I would not have confided in him.

TURN INTO FRENCH.

If you think[1] him *adequate*-to-the-task,[2] if you think he *is* capable of it, entrust him with it. Let us go, if you think it *will be* fine. If it appears to you that it *be* so. If you think that I *am in the wrong*, do tell me. If it is a thing that *can be* done, I shall be overjoyed at it. If it were I who *had done* it, who *had said* it.

If I thought you *were* now in London, I would repair thither. Had I thought that matters[3] *would-have-taken*-such-a-turn[4] since I saw you, I would have started sooner. If I thought you *would bring* me the things I want, I would wait for you. If I thought you *would return* before the end of the month, I would stay a little longer. I think your friend would have started sooner, *had* he *known* that you were not coming.

If we had supposed-that[5] we *should have been admitted* into that house, we would have accompanied you. If I thought your lawsuit *would-come-on*[6] before the judge in a fortnight, I would-undertake-to-defend-you.[7] If the deserters had supposed the enemy *would have been conquered* in so short a time, they would not have abandoned our army.

1. Juger.—2. Pouvoir remplir cette mission.—3. Choses.—4. Se passer ainsi.—5. Penser que.—6. Etre porté.—7. Se charger de plaider une cause.

CXVII.—After *Si*, expressed or understood, the Pluperfect of the Indicative and the Compound Conditional are often elegantly translated by the Imperfect of the Subjunctive.

S'ils m'eussent vu fuir (*i.e.*, S'ILS M'AVAIENT VU FUIR), *ils se seraient mis à mes trousses, et m'auraient eu bientôt rattrapé.* Had they seen me running away, they would have been at my heels in an instant and would soon have caught me.

Elle eût voulu (*i.e.*, ELLE AURAIT VOULU), *que la mort la plus prompte fermât ses yeux et terminât sa honte.* She wished that a sudden death would put an end to her life and shame.

Si cet arrangement eût réussi, il était en état de faire

face à tout. If that scheme had succeeded, he was able to stand all demands.

TURN INTO FRENCH.

My dear guests, *had*-you-*alighted*-at-the-house-of[1] some other inhabitant of Arcadia, or *had* you *come*[2] this way a few years ago, you *would have been* still better *received.* She *would have been* so happy to see her son again. If you *had drunk* nothing else than pure[3] water all your life, and *had-been-satisfied*[4] with simple nourishment, you would not now be tormented with the gout.

I believe he would-have-run-mad-on-the-occasion,[5] *had*-I-not-*been*-at-great-pains-to-calm-him.[6] They *would have accused* him of servile copying.[7] Any-person-but[8] you *would have kept* it. Nobody *thought* that this would come-to-pass.[9] *Had* he *conducted himself* with common[10] prudence, he would have succeeded.

1. Etre descendu chez.—2. Passer.—3. Claire.—4. Se contenter.—5. Devenir fou.—6. Prendre soin de lui remettre l'esprit.—7. Avoir copié.—8. Tout autre que.—9. Arriver.—10. Ordinaire.

ON THE IMPERATIVE.

CXVIII.—Every second person of the Imperative not ending in *S*, takes one when followed by the pronouns *En* or *Y*. But no *S* is added to the Imperative before *En* a preposition.

Je veux entrer dans cette chambre, ouvres-en la porte. I wish to go into that room; open the door of it.

Vas-y. Go thither. *Portes-y.* Carry thither.

Va en trois jours à Paris. Go in three days to Paris.

CXIX.—In the Imperative Affirmative, the Pronouns always come after the Verb which governs them, and must be united to them by a hyphen.

Voulez-vous me conduire à ma chambre? Menez-y-moi. Will you show me to my room? Show me the way.

Donnez-leur-moi sur les oreilles. Box their ears for me.

Quelques amis que tu aies, fie-toi plutôt à toi-même qu'à eux. Though you have ever so many friends, trust to yourself.

CXX.—But if the Pronouns are governed by another Verb in the Infinitive, no hyphen should be used.

Va t'amuser. Go and amuse yourself.

In this case, *Va* must be written without an *S* when *En* or *Y* depends on another Verb.

Va y donner ordre. Go and settle the matter.

Va en chercher. Go and get some.

CXXI.—*Moi* and *Toi* are used after the Imperative instead of *Me* and *Te*.

Laisse-moi m'asseoir. Let me sit down.

Souviens-toi de la fragilité des choses humaines. Remember the instability of all human things.

Except before *En*, or before a second Imperative, or when the Imperative is used negatively.

Ne m'étourdis pas, va-t'en. Don't deafen me, get you gone.

Pour des injures, dis-m'en tant que tu voudras. As for names, call me as many as you like.

Blâmez-moi ou me louez, j'en veux désormais faire à ma tête. Blame me or praise me, I will henceforth act as I please.

CXXII.—If two Imperatives come together, with a CONJUNCTION between them, the second Objective Pronoun is generally placed before the second Imperative.

Ecrivez-le-lui et le lui envoyez. Write it to him and send it to him.

Quand on proposa à une tribu d'Indiens sauvages d'émigrer, son chef répondit: Dirons-nous aux ossements de nos pères: Levez-vous et suivez-nous à l'étranger! When a tribe of wild Indians had proposed to emigrate, their chief replied: Shall we say to the bones of our fathers: Arise and follow us to a foreign land!

CXXIII.—When passing from Negation to Affirmation, the second Objective Pronoun is placed after the second Imperative.

Ne le punissez pas, mais punissez-moi. Do not punish him but punish me.

TURN INTO FRENCH.

Follow me. *Let us take* it. *Give* us. *Tell* it. *Do* it. *Let* me do. *Give* me several. *Describe*[1] or *show* them to me. *Sell* or *lend* me this book. As soon as you have done your exercise, *bring* it to me. *Give* it to me or *lend* it to me. *Make haste*[2] and dress yourself. *Prepare* thyself to die.

Take some there for thy brother. *Seek out* the cause of it. *Exhibit*-on[3] that occasion proofs of your zeal. *Do* not *give* it, but *sell* it to her. Do not *weary* me. *Send* them some there. Do not *send* them any there. *Take* them some there. Do not *offer* them any there. *Give* it to him. *Take* me there. *Make*-them[4] return thee thy money. *Go* and tell him to come. *Think* of it. *Admit* him, be-he-who-or-what-he-may.[5] *Ask* him to come and speak to me. *Run* thither as fast as you can.

1. Peindre.—2. Se dépêcher.—3. Donner en.—4. Fais toi.—5. Quel qu'il soit, ou qu'il soit qui il voudra.

CXXIV.—When *Que,* let, the so-called sign of the Imperative, denotes order, command, prayer, assent, the following Verb is invariably put in the Subjunctive.

Prenne l'autre qui voudra. Let who will take the other.

Que celui ou celle qui l'a vu faire le fasse. Let him or her who saw it done do it.

CXXV.—After the Imperative, *Que,* denoting purpose, requires the Subjunctive.

Suivez-moi que j'aille un peu montrer mon habit par la ville. Follow me, that I may go and show my clothes through the town.

Mettez ordre à ce que je sois payé. See that I am paid.

Donnez l'ordre à mes domestiques qu'ils n'aient l'air de se douter de mon absence. Give orders to my servants, that they take no notice of my absence.

TURN INTO FRENCH.

Let him or her who saw it *say* so. Let him who sat near him *say* what he heard. Let those who have done their exercise *go* and play. Let her or-anybody[1] who is of a different opinion *act* and *do* as he thinks-proper.[2] Let those *go* that choose to go. Let such *come* as choose to come.

Let them *speak* the truth. Let me *tell* you my mind. Come-hither[3] that I *may tell* you something. Draw your plate near that I *may help* you to some soup. Let us pray to God that he *may avert* such a misfortune. Take care that the meat *be*-not-*over-roasted.*[4] Take care lest he *should do* it. Take care that you *come*-to-no-harm-by-it.[5] Take care that the rope *do* not *slip.*[6] Do nothing till you *hear*-from-me.[7] Let me *hear*[8] no more about it.

Let him *come again* when he is sober.[9] Let me *think.*[10]

Let me not *be disturbed*. Don't let me *disturb* you. Let not one *say* that virtue is despised. Let one *be forewarned*[11] against every event. Let me *die* if it is not true. When the signal is given to-engage,[12] let every man *do* his duty.

Let the means *correspond*[13] with the end. Let religion *enjoin*-the-countenance[14] of the law. Let her *do* as she thinks proper. Let him *say* what he will. *Out*-with-him.[15] Let them *slacken*[16] their steps. Let him *come down* as soon as he has his boots on. Let him *come in*. We only want one dish, but let it *be* good.

Let me *sink-down*-into-my[17] grave unmentioned.[18] Let all things *be* ready against-we-come-back.[19]

Let him *stay* or *go*, it is alike[20] indifferent to me. Let him *avail-himself*-of[21] his right. Let me *hear* no more of this. Let the boundary of thy heritage *be* to-thee-the-boundary[22] of the world.

Let me *hear-again*[23] a complaint, a murmur, and I shall speak to you. Let him *prescribe* what is to be done. Let him *give* in a-statement[24] of his disbursements. Let her *be doing* no-matter-what,[25] she must come. Let her *do* as much for-herself[26] as I do for her. Let her *do* it hereafter.[27] Let every-man[28] *know* his own importance. Let him *get* his house painted as soon as he can. Let him *be taken* alive or dead. If any mischief happens to him, let him *blame*[29] himself. Let him *refrain*[30] from swearing.

1. Ou qui que ce soit.—2. Juger convenable.—3. Approcher.—4. Ne rôtir trop.—5. En mésarriver.—6. Lâcher.—7. Avoir de mes nouvelles. —8. Entendre parler de.—9. Dégriser.—10. Réfléchir.—11. Prémunir. —12. Pour en venir aux mains.—13. Etre en rapport.—14. Prescrire le respect.—15. Mettre à la porte.—16. Ralentir.—17. Descendre dans la.—18. Inconnu.—19. à notre retour.—20. Parfaitement.—21. Faire valoir son droit.—22. Pour toi celles.—23. Revenir.—24. Le mémoire. —25. N'importe quoi.—26. Pour soi.—27. à l'avenir.—28. Chacun. 29. S'en prendre à.—30. S'abstenir.

ON THE SUBJUNCTIVE CONSTRUCTION.

APPLICATION OF THE TENSES OF THE SUBJUNCTIVE.*

CXXVI.—RULE 1ST. When the first Verb is in the Present or in the Future of the Indicative, the second Verb is in the Present of the Subjunctive, if the second Verb denotes a Present or a Future action.

La sagesse exige que nous soyons sur nos gardes. It is wisdom to keep ourselves on our guard.

J'ai bien affaire qu'il me vienne rompre la tête de ses folies. What business have I to have my head stunned with his nonsense?

TURN INTO FRENCH.

I ardently long[1] that a bond[2] of friendship *might unite* us. He may or may not *come.* I may *go* this afternoon. I wish that you *would fulfil* your duties. I wish you *would make* him your friend.

You will have[3] *to come.* I shall not believe it until I *see* it. I will-have[4] him *do* it. I have no hope that she *will come.* Is-it-your-pleasure[5] that we *should go* and fetch it? We apprehend[6] it *is* not to-the-purpose.[7] You will not like[8] to *hear*[9] the truth.

That is strange that you never *trust*[10] your friends. How-lucky-it-is-for-him[11] that I *am* such a coward! If you think I *am* pleased, you are mistaken. If I go and *should* you not *be* there? I must *start* in a week. I will not allow you *to go* and lodge at a hotel.

* For all cases connected with, or relating to the Subjunctive, see Festu's Treatise on the French Subjunctive and its Negatives.

Suppose the-case-*were*-yours.[12] Suppose he *should surprise* me. At what o'clock do you desire us *to start?* Do you allow us *to go out* this afternoon? It is disagreeable that we[13] *should-be-kept*-waiting[14] so long.

It is better that he *should make* them come. Whatever[15] he *may do*, he will not succeed. He will not suffer his compassion[16] *to be abused.* Do you suppose one *ought*-to-believe[17] all she says? Do not expect me *to side*[18] with you. Do you think he *will come* after such singular usage? The thing must *be done* whether *he will* or not.

I shall take care[19] that he *know* his lesson. See that[20] it *be done* directly. Take care that no one *come* and interrupt us. See that nothing *be overlooked.* See that the children *make* no noise.

1. Brûler.—2. Nœud.—3. Falloir.—4. Vouloir.—5. Plaire.—6. Ne pas croire.—7. à propos.—8. Etre bien aise.—9. Dire.—10. Croire.—11. Qu'il est heureux.—12. S'agir de vous.—13. On.—14. Faire attendre.—15. Quoi qu'il.—16. Pitié.—17. Falloir croire.—18. Prendre parti.—19. Avoir soin.—20. Voir à ce que.

CXXVII.—Rule 2nd. When the first Verb is in the Present, or in the Future of the Indicative, the second Verb must be in the Past of the Subjunctive, if this second Verb indicate a mere Indefinite Past Time.

Croyez-vous que les hommes soient nés pour les rois, comme les animaux pour les hommes? Do you think that men are born for kings, as beasts for men?

C'est le meilleur homme qui ait jamais vécu. He is the best man that ever lived.

Il faudra que vous ayez fini, quand je reviendrai. You must have done when I come back.

TURN INTO FRENCH.

I doubt whether he *has* ever *known* it. For-anything[1] that *has* yet *happened*, it will be impossible for you *to have* any hold upon him. I am surprised that you *had* so much patience. I am very glad that you *warned* me. Is it true that you *made*-a-mistake?[2]

I doubt whether you *were able* to do it. He-must-have[3] *asked* for it. You are the first to whom we *said* it. I do-not-know[4] that he *is arrived.* He denies that he *has taken* it. He will not come till[5] you *send* for him. Wait till the rain *is over.*

I regret you *did* not *hear* that sermon. I cannot believe that you *deceived* him. I-am-anxious[6] you *should be satisfied.* I am astonished he *should have said* nothing about it. I am astonished you *should* not *have foreseen* such-an[7] accident. You-will-hardly-conceive[8] him *to have been* so stupid. You-are-found-fault-with[9] for *having* done so.

This is the best information[10] I *can have.* I wonder you *had* not so much courage as to tell him you would never consent to it. I am afraid it will rain before the day *is over.*

1. Quelque chose.—2. Se tromper.—3. Il aura fallu.—4. Ignorer.—5. Que.—6. Tenir à ce que.—7. Cet.—8. Avoir de la peine à croire.—9. On trouve à redire que.—10. Avis.

CXXVIII.—RULE 3RD. When the first Verb is in the Present, or in the Future of the Indicative, the second Verb is put in the Imperfect of the Subjunctive in two cases:

1st. When the second Verb expresses a Present or a Future Time, with a condition expressed or implied.

Je doute que vous pussiez le faire, si l'on vous en priait. I doubt whether you could do it, if you were asked or requested.

Je ne croirai jamais que vous pussiez le faire, si l'on vous en priait. I shall never believe that you could do it if you were requested.

2nd. When the second Verb, though expressive of a

past event, carries the mind back to the very time at which it occurred.

Penses-tu qu'Alexandre en terre ait eu cette mine et qu'il sentît aussi mauvais? Dost thou think that Alexander looked in this fashion in the earth and smelt so?

Je n'assurerai pas que ce prince vécût à l'époque que vous citez. I shall not affirm that this prince lived at the time you mention.

TURN INTO FRENCH.

If you were requested to do it, I shall never deny that you *were thinking* of doing it. If we were requested to do it, are you afraid that we *would consent* to it?

I do not doubt but-he[1] *would come,* if he were asked. I doubt whether he *would come,* if he knew that. I question whether you *would study,* if you were not compelled. I do not think you *would do* it, if you were not compelled.

I doubt whether I *would stay,* if you were going away. Do you think I *could see* her, if I went now? I do not think she *would play,* if you were present. Where will you find a man who *would not commit* the same mistake, if he were exposed to the same temptation?

I question whether this gentleman *would succeed* without your assistance. I shall never believe he *would succeed* without them. I shall not say that you *were* in the wrong at-that-time.[2] I do not say that you *had* then bad intentions, but I do not think that at that time you *were* right on this point.

1. Qu'il ne.—2. Alors.

CXXIX.—Rule 4th. When the first Verb is in the Present or in the Future of the Indicative, the second is in the Pluperfect of the Subjunctive, if it refers to a Past Action, with a condition expressed or implied.

Je doute que vous eussiez pu le faire, si l'on vous en avait prié. I doubt whether you could have done it, had you been asked.

Je ne croirai jamais que vous eussiez pu le faire, si l'on ne vous avait pas aidé. I shall never believe you could have done it, had you not been helped.

TURN INTO FRENCH.

Had she been asked, I cannot think she *could have consented.* I question whether she *would have written,* had she known that. I doubt whether your brother *would have set off* without you. I do not think you *would have done* it, had you not been compelled.

I do not know whether this affair *would have succeeded* without her. I doubt whether I *would have said* it, had he not forced me to it. I doubt whether we *would have lent* the money, had you not asked us to do it. Do you think your sisters *would have come,* had it been fine weather? I do not think they *would have come,* if I had not gone for them.

It is probable you *could-have-got*[1] the situation, had you applied-for[2] it. Do you think your brothers *would have learned* French, had they been taught properly?[3]

1. Obtenir.—2. Demander.—3. Bien.

CXXX.—Rule 5th. The Imperfect, the Past Tenses, and the Conditionals require the Imperfect and the Pluperfect of the Subjunctive.

The Imperfect, to indicate a Present or a Future Time.

J'ignorais qu'il fût encore en vie. I was not aware that he was still alive.

Il ne se doutait pas que vous demeurassiez ici. He had no idea that you were living here.

Je serais charmé que vous voulussiez m'accompagner dans mon voyage. I should be happy to have the pleasure of your company on my journey.

The Pluperfect, if the event it expresses was Prior to that expressed by the first Verb.

Nous ignorions qu'il eût été blessé. We did not know he had been wounded.

On n'avait pas cru que nous eussions si complètement réussi. At first they did not believe that we had so completely succeeded.

TURN INTO FRENCH.

I was not certain you *would come.* I did not think you *would be back* so soon. It was proper he *should be* there himself. I was surprised at *his arriving* so soon. I would have-her-*make-haste.*[1] She seemed interested that[2] I *should* not *lose* myself. He consented that his son *should return.* I desired[3] the note *to be sent* early. I never should have supposed your sisters *were* English.

Did you think I *should-have-gone?*[4] I was not sure you *would have come.* I did not know that you *had studied* French. I went before he *had arrived.* I did not know that *had cost* so much money. Would you have thought he *would have bought* the horse? I did not know he *had lost* his lawsuit. I *would-have-been-obliged*[5] to write.

I wish you *had mentioned* it to me long ago, all would be right[6] now. It were to be wished that you *would apply* yourself more seriously to your studies. Oh, that my friend *were come!* He was not convinced of the fact, nor was it likely he *should.* I wish you *could* lend me ten pounds.

I wish you *would* never *have troubled-yourself*[7] with my son. He did not think I *had anticipated*[8] him. I wish he *would settle* in this country. I would they *were-out*-of[9] the room.

That child ought[10] *to be whipped,* to teach-him-better-manners.[11] I did not suppose he *was* impudent enough to answer so. It is getting-late.[12] I did not think it *was* so late.

1. Se dépêcher.—2. à ce que.—3. Donner l'ordre qu'on.—4. Devoir y aller.—5. Falloir.—6. En règle.—7. S'occuper.—8. Prévenir.—9. N'être plus dans.—10. Mériterait qu'on.—11. Lui apprendre à vivre.—12. Commencer à se faire tard.

CXXXI.—Rule 6th. With the Past Indefinite, or the Conditionals, we use the Present of the Subjunctive, to denote Present Actuality, or Something which can be done at all times; but, the second Verb should be in the Imperfect, if the state or action is over at the time of speaking.

Je n'ai pas pu aller au spectacle, quelque envie que j'en aie. I was not able to go to the theatre, though I am ever so fain.

Je n'ai pas pu aller au spectacle, quelque envie que j'en eusse. I was not able to go to the theatre, though I was ever so fain.

Il m'aurait trompé quoiqu'il dise que je sois son meilleur ami. He would have deceived me, though he says I am his best friend.

Je ne saurais croire qu'il veuille vous tromper ni qu'il le puisse. I cannot believe that he was willing or able to deceive you.

TURN INTO FRENCH.

God has given us eyes that we *may* see. God has created us that we *may* love, revere, and serve him. He gave us reason that we *may* discern good from evil. He refused me this favour, although he *is* my friend. I wrote him *to be* here at four o'clock.

Although he *is recovering*[1] from illness, and (*is*) still very weak, he would-set-out.[2] I have used no expression that *is* not the truth. It-has-been-God's-will-that[3] we *should be* poor and needy. Who could[4] doubt his *being* an honest man, unless-perchance[5] his creditors? I-cannot-think[6] it *is* as they relate it.

She did me too many services for me *to-doubt*[7] her friendship. He has neglected us too long for us *to-expect*-anything[8] from him. I cannot help his *doing* such things.

1. Relever.—2. Se mettre en route.—3. Dieu a voulu que.—4. Pourrait.—5. Si ce n'est peut-être.—6. Je ne saurais m'imaginer.—7. Pouvoir douter.—8. Pouvoir rien espérer.

ON OPTATIVE PROPOSITIONS.

CXXXII.—In Optative Propositions, in Adjurations, in Imprecations, a sentence will often commence with a Subjunctive Clause, the Verb of the leading Proposition being left out, with the Conjunction *Que* sometimes expressed and very often omitted.

Plût à Dieu que mon indignation fût pesée et qu'on mît ensemble dans une balance ma calamité! Oh, that my grief were thoroughly weighed, and my calamity laid in the balance together.

Puisse cet océan où vous l'exposez ne jamais vous la rendre! Puissent ses flots vous rapporter mon corps, et, le roulant avec le sien parmi les cailloux de ces rivages, vous donner, par la perte de vos deux enfants, un sujet éternel de douleur! May the ocean, to which you trust her, restore her to you no more! May the waves, rolling back our corpses amidst the stones of the beach, give you, in the loss of your two children, an eternal subject of remorse!

TURN INTO FRENCH.

God *bless* her! *May* I see her happy! *May* the Gods destroy[1] me, rather than suffer me to be enslaved by effeminacy![1] Success-*attend*[2] you! *May* you live happily! *May* he live these fifty years! *Heaven-grant*[4] that he may repent in time! *May* God reward[5] you!

Would-to[6] heaven it had been otherwise! *Would* to God you had taken[7] my advice! God-*forbid*[8] he should die! Heaven *grant* that this do not happen! *May* I see[9] them in good health! *Please* God that you may return!

Accursed be the day on-which[10] I was born! *Cursed* be the man before the Lord that raiseth up and buildeth this city of Jericho! Far-*be*-it-from-me[11] to leave her! Much-good[12] *may* it do you!

May-it-please[13] your Excellency. *May* they come back safe![14] *Mayest* thou ever be what now thou art! If ever I dreamt-of-such-a-thing,[15] *may* I ——!

God *grant* it-may-not-be-too-late![16] *May* the gods make them feel the joy of living under so good a father! God *grant* we may never have need of you! God-*preserve*[17] me from having any such thought! Heaven *preserve* me from it!

Would to God you were married! I *wish* to God I had done it! *May* I die if I know it! *May* the monster who committed so horrible an action perish! *May* God punish me if I deceive you!

1. Faire périr.—2. La mollesse.—3. Pouvoir réussir.—4. Fasse le ciel.—5. Le rendre.—6. Plût au.—7. Suivre.—8. à Dieu ne plaise que.—9. Revoir.—10. Où.—11. à Dieu ne plaise que.—12. Grand bien.—13. Vouloir bien.—14. Sains et saufs.—15. Songer à cela.—16. En être encore temps.—17. Plaise au ciel.

ON NEGATIVE PROPOSITIONS.

CXXXIII.—After Negative Propositions, if what is stated in the subordinate clause is asserted as being positive and true, the Indicative is used.

Il ne s'apercevait pas qu'on le persiflait. He did not perceive that he was sneered at.

But the Subjunctive must be used in the subordinate clause, whenever doubt or ignorance arises in the speaker's mind as to the existence of a thing, the actuality of a fact or of an occurrence.

J'ignorais où pouvait être cette prétendue bibliothèque, je ne m'étais point aperçu qu'il y en eût dans la maison. I could not conceive where this pretended library could be, having never perceived any such thing in the house.

Il n'y a guère lieu de douter qu'il vous eût secondé. It is scarcely to be doubted but he would have seconded you.

Je ne conçois pas qu'il puisse s'oublier jusqu'à vous manquer de respect. I cannot conceive he should so far forget himself as to be disrespectful to you.

TURN INTO FRENCH.

Darius did not think he *would be conquered* by Alexander. The good citizens did not believe that Socrates *would be condemned* by the judges. He does not know that the king *passed* through this town. I did not believe that the affair *would be* so soon *over*.

I am-by-no-means-certain[1] that she *will-take*[2] him. I am not astonished at *his knowing* it. I do not think he *is* here. There was no likelihood[3] of *his-losing*-his-way.[4] There was no necessity[5] for *his measuring* the cloth after you.

My father would not consent to *his-devoting*-himself[6] to this profession. It is not comforting[7] that your business *should take* such-an-ill[8] turn. It is not proper that children *should-have*-their-own-way.[9] It was not possible for you *to arrive* in two days. It was not time for us *to begin*. It is not proper[10] for you *to offend* any-one.[11]

It was not sufficient that you *should know* the essential of the matter,[12] it was still necessary that I *should-inform*[13] you of the details. I do not think it *will rain*. I did not think it *would rain*.

The king does not mean[14] that his subjects *should be oppressed* upon-any-account-whatever.[15] I could never get[16] him *to do* it. You would not like *to-be-caught*[17] playing. The disease is dangerous, but I do not think he *will die of* it.

1. N'être pas sûr.—2. Accepter.—3. Probable.—4. S'égarer.—5. Nécessaire.—6. Se vouer.—7. Consolant.—8. Un si mauvais.—9. Etre abandonné à leur volonté.—10. Convenir.—11. Qui que ce soit.—12. Affaire.—13. Instruire.—14. Entendre.—15. Sous quelque pretexte que ce soit.—16. Obtenir.—17. Surprendre.

ON INTERROGATIVE PROPOSITIONS.

CXXXIV.—In Interrogations, the speaker either wants to communicate or impart his own impressions, or asks the sentiment of another.

Direz-vous après cela que je ne suis pas de vos amis? Will you say after that that I am no friend of yours?

The speaker here means to convey that he is a friend of yours, and challenges you to refute his assertion.

Quoi! vous croyez bonnement qu'il vous paiera? What! are you simple enough to believe that he will pay you?

Here we must use the Indicative, for, in addition to the irony it contains, the Interrogation involves a negation, that you will not be paid; it is tantamount to this: "If you fancy he will pay you, I wish you may get it."

CXXXV.—Should the speaker, for the mere satisfaction of his own mind, ask the person he speaks to whether a thing is possibly so, was actually so, or is likely to be so, the Indicative should be used.

Combien voit-on de parvenus qui sont hautains et insolents? How many haughty and insolent upstarts do we see?

Parlez-moi franchement, pensez-vous que mon ouvrage

ndra quelque succès ? Be plain with me, do you ɛ my work will meet with some success ?

ıt should the same question be asked with an in-ıl feeling of despondency, fear, doubt, or apprehen- in the speaker, the Subjunctive must be used.

ɔmbien voit-on de parvenus qui soient affables et ɘstes ? How many affable and modest upstarts do ee ?

ɑrlez-moi franchement, pensez-vous que mon ouvrage nne quelque succès ?

TURN INTO FRENCH WITH THE INDICATIVE.

› you think I *shall speak* French easily ? Do you think *ll pronounce* it well ? Do you think his protection *is* very ıl to me ? Do you think this *will-keep*[1] till to-morrow ? ou expect the sum *will be paid* ? Do you think it *will* ? Do you think we *shall have* rain ? Have I told you his father *is* dead ? Do you know that I *have bought* a e ?

.d you not perceive they *wanted* to deceive you ? You that your friend will-be-a-gainer-by[2] the bargain, but you yourself shall-be-a-loser-by[4] it ; do you really be- you *shall* (be a loser) ? Do you think this affair *will be* terminated ? Don't you think I am right, that this 's-quite-as-good-as[5] the other ?

› you think he *will come* ? Would you actually think it *was* in the very Bastille that Voltaire wrote[6] the two cantos of his Henriade ? Who would have thought a of his cloth[7] *would commit*[8] such an action ?

ʒe garder.—2. Prétendre.—3. Gagner à.—4. Perdre à.—5. Valoir —6. Composer.—7. Robe.—8. Faire.

TURN INTO FRENCH WITH THE SUBJUNCTIVE.

o you think he *distinguished himself* as much as they say ? 'ou not think[1] that such reflections *are* ill-placed ? Did she think that we *had-a-mind*[2] to wait here till to-morrow? Does he hope that she *is* well-disposed towards[3] him? Do you doubt[4] that he *was* there?

Would you have me *be-out-*of[5] the fashion? Do you think the horse *is* up-to-my-weight?[6] Is it fit[7] for you *to-be-*riding[8] when your poor old father is walking?[9] Would you have me *applaud* what I condemn? Because he is a liar, does-it-follow-that[10] I am one?

Do you think the chops *are* done-enough?[11] Do you suppose such-to-be[12] his genuine sentiments? Would you like the horse *to-be-brought?*[13] In[14] what manner would you have me *behave* to him? Do you think that he *can* stoop[15] to such caprice?

Do you want me *to come* and see you? I do. Do you fear it *will rain?* I do. Do you think this book *is well written?* I do not. Do you think you *are right?* I do. Do you think it *belongs* to man to penetrate the future? I do not. Do you think that *will suit* her? Do you think the weather *will clear up* to-day? I do. Do you think the question discussed at the meeting *has been well-put?*[16] I do not.

1. Trouver.—2. Avoir envie.—3. Pour.—4. Soupçonner.—5. N'être pas.—6. De force à supporter mon poids.—7. Convenable.—8. Aller à cheval.—9. Aller à pied.—10. Est-ce à dire que.—11. Suffisamment cuites.—12. Etre là.—13. Amener.—14. De.—15. Se soumettre.—16. Bien posée.

ON THE DOUBLE NEGATIVES.

CXXXVI. — Though bordering on Affirmation, Double Negatives in Subjunctive clauses are not quite affirmative.

Je ne doute pas qu'elle ne soit vertueuse. I do not doubt but she is honest.

The chances, the probabilities are in her favour; yet there is no saying, there is no assertion of her being so; she may or she may not. Lingering doubt still awakens suspicion.

It is no such assertion as: *Je crois qu'elle est vertueuse*, which implies no surmising, no after-thought, no misgiving whatever in the mind.

In any other Mood, Double Negatives are affirmative.

Je ne dis pas que je ne vous paierai pas, mais donnez-moi du temps. I do not say I shall not pay you, but give me time.

Je n'ai pas pu ne pas me réjouir au fond de mon cœur. I could not help rejoicing in the depth of my heart.

Je ne puis pas ne point citer ici le jugement singulier que le Prince de Conti fait de Cinna. I cannot help quoting here the singular judgment which the Prince of Conti passed on Cinna.

CXXXVII.—When the first of two Propositions, connected by *Que*, or a Relative Clause, contains a Negative idea, and the second a Positive idea, *Ne* is used before each Verb, excluding *Pas, point, rien, personne*, &c., in the Subjunctive Clause.

Il n'est rien que je ne fasse pour vous obliger. There is nothing I would not do to oblige you. I would do anything, *i.e.*, if it is possible, if I see my way to it, if it will not compromise me, if I can consistently do it, &c., &c.

Though seemingly affirmative, yet there is always in these Propositions a mental reservation for all that.

But should the Subjunctive Clause involve a negation, *Ne* is omitted before the Subjunctive Verb.

Allez-vous-en, il n'est rien que je fasse pour vous

obliger. Be off, there is nothing that I would do to oblige you.

TURN INTO FRENCH.

There is nobody who *does not pity* me. There is nobody who *pities* me. There is not-a-man[1] but *knows* it. There is no man who *knows* it. There is no one but *wishes*-her-well.[2] There is no one *wishes* him well. There was nobody at the ball whom I *did not know*. There was nobody whom she *knew*.

There is not one who *is not willing* to answer for[3] him. There is not one *willing* to answer for him. I do not know anybody who *does not like* him. Out-of[4] all his friends, I do not know any one *willing* to-serve[5] him.

I saw nobody who *praised* you. I saw nobody but *praised* you. I assert[6] nothing for-which[7] I *have not* good proof (*pl.*). There is nothing about which I *am* less *informed*. I have-said-nothing-but[8] what *is approved of* by experience. I shall not make any objection to you but what *shall be grounded*[9] on good proof (*pl.*). Not a housemaid but *has* a husband running-in-her-head.[10] There is no one but *knows* it.

There is nothing of which my son *would not be capable*, if he were not idle. There is nothing that I *would not do* for him, if he would work. There is nobody to whom he *is* not a-burden.[11] He cannot be employed in[12] anything but he *commits*-stupid-blunders.[13] There are few animals that-*have*-a-more-sure-foot[14] than goats and mules. There are few animals but *can be tamed*.[15]

I will not give you any book to read which *is not* fit[16] for a young person. There are no books in my library but I *have read*.

There is no one but what *has* his good points.[17] There is no rule so general but *has* its exceptions. There is no one who *would not prefer* to die, rather than drag-out[18] such a miserable existence. There is no man so stupid as-not[19] *to acknowledge* a Divinity.

Not-a-day-passes[20] but the family *meet*. Not a day passes but she *comes* to my house. He is not so poor as *not to-be-able-to-give-alms*.[21] There-is-not[22] any Spaniard but *has* some claims[23] to a high-pedigree.[24] There is nothing which a good-man[25] *hates* more than flattery.

There is nothing on earth which man *has not appropriated.*[26] Do nothing in secret which you *cannot* acknowledge-before[27] everybody. There was no nation which Alexander *did not wish* to-conquer.[28] There is nothing that-he-*would-not*[29] *do* for her. He is not so foolish[30] but he *knows* well what he does. There is no man alive who *will* undertake it. There is no man but *will* undertake it. There-is-scarcely-a-day[31] but he *comes* to my house.

1. Personne.—2. Lui vouloir du bien.—3. De.—4. De.—5. Rendre service à.—6. Avancer.—7. Dont.—8. Avancer qui ne.—9. Confirmer.—10. Trotter dans l'esprit.—11. à charge.—12. à.—13. Faire des balourdises.—14. Dont le pied ait plus de sûreté.—15. Apprivoiser.—16. Convenables.—17. Qualités.—18. Mener.—19. Qui ne.—20. Il n'est pas de jour.—21. Pouvoir faire l'aumône.—22. Il n'est pas.—23. Prétentions.—24. Illustre généalogie.—25. Homme de bien.—26. S'approprier.—27. Avouer à.—28. Soumettre.—29. Qu'il ne soit prêt à.—30. Fou.—31. Il n'y a presque pas de jour.

CXXXVIII.—In Interrogative Propositions, however, *Ne* alone is used in the Subjunctive Clause to express a positive idea, and omitted to convey a negative idea.

Avez-vous un ami qui ne soit des miens? Have you a friend who is not likewise mine? *i.e.*, You have not a friend but he is mine also.

Avez-vous un ami qui soit des miens? Have you a single friend who is mine? *i.e.*, You have not one. They may possibly be yours, but I repudiate them.

The above interrogations are called questions of Appeal. A question is said to be of appeal whenever the speaker challenges the person spoken to, to refute what is stated. In instances of this kind, the tone and accentuation of the voice should always convey a something of the feelings pervading the speaker's mind, or else this Interrogation might be mistaken for Questions of uncertainty, doubt, or ignorance, as,

Avez-vous un ami qui soit des miens? Have you a friend, any friend who is likewise mine? who is our mutual friend?

CXXXIX.—The Interrogation, moreover, as a Question of appeal, offers this peculiarity, that when it is without a Negative in the Indicative Mood, it conveys a negative meaning; and when used with *Ne pas, Ne point,* it implies an affirmative sense.

De tous ceux qui se disaient mes amis, aucun m'a-t-il secouru? Did any of all those who called themselves my friends assist me? *i.e.,* Nobody did.

Le Seigneur ne tient-il pas entre ses mains les cœurs de tous les hommes? Does not the Lord hold in his hands the hearts of all men? *i.e.,* He does hold them.

TURN INTO FRENCH.

Is there any one she *does not slander?* Is there any one she *speaks-ill-of?*[1] Is there a man whom he *does not despise?* Is there a man whom he *despises?* Is there any one she *does-not-speak*-well-of?[2] Is there any one she *speaks*-favourably-of? What knowest thou that we *know not?* What understandest thou which we *do not?* Is there a man who *is pleased* with his lot?

Is there anything you *recollect*-of[3] in that work? Have I a friend who *is not* also his?[4] Is there any hope that he *will submit?* Is there any[5] injustice which he *does not commit?*

Is there any hope that she *can succeed?* Was there a sedition of which he *was not* the ringleader? Is there a town in the kingdom which *is* more submissive?

I am a Jew: *hath*-not-a-Jew-eyes?[6] *hath* not a Jew

hands, organs, senses, affections, passions? *Is* he *not fed* with-the[7] same-food,[8] *hurt* with the same weapons, subject to the same diseases as-a-Christian-is?[9] If you prick us, *do* we *not bleed?* If you tickle us, *do* we *not laugh?* If you poison us, *do* we *not die?*

Can you add[10] to the glory of Jesus Christ by the pleasures of the theatre? *Can* Jesus Christ be-a-participator[11] in such-kinds-of-pleasures,[12] and, before going to them, *could you* tell him that-your-only-object-in-so-doing-is[13] his glory and the desire to please him?

1. Médire de.—2. Dire du bien de.—3. Se souvenir.—4. Des siens.—5. Aucune.—6. Est-ce qu'un Juif n'a pas des yeux.—7. Des.—8. Aliments.—9. Qu'un Chrétien.—10. Rapporter.—11. Entrer pour quelque chose.—12. Ces sortes de délassements.—13. Que vous ne vous proposez dans cette action que.

CXL.—Sometimes Subjunctive Clauses are to be found without any Negation expressed, but then the negation is tacit in the mind or involved in the context of the passage.

Charité, humilité, vertus si belles! êtes-vous donc trop pures pour la terre? êtes-vous donc remontées avec mon Sauveur au céleste séjour? Autrefois, j'ai vu, parmi la foule des cités, quelques hommes vous vouer un culte sublime. Néanmoins, à de si rares exemples, mes yeux attristés se portaient avec espoir vers les campagnes et je croyais que ces paisibles champs dussent être votre asile! Charity, humility, virtues so lovely! are you too pure for this earth? Did you reascend with my Saviour into celestial bliss? Formerly, among the throng of cities, I saw but few men paying you a sublime worship. Nevertheless, from such rare instances, my saddened eyes turned with hope towards the country, and I thought that these peaceful fields should have been your abode!

And in this example, the context clearly involves that after all these peaceful fields were not the abode of charity, humility, &c., &c.

ON THE CONSTRUCTION OF VERBS OF FEAR.

CXLI.—When, in English, the Verb that comes after *Craindre* is in the same person as *Craindre,* the French use *De* before the Infinitive.

Je crains de laisser échapper l'occasion. I am afraid I shall let the opportunity escape.

TURN INTO FRENCH.

I am afraid *I shall lose* his money. I fear *being discovered.* He is afraid *he shall not* see you. He is afraid *he-shall-be-troublesome*[1] to you. She was afraid *she might be* too-late.[2] She fears to *fall.* We are afraid *we shall lose* his money. We are afraid we *shall get* him summoned.[3] Are you afraid *to get-wet*?[4] Are you afraid *to-catch*-cold?[5]

They became-afraid-that-they[6] *might be put* to death. I fear I *am intruding.*[7]

1. Incommoder.—2. En retard.—3. Avoir à faire assigner.—4. Se mouiller.—5. S'enrhûmer.—6. Ils furent saisis de la crainte de. —7. Importun.

CXLII.—Conjugated affirmatively, interrogatively, or with negation and interrogation united, *Appréhender, Avoir peur, Craindre, Il est dangereux, Trembler, Redouter,* require *Ne* before the Subjunctive, if afraid lest something should occur, or should have occurred, contrary to our desires.

Je crains que mon enfant ne meure. I am afraid my child will die.

Elle est très-emportée, il est à craindre qu'elle ne fasse quelque éclat mal à propos. She is very passionate, it is to be feared she will make some unseasonable disturbance.

Mon frère ne craint-il pas que je n'aie les poumons attaqués ? Is not my brother afraid of my lungs being affected ?

TURN INTO FRENCH.

He is better, but we are afraid the fever *may return.* I am afraid lest the disease *should-prove*-fatal.[1] We are afraid that the merchant at whose house we dined yesterday *will-fail*[2] sooner or later. Whatever[3] we may do, I am afraid he *will* sooner or later *gain*-his-ends.[4] After so violent-a-shock,[5] it is to be feared the wall *will tumble down.*

Do you fear we *shall have* a storm and that the vessel *will be wrecked?* Are you afraid that he *will come* and disturb us? Are you afraid that my friend *will die?* Do you fear that he *will take* your money? Are you afraid that I *will undertake* the business without consulting you?

Are you not afraid that child *will be punished?* Do you not fear that the disease *will be* fatal? Do you not dread[6] her *knowing* it? Do you not tremble lest this *should happen?* Are you not afraid that she *will chide* you?

I was-mortally-afraid[7] lest the road we took *would conduct* us to Mansilla, and that we *should meet with* Rolando and his confederates.[8] I was-afraid[9] they *would search* for me even-in-the-night.[10] I am apprehensive lest he *should arrive* suddenly, and I fear above all lest he *should surprise* us.

Are you not afraid that the sky *will-become*-cloudy?[11] Are you not afraid that the hail *will-injure*[12] your wall-trees?[13] Are you not afraid your tooth *will-decay?*[14] Do you not fear I *shall lose* my lawsuit?

Is it to be feared that it *will rain?* Is it to be feared that it *will be* bad weather? I fear it *is* too true. I doubt[15] there *is* something.

I am afraid they *made* them talk, and *made* them say what they ought not to have said. Are you not afraid your gown *will-lose*-its-colour?[16]

1. Devenir mortelle.—2. Faire faillite.—3. Quelque chose que.—4. Arriver à ses fins.—5. Grand ébranlement.—6. Redouter.—7. Mourir de peur.—8. Camarades.—9. Appréhender.—10. Dès la nuit même.—11. Se couvrir.—12. Endommager.—13. Espaliers.—14. Se carier.—15. Craindre.—16. Se déteindre.

CXLIII.—Should we wish the thing to happen, *Ne pas* or *Ne point* is necessary; and this, whatever be the form of the leading Proposition, Affirmative, Interrogative, or both with Negation and Interrogation.

Je vois que vous prenez sur vous toutes les fatigues, je crains que vous n'y résistiez pas. I see that you take all the fatigue upon yourself, I am afraid you will not stand it.

Craignez-vous que ce fripon ne soit pas puni? Are you afraid that this knave will not be punished?

Ne craignez-vous pas qu'il ne perde pas son procès? Are you not afraid that he will not lose his lawsuit?

TURN INTO FRENCH.

I am afraid this boy *will not be punished.* Do you not also fear he *will not be punished*? It is feared that this man *will not end* well. I fear my brother *will not come* to-night. Does she fear I *shall not come*? She fears your not *doing* it. Are you not afraid that they[1] *will-not-set*[2] his leg well? I am apprehensive that they *will not do* it well.

The ministers do their utmost[3] to lay-the-storm,[4] but I am afraid they *will* not *succeed.* You are afraid lest this should happen, and I[5] am afraid lest it *should not.* You-look-as-if-you-were-afraid[6] lest I *should not have received* your letter.

I am not afraid that my letter *will not be delivered*[7] to her, but I am afraid it *will be delivered* too late. I am apprehensive of her not *knowing* it in time. I am afraid that he *will not come* in time, but I am not afraid that he *will not come* at all.

I am afraid it *will not rain*. I am afraid that you *will not be able* to carry them over.[8] He was-much-afraid[9] the sum *would* not *be allowed* him. I was beginning to fear that you *would* not *come*.

You are greatly-behind-hand,[10] and I am afraid your task *will* not *be done*-in[11] time. I am afraid that a man of my age *will* not *be* after[12] her taste. Are you afraid it-*will-hurt*-her-feelings?[13] I am greatly afraid it *will*, and that she *will* not *come*.

1. On.—2. Remettre.—3. Possible.—4. Conjurer la tempête.—5. Et moi, je.—6. Il semble que vous ayez peur.—7. Remettre.—8. De l'autre côté.—9. Avoir bien peur qu'on.—10. Bien en arrière.—11. Achevée à.—12. De.—13. Lui faire de la peine.

CXLIV.—The conjunctive expressions, *De crainte que, De peur que*, follow the same Syntax, *i.e.*, they require *Ne*, in the Subjunctive clause, when expressing something contrary to our desire, and *Ne pas* when agreeable to it.

Coupez les aîles à cet oiseau de peur qu'il ne s'envole.
Cut the wings of this bird lest it should fly away.

Passez chez elle de crainte qu'elle ne vienne pas.
Call on her lest she should not come.

TURN INTO FRENCH.

Speak mildly to him lest he *should-become-exasperated*[1] and *repulse*[2] you. Shun drunkenness, lest good men *should shun* you. They never allow[3] their king to build any fortresses, for fear he *should-use*-them[4] less to defend than to oppress them.

1. S'aigrir.—2. Rebuter.—3. Souffrir.—4. S'en servir.

CXLV.—Conjugated Negatively in the first Clause, *Ne* is omitted before the Subjunctive.

Je n'appréhende pas que ce ressort rompe à la détente. I am not afraid of the spring breaking when on the strain.

CXLVI.—When *Si*, *Peu*, *Guère*, *Sans*, &c., involve a negation, *Ne* is omitted in the Subjunctive Clause.

Si je craignais qu'ils fussent partis, je ne sortirais pas. If I were afraid they were gone, I would not go out.

On appréhende peu, on appréhende guère qu'il vienne. They little, they but little dread his coming.

Je puis vous assûrer que nous partirons, Ambroise et moi, sans appréhender que vous nous souffliez ce précieux nantissement. I can assure you that Ambrose and I will set out, without the least apprehension of your giving us the slip.

CXLVII.—But should *Si* and *Ne* be used in the same clause, *Ne* is required before the Subjunctive.

Je le ferais, si je ne craignais que vous ne vous fâchiez ou *que vous ne vous fâchassiez.* I would do it, if I were not afraid to make you angry.

CXLVIII.—When the Interrogation, though affirmative in form, involves a Negation, *Ne* is not used in the Subjunctive Clause.

Peut-on craindre que la terre manque aux hommes? What need we fear that this earth will fail men? *i.e.*, we need not fear.

Craignez-vous que mes yeux versent trop peu de larmes? Are you afraid that my eyes will not shed tears enough?

TURN INTO FRENCH.

Do not fear that *I shall come* after the last reception you gave[1] me. I am not afraid that you *will commit* any act of weakness. I do not fear that he *will dare* to do it. With-the-help-of[2] printing, it is no longer to be feared that sciences *will* ever *be lost*. I do not fear that the moderation of my life *will-be*-of-no-small-avail[3] against calumnies.

I had no apprehension of my friend's *hurting* himself. I had no apprehension of their *imitating* our design. I had no apprehension of the minister's *impeaching*[4] my conduct. She had-no-apprehension[5] of his ever *injuring* her interest. There is no fear of his *invading* our country. I had no apprehension of my servant's *letting* them in. There is no fear of his *opposing* your will.

If I were afraid or dreading his *coming*, I would have taken measures. I would forbid that, if I feared you *would do* it. I would have posted soldiers on yon hill, had I feared the enemy *would occupy* it. If I feared her *coming*, I would not have sent for you.

I would speak to him about it, were I not afraid of his *having changed* his-mind.[6]

I am not afraid of his *coming*, nor am I afraid of his *surprising* us. She is not afraid that this stuff *will shrink* when washing. Do not be afraid that abundance of water *will weaken* or-*relax*[7] your stomach. Do not be afraid of my *exposing*[8] you, but explain yourself freely.[9]

What-need-we-be-apprehensive[10] of his *coming?* When one is in good health, what need we fear, can one fear, is it to be feared that an excess *should-upset*-one's-health[11] or *make* one unwell? We little dread his *coming*.

I am not afraid of people's *descanting*[12] on my actions.

1. Faire.—2. Au moyen de.—3. Avoir peu de force.—4. Attaquer.—5. N'avoir aucune crainte.—6. D'avis.—7. Et refroidir.—8. Commettre.—9. Hardiment.—10. Que peut-on craindre.—11. Incommoder.—12. Commenter.

CXLIX.—*Douter*, followed by *Que*, requires the Subjunctive.

Je doute que le moment soit opportun. I doubt the fitness of the time.

On doutait fort qu'il pût payer. His power to pay was much questioned.

CL.—When *Douter* is negative or interrogative, *Ne* is used in the Subordinate Clause.

On ne doit pas douter qu'il n'y ait eu des poètes avant Homère. It is not to be doubted but there were poets before Homer.

Qui doute que la vertu ne soit aimable? Who doubts but virtue is lovely?

CLI.—However, *Ne* should be omitted, when we want to convey something positive, manifest, or incontestable.

Je n'ai jamais douté que vous pussiez le faire, quoique je doutasse fort que vous le voulussiez. I never questioned your being able, though I very much doubted your being willing to do it.

Doutez-vous que je sois malade? Do you doubt my being unwell?

TURN INTO FRENCH.

It-is-questionable[1] whether the moon *has* an atmosphere. I doubt whether it[2] be so. I doubt whether he *has ever known* it. They doubt your *ability*-to-execute[3] that office. She doubts his *returning*. I doubt whether any of them *will do* it.

I do not doubt that you *are* very clever, though you look[4] very young. I-had-no-doubt-*of*[5] *finding* some good place.

I do not doubt but he *will-be-asked.*[6] I do not doubt but they *are*-extremely-impatient-to-hear-from-me.[7] I do not doubt but I *may* avoid him. I did not doubt but she *would come.*

Who can doubt but the Romans *were*[8] very cruel? Who can doubt but life *is* a present from God? Do you doubt that he *will obey?* When we see him behaving so,[9] can we not question his *being* happy? No[10] doubt but it *is* so. Do you doubt that the second edition of this book *has just been* published? Do you doubt that this merchant *has just* dismissed[11] his clerk?

I-am-afraid[12] his eye, his leg, or limb *will* never *heal.*[13] We did not doubt that they *would die.* I doubt whether he will *answer* your expectation. I do not doubt but she *will know* it.

1. On doute.—2. Cela.—3. Etre capable de remplir.—4. Paraître.—5. Je ne doutais point que.—6. Inviter.—7. Avoir extrême impatience d'apprendre de mes nouvelles.—8. Avoir été.—9. Ainsi.—10. Nul.—11. Remercier.—12. Douter.—13. Se guérir.

CLII.—*Nier* governs the Subjunctive without *Ne,* when the sense is positive.

Je nie que cela soit. I deny that it is so.

CLIII.—Negatively, according to the Académie, we might indifferently say: *Je ne nie pas, Je ne disconviens pas, Je ne conteste pas qu'il ait fait,* ou *qu'il n'ait fait cela.* I do not deny, I allow, I do not dispute that he did that.

Yet, generally, the Subordinate Verb takes *Ne,* if the Principal Verb does.

CLIV.—Should the Subordinate come first, *Ne* is not used before it: *Que Toussaint ait été cruel, hypocrite et traitre, je ne prétends pas le nier.* That Toussaint was cruel, hypocritical, and a traitor, I do not intend to deny.

CLV.—Interrogatively, *Ne* is generally expressed: *Peut-on nier qu'il n'ait avancé cette proposition?* Can any one deny but he laid down the proposition?

Yet, we could say: *Qui est-ce qui nie que les savants sachent mille choses vraies que les ignorants ne sauront jamais?* Who denies but that learned men know a thousand things which the ignorant will never know?

CLVI.—Should *Nier* be both interrogative and negative, *Ne* is left out in the Subjunctive Clause: *Puisque personne ne vous accusait, ne pouviez-vous pas nier que vous l'eussiez fait?* Since nobody did accuse you, could you not have denied your having done it?

CLVII.—After *Contester, Disputer, Disconvenir, Désespérer,* the subordinate takes *Ne,* if the principal is Negative or Interrogative.

On ne désespérait pas que vous ne devinssiez riche. We had no fear but you would become rich.

Vous ne sauriez disconvenir qu'il ne vous ait parlé. You cannot deny that he did speak to you.

And with the Indicative, but without negation, in the subordinate: *Vous ne sauriez disconvenir qu'il vous a parlé.*

TURN INTO FRENCH.

He does not deny[1] that I *said* so to him. I question, nay,[2] I deny, that he *is* happy. I do not question, I do not deny that he *is* happy. I do not despair of her *recovering.*[3]

He denied flat[4] his *having* said anything about it. I do not dispute[5] but you *may* find better examples. I do not deny but that *may be* so.

I do not dispute[6] your *being learned;* but be modest. He does-not-deny[7] that she *behaved* very badly to him. It must be allowed that he *is* brave. I *allow* that he *is* a better swordsman than I am, but he is too-much-of-a-boaster.[8] Do you deny that he *said* that? Can he deny that he *did* it?

I do not despair *of-fine-weather.*[9] We must not despair that the truth *will appear* in time. Why will you not allow that this remedy *is* better than the other? You cannot deny that this remedy *is* better than the other. Can any one deny that he *committed* the blunder?

1. Disconvenir.—2. Même.—3. Se rétablir.—4. Tout plat.—5. Contester.—6. Disconvenir.—7. Ne pas disconvenir.—8. Un peu fanfaron. —9. Avoir du beau temps.

CLVIII.—After *Empêcher, Éviter, Prendre garde, Garder,* in the sense of taking care that something do not happen, the Subordinate Verb *generally* takes *Ne,* whether the Principal Verb be negative, affirmative, or interrogative.

J'ai eu toutes les peines imaginables pour empêcher qu'on ne le battît. It was as much as I could do to keep him from a beating.

Cela n'empêcha pas qu'il ne le fît. He did it nevertheless; notwithstanding that, he did it.

Prenez garde que cette plaisanterie ne devienne sérieuse. Take heed this jest do not become serious.

Ne, with *empêcher,* is omitted when we neither prohibit, prevent, or oppose a thing.

Si l'on ne veut pas faire le bien, il ne faut pas empêcher que les autres le fassent. If we do not want to do good, we should not prevent others from doing so.

Je n'empêche pas qu'il sorte. I do not oppose his going out, I do not object to his going out.

Whereas *Je n'empêche pas qu'il ne sorte* would imply that the leave, the permission is more or less in the power of the speaker, who possibly might raise obstacles or objections to the going out.

We must also say without *Ne, Il faut prendre garde que les futailles soient bonnes avant d'y entonner le vin.* We must take care to have good casks before putting the wine into them.

The *Ne* is not used before the Subjunctive because it would imply a contradiction of the intention.

Observe that when *Prendre garde* means to notice, to observe, it requires the Indicative.

La plupart des hommes ne prennent pas garde que la vie passe promptement. Most men do not observe that life passes swiftly away.

Although *Défendre* bears a great analogy to *Empêcher,* it never requires *Ne.*

J'ai défendu que vous fissiez telle chose, ou *Je vous ai défendu de faire telle chose.* I forbade you to do such thing.

TURN INTO FRENCH.

I do not *prevent* him *doing* what he pleases.[1] The interposition of a cloud *prevents* the sun's rays from *reaching*-us.[2] *Prevent* his *going out.* Do not *prevent* his *going out.* I cannot *help* his *going out.* I cannot[3] *help* his *doing* such a thing.

I will not *hinder* your *coming.* The rain *prevented* him from *taking* a walk. I *prevent,* I do not *prevent,* can I *prevent,* without *preventing,* ought I to *prevent* his or her *coming?*

Avoid his *speaking* to you. Henry wished to *prevent*[4]

Lewis from *taking a part.* *Avoid* her *coming.* The blown[5] glass has been baked-over-again[6] to *prevent* its *cracking.*[7]

Take care or *take heed* of *being wronged.*[8] *Take care* lest he *should do* it. Be-very-careful[9] that nobody come. *Take care* that the meat *be-not-overdone.*[10] *Take care* that your intention do not appear.[11] *Take care* lest you *be seen* or[12] *heard.* We must moreover[13] *take care* that the punishment[14] *be* not greater than the offence.[15]

Take care to-have-everything-ready.[16] Have you *taken care* lest that man *should deceive* you? *Take heed* lest there *should-be*[17] pride in despising his liberality. I always took care to *have* them ready.

We ought during our life to take care that the isolation and youth of our children *should have* a firm support.[18]

1. Vouloir.—2. Venir jusqu'à nous.—3. Je ne saurais.—4. Eviter.—5. Soufflé.—6. Recuire.—7. Se fendre.—8. Faire du tort à.—9. Prendre garde.—10. Ne rôtir trop.—11. Eclater.—12. Et qu'on.—13. De plus.—14. Peine.—15. Faute.—16. Que tout être prêt.—17. Y avoir.—18. Appui.

CLIX.—When a Subjoined Clause, connected by *Qui, que, dont, à quoi, lequel, où,* expresses an affirmative sense, the Indicative is used.

Indiquez-moi le lieu où je pourrai le trouver. Let me know the place where I can find him.

Passez-moi le livre qui est sur la table. Hand me that book on the table there.

TURN INTO FRENCH.

I am looking out for a friend *who is willing* and *able* to oblige me. That was a business *from which* I-*reaped*[1] no benefit. It is not well known *who was* the inventor of printing. He reposed-an-entire-confidence-in[2] persons *that betrayed* him. The army was-drawn-up[3] in-such-a-manner-*as*[4] *to make*-it-appear more numerous than it really was.

She is working at something *which will be* very handsome. The swallow has found a nest *where she may* lay[5] her young.

1. Je n'ai retiré.—2. Se livrer entièrement à des.—3. Ranger en bataille.—4. D'une manière qui.—5. Déposer.

CLX.—When a Subjoined Clause, connected by *Qui, que, dont, à quoi, lequel, où,* conveys doubt or uncertainty, wonder and surprise, desire, need, or purpose, the Subjunctive Mood is used, especially if these Relatives are preceded by *Aucun, peu, guère, quelque chose, rien, nul, personne, quelqu'un,* and, in short, any noun expressed in an Indefinite sense.

Ma maîtresse veut avoir une espèce d'homme d'affaires qui entende bien l'économie et qui tienne un compte exact de l'argent déboursé. My mistress should like to have a kind of a steward who should understand economy and keep an exact account of the money disbursed.

Ce n'est pas une chose dont il faille disputer. There needs be no dispute about the matter.

Avez-vous un domestique qui vous convienne? Are you well suited with a servant?

Est-ce un homme sur lequel on puisse compter? Is he a man to be depended upon?

TURN INTO FRENCH.

Could he find no one *who had lost* the money? Do not set them examples *that are* pernicious. I want a trade *that will support*[1] me and my children. Let-us-forbear-doing-anything[2] *that may commit* us. Give[3] me a proof *which may be* more convincing.

I want shoes *which I can* put on easily. I wish to have shoes *that will fit* easily. Wanted,[4] a governess *who can* teach French, music, drawing, &c., &c., &c., salary twenty pounds a year!! Wanted, a valet de place *who knows* several languages. Do you know anybody *going* to Paris? Do you know a tailor *who is* honest? Do you know any one *who understands* it? I know nothing *that is* better for our happiness than friendship. I know nobody *who is* so happy as you are.

Is there anybody in the world *that cherishes* you more than I do? I do not know any one *whom I would oblige* sooner than you. Is there anybody here *that knows* you?

Is there a man *who is willing* to come with us? There is nobody *that I know.* Do you know any one *that is* on good terms with him? I hope to find a friend *that will* not *be* ungrateful. I see only us two *who are* reasonable.

1. Nourrir.—2. Se garder de rien faire.—3. Citer.—4. On demande.

CLXI.—Indicative after Superlatives, after *le seul, le premier, le dernier,* &c.

Ils sont cinq ou six frères, mais c'est le plus jeune que je connais. There are five or six brothers of them, but it is the youngest I know or am acquainted with.

L'expérience tient une école où les leçons coûtent cher, mais c'est la seule où les insensés peuvent s'instruire. Experience keeps a school where lessons are expensive, but it is the only one where fools can be taught.

TURN INTO FRENCH.

He had taken at Vernon *the smallest* house he *could* find. That was *the-least*-reward[1] that *could* be given to him. I shall bring you back *the best* and *finest* muslin I *can* find.

It was *the most afflicted* woman we comforted.[2] You will go for *my finest* gown which *is hung* in my wardrobe. I will choose the *prettiest* frock that I *can* find. I shall sell you *the best* gloves which *are* in the small parcel. You will bring me *my best* gun, which *I wish* to clean.

The next time you *happen* to do such a thing, you shall have to-deal-with-me.[3] *Next*[4] *time I see* him, I will punish him. They made me a present of their blessing, *which-was-the-only-thing*[5] *I expected* from them. It is *the first thing I shall do* on arriving. It is in *the first* house which you *will see* on the right.

You must take[6] *the first* street which you *will meet* on the left. It is *the last* volume which *is* the best. It is *the only* town wherein we *shall stop*. *The last* time I *went* to a ball, we-kept-it-up-till[7] morning. You are *the last* man I *should*[8] consult. How pretty she was *the last* time *I saw* her. This is *the last* place where I-*should-expect*[9] to find you. He was *the first to*[10] *perceive* that truth. It is not *the first* time they *fell-out*.[11]

1. La moindre des récompenses.—2. Consoler.—3. Affaire à moi.—4. La première.—5. C'était le seul bien.—6. Entrer dans.—7. Nous restâmes jusqu'au.—8. Voudrais.—9. Je me serais attendu de.—10. Qui.—11. Se brouiller.

CLXII.—When we do not wish to express ourselves in too positive a manner,—when choice, selection, preference, or comparison is implied, and, of course, doubt or hesitation in the mind of the speaker,—the Subjunctive is used after Superlatives, after *Le seul, l'unique, le premier, le dernier*, &c.

C'était l'homme le plus loyal que je connusse. He was the most upright man I ever knew.

If in this case the Indicative were used, the phrase would convey: *Que je connaissais l'homme le plus loyal, et non un autre*, that I knew the most upright man, and no other upright man but him.

C'est le seul reproche que je lui fis, et c'était justement le seul qu'il ne méritât pas. This was the only reproach I made him, and this was the only one he did not deserve.

TURN INTO FRENCH.

He is *the most stupid* man I *know.* He is *as-good-a-man-as*[1] ever *lived.* They are *the best* sort-of-people[2] I ever *saw.* He is *the-most-open*-fellow[3] I ever *met with.* These are *the finest* goods I *have received* this long while. It is *the best* pen I ever *used.*[4]

It is *the greatest* happiness I *can* enjoy. It was *the sweetest* reward I *could have*[5] expected. We bring you back *the finest* and *best* muslin that we *have been able* to find.

The *greatest* harm which an enemy *can* do us is to accustom our heart to hatred. Famine is one of *the greatest* scourges that *can* visit[6] a country. Addison is *the greatest* prose writer the English *have had* yet. Nero was *the greatest* tyrant that ever *disgraced* the name of man. It was one of *the bitterest*[7] winters I *have* ever *seen.*

I will give you *the soundest*-thrashing[8] you ever *got.* That is the *best* laid[9] snare it *is* possible to imagine. That is *the most natural* explanation that *can* be given of his conduct.

The Egyptians were *the first* who *listened* to these wonderful masters. Pythagoras was *the first* among the Greeks who *took* the name of Philosopher. The-main-point[10] is to look (that you should look) to your health.

Virtue was *the only* wealth[11] he *inherited* from his father. That is not the *first* failure of that commercial house (Translate—It is not the first time that, &c.). You are *the first* to whom we *said* it. It is *the only* piece-of-indiscretion[12] he ever *was* guilty of. The Battle of Crécy was *the first* in which they made-use-of[13] cannon.

He is *the last* who *did* it. It is *the last* letter she *wrote.* It is *the last* volume I *read.* If he does not follow this advice, it will be *the last* we *shall give* him. It is *the only* money I *can* dispose of. It was *the only* thing on which he set-any-value.[14] This was the only consolation (which was) *left me.*

1. Le meilleur homme.—2. Gens.—3. L'individu le plus franc.—4. Se servir.—5. Pouvoir.—6. Désoler.—7. Rude.—8. La meilleure volée *ou* raclée.—9. Dressé.—10. Le principal.—11. Bien.—12. Indiscrétion.—13. Employer.—14. Attacher quelque prix.

CLXIII.—Adjectives, Verbs, Words or Forms of speech expressive of joy, grief, approbation, wonder, or surprise, require the Subjunctive when there are two Nominatives, the Infinitive if there is but one.

Il est inoui que pareille chose soit jamais arrivée. It is unheard of that such a thing should have ever happened.

C'est un de mes étonnements qu'il ait pu réussir par ce moyen-là! One of my wonders, *or* the thing I wonder at is, how possibly, he could have succeeded by such means!

Nous sommes heureux d'avoir pu vous plaire. We are glad we were able to please you.

TURN INTO FRENCH.

We have been delighted that you *struck-up*-a-friendship[1] with that honest man. I am very glad you *told*[2] me. We shall be very glad if your brother *will keep* us company. He would be very glad if you *would be* one-of-the-party.[3] It is a pity that his brother *is* so wild.[4]

I would be sorry that you *should entertain*-about-me[5] a thought so contrary to the friendship which exists between us. We are happy that he *knew* nothing about-it.[6] It is fortunate for him that you *interested*-yourself-for-his-concerns.[7] It is a-misfortune[8] you *did* not *write* sooner. I am exceedingly-glad[9] that *has happened.*

I am amazed he *should have told* me nothing about it. I am surprised you *found* him in-so-bad-a-condition.[10] I am sorry you *did* not *inform*[11] me of it sooner. I-am-sorry[12] you *do* not *wish* to do it.

I am very much mortified that you *are prohibited*[13] from going to court. I should be very-glad[14] to have my doubts *cleared-up.*[15] It is a-pity[16] he *does* not *keep* his word. I am glad that somebody *should pre-engage*[17] him in my behalf before I see him.

I wonder you *keep-company-with*-such-fellows.[18] I regret your *being*[19] absent. It is very lucky for them their master *did* not *hear* them speak-back.[20] I am delighted that you *are* not *acquainted* with him. I am delighted that it *is* so. I am surprised that you *have* not *done*-your-task.[21] I wonder he *does* not *see* the danger he-is-in.[22]

1. Lier d'amitié.—2. Avertir.—3. De la partie.—4. Dérangé.—5. Avoir de moi.—6. En.—7. S'intéresser pour lui.—8. Mal.—9. Ravi.—10. Si mauvais état.—11. Dire.—12. Il me fâche que.—13. Interdire.—14. Bien aise qu'on.—15. Eclaircir de.—16. Fâcheux.—17. Prévenir.—18. Fréquenter des gens de cette espèce.—19. Avoir été.—20. Répondre.—21. Faire votre devoir.—22. Où il est.

CLXIV.—After Impersonal Verbs expressing doubt, impossibility, will, necessity, or propriety, the Subjunctive is very commonly used.

Il semble que la liberté soit faite pour le génie des peuples de l'Europe, et la servitude pour celui des peuples de l'Asie. Liberty seems to be suited to the genius of the people of Europe, and slavery to those of Asia.

Il ne vaut pas la peine que vous lui répondiez. He is beneath your notice.

CLXV.—Many Verbs, as *Il me semble, il résulte, il paraît*, &c., which take the Indicative when affirmatively used, require the Subjunctive, if expressive of doubt, in Negative or Interrogative Propositions.

Il n'est pas à présumer qu'il en restera là. It is not likely that he will be satisfied with that.

Est-il à présumer qu'il y consente? Il n'est pas à présumer qu'il le fasse. Is it likely that he will consent to it? It is not very likely that he will do it.

CLXVI.—After *Sembler, Suffire, S'ensuivre,* &c., the Indicative or the Subjunctive is used according to the positive or doubtful sense of the assertion.

Parce que vous n'avez pas arrosé vos fleurs, s'ensuit-il qu'elles vont mourir? Because you have not watered your flowers, does it follow that they will die?

De ce qu'un homme est plus adroit ou plus fort qu'un autre, il ne s'ensuit pas qu'il ait de meilleures raisons. Because one man is stronger or more dexterous than another, it does not follow that he has the better cause.

TURN INTO FRENCH.

It is proper every-man[1] *should have* his place in society. I must *have* a little talk[2] with her. It is proper that you *should be dressed*[3] decently. It is not proper that you *should offend anybody.*[4] It was proper that we *should retire.*

One-would-think[5] he *is paid* to do that. One would think he *had sworn* my destruction.[6] He paints[7] things in-such-lively-colours[8] that one thinks one *sees* them. Do you think this pair of boots *is-worth*[9] mending? Does it not appear to you that this tree *is* higher than that one? It does not appear to me *to be* higher. It appears *to be* higher.

It is-sufficient,[10] or it is enough you *should know* the will of your father to obey. Your *having informed* him is sufficient. You-ought-to-be-satisfied[11] that I *have* already *warned* you once. Let it be sufficient for you that I *wished* for it. It is sufficient that she *is* in the wrong.

It-is-of-importance[12] that he *should be informed* of what is going on. It is necessary that we *should write* that we may see them. It is of consequence to your partners that you *should set out* immediately. It concerns-the-public-welfare[13] that it *should be governed* by wise people.

What-though[14] he *refused* us the favour; is that a reason for being ungrateful? "What though your general *is* dead," exclaimed Rasi, a Mussulman captain; "God is living and sees you."

I-do-not-choose[15] that she *should go* thither, nor that he *should come*. I-am[16] extremely displeased that things *should-have-been-transacted*-in-this-manner.[17] What matter whether the thing *be* true or false? What signifies[18] whether he *go* or *stay*? It-is-not-possible[19] that you *should see* them.

I must *make-myself-acquainted*-with[20] this affair. He must either *fall*[21] or *fly*. You must *have-been-out*[22] very late. He must *go*, or else *find*-some-one-to-go-for-him.[23] She must *lower*[24] her pretensions.

I recollected that in order to teach Dutchmen English, it was necessary that they *should teach* me Dutch.

1. Chacun.—2. Entretien.—3. Mettre.—4. Qui que ce soit.—5. Il semble.—6. Perte.—7. Dépeindre.—8. Si vivement.—9. Valoir la peine. —10. Suffire.—11. Il doit vous suffire.—12. Importer.—13. Important pour le bien de la république.—14. Qu'importe.—15. Il ne me plaît pas. —16. Il me.—17. Se passer de la sorte.—18. Importer.—19. N'y avoir pas moyen.—20. Se mettre au courant de.—21. Succomber.—22. Etre rentré.—23. Se faire remplacer par quelqu'un.—24. Rabattre de.

CLXVII.—*Etre*, impersonal, and accompanied by an Adjective of evidence, certainty, probability, requires the Indicative when used affirmatively; the Subjunctive when used interrogatively or negatively, if doubt is implied in the speaker's mind; if not, the Indicative should be used.

. . . . *Est-il vrai que ma tante*
Ait du goût pour Lindor, et qu'il en soit épris?
Est-il bien vrai, Pasquin, que tu les as surpris
Se jurant un amour?

Is it true that my aunt has an inclination for Lindor, and that he is enamoured with her? Is it really true, Pasquin, that you caught them plighting love to one another?

CLXVIII.—*Etre* impersonal governs the Subjunctive, when accompanied by Adjectives, Words, or Forms of Speech requiring that mood.

Il n'est pas besoin qu'on lui dise deux fois la même chose. There is no occasion for your telling him the same thing twice.

Il est étonnant qu'on prenne de si grandes libertés. It is surprising how people should take such liberties.

Il était de leur intérêt que la guerre ne traînât pas en longueur. It concerned them that the war should not be protracted.

Ce before *Etre,* and followed by *Que,* generally requires the second Verb to be put in the Subjunctive.

C'est un miracle qu'il en ait échappé. It is a wonder he escaped.

C'est dommage qu'il se conduise si mal, ayant tant de talent. It is a pity that, having so much talent, he behaves himself so ill.

C'est assez qu'il soit pédant pour qu'il prenne un ton si arrogant. His being a pedant is enough for him to assume an arrogant tone.

TURN INTO FRENCH.

It is not probable that the thing *should be* as you say. It is rather unlikely he *did* or *said* that. It is not meet[1] he *should know* it. It is indifferent[2] *to take* this way or the other.

His *having* once *mistaken* is-enough.[3] His *having retracted* what he said is sufficient. It is enough for you *to be* warned. Such stupid questions deserve no answer; your *having asked*[4] them is sufficient.

It is a pity you *had* no time to say more. It is not a thing that *will be* beneficial[5] to you. It is not good that man *should be* alone. It is no disparagement to him that his father *is* poor. It is not surprising he *should be* a bad father, who was a bad son. It is but fair you should *indemnify* him. It is proper that you *should begin* this exercise again; it is fit that you *should do* so.

There was little probability of the event *taking* place. It is advisable for you to do that. When Arnauld wished Nicole to help him in a new work, the latter replied: "Are we not now too old, is it not time we *should rest?*" "Rest!"[6] replied Arnauld, "have we not eternity to rest in?"

I am not sure that he *can do* it. Are you sure he *arrived* in time? He does not deserve *to be believed.* There is a possibility that he *may return.* Is it possible that you *are* the-sublime-genius[7] whose reputation is so great in this country? I am not certain that you *are* in the right. Is it true that you *said* it? It is not true that I *said* it.

My-having[8] saluted wicked people does not imply that I *am* one. Not that I *doubted* the death of Don Alvaro, or *was restrained* by the fear of seeing him again when I least expected. Not but that I *am* satisfied with my condition.

1. à propos.—2. Indifférent qu'on.—3. C'est assez qu'il.—4. Faire.—5. Avantageuse.—6. Nous reposer.—7. Ce bel esprit.—8. Parce que j'ai.

CLXIX.—After *Quel que* (*Predicate*), *quelque* (before Adjectives or Adverbs); *quelque* (before Nouns); *qui que, quoi que, si que, si peu que,* the Subjunctive is invariably used.

Voici trois chemins, quel que soit celui que vous preniez, il vous conduira chez vous. Here are three roads, whichever you take will lead you home.

Quelque amitié que j'aie pour vous, ne croyez pas que je fasse cela. Much as I love you, do not think I shall do that.

De quelques superbes distinctions que se flattent les hommes, ils ont tous la même origine. With whatever proud distinction men may flatter themselves, they have all the same origin.

Il lui accordera sa demande quelque considérable qu'elle soit. He will give her what she asks, though she asks ever so much.

Quoi que vous ou lui, vous puissez penser, j'agirai comme je jugerai convenable. Whatever you or he may think, I shall act as I think proper.

Si fort que vous soyez, si grand qu'on vous proclame,
Aimez qui vous résiste et croyez qui vous blâme.

How mighty soever you may be, how great soever you may be proclaimed, love whoever resists you and believe whoever blames you.

TURN INTO FRENCH.

Whatever your intentions *may be*, shall you follow his advice, *whatever* it *may be?* I do not know who has done it; but *whoever* he *may be*, I will punish him. *Whoever* those ladies *may be*, I will not let them in. Rich or poor, *whatever* he *may be*, he shall be welcome. Tell me your reasons, *whatever* they *may be*. Two roads are-before-you[1] on your entrance into the world,—the one leads to vice, the other to virtue; *whichever way* you *take*, you will soon reach the term of this mortal life to enter into eternal life. *Let* the laws *be* what *they will*, they should be adhered to. I will follow him *whichever* road he *takes*. *However* good his mother *may be*, she is too indulgent.[2] *Though* a-man[3] *be* ever so good a musician, it does not follow that he is a good singer. *As* brave a soldier as he *is*. Rich *as* he *is*. Big *as* he *is*. False *as* these reports *may be*.

However anxious[4] *I am* to break off with him, I must, however, keep-fair[5] with him for a little while yet. *Though* I *be* ever so attentive, they always find fault with what I do. *However* guilty men *may be*. *However* corrupted our morals *may be*. *However* estimable glory *may be*.

How cleverly *soever* he *contrives*,[6] he shall not succeed. *How* well *soever* you *may act*, still-you-will-meet[7] with traducers for all that.

Whatever difference there *appears* to be between ranks of life, there is nevertheless certain compensations of good and evil which render them equal. The spendthrift is always poor, *whatever* riches he *may have*. *How* desirous *soever* he *was* of sending home the audience[8] satisfied, he could by-no-means-effect-it.[9]

Whoever knows it, I do not care. *Whoever*[10] *spoke* to him, he answered nothing. *Whoever speaks* to you about it, say that you know nothing about it. *Whichever* of the parties *gains*[11] the victory, we shall perish. *Whoever told* it to you, he is mistaken. *Whoever asks* for me, say that I am busy.[12] *Whoever used*-this-language[13] does not deserve to be believed. *Whoever did* it, he is a clever man.

Be he who he may, I take-it-kindly-of[14] him. *Be he who he may* who *told* it to me, he-did-right.[15] *Let him be who he will*, or *whoever* he *may be*, he shall repent it.

To whomsoever you *may-speak*,[16] be civil. *Of whomsoever* you speak, avoid slander. We ought never to speak ill of *any one* in his absence. *To whomsoever* you *may apply*, they will give you the same advice.[17] *Nobody whatever* prejudiced-me[18] against him.

He mistrusted[19] *nobody at all*. Tell your master I fear *nobody whatever*, and that I will not obey him in-*anything-whatever*.[20] The wise man does not envy *anybody's* fortune. There is[21] *nobody whatever* perfectly-happy.[22]

Whatever you or he *may say*, *whatever* you or he *may do*, she will never speak to you again. Whatever you may propose, that man will always uphold the opposite.[23] *Whatever* she *may say*, I cannot believe he did it.

Let the weather *be-ever*-so-hot,[24] we shall never go out. *Let* the temptation *be ever* so-weak,[25] man runs the risk of yielding to it when he does not repulse it immediately. *Let* a man *be* ever so-great,[26] he is a man for all that. *Though* you *give* ever so-little,[27] I shall for ever be grateful.

1. Se présentent à vous.—2. Faible.—3. On.—4. Désireux.—5. Ménager un peu.—6. S'y prendre.—7. Vous n'en trouverez pas moins.—

8. Spectateurs.—9. En venir à bout.—10. Qui que ce fût qui.—11. Remporter.—12. En affaire.—13. Avoir tenu ce discours.—14. En savoir bon gré.—15. Il a bien fait.—16. S'adresser.—17. Conseil.—18. Ne m'a prévenu.—19. Se défier de.—20. En quoi que ce soit.—21. Il n'y a.—22. De véritablement heureux.—23. Le contraire.—24. Si forte que soit.—25. Si faible que.—26. Si grand que.—27. Si peu que.

CLXX.—Conjunctions and Conjunctive Expressions requiring the Subjunctive Mood.

Le feu me monta au visage, et je crois que, pour peu que j'eusse parlé, je n'aurais pu m'empêcher de le brusquer. I began to redden, and I believe, had I gone a little further, I should have affronted him.

Ne fera-t-elle pas bien de faire en sorte qu'ils n'aient pas lieu de se plaindre ? Had she not better manage it so as to give them no cause to complain ?

Quoiqu'il dise qu'il ait fait tout son possible, ne faites pas fond sur ce qu'il dit. Although he says he did all he could, do not rely on what he says.

TURN INTO FRENCH.

Though the same room *served* us as a parlour and kitchen, that only made[1] it warmer. *Although* we[2] often *ask for*, we seldom listen to advice. I suspect *though* I *do* not *fear* him.

If he should-call[3] during my absence, beg him to wait, *unless* he *should be* in too great a hurry. Have you wept for your sin *so-that*[4] your spirit *be* sorrowful ?[5] *Whether* a liar *lie* or *tell* the truth, he is no longer believed.

This disgrace has befallen[6] them, *not because* they *deserve* it, but because people like new-faces.[7] Contrive[8] your intrigues *so* as not *to involve*-me.[9] We must live in such a way *as*[10] *to do harm* to nobody.

Far[11] *from being* your enemy, *if*[12] he *has* any money at all, he will help you. Do things *so that* everybody *may be* contented or pleased. I will do it, *not that* I *am* obliged, but to have peace. We shall-be-off[13] *without being-observed*.[14]

We cannot thrive *unless* we *are* industrious and frugal.[15] He dropped-*ere*[16] I *could come* to his assistance. Behave *so that* man *may see* your good deeds. Pull the bell *in order that* they *may* come and open the door.

1. Rendre.—2. Nous en.—3. Venir à passer.—4. De manière à ce que.—5. Contristée.—6. Arriver.—7. Changement.—8. Nouer.—9. M'y mêler.—10. De façon à ce que.—11. Loin que.—12. Pour peu que.—13. S'esquiver.—14. S'en apercevoir.—15. Econome.—16. Tomber avant que.

CLXXI.—*Que* used for *Afin que, pour que, jusqu'à ce que, soit que,* requires the Subjunctive, *Que* used instead of *à moins que, sans que, de peur que, de crainte que, avant que,* requires *Ne* before the Subjunctive.

Sylla ne cessa point de faire couler le sang de ses concitoyens qu'il n'eût assouvi sa cruauté. Sylla did not cease from shedding the blood of his fellow-citizens until he had sated his cruelty.

Un pilote ne s'embarque point qu'il n'ait pris auparavant toutes les précautions pour arriver à bon port. A pilot does not embark until he has taken every precaution to arrive successfully in port.

TURN INTO FRENCH.

Whether it *rains* or not, must you go out? Must a soldier fight, *whether* he *is* brave or not? It is immaterial[1] to me *whether* it *is* so or not.

I shall not be contented *unless* I *know* it. I will not go[2] thither, *before* she *comes*. Do not go near that dog *lest* he *bite* you. Let us make haste *for fear* anybody *should come*. I will not speak *unless* he *goes* out. I will not do it *unless* you come.

Provided our wives *consent* to it, and you *promise* to settle two hundred pounds upon your daughter. Though we are convinced of the truth of the assertion, and *are willing*[3] to believe you, yet we require time for reflection. Unless you come or *write* to me, I shall not go.

A prudent man does not undertake an affair *until* he *has taken* every measure (*pl.*) to succeed. I shall not go to Paris *until* you *go* there yourself. Do nothing *till* you *hear* from me. Wait *till* the theatre-*empties*.[4] I shall not believe myself safe[5] *until* I *have obtained* his consent.

1. Indifférent.—2. Se rendre.—3. Disposés.—4. La salle se dégarnir —5. En sûreté.

CONSTRUCTION OF S'EN FALLOIR WITH NE.

CLXXII.—*S'en falloir* requires *Ne* before the Subjunctive, when the principal Verb expresses doubt, negation, interrogation, or is attended by words of a negative import, such as *Peu, bien peu, rien, presque rien, presque*, &c.

Mes pieds m'ont presque manqué ; il s'en est peu fallu que mes pas n'aient glissé. My feet were almost gone ; my steps had well-nigh slipped.

Peu s'en faut que je ne sois malade. I am anything but well.

Il ne s'en faut pas beaucoup que la somme n'y soit. There does not want much to complete the sum.

The *Ne* is used in the Subjunctive Clause to convey that notwithstanding the littleness of the deficiency, yet there is still a trifle wanting, a falling short of the whole sum.

TURN INTO FRENCH.

I have-been-very-near[1] *being deceived.* He-was-as-near-as-possible[2] *being killed.* I-do-not-know-what-prevents-me-from[3] *beating* you. I was well-nigh *being beaten.* A little more and[4] he *had-been-run-over.*[5] He had like[6] *to be defeated.* He was very near[7] *failing*[8] in that undertaking. How-near-were[9] these two friends *quarrelling.*[10]

You say it wants twenty pounds to complete the sum; we-are-far-from[11] *agreeing.*[12] He-was-within-an-ace[13] of *losing* his cause.[14]

He was near *obtaining* the prize. You have been very near *meeting* him. I was very near *coming* here before your brother. We were very near *giving up*[15] our project. He was very near *ripping up* my side[16] with-a-sabre.[17]

Your cousin is not far from *being* as learned as you are. He was so rash that he was not far from *being* killed.

1. Peu s'en falloir.—2. S'en falloir presque rien.—3. Peu s'en falloir que.—4. Peu s'en falloir.—5. Avoir été écrasé.—6. Peu s'en falloir.—7. Peu s'en falloir.—8. Succomber.—9. Que s'en est-il fallu.—10. Se brouiller.—11. S'en falloir beaucoup.—12. Etre d'accord.—13. Peu s'en falloir.—14. Procès.—15. Renoncer à.—16. M'ouvrir le côté.—17. D'un coup de sabre.

CONSTRUCTION OF S'EN FALLOIR WITHOUT NE.

CLXXIII.—But when *S'en falloir* is unattended by any word of a negative meaning, it involves a negation and, of course, does not require *Ne* in the Subjunctive Clause.

Il s'en faut bien que la chose se soit passée comme vous le dites. The thing occurred in quite a different manner from what you say.

TURN INTO FRENCH.

Your brother fell from his horse; *he-had-like*[1] *to have broken* his leg. He *is far from* being as clever as-he-thinks.[2] I *was far*[3] *from* approving-your-conduct[4] on that occasion. The one *is far from* having-the[5] merit of the other. He *is far from* having satisfied[6] public expectation.

It-*is-far*[7] *from*-being-so-here.[8] This *was far from* being the case.[9] You *are far from* surpassing your school-fellows.[10] Their apartments *were far from* being as well lighted as ours. He *is far from* drawing as well as your sister. He writes *nearly*[11] as well as his master. I *was very far from* expecting[12] such an act[13] of ingratitude from you. The crime *is far from* being equal.

I *am far from* being in good-health.[14] She seems prudent; *she-is-however-by-no-means-so.*[15] The countess's hand *is far from* being-as-fine.[16] Riches and honours, and even science, *are-far*[17] *from* rendering a man happy; virtue alone has that privilege. *Far-be-it-from*-me-to-suppose-that[18] those men, so intrepid in battles, display the same courage when death comes and strikes them on their beds!

1. Il s'en est peu fallu.—2. Qu'il croit l'être.—3. Beaucoup que.—4. Vous approuver.—5. Etre du.—6. Satisfaire à.—7. S'en falloir bien.—8. En être ici de même.—9. Ainsi.—10. Condisciples.—11. S'en falloir peu.—12. S'attendre.—13. Trait.—14. Bien portant.—15. Il s'en faut bien qu'elle le soit.—16. Avoir la main aussi belle.—17. Il s'en faut bien que, &c.—18. Combien s'en faut-il que.

CLXXIV.—*S'en falloir* is followed by *De,* when the quantity or number alluded to falls short of what is required; it then conveys an idea of size or quantity rather than of quality.

Il s'en fallait de cinq minutes qu'il fût huit heures. It wanted five minutes to eight.

Il s'en fallait de cent francs que la somme y fût. The sum was short of a hundred francs.

TURN INTO FRENCH.

The ladders *wanted* a great deal of-the-ordinary-length.[1] His work *is far* from being being finished. His works *are far* from being well written. We are not *by* a few months of the same age. *There is not* a fortnight's difference between-our-ages.[2]

1. Avoir la longueur ordinaire.—2. Etre du même age.

CLXXV.—*Tant s'en faut que.* Far from, so far from.

Tant s'en faut que la mort soit un mal, qu'au contraire elle met fin à tous nos maux. Death is so far from being an evil, that, on the contrary, it puts an end to all our evils.

TURN INTO FRENCH.

So far is this play *from* pleasing me, that[1] I think it insufferable.[2] *Far from* scolding you, I on the contrary congratulate you. *So far from* owing you money, on the contrary, it is you who owe me some.

So far from consenting to it, on the contrary, he-is-reluctant-to-it.[3] *So far from* hating you, on the contrary, he loves you. You *are far from* doing him good. I *am far from* doing you any-mischief.[4] I *am far from* being powerful. You *are far from* being pitied.

The fruits of the earth *are so far from* being intended-for[5] beasts, that, on the contrary, we see that beasts themselves have been created for-the-use-of-man.[6]

1. Au contraire.—2. Détestable.—3. Il y répugne.—4. Aucun mal.—5. Destiner à.—6. Pour l'homme.

CLXXVI.—*Tenir à*, to have it in one's power.

Tenir à moi, à lui, &c., negatively or interrogatively used, generally require *Ne*.

Je ne sais pas à quoi il tient que je ne vous batte. I don't know what prevents me from beating you.

A quoi tient-il que cela ne se fasse? What prevents that from being done?

CLXXVII.—After *Il tient à moi, à lui*, &c., affirmatively used, no negation is required in the Subjunctive Clause.

Il tient à moi que l'affaire se fasse. The transaction of the thing lies or rests with me.

Tenir, with *Ne que*, generally excludes *Ne*.

Il ne tient qu'à moi que l'affaire se fasse. The transaction of the thing only lies with me.

CLXXVIII.—Yet, *Il ne tient qu'à* may sometimes take *Ne* in the Subjunctive Clause, whenever it suggests an idea of an opposition, an obstacle thwarting our designs or intents.

Il n'a tenu qu'à vous que je n'aie plus tôt rendu justice à M. de Lagarde. It was all along your fault, if I did not do justice to M. de Lagarde.

CLXXIX.—If *Il tient* be both Negative and Interrogative, *Ne* is omitted in the Subjunctive Clause.

Ne tient-il pas à moi que tout cela se fasse? Does not the doing of all this depend upon me?

TURN INTO FRENCH.

What-is-the-cause[1] that we do not *set out* immediately? It *was-not-my-fault*[2] if you *did* not *receive* the letter that you expected. What *can prevent* its *being* so? He-*was-near*[3] *killing* himself. It *will be no fault of mine* if he *does* not *succeed*. It *is* not *my fault* if he *is* not *satisfied*.

They-*were*-very-*near*[4] *coming-to-blows*.[5] What *prevents* men from *enjoying* real[6] happiness. I do not know what-*hinders*-me-from[7] *splitting* your skull with the fragments[8] of the feast you (*f.*) came to disturb.

Cæsar *was very near* being *proscribed* by Sylla. We-*were-very-near*[9] *losing* the battle. I know that *it was no fault of yours* if I *did not obtain* what I was asking for. *Does his being condemned depend-on-you-only?*[10] *It does not depend upon me* that she *should be* happy.

I-was-told[11] that it *was in your power* to *put an end* to this affair. It *shall be no fault of mine* if[12] you are not paid[13] all the honours you are entitled-to.[14]

1. à quoi tient il.—2. Il n'a pas tenu à moi.—3. Il ne tint à rien qu'il.—4. Il ne tint presqu'à rien.—5. Se battre.—6. Véritable.—7. Qui me tient que je.—8. Les pièces.—9. Il n'a tenu presqu'à rien que la.—10. Ne tient-il qu'à vous.—11. J'ai appris.—12. Qu'on.—13. Rendre.—14. Devoir.

ON THE PASSIVE CONSTRUCTION.

CLXXX.—Passive Verbs are either followed by *De* or *Par*.

Les génies tracassiers sont haïs de tout le monde. Troublesome geniuses are hated by everybody.

Elle fut immolée par le vainqueur sous les yeux mêmes de son père. She was immolated by the conqueror under the very eyes of her father.

Often the French prefer the Active Voice when the English would use the Passive.

La fréquentation des personnes qui parlent mal corrompt le style et le langage. By associating with people who speak badly, the style and language are corrupted.

CLXXXI.—With the Possessive Pronouns, the object spoken of is often the Nominative of the English Passive Construction; in French the person, rather than the thing spoken of, becomes the Nominative of the Active Construction.

Il avait les jambes tellement enflées qu'on fut obligé de fendre ses bottes. His legs were so much swollen that they were obliged to cut his boots.

TURN INTO FRENCH.

Romulus and Remus were-suckled[1] by a *wolf*. *Sam* was desired by his *mamma* not to eat sour apples. *I* am amused by their *follies*. *I* was shocked with two or three *things* in her performance. *He* was proclaimed *king* by the *army*.

He was choked by a *quinsy*.[2] The *mouse* was eaten by the *cat*. *Riches* are desired by all.

His hands *were tied* behind his back. His eyes *were* all on[3] fire, and face enflamed.[4] Her eyes *are* lively,[5] and full of fire. His hair and beard *are* red.[6] His feet *are* warm. His body and limbs *are* well proportioned. His neck *is* too long, his head is too small, his ears too short, and he has a kind of hump on his back. *Is* her hand as small as mine.[7] His face *is* as young looking as if he were but twenty. That horse's legs *are* swelled.[8]

1. Allaiter.—2. Esquinancie.—3. En.—4. Enluminé.—5. Vifs.—6. Roux.—7. Moi.—8. Gorgées.

CLXXXII.—In Indeterminate Propositions, the Passive voice, used in English, is rendered in French by the Active voice, with *On* as its Nominative, or by a Reflective Form or an Impersonal Construction.

On ne peut le dire trop de fois, assez de fois, regardez-y à deux fois. That cannot be said too often, or often enough, look at it twice.

J'ordonnai qu'on le saignât et qu'on ne lui plaignît pas l'eau. I ordered him to be bled and not to be begrudged water.

L'air atmosphérique se compose de gaz oxygène, de gaz azote et de gaz acide carbonique. Atmospheric air is composed of oxygen, nitrogen, and carbonic acid gas.

Ces propos incendiaires se tiennent publiquement. These inflammatory discourses are publicly spoken.

Il se couve quelque chose. There is something brewing.

Il court beaucoup de fausse monnaie. There is a good deal of bad money about.

CLXXXIII.—Passive Verbs, followed in English by an Objective, are rendered by the Active voice in French, with *On* as Nominative.

On lui donna une bonne place en récompense des services qu'il avait rendus. He was given a good situation as a reward for the services he had rendered.

TURN INTO FRENCH.

The soup and fish *are* first[1] *served up.* These houses *are to-be-knocked-down.*[2] The houses *have been pulled-down*[3] on each side in-order-to-make-the-square-larger.[4] No[5] trace of that event *is to be found* in history. The father *is beloved* and the son *is feared.* Tyrants *are feared* but *are* not *loved.*

He swallows-down[6] everything that *is laid* to him. It *was* formerly *believed* that ants, during-the[7] summer, laid-up[8] provisions for the winter. It *is said* that Achilles could not be wounded but in the heel. It *was believed* that the water-spout sucked-up[9] the water of the sea.

The masts of certain vessels *are sloped* a little towards-the-stern.[10] A man *is* not *condemned* merely on-probable-evidence.[11] Where-*could*-there[12] *be found* so idle a boy? You deserve *to be punished.* I hate *to be paid* compliments, *to be interrupted* incessantly.

The curtain[13] *rises, falls.*[14] The sea *is discovered* in the distance.[15] It *may be lowered* and *raised*-at-pleasure.[16] That *is seen* at a distance. *Does* this door *open* easily? That door is ill-made, it *does* not *shut* close.[17]

That news *is whispered-about.*[18] Bad news (*pl.*) *is* sooner[19] *spread* than good. That *is-grounded*[20] on false report. Air *is dilated, rarefied, condensed, compressed.* Such[21] things *ought* not *to be said, ought* not *to be asked for, should not be entrusted* to everybody. Languages *are learnt* by custom. This noun *is declined* after[22] such a noun.[23] Water *is changed* into ice by the action of the cold. *Is* not light *refracted* in passing through transparent bodies? Does not iron expand[24] when it *is heated?* Radishes, figs, butter, anchovies, melons, are served-up as-by-dishes.[25] Can you tell me where the book *is to be had?* The book *is to be had* only at one bookseller's. Wine *may be had* at almost any price.

There *is* good wine *drunk* in France. Sincere friends *are* sometimes *to be found.* A council *was held* yesterday. Houses *are building* along-the-whole[26] line. Preparations *are making* on all sides. Fine things *are to be found* there. A rumour *was spread.* I *am forbidden* to drink wine. Troops *are coming* from-all-quarters.[27]

There *happened*-to-be[28] a man who gave me the information[29] I required. His fever is gone; there-*remains*-behind[30] a great weakness. I-*have-taken-in*-bad-cards.[31] I *have taken in* two aces and two trumps. Each member *shall be allowed* to introduce a friend.

He *was asked* his opinion. John *was taught* grammar. William *was promised* a reward. Peter *was paid* the-balance-due-him.[32] He *has-been-allowed*[33] his travelling-expenses.[34] She *was denied* the privilege. She *has been taught* music. She *has been told* the secret.

She *was told* the whole affair. He *was allowed* great liberty. She *was refused* entrance into the house. He *was asked* several questions. She would not accept the jewels, though she *was offered* them by her mother. Have patience and you *shall be paid* all. Were you *paid-back*[35] the money? We *were told* quite a different story.

1. D'abord.—2. Démolir.—3. Abattre.—4. Pour l'agrandissement de la place.—5. Aucune.—6. Gober.—7. En.—8. Faire.—9. Pomper.—10. Sur l'arrière.—11. Sur de simples indices.—12. Où pourrait-on.—13. La toile.—14. Se baisser.—15. Lointain.—16. Se hausser à volonté.—17. Bien.—18. Se murmurer.—19. Plus promptement.—20. Se fonder.—21. De telles.—22. Sur.—23. Autre.—24. Se dilater.—25. En hors d'œuvre.—26. Tout le long de.—27. De toutes parts.—28. Se trouver.—29. Renseignement.—30. Il lui est resté.—31. Il m'est rentré un vilain jeu.—32. Le solde qu'on lui devait.—33. Allouer.—34. Frais de voyage.—35. Rendre.

ON DEVOIR.

CLXXXIV.—*Devoir* literally means to owe.

Doit-il quelque chose à cet homme? Il doit au tiers et au quart. Does he owe that man anything? He is in everybody's debt.

Devoir is rendered by *ought, should,* or *to be bound,* when it conveys an idea of duty, fitness, propriety or expediency in a moral point of view.

Il n'est rien qu'on doive recommander davantage aux jeunes gens que de prendre garde aux liaisons qu'ils forment. There is nothing that ought to be more recommended to youth than to mind what connexions they form.

Oh, que les rois doivent bien prendre garde aux guerres qu'ils entreprennent! Oh, how cautious ought kings to be with respect to the wars they undertake!

Un ami doit supporter les infirmités d'un ami. A friend should bear a friend's infirmities.

Si je dois obliger mon prochain, à plus forte raison dois-je secourir mon frère. If I am bound to oblige my neighbour, I am still more so to assist my brother.

Devoir, denoting conjunctures, probability, inference, or supposition, is expressed by *Must.*

À la vie que mène cet homme, il doit être bien riche. At the rate the man lives, he must be very rich.

À son ton impérieux, je pensai que ce devait être un homme d'importance. From his being so lordly, I thought he must be a man of importance.

Devoir, denoting a future action as likely or intended to be, is translated by *to be.*

Si vous supposez que je doive céder à vos caprices vous êtes singulièrement dans l'erreur. If you suppose that I am to give in to your humours you are egregiously mistaken.

TURN INTO FRENCH.

Every man *ought* to live according to his rank.[1] There is something servile and fawning-about-his-general-character,[2] though I who am his cousin *ought* to be the last person to say so.

Greatness is not of such-high-value[3] that we *should* sacrifice our rest to it. Do you imagine[4] it *should* be so? What do you think I ought to do? *Should* a king treat a man more harshly than the law would treat him? It is as it *should* be. It was as it *should* be. Things are not as they *should* be.

Here is a fine horse, it *must* be dear. You *must* be tired since you come from so far. It *must* have-been[5] very cold last night, for the river is frozen. One *must* needs be very cold with so light a coat. Do you imagine that people *must* obey you? His best friend *must* allow[6] he is a-little-quiz.[7]

Men must bear-with[8] one another. Think now[9] of old age which *must* inevitably come: this is the way-of-spending[10] your youth well.

What *am* I to do in such[11] a case? What do you think I *ought* to do? *Are* you to go anywhere? I *am* not to go anywhere. *Is* anything to happen? *Is* there a race to-be-run[12] to-morrow? Do you believe the Caliph *is* to pay your ignorance? Either he or I *am* to do it. And for whose sake *am* I to do it? *Were* you not to go and spend a week at your uncle's? We *are* to go to him one-of-these-days.[13]

1. Condition.—2. De rampant dans sa manière d'être.—3. D'un si haut prix.—4. Sembler.—5. Avoir fait.—6. Convenir.—7. Un peu persifleur.—8. Se supporter.—9. Dès à présent.—10. Moyen d'employer.—11. Pareil.—12. Se faire.—13. De jour à autre.

SELECTED PIECES

FOR

FRENCH ELEMENTARY COMPOSITION.

THE STORY OF MACBETH.

THERE was a king of Scotland called Duncan, a very good old man. He had two sons; one was called Malcolm, and the other Donaldbane. At this time Scotland, and indeed France and England, and all the other countries of Europe, were much harassed by the Danes. These were a very fierce, warlike people, who sailed from one place to another, and landed their armies on the coast, burning and destroying everything wherever they came. They were heathens, and did not believe in the Bible, but thought of nothing but battle and slaughter, and making plunder. When they came to countries where the inhabitants were cowardly, they took possession of the land. At other times, they landed with their soldiers, took what spoil they could find, burned the houses, and then got on board, hoisted sails, and away again. They did so much mischief, that people put up prayers to God in the churches to deliver them from the rage of the Danes.

Now, it happened in the time of King Duncan, that a great fleet of these Danes came to Scotland, and landed their men in Fife, and threatened to take possession of that province. So a numerous Scottish army was levied to go to fight with them. The good King Duncan was too old to command his army, and his sons were too young. So he sent out one of his near relations, who was called Macbeth;

he was son of the thane, or governor of Glamis. This Macbeth, who was a brave soldier, put himself at the head of the Scottish army, and marched against the Danes. And he carried with him a relation of his own, called Banquo, who was thane of Lochaber, and was also a very brave man. So there was a great battle fought between the Danes and the Scots, and Macbeth and Banquo defeated the Danes, and drove them back to their ships, leaving a great many of their soldiers both killed and wounded. Then Macbeth and his army marched back to a town in the north of Scotland, called Forres, rejoicing on account of their victory.

Now there lived at this time three old women in the town of Forres, whom people thought were witches; for, in those early times, ignorance and superstition were common among the people, and even great men, like Macbeth, believed that such persons as these witches of Forres could tell what was to come to pass afterwards, and listened to the nonsense which they told them, as if the old women had really been prophetesses. The old women saw that they were respected and feared, so that they were tempted to impose upon people, by pretending to tell what was to happen to them, and they got presents for doing so. So the three old women went and stood by the wayside, on a heath near Forres, and waited till Macbeth came up. And then, stepping before him as he was marching at the head of his soldiers, the first woman said, "All hail, Macbeth—hail to thee, thane of Glamis." The second said, "All hail, Macbeth—hail to thee, thane of Cawdor." Then the third, wishing to pay him a higher compliment than the other two, said, "All hail, Macbeth, that shall be king of Scotland."

Macbeth was very much surprised to hear the witches give him these titles; and while he was wondering what they could mean, Banquo stepped forward, and asked them whether they had nothing to tell about him as well as about Macbeth. And they said that he should not be so great as Macbeth, but that though he himself should never be a king, yet his children should succeed to the throne of Scotland, and be kings for a great number of years. Before Macbeth was recovered from his surprise, there came a messenger to tell him that his father was dead, so that he was become thane of Glamis by inheritance. And there came a second messenger from the king, to thank Macbeth for the great victory over the Danes, and tell him that the thane of Cawdor had rebelled against the king, and that the king had taken his office from him, and had sent to make Macbeth thane of Cawdor as well as Glamis. Thus the two first old women seemed to be right in giving Macbeth these two titles. I dare say that they knew something of the death of his father, and that the government of Cawdor was intended for Macbeth, though he had not heard of it. However, Macbeth, seeing a part of their words come to be true, began to think how he was to bring the rest to pass, and make himself king. And Macbeth had a wife, who was a very ambitious wicked woman, and when she found out that her husband thought of raising up himself to be king of Scotland, she encouraged him by all means in her power, and persuaded him that the only way to get possession of the crown was to kill the good old king, Duncan.

Macbeth was very unwilling to commit so great a crime, for he knew what a good king Duncan had been, and he recollected that he was his relation, and had been always very kind to him. But his wife continued telling him what a foolish cowardly thing it was in him not to take the opportunity of making himself king, when it was in his power to gain what the witches promised him. So the wicked advice of his wife, and the prophecy of these wretched old women, at last brought Macbeth to think of murdering his king and his friend. The way in which he accomplished his crime, made it still more abominable. Macbeth invited Duncan to come to visit him, at a great castle near Inverness; and the good king, who had no suspicions of his kinsman, accepted the invitation very willingly. Macbeth and his lady received the king and all his retinue with much appearance of joy, and made a great feast, as a subject would do to make his king welcome. About the middle of the night, the king desired to go to his apartment, and Macbeth conducted him to a fine room, which had been prepared for him.

Now, it was the custom, in those barbarous times, that wherever the king slept, two armed men slept in the same chamber, in order to defend his person, in case he should be attacked by any one during the night. But the wicked Lady Macbeth had made these two watchmen drink a great deal of wine, and had besides put some drugs into the liquor, so that when they went to the royal apartment they both fell asleep, and slept so soundly, that nothing could awaken them. Then the cruel Macbeth came into the bedroom of King Duncan about two in the morning. It was a terrible stormy night; but the noise of the wind and of the thunder could not awaken the king, as he was old, and weary with his journey; neither could it awaken the two sentinels. They all slept soundly. So Macbeth having come into the room, and stepped gently over the floor, he took the two dirks which belonged to the sentinels, and stabbed poor old King Duncan to the heart, and that so effectually, that he died without giving even a groan. Then Macbeth put the bloody daggers into the hands of the sentinels, and daubed their faces over with blood, that it might appear as if they had committed the murder. Macbeth was frightened at what he had done, but his wife made him wash his hands and go to bed.

Early in the morning, the nobles and gentlemen who attended on the king, assembled in the great hall of the castle, and there they began to talk of what a dreadful storm it had been the night before. But Macbeth could scarcely understand what they said, for he was thinking on something much worse and more frightful than the storm, and was wondering what would be said when they heard of the murder. They waited for some time, but finding that the king did not come from his apartment, one of the noblemen went to see whether he was well or not. But when he came into the room, he found poor King Duncan lying stiff, and cold, and bloody, and the two sentinels, with their dirks or daggers covered with blood, both fast asleep. As soon as the Scottish nobles saw this terrible sight, they were greatly astonished and enraged; and Macbeth made believe as if he were more enraged than any of them, and, drawing his sword, before any one could prevent him, he killed the two attendants who were in the sleeping apartment of the king, pretending to think that they had been guilty of murdering King Duncan.

When Malcolm and Donaldbane, the two sons of the good king, saw their father slain in this strange manner within Macbeth's castle, they became afraid that they might be put to death likewise, and fled away out of Scotland; for, notwithstanding all the excuses which he could make, they still believed that Macbeth had killed their father. Donaldbane fled into some distant island, but Malcolm, the eldest son of Duncan, went to the court of England, where he begged for assistance from the English king, to place him on the throne of Scotland as his father's successor. In the meantime, Macbeth took possession of the kingdom of Scotland, and thus all his wicked wishes seemed to be fulfilled. But he was not happy. He began to reflect how wicked he had been in killing his friend and benefactor, and how some other person, as ambitious as he was himself, might do the same thing to him. He remembered, too, that the old women had said, that the children of Banquo should succeed to the throne after his death, and therefore he concluded that Banquo might be tempted to conspire against him, as he had himself done against King Duncan. The wicked always think that other people are as bad as themselves.

In order to prevent this supposed danger, he hired ruffians to watch in a wood, where Banquo and his son Fleance sometimes used to walk in the evening, with instructions to attack them, and kill both father and son. The villains did as they were ordered by Macbeth; but while they were killing Banquo, the boy Fleance made his escape from their wicked hands, and fled into Wales. And it is said, that long afterwards, his children came to possess the Scottish crown. Macbeth was not the more happy that he had slain his brave friend and cousin Banquo. He knew that men began to suspect the wicked deeds which he had done, and he was constantly afraid that some one would put him to death as he had done his old sovereign, or that Malcolm would obtain Edward the king of England's assistance, and come to make war against him, and take from him the Scottish kingdom. So, in this great perplexity of mind, he thought that he would go to the old women, whose words had first put into his mind the desire of becoming a king. It is to be supposed, that he offered them presents, and that they were cunning enough to study how to give him some answer, which should make him continue in the belief that they could prophesy what was to happen in future times. So they answered to him that he should not be conquered, or lose the crown of Scotland, until a great forest, called Birnam Wood, should come to attack him in a strong castle situated on a high hill called Dunsinane.

Now, the hill of Dunsinane is upon the one side of a valley, and the forest of Birnam is upon the other. There are twelve miles distant betwixt them, and besides that, Macbeth thought that it was impossible that the trees could ever come to the assault of the castle. He therefore resolved to fortify his castle on the hill of Dunsinane very strongly, as being a place in which he would always be sure to be safe. For this purpose he caused all his great nobility and thanes to send in stones, and wood, and other things wanted in building, and to drag them with oxen up to the top of the steep hill where he was building the castle. Now, among other nobles who were obliged to send oxen, and horses, and materials, to this laborious work, was one called Macduff, the thane of Fife. Macbeth was afraid of this thane, for he was very powerful, and was accounted both brave and wise; and Macbeth thought that he most probably would join with Prince Malcolm, if ever he should come from England with an army. The king, therefore, had a private hatred against the thane of Fife, which he kept concealed from all men, until he should have some opportunity of putting him to death, as he had done Duncan and Banquo. Macduff, on his part, kept upon his guard, and went to the king's court as seldom as he could, thinking himself never safe unless while in his own castle of Kennoway, which is on the coast of Fife, near to the mouth of the Frith of Forth.

It happened, however, that the king had summoned several

of his nobles, and Macduff, the thane of Fife, amongst others, to attend him at his new castle of Dunsinane; and they were all obliged to come, none dared stay behind. Now, the king was to give the nobles a great entertainment, and preparations were made for it. In the meantime, Macbeth rode out with a few attendants, to see some oxen drag the wood and the stones up the hill, for enlarging and strengthening the castle. So they saw most of the oxen trudging up the hill with great difficulty, for the ascent is very steep, and the burdens were heavy, and the weather was extremely hot. At length Macbeth saw a pair of oxen so tired that they could go no farther up the hill, but fell down under their load. Then the king was very angry, and demanded to know who it was among his thanes that had sent oxen so weak and so unfit for labour, when he had so much work for them to do. Some one replied that the oxen belonged to Macduff, the thane of Fife. "Then," said the king, in great anger, "since the thane of Fife sends such worthless cattle as these to do my labour, I will put his own neck into the yoke, and make him drag the burdens himself."

There was a friend of Macduff who heard these angry expressions of the king, and who hastened to communicate them to the thane of Fife, who was walking in the hall of the king's castle while dinner was preparing. The instant that Macduff heard what the king had said, he knew that he had no time to lose in making his escape; for whenever Macbeth threatened to do mischief to any one, he was sure to keep his word.

So Macduff snatched up from the table a loaf of bread, called for his horses and his servants, and was galloping back to his own province of Fife before Macbeth and the rest of the nobility were returned to the castle. The first question which the king asked was, what had become of Macduff? and being informed that he had fled from Dunsinane, he ordered a body of his guards to attend him, and mounted on horseback himself to pursue the thane, with the purpose of putting him to death. Macduff, in the meantime, fled as fast as horses' feet could carry him; but he was so ill provided with money for his expenses, that when he came to the great ferry over the river Tay, he had nothing to give to the boatmen who took him across, excepting the loaf of bread which he had taken from the king's table. When Macduff got into his province of Fife, he rode on faster than before, towards his own castle of Kennoway, which stands close by the seaside; and when he reached it, the king and his guards were not far behind him. Macduff ordered his wife to shut the gates of the castle, draw up the drawbridge, and on no account to permit the king or any of his soldiers to enter. In the meantime, he went to the small harbour belonging to the castle, and caused a ship which was lying there to be fitted out for sea in all haste, and got on board himself, in order to escape from Macbeth.

In the meantime, Macbeth summoned the lady to surrender the castle, and to deliver up her husband. But Lady Macduff, who was a wise and a brave woman, made many excuses and delays, until she knew her husband was safely on board the ship, and had sailed from the harbour. Then she spoke boldly from the wall of the castle to the king. "Do you see," she said, "yon white sail upon the sea? Yonder goes Macduff to the court of England. You will never see him again, till he comes back with young Prince Malcolm to pull you down from the throne, and to put you to death. You will never be able to put your yoke, as you threatened, on the thane of Fife's neck." Some say Macbeth was so much incensed at this bold answer, that he and his guards attacked the castle and took it, killing the brave lady and all whom they found there. But others say, that the king, seeing that the castle of Kennoway was very strong, and that Macduff had escaped from him, departed back to Dunsinane without attempting to take Macduff's castle of Kennoway. The ruins of the castle are still to be seen. There reigned at that time in England a very good king, called Edward the Confessor. I told you Prince Malcolm, the son of Duncan, was at his court, soliciting assistance to recover the Scottish throne. The arrival of Macduff greatly aided the success of the request the prince had made; for the English king knew Macduff was a brave and a wise man. As he assured

Edward that the Scots were tired of the cruel Macbeth, and would join Prince Malcolm if he were to enter Scotland at the head of an army, the king ordered the Earl of Northumberland to enter Scotland with an army, and assist Prince Malcolm in the recovery of his father's crown.

Then it happened as Macduff had said, for the Scottish nobles would not fight for Macbeth, but joined Prince Malcolm and Macduff against him; so that at length he shut himself up in his castle of Dunsinane where he thought himself safe, according to the old women's prophecy, until Birnam Wood should come against him. At this time Malcolm and Macduff were come as far as Birnam Wood, and lay encamped there with their army. The next morning, when they were to march across the broad valley to attack the castle of Dunsinane, Macduff advised that every soldier should cut down a bough of a tree and carry it in his hand, that the enemy might not be able to see how many men were coming against them. Now the sentinel who stood on Macbeth's castle-wall, when he saw all these branches which the soldiers of Prince Malcolm carried, ran to the king, and informed him that the wood of Birnam was moving towards the castle of Dunsinane. The king at first called him a liar, and threatened to put him to death; but when he looked from the walls himself, and saw the appearance of a forest approaching from Birnam, he knew the hour of his destruction was come. His followers, too, began to be disheartened, and to fly from the castle, seeing their master had lost all hopes. Macbeth, however, recollected his own bravery, and sallied out desperately at the head of the few followers who remained faithful to him. He was killed after a furious resistance, fighting hand to hand with Macduff in the thick of the battle. Prince Malcolm mounted the throne of Scotland, and reigned long and prosperously.—WALTER SCOTT, "*Tales of a Grandfather.*"

MURAD THE UNLUCKY.

It is well known that the grand seignior amuses himself by going at night, in disguise, through the streets of Constantinople, as the caliph, Haroun Al Raschid, used formerly to do in Bagdad.

One moonlight night, accompanied by his grand vizier, he traversed several of the principal streets of the city, without seeing anything remarkable. At length, as they were passing a rope-maker's, the sultan recollected the Arabian story of Cogia-Hassan, the rope-maker, and his two friends, Saad and Saadi, who differed so much in their opinion concerning the influence of fortune over human affairs.

"What is your opinion on this subject?" said the grand seignior to his vizier.

"I am inclined, please your majesty," replied the vizier, "to think that success in the world depends more upon prudence than upon what is called luck, or fortune."

"And I," said the sultan," am persuaded that fortune does more for men than prudence. Do you not every day hear of persons who are said to be fortunate or unfortunate? How comes it that this opinion should prevail amongst men, if it be not justified by experience?"

"It is not for me to dispute with your majesty," replied the prudent vizier.

"Speak your mind freely; I desire and command it," said the sultan.

"Then I am of opinion," answered the vizier, "that people are often led to believe others fortunate, or unfortunate, merely because they only know the general outline of their histories, and are ignorant of the incidents and events in which they have shown prudence or imprudence. I have heard, for instance, that there are at present in this city two men who are remarkable for their good and bad fortune; one is called *Murad the Unlucky*, and the other *Saladin the Lucky*. Now, I am inclined to think, if we could hear their stories, we should find that one is a prudent and the other an imprudent character."

"Where do these men live?" interrupted the sultan. "I will hear their histories from their own lips before I sleep."

"Murad the Unlucky lives in the next square," said the vizier.

The sultan desired to go thither immediately. Scarcely had they entered the square when they heard the cry of loud lamentations. They followed the sound till they came to a house, of which the door was open, and where there was a man tearing his turban and weeping bitterly. They asked the cause of his distress, and he pointed to the fragments of a china vase which lay on the pavement at his door.

"This seems undoubtedly to be beautiful china," said the sultan, taking up one of the broken pieces; "but can the loss of a china vase be the cause of such violent grief and despair?"

"Ah, gentlemen," said the owner of the vase, suspending his lamentations, and looking at the dress of the pretended merchants, "I see that you are strangers: you do not know how much cause I have for grief and despair! You do not know that you are speaking to Murad the Unlucky! Were you to hear all the unfortunate accidents that have happened to me, from the time I was born till this instant, you would perhaps pity me, and acknowledge I have just cause for despair."

Curiosity was strongly expressed by the sultan; and the hope of obtaining sympathy inclined Murad to gratify it by the recital of his adventures. "Gentlemen," said he, "I scarcely dare invite you into the house of such an unlucky being as I am; but, if you will venture to take a night's lodging under my roof, you shall hear at your leisure the the story of my misfortunes."

The sultan and the vizier excused themselves from spending the night with Murad, saying that they were obliged to proceed to their khan, where they should be expected by their companions; but they begged permission to repose themselves for half an hour in his house, and besought him to relate the history of his life, if it would not renew his grief too much to recollect his misfortunes.

As soon as the pretended merchants were seated, Murad began his story in the following manner:—

"My father was a merchant of this city. The night before I was born, he dreamed that I came into the world with the head of a dog and the tail of a dragon; and that, in haste to conceal my deformity, he rolled me up in a piece of linen, which unluckily proved to be the grand seignior's turban, who, enraged at his insolence in touching his turban, commanded that his head should be struck off.

"My father awaked before he lost his head; but not before he had half lost his wits from the terror of his dream. Being a firm believer in predestination, he was persuaded that I should be the cause of some great evil to him, and he took an aversion to me even before I was born. He considered his dream as a warning sent from above, and consequently determined to avoid the sight of me. He would not stay to see whether I should really be born with the head of a dog and the tail of a dragon, but he set out the next morning on a voyage to Aleppo.

"He was absent for upwards of seven years; and, during that time, my education was totally neglected. One day I inquired from my mother why I had been named Murad the Unlucky? She told me that this name was given to me in consequence of my father's dream; but she added that, perhaps, it might be forgotten, if I proved fortunate in my future life. My nurse, a very old woman, who was present, shook her head, with a look which I never shall forget, and whispered to my mother, loud enough for me to hear, 'Unlucky he was, and is, and ever will be. Those that are born to ill luck cannot help themselves: nor can any but the great prophet, Mahomet himself, do any thing for them. It is a folly for unlucky persons to strive with their fate: it is better to yield to it at once.'

"This speech made a terrible impression upon me, young as I then was; and every accident that happened to me afterwards confirmed my belief in my nurse's prognostic. I was in my eighth year when my father returned from abroad. The year after he came home my brother Saladin was born, who was named Saladin the Lucky, because the day he was born a vessel freighted with rich merchandise for my father arrived safely in port.

"I will not weary you with a relation of all the little instances of good fortune by which my brother Saladin was distinguished, even during his childhood. As he grew up, his success in every thing he undertook was as remarkable as my ill luck in all that I attempted. From the time the rich vessel arrived, we lived in splendour; and the supposed prosperous state of my father's affairs was of course attributed to the influence of my brother Saladin's happy destiny.

"When Saladin was about twenty, my father was taken dangerously ill; and, as he felt that he should not recover, he sent for my brother to the side of his bed, and, to his great susprise, informed him that the magnificence in which we had lived had exhausted all his wealth, that his affairs were in the greatest disorder; for, having trusted to the hope of continual success, he had embarked in projects beyond his powers.

"The sequel was, he had nothing remaining to leave to his children but two large china vases, remarkable for their beauty, but still more valuable on account of certain verses inscribed upon them in an unknown character, which were supposed to operate as a talisman or charm in favour of their possessors.

"Both these vases my father bequeathed to my brother Saladin; declaring he could not venture to leave either of them to me, because I was so unlucky that I should inevitably break it. After his death, however, my brother Saladin, who was blessed with a generous temper, gave me my choice of the two vases; and endeavoured to raise my spirits, by repeating frequently that he had no faith either in good fortune or ill fortune.

"I could not be of his opinion; though I felt and acknowledged his kindness in trying to persuade me out of my settled melancholy. I knew it was in vain for me to exert myself, because I was sure that, do what I would, I should still be Murad the Unlucky. My brother, on the contrary, was nowise cast down, even by the poverty in which my father left us: he said he was sure he should find some means of maintaining himself, and so he did.

"On examining our china vases, he found in them a powder of a bright scarlet colour; and it occurred to him that it would make a fine dye. He tried it; and, after some trouble, it succeeded to admiration.

"During my father's lifetime, my mother had been supplied with rich dresses by one of the merchants who were employed by the ladies of the grand seignior's seraglio. My brother had done this merchant some trifling favours, and, upon application to him, he readily engaged to recommend the new scarlet dye. Indeed it was so beautiful that, the moment it was seen, it was preferred to every other colour. Saladin's shop was soon crowded with customers; and his winning manners and pleasant conversation were almost as advantageous to him as his scarlet dye. On the contrary, I observed that the first glance of my melancholy countenance was sufficient to disgust every one who saw me. I perceived this plainly; and it only confirmed me the more in my belief in my own evil destiny.

"It happened one day that a lady, richly apparelled and attended by two female slaves, came to my brother's house to make some purchases. He was out, and I alone was left to attend the shop. After she had looked over some goods, she chanced to see my china vase, which was in the room. She took a prodigious fancy to it, and offered me any price, if I would part with it: but this I declined doing, because I believed that I should draw down upon my head some dreadful calamity, if I voluntarily relinquished the talisman. Irritated by my refusal, the lady, according to the custom of her sex, became more resolute in her purpose; but neither entreaties nor money could change my determination. Provoked beyond measure at my obstinacy, as she called it, she left the house.

"On my brother's return, I related to him what had happened, and expected that he would have praised me for my prudence: but, on the contrary, he blamed me for the superstitious value I set upon the verses of my vase; and observed that it would be the height of folly to lose a certain means of advancing my fortune, for the uncertain hope of magical protection. I could not bring myself to be of his opinion; I had not the courage to follow the advice he gave. The next day the lady returned, and my brother sold his vase to her for ten thousand pieces of gold. This money he laid out in the most advantageous manner, by purchasing a new stock of merchandise.

"The lady, who bought my brother Saladin's vase, was the favourite of the sultana, and all-powerful in the seraglio. Her dislike to me, in consequence of my opposition to her wishes, was so violent, that she refused to return to my brother's house while I remained there. He was unwilling to part with me; but I could not bear to be the ruin of so good a brother. Without telling him my design, I left his house, careless of what should become of me. Hunger, however, soon compelled me to think of some immediate mode of obtaining relief. I sat down upon a stone, before the door of a baker's shop: the smell of hot bread tempted me in, and with a feeble voice I demanded charity.

"The master baker gave me as much bread as I could eat, upon condition that I should change dresses with him, and carry the rolls for him through the city this day. To this I readily consented; but I had soon reason to repent of my compliance. Indeed, if my ill luck had not, as usual, deprived me at the critical moment of memory and judgment, I should never have complied with the baker's treacherous proposal. For some time before, the people of Constantinople had been much dissatisfied with the weight and quality of the bread furnished by the bakers. This species of discontent has often been the sure forerunner of an insurrection; and in these disturbances the master bakers frequently lose their lives. All these circumstances I knew; but they did not occur to my memory when they might have been useful.

"I changed dresses with the baker; but scarcely had I proceeded through the adjoining street with my rolls, before the mob began to gather round me with reproaches and execrations. The crowd pursued me even to the gates of the grand seignior's palace; and the grand vizier, alarmed at their violence, sent out an order to have my head struck off: the usual remedy, in such cases, being to strike off the baker's head.

"I now fell upon my knees, and protested I was not the baker for whom they took me; that I had no connexion with him; and that I had never furnished the people of Constantinople with bread that was not weight. I declared I had merely changed clothes with a master baker, for this day; and that I should not have done so, but for the evil destiny which governs all my actions. Some of the mob exclaimed that I deserved to lose my head for my folly; but others took pity on me, and whilst the officer, who was sent to execute the vizier's order, turned to speak to some of the noisy rioters, those who were touched by my misfortune opened a passage for me through the crowd, and, thus favoured, I effected my escape.

"I quitted Constantinople. My vase I had left in the care of my brother. At some miles' distance from the city, I overtook a party of soldiers. I joined them; and learning that they were going to embark with the rest of the grand seignior's army for Egypt, I resolved to accompany them. If it be, thought I, the will of Mahomet that I should perish, the sooner I meet my fate the better. The despondency into which I was sunk was attended by so great a degree of indolence, that I scarcely would take the necessary means to preserve my existence. During our passage to Egypt I sat all day long upon the deck of the vessel, smoking my pipe; and I am convinced that, if a storm had risen, as I expected, I should not have taken my pipe from my mouth: nor should I have handled a rope, to save myself from destruction.

"We landed, however, safely, contrary to my melancholy forebodings. By a trifling accident, not worth relating, I was detained longer than any of my companions in the vessel when we disembarked; and I did not arrive at the camp at El Arish till late at night. It was moonlight, and I could see the whole scene distinctly. There was a vast number of small tents scattered over a desert of white sand; a few date trees were visible at a distance; all was gloomy, and all was still; no sound was to be heard but that of the camels, feeding near the tents; and, as I walked on, I met with no human creature.

"My pipe was now out, and I quickened my pace a little towards a fire, which I saw near one of the tents. As I proceeded, my eye was caught by something sparkling in the sand: it was a ring. I picked it up, and put it on my finger, resolving to give it to the public crier the next morning, who might find out its rightful owner; but, by ill luck, I put it on my little finger, for which it was much too large, and as I hastened towards the fire to light my pipe, I dropped the ring. I stooped to search for it amongst the provender on which a mule was feeding; and the cruel animal gave me so violent a kick on the head, that I could not help roaring aloud.

"My cries awakened those who slept in the tent, near which the mule was feeding. Provoked at being disturbed, the soldiers were ready enough to think ill of me, and they took it for granted that I was a thief, who had stolen the ring I pretended to have just found. The ring was taken from me by force; and the next morning I was bastinadoed for having found it: the officer persisting in the belief that stripes would make me confess where I had concealed certain other articles of value which had lately been missed in the camp. All this was the consequence of my being in a hurry to light my pipe, and of my having put the ring on a finger that was too little for it.

"When I was able to walk again, after my wounds were healed, I went into one of the tents distinguished by a red flag, having been told that these were coffee-houses. Whilst I was drinking coffee, I heard a stranger near me complaining that he had not been able to recover a valuable ring he had lost, although he had caused his loss to be published for three days by the public crier, offering a reward of two hundred sequins to whomever should restore it. I guessed that this was the very ring which I had unfortunately found. I addressed myself to the stranger, and promised to point out to him the person who had forced it from me. The stranger recovered his ring, and being convinced that I had acted honestly, he made me a present of two hundred sequins, as some amends for the punishment which I had unjustly suffered on his account.

"Now you would imagine that this purse of gold was advantageous to me: far the contrary; it was the cause of new misfortunes.

"One night, when I thought that the soldiers who were in the same tent with me were all fast asleep, I indulged myself in the pleasure of counting my treasure. The next day, I was invited by my companions to drink sherbet with them. What they mixed with the sherbet which I drank, I know not: but I could not resist the drowsiness it brought on. I fell into a profound slumber; and, when I awoke, I found myself lying under a date tree, at some distance from the camp.

"The first thing I thought of, when I came to my recollection, was my purse of sequins. The purse I found still safe in my girdle; but, on opening it, I perceived that it was filled with pebbles, and not a single sequin was left. I had no doubt that I had been robbed by the soldiers with whom I had drunk sherbet; and I am certain that some of them must have been awake the night I counted my money: otherwise, as I had never trusted the secret of my riches to any one, they could not have suspected me of possessing any property; for, ever since I kept company with them, I had appeared to be in great indigence.

"I applied in vain to the superior officers for redress: the soldiers protested they were innocent; no positive proof appeared against them, and I gained nothing by my complaint but ridicule and ill-will. I called myself, in the first transport of my grief, by that name which, since my arrival in Egypt, I had avoided to pronounce: I called myself Murad the Unlucky! The name and the story ran through the camp; and I was accosted afterwards, very frequently, by this appellation. Some indeed varied their wit, by calling me Murad with the purse of pebbles.

"All that I had yet suffered is nothing compared to my succeeding misfortunes.

"It was the custom at this time, in the Turkish camp, for the soldiers to amuse themselves with firing at a mark.

The superior officers remonstrated against this dangerous practice, but ineffectually. Sometimes a party of soldiers would stop firing for a few minutes after a message was brought them from their commanders, and then they would begin again in defiance of all orders. Such was the want of discipline in our army, that this disobedience went unpunished. In the meantime, the frequency of the danger made most men totally regardless of it. I have seen tents pierced with bullets, in which parties were quietly seated, smoking their pipes, whilst those without were preparing to take fresh aim at the red flag on the top.

"This apathy proceeded, in some, from unconquerable indolence of body; in others, from the intoxication produced by the fumes of tobacco and of opium; but in most of my brother Turks, it arose from the confidence the belief in predestination inspired. When a bullet killed one of their companions, they only observed, scarcely taking the pipes from their mouths, 'Our hour is not yet come: it is not the will of Mahomet that we should fall.'

"I own that this rash security appeared to me at first surprising, but it soon ceased to strike me with wonder. I became almost as careless as my companions from following the same course of reasoning. It is not, thought I, in the power of human prudence to avert the stroke of destiny. I shall perhaps die to-morrow; let me therefore enjoy to-day.

"I now made it my study, every day, to procure as much amusement as possible. My poverty, as you will imagine, restricted me from indulgence and excess; but I soon found means to spend what did not actually belong to me. There were certain Jews, who were followers of the camp, and who, calculating on the probability of victory for our troops, advanced money to the soldiers; for which they engaged to pay these usurers exorbitant interest. The Jew to whom I applied traded with me also upon the belief that my brother Saladin, with whose character and circumstances he was acquainted, would pay my debts, if I should fall. With the money I raised from the Jew I continually bought coffee and opium, of which I grew immoderately fond. In the delirium it created, I forgot all my misfortunes, all fear of the future.

"One day, when I had raised my spirits by an unusual quantity of opium, I was strolling through the camp, sometimes singing, sometimes dancing like a madman, and repeating that I was not now Murad the Unlucky. Whilst these words were on my lips, a friendly spectator, who was in possession of his sober senses, caught me by the arm, and attempted to drag me from the place where I was exposing myself. 'Do you not see,' said he, 'those soldiers, who are firing at a mark? I saw one of them, just now, deliberately taking aim at your turban; and, observe, he is now reloading his piece.' I struggled with my adviser, repeating, 'I am not the wretch you take me for; I am not Murad the Unlucky.' He fled from the danger himself: I remained, and in a few seconds afterwards a ball reached me, and I fell senseless on the sand.

"The ball was cut out of my body by an awkward surgeon, who gave me ten times more pain than was necessary. He was particularly hurried at this time, because the army had just received orders to march in a few hours, and all was confusion in the camp. My wound was exceedingly painful, and the fear of being left behind with those who were deemed incurable added to my torments.

"During that day, when my fever was at the height, and when my orders were to keep my bed, contrary to my natural habits of indolence, I rose a hundred times and went out of my tent, in the very heat of the day, to satisfy my curiosity as to the number of the tents which had not been struck, and of the soldiers who had not yet marched. The orders to march were tardily obeyed, and many hours escaped before our encampment was raised. Had I submitted to my surgeon's orders, I might have been in a state to accompany the most dilatory of the stragglers; I could have borne, perhaps, the slow motion of a litter on which some of the sick were transported; but in the evening, when the surgeon came to dress my wounds, he found me in such a situation that it was scarcely possible to remove me.

"He desired a party of soldiers, who were left to bring

up the rear, to call for me the next morning. They did so; but they wanted to put me upon the mule which I recollected, by a white stroke on its back, to be the cursed animal that had kicked me whilst I was looking for the ring. I could not be prevailed upon to go upon this unlucky animal. I tried to persuade the soldiers to carry me, and they took me a little way; but, soon growing weary of their burden, they laid me down upon the sand, pretending that they were going to fill a skin with water at a spring they had discovered, and bade me lie still and wait for their return.

"I waited and waited, longing for the water to moisten my parched lips; but no water came—no soldiers returned, and there I lay for several hours, expecting every moment to breathe my last. I made no effort to move, for I was now convinced my hour was come; and that it was the will of Mahomet that I should perish in this miserable manner, and lie unburied like a dog—a death, thought I, worthy of Murad the Unlucky.

"My forebodings were not this time just; a detachment of English soldiers passed near the place where I lay; my groans were heard by them, and they humanely came to my assistance. They carried me with them, dressed my wound, and treated me with the utmost tenderness.

"Under their care I recovered, but scarcely had I regained my strength before I fell into new disasters. It was hot weather, and my thirst was excessive. I went out, with a party, in hopes of finding a spring of water. The English soldiers began to dig for a well, in a place pointed out to them by one of their men of science. I was not inclined to such hard labour, but preferred sauntering on in search of a spring. I saw at a distance something that looked like a pool of water; and I pointed it out to my companions. Their man of science warned me, by his interpreter, not to trust to this deceitful appearance; for that such were common in this country, and that when I came close to the spot, I should find no water there. He added that it was a greater distance than I imagined; and that I should in all probability be lost in the desert, if I attempted to follow this phantom.

"I was so unfortunate as not to attend to his advice: I set out in pursuit of this accursed delusion, which assuredly was the work of evil spirits, who clouded my reason, and allured me into their dominion. I went on, hour after hour, in expectation continually of reaching the object of my wishes; but it fled faster than I pursued, and I discovered at last that the Englishman, who had doubtless gained his information from the people of the country, was right, and that the shining appearance which I had taken for water was a mere deception.

"I was now exhausted with fatigue: I looked back in vain after the companions I had left; I could see neither men, animals, nor any trace of vegetation in the sandy desert. I had no resource but, weary as I was, to measure back my footsteps which were imprinted in the sand.

"I slowly and sorrowfully traced them as my guides in this unknown land. Instead of yielding to my indolent inclinations, I ought however to have made the best of my way back before the evening breeze sprung up. I felt the breeze rising, and unconscious of my danger, I rejoiced, and opened my bosom to meet it; but what was my dismay when I saw that the wind swept before it all trace of my footsteps in the sand. I knew not which way to proceed; I was struck with despair, tore my garments, threw off my turban, and cried aloud; but neither human voice nor echo answered me. The silence was dreadful. I had tasted no food for many hours, and I now became sick and faint. I recollected that I put a supply of opium into the folds of my turban; but, alas! when I took my turban up I found that the opium had fallen out. I searched for it in vain on the sand where I had thrown the turban.

"I stretched myself out upon the ground, and yielded without further struggle to my evil destiny. What I suffered from thirst, hunger, and heat, cannot be described! At last I fell into a sort of trance, during which images of various kinds seemed to flit before my eyes. How long I remained in this state I know not; but I remember that I was brought to my senses by a loud shout, which came from persons belonging to a caravan returning from Mecca. This was a shout of joy for their safe arrival at a certain spring, well known to them in this part of the desert.

"The spring was not a hundred yards from the spot where I lay; yet, such had been the fate of Murad the Unlucky, that he missed the reality, whilst he had been hours in pursuit of the phantom. Feeble and spiritless as I was, I sent forth as loud a cry as I could, in hopes of obtaining assistance, and I endeavoured to crawl to the place from which the voices appeared to come. The caravan rested for a considerable time, whilst the slaves filled the skins with water, and whilst the camels took in their supply. I worked myself on towards them; yet, notwithstanding my efforts, I was persuaded that, according to my usual ill fortune, I should never be able to make them hear my voice. I saw them mount their camels! I took off my turban, unrolled it, and waved it in the air. My signal was seen! The caravan came towards me!

"I had scarcely strength to speak; a slave gave me some water, and, after I had drunk, I explained to them who I was, and how I came into this situation.

"Whilst I was speaking, one of the travellers observed the purse which hung to my girdle: it was the same the merchant, for whom I recovered the ring, had given to me; I had carefully preserved it, because the initials of my benefactor's name, and a passage from the Koran, were worked upon it. When he gave it to me, he said that, perhaps, we should meet again, in some other part of the world, and he should recognize me by this token. The person who now took notice of the purse was his brother; and, when I related to him how I had obtained it, he had the goodness to take me under his protection. He was a merchant, who was now going with the caravan to Grand Cairo; he offered to take me with him, and I willingly accepted the proposal, promising to serve him as faithfully as any of his slaves. The caravan proceeded, and I was carried with it.—Miss Edgeworth.

THE MOOR'S LEGACY.

Just within the fortress of the Alhambra, in front of the royal palace, is a broad open esplanade called the Place or Square of the Cisterns (la Plaza de los Algibes), so called from being undermined by reservoirs of water hidden from sight, and which have existed from the time of the Moors. At one corner of this esplanade is a Moorish well cut through the living rock to a great depth, the water of which is cold as ice and clear as crystal. The wells made by the Moors are always in repute; for it is well known what pains they took to penetrate to the purest and sweetest springs and fountains. The one of which we now speak is famous throughout Granada, insomuch that the water-carriers, some bearing great water jars on their shoulders, others driving asses before them, laden with earthen vessels, are ascending and descending the steep woody avenues of the Alhambra, from early dawn until a late hour of the night.

Fountains and wells, ever since the scriptural days, have been noted gossiping places in hot climates; and, at the well in question, there is a kind of perpetual club kept up during the livelong day, by the invalids, old women, and other curious do-nothing folk of the fortress, who sit here on the stone benches, under an awning spread over the well to shelter the toll-gatherer from the sun, and dawdle over the gossip of the fortress, and question every water-carrier that arrives about the news of the city, and make long comments on every thing they hear and see. Not an hour of the day but loitering housewives and idle maid-servants may be seen, lingering with pitcher on head or in hand, to hear the last of the endless tattle of these worthies.

Among the water-carriers who once resorted to this well, there was a sturdy, strong-backed, bandy-legged, little fellow, named Pedro Gil, but called Peregil for shortness. Being a water-carrier, he was a Gallego, or native of Galicia, of course. Nature seems to have formed races of men, as she has of animals, for different kinds of drudgery. In France the shoeblacks are all Savoyards, the porters of hotels all Swiss—and, in the days of hoops and hair-powder in England, no man could give the regular swing to a sedan-chair but a bog-trotting Irishman. So in Spain, the carriers of water and bearers of burdens are all sturdy little natives of Gallicia. No man says, "Get me a porter,"—but, "Call a Gallego."

To return from this disgression, Peregil the Gallego had begun business with merely a great earthen jar which he carried upon his shoulder. By degrees he rose in the world, and was enabled to purchase an assistant of a correspondent class of animals,—being a stout, shaggy-haired donkey.. On each side of this his long-eared aid-de-camp, in a kind of pannier, were slung his water-jars, covered with fig leaves to protect them from the sun. There was not a more industrious water-carrier in all Granada, nor one more merry withal. The streets rang with his cheerful voice as he trudged after his donkey, singing forth the usual summer note that resounds through the Spanish towns: "*Quien quiere agua—agua mas frai que la nieve?*" "Who wants water—water colder than snow? Who wants water from the well of the Alhambra, cold as ice and clear as crystal?" When he served a customer with a sparkling glass, it was always with a pleasant word that caused a smile; and if, perchance, it was a comely dame or dimpling damsel, it was always with a sly leer and a compliment to her beauty that was irresistible. Thus Peregil the Gallego was noted throughout all Granada for being one of the civilest, pleasantest, and happiest of mortals. Yet it is not he who sings loudest and jokes most that has the lightest heart. Under all this air of merriment, honest Peregil had his cares and troubles. He had a large family of ragged children to support, who were hungry and clamorous as a nest of young swallows, and beset him with their out-cries for food whenever he came home of an evening. He had a helpmate, too, who was any thing but a help to him. She had been a village beauty before marriage,—noted for her skill at dancing the bolero and rattling the castanets; and she still retained her early propensities, spending the hard earnings of honest Peregil in frippery, and laying the very donkey under requisition for junketing parties into the country on Sundays and Saints'-days, and those innumerable holidays which are rather more numerous in Spain than the days of the week. With all this she was a little of a slattern, something more of a lie-a-bed, and above all a gossip of the first water—neglecting house, household, and every thing else, to loiter slip-shod in the houses of her gossip neighbours.

He, however, who tempers the wind to the shorn lamb, accommodates the yoke of matrimony to the submissive neck. Peregil bore all the heavy dispensations of wife and children with as meek a spirit as his donkey bore the water-jars; and, however he might shake his ears in private, never ventured to question the household virtues of his slattern spouse.

He loved his children, too, even as an owl loves its owlets, seeing in them his own image multiplied and perpetuated; for they were a sturdy, long-backed, bandy-legged little brood. The great pleasure of honest Peregil was, whenever he could afford himself a scanty holiday, and had a handful of maravedis to spare, to take the whole litter forth with him,—some in his arms, some tugging at his skirts, and some trudging at his heels,—and to treat them to a gambol among the orchards of the Vega, whilst his wife was dancing with her holiday friends in the Angosturas of the Darro.

It was a late hour one summer night, and most of the water-carriers had desisted from their toils. The day had been uncommonly sultry; the night was one of those delicious moonlights which tempt the inhabitants of those southern climes to indemnify themselves for the heat and inaction of the day, by lingering in the open air and enjoying its tempered sweetness until after midnight. Customers for water were therefore still abroad. Peregil, like a considerate pains-taking little father, thought of his hungry children. "One more journey to the well," said he to himself, "to earn a Sunday's puchero for the little ones." So saying, he trudged manfully up the steep avenue of the Alhambra,—singing as he went, and now and then bestowing a hearty thwack with a cudgel on the flanks of his donkey, either by way of cadence to the song, or refreshment to the animal; for dry blows serve in lieu of provender, in Spain, for all beasts of burthen.

When arrived at the well, he found it deserted by every one except a solitary stranger in Moorish garb, seated on the stone bench in the moonlight. Peregil paused at first, and regarded him with surprise, not unmixed with awe, but the Moor feebly beckoned him to approach. "I am faint and ill," said he, "aid me to return to the city, and I will pay thee double what thou couldst gain by thy jars of water.

The honest heart of the little water-carrier was touched with compassion at the appeal of the stranger. "God forbid," said he, "that I should ask fee or reward for doing a common act of humanity. He accordingly helped the Moor on his donkey, and set off slowly for Granada: the poor Moslem being so weak, that it was necessary to hold him on the animal to keep him from falling to the earth.

When they entered the city, the water-carrier demanded whither he should conduct him. "Alas!" said the Moor faintly, "I have neither home nor habitation; I am a stranger in the land. Suffer me to lay my head this night beneath thy roof, and thou shalt be amply repaid."

Honest Peregil thus saw himself unexpectedly saddled with an infidel guest, but he was too humane to refuse a night's shelter to a fellow-being in so forlorn a plight; so he conducted the Moor to his dwelling. The children, who had sallied forth open-mouthed as usual, on hearing the tramp of the donkey, ran back with affright when they beheld the turbaned stranger, and hid themselves behind their mother. The latter stepped forth intrepidly, like a ruffling hen before her brood when a vagrant dog approaches.

"What infidel companion," cried she, "is this you have brought home at this late hour, to draw upon us the eyes of the Inquisition?"

"Be quiet, wife," replied the Gallego, "here is a poor sick stranger, without friend or home; wouldst thou turn him forth to perish in the streets?"

The wife would still have remonstrated; for, although she lived in a hovel, she was a furious stickler for the credit of her house; the little water-carrier, however, for once was stiff-necked, and refused to bend beneath the yoke. He assisted the poor Moslem to alight, and spread a mat and a sheep-skin for him on the ground in the coolest part of the house, being the only kind of bed that his poverty afforded.

In a little while the Moor was seized with violent convulsions, which defied all the ministering skill of the simple water-carrier. The eye of the poor patient acknowledged his kindness. During an interval of his fits, he called him to his side, and addressing him in a low voice, "My end," said he, "I fear, is at hand. If I die, I bequeath you this box, as a reward for your charity." So saying, he opened his albornoz, or cloak, and showed a small box of sandal-wood, strapped round his body. "God grant, my friend," replied the worthy little Gallego, "that you may live many years to enjoy your treasure, whatever it may be." The Moor shook his head; he laid his hand upon the box, and would have said something more concerning it, but his convulsions returned with increased violence, and in a little while he expired.

The water-carrier's wife was now as one distracted. "This comes," said she, "of your foolish good-nature, always running into scrapes to oblige others. What will become of us when this corpse is found in our house? We shall be sent to prison as murderers; and if we escape with our lives, shall be ruined by notaries and alguazils."

Poor Peregil was in equal tribulation, and almost repented himself of having done a good deed. At length a thought struck him. "It is not yet day," said he, "I can convey the dead body out of the city, and bury it in the sands on the banks of the Xenil. No one saw the Moor enter our dwelling, and no one will know any thing of his death."

So said, so done. The wife aided him; they rolled the body of the unfortunate Moslem in the mat on which he had expired; laid it across the ass, and Peregil set out with it for the banks of the river.

As ill-luck would have it, there lived opposite to the

water-carrier a barber named Pedrillo Pedrugo, one of the most prying, tattling, and mischief-making of his gossip tribe. He was a weasel-faced, spider-legged varlet, supple and insinuating; the famous barber of Seville could not surpass him for his universal knowledge of the affairs of others, and he had no more power of retention than a sieve. It was said that he slept but with one eye at a time, and kept one ear uncovered, so that, even in his sleep, he might see and hear all that was going on. Certain it is he was a sort of scandalous chronicle for the quid-nuncs of Granada, and had more customers than all the rest of his fraternity.

The meddlesome barber heard Peregil arrive at an unusual hour at night, and the exclamations of his wife and children. His head was instantly popped out of a little window which served him as a look-out, and he saw his neighbour assist a man in Moorish garb into his dwelling. This was so strange an occurrence, that Pedrillo Pedrugo slept not a wink that night. Every five minutes he was at his loop-hole watching the lights that gleamed through the chinks of his neighbour's door, and before daylight he beheld Peregil sally forth with his donkey unusually laden.

The inquisitive barber was in a fidget; he slipped on his clothes, and, stealing forth silently, followed the water-carrier at a distance, until he saw him dig a hole in the sandy bank of the Xenil, and bury something that had the appearance of a dead body.

The barber hied him home, and fidgetted about his shop, setting every thing upside down until sunrise. He then took a basin under his arm, and sallied forth to the house of his daily customer the alcaid.

The alcaid was just risen. Pedrillo Pedrugo seated him in a chair, threw a napkin round his neck, put a basin of hot water under his chin, and began to mollify his beard with his fingers.

"Strange doings!" said Pedrugo, who played barber and newsmonger at the same time—"Strange doings! Robbery, and murder, and burial, all in one night!"

"Hey!—how! what is that you say?" cried the alcaid.

"I say," replied the barber, rubbing a piece of soap over

the nose and mouth of the dignitary, for a Spanish barber disdains to employ a brush—"I say that Peregil the Gallego has robbed and murdered a Moorish Mussulman, and buried him this blessed night: *Maldita sea la noche*—accursed be the night for the same!"

"But how do you know all this?" demanded the alcaid.

"Be patient, Senor, and you shall hear all about it," replied Pedrillo, taking him by the nose and sliding a razor over his cheek. He then recounted all that he had seen, going through both operations at the same time, shaving his beard, washing his chin, and wiping him dry with a dirty napkin, while he was robbing, murdering, and burying the Moslem.

Now it so happened that this alcaid was one of the most overbearing, and, at the same time, most griping and corrupt curmudgeons in all Granada. It could not be denied, however, that he set a high value upon justice, for he sold it at its weight in gold. He presumed the case in point to be one of murder and robbery; doubtless there must be rich spoil; how was it to be secured into the legitimate hands of the law? for as to merely entrapping the delinquent—that would be feeding the gallows; but entrapping the booty—that would be enriching the judge, and such, according to his creed, was the great end of justice. So thinking, he summoned to his presence his trustiest alguazil—a gaunt, hungry-looking varlet, clad according to the custom of his order in the ancient Spanish garb—a broad black beaver turned up at the sides, a quaint ruff, a small black cloak dangling from his shoulders, rusty black under-clothes that set off his spare wiry frame, while in his hand he bore a slender white wand, the dreaded insignia of his office. Such was the legal bloodhound of the ancient Spanish breed, that he put upon the traces of the unlucky water-carrier; and such was his speed and certainty, that he was upon the haunches of Peregil before he had returned to his dwelling, and brought both him and his donkey before the dispenser of justice.

The alcaid bent upon him one of his most terrific frowns. "Hark ye, culprit!" roared he in a voice that made the knees of the little Gallego smite together—"hark ye, culprit! there is no need of denying thy guilt; every thing is known to me. A gallows is the proper reward for the crime thou hast committed; but I am merciful, and readily listen to reason. The man that has been murdered in thy house was a Moor, an infidel, the enemy of your faith. It was doubtless in a fit of religious zeal that thou hast slain him. I will be indulgent therefore; render up the property of which thou hast robbed him, and we will hush the matter up."

The poor water-carrier called upon all the saints to witness his innocence; alas! not one of them appeared; and, if they had, the alcaid would have disbelieved the whole calendar. The water-carrier related the whole story of the dying Moor, with the straight-forward simplicity of truth, but it was all in vain. "Wilt thou persist in saying," demanded the judge, "that this Moslem had neither gold nor jewels, which were the objects of thy cupidity?"

"As I hope to be saved, your worship," replied the water-carrier, he had nothing but a small box of sandal-wood, which he bequeathed to me in reward for my services."

"A box of sandal-wood! a box of sandal-wood!" exclaimed the alcaid, his eyes sparkling at the idea of precious jewels. "And where is this box? where have you concealed it?"

"An it please your grace, replied the water-carrier, "it is in one of the panniers of my mule, and heartily at the service of your worship."

He had hardly spoken the words, when the keen alguazil darted off and re-appeared in an instant with the mysterious box of sandal-wood. The alcaid opened it with an eager and trembling hand; all pressed forward to gaze upon the treasures it was expected to contain, when, to their disappointment, nothing appeared within but a parchment scroll covered with Arabic characters and an end of a waxen taper.

When there is nothing to be gained by the conviction of a prisoner, justice, even in Spain, is apt to be impartial. The alcaid having recovered from his disappointment, and found that there was really no booty in the case, now listened dispassionately to the explanation of the water-carrier, which was corroborated by the testimony of his wife. Being convinced, therefore, of his innocence, he discharged him from arrest; nay more, he permitted him to carry off the Moor's legacy, the box of sandal-wood and its contents, as the well merited reward of his humanity, but he retained his donkey in payment of costs and charges.

Behold the unfortunate little Gallego reduced once more to the necessity of being his own water-carrier, and trudging up to the well of the Alhambra with a great earthen jar upon his shoulder.

As he toiled up the hill in the heat of a summer noon, his usual good humour forsook him. "Dog of an alcaid!" would he cry, "to rob a poor man of the means of his subsistence, of the best friend he had in the world!" And then, at the remembrance of the beloved companion of his labours, all the kindness of his nature would break forth: "Ah, donkey of my heart!" would he exclaim, resting his burden on a stone, and wiping the sweat from his brow—"Ah, donkey of my heart! I warrant me thou thinkest of thy old master! I warrant me thou missest the water-jars—poor beast!"

To add to his afflictions, his wife received him, on his return home, with whimperings and repinings; she had clearly the vantage-ground of him, having warned him not to commit the egregious act of hospitality that had brought on him all these misfortunes; and, like a knowing woman, she took every occasion to throw her superior sagacity in his teeth. If ever her children lacked food, or needed a new garment, she could answer with a sneer—"Go to your father—he is heir to king Chico of the Alhambra: ask him to help you out of the Moor's strong-box.

Was ever poor mortal so soundly punished for having done a good action? The unlucky Peregil was grieved in flesh and spirit, but still he bore meekly with the railings of his spouse. At length, one evening, when, after a hot day's toil, she taunted him in the usual manner, he lost all patience. He did not venture to retort upon her, but his eye rested upon the box of sandal-wood, which lay on a shelf with the lid half open, as if laughing in mockery at his vexation. Seizing it up, he dashed it with indignation to the floor:—"Unlucky was the day that I ever set eyes on thee," he cried, "or sheltered thy master beneath my roof!"

As the box struck the floor, the lid flew wide open, and the parchment scroll rolled forth. Peregil sat regarding the scroll for some time in moody silence. At length, rallying his ideas—"Who knows," thought he, "but this writing may be of some importance, as the Moor seems to have guarded it with such care?" Picking it up, therefore, he put it in his bosom; and the next morning, as he was crying water through the streets, he stopped at the shop of a Moor, a native of Tangiers, who sold trinkets and perfumery in the Zacatin, and asked him to explain the contents.

The Moor read the scroll attentively, then stroked his beard and smiled. "This manuscript," said he, "is a form of incantation for the recovery of hidden treasure that is under the power of enchantment. It is said to have such virtue, that the strongest bolts and bars, nay, the adamantine rock itself, will yield before it!"

"Bah!" cried the little Gallego, "what is all that to me? I am no enchanter, and know nothing of buried treasure." So saying, he shouldered his water-jar, left the scroll in the hands of the Moor, and trudged forward on his daily rounds.

That evening, however, as he rested himself about twilight at the well of the Alhambra, he found a number of gossips assembled at the place, and their conversation, as is not unusual at that shadowy hour, turned upon old tales and traditions of a supernatural nature. Being all poor as rats, they dwelt with peculiar fondness upon the popular theme of enchanted riches left by the Moors in various parts of the Alhambra. Above all, they concurred in the belief that there were great treasures buried deep in the earth, under the tower of the seven floors.

The stories made an unusual impression on the mind of honest Peregil, and they sank deeper and deeper into his thoughts as he returned alone down the darkling avenues. "If, after all, there should be treasure hid beneath that tower, and if the scroll I left with the Moor should enable me to get at it!" In the sudden ecstacy of the thought he had well nigh let fall his water-jar.

That night he tumbled and tossed, and could scarcely get a wink of sleep for the thoughts that were bewildering his brain. Bright and early he repaired to the shop of the Moor, and told him all that was passing in his mind. "You can read Arabic," said he; "suppose we go together to the tower and try the effect of the charm; if it fails we are no worse off than before, but if it succeeds we will share equally all the treasure we may discover."

"Hold," replied the Moslem, "this writing is not sufficient of itself; it must be read at midnight, by the light of a taper singularly compounded and prepared, the ingredients of which are not within my reach. Without such taper the scroll is of no avail."

"Say no more!" cried the little Gallego, "I have such a taper at hand, and will bring it here in a moment." So saying, he hastened home, and soon returned with the end of yellow wax taper that he had found in the box of sandal-wood.

The Moor felt it and smelt to it. "Here are rare and costly perfumes," said he, "combined with this yellow wax. This is the kind of taper specified in the scroll. While this burns, the strongest walls and most secret caverns will remain open. Woe to him, however, who lingers within until it be extinguished. He will remain enchanted with the treasure."

It was now agreed between them to try the charm that very night. At a late hour, therefore, when nothing was stirring but bats and owls, they ascended the woody hill of the Alhambra, and approached that awful tower, shrouded by trees and rendered formidable by so many traditionary tales. By the light of a lantern, they groped their way through bushes, and over fallen stones, to the door of a vault beneath the tower. With fear and trembling, they descended a flight of steps cut into the rock. It led to an empty chamber, damp and drear, from which another flight of steps led to a deeper vault. In this way they descended four several flights, leading into as many vaults, one below the other, but the floor of the fourth was solid; and though, according to tradition, there remained three vaults still below, it was said to be impossible to penetrate further, the residue being shut up by strong enchantment. The air of this vault was damp and chilly, and had an earthy smell, and the light scarce cast forth any rays. They paused here for a time in breathless surprise, until they faintly heard the clock of the watch-tower strike midnight; upon this they lit the waxen taper, which diffused an odour of myrrh and frankincense and storax.

The Moor began to read in a hurried voice. He had scarce finished when there was a noise as of subterraneous thunder. The earth shook, and the floor yawning open, disclosed a flight of steps. Trembling with awe they descended, and, by the light of the lantern, found themselves in another vault covered with Arabic inscriptions. In the centre stood a great chest secured with seven bands of steel, at each end of which sat an enchanted Moor in armour, but motionless as a statue, being controlled by the power of the incantation. Before the chest were several jars filled with gold and silver, and precious stones. In the largest of these they thrust their arms up to the elbow, and at every dip hauled forth handfuls of broad yellow pieces of Moorish gold, or bracelets and ornaments of the same precious metal, while occasionally a necklace of oriental pearl would stick to their fingers. Still they trembled and breathed short while cramming their pockets with the spoils, and cast many a fearful glance at the two enchanted Moors who sat grim and motionless, glaring upon them with unwinking eyes. At length, struck with a sudden panic at some fancied noise, they both rushed up the staircase, tumbled over one another into the upper apartment, overturned and extinguished the waxen taper, and the pavement again closed with a thundering sound.

Filled with dismay, they did not pause until they had groped their way out of the tower, and beheld the stars shining through the trees. Then, seating themselves upon the grass, they divided the spoil, determining to content themselves for the present with this mere skimming of the jars, but to return on some future night and drain them to the bottom. To make sure of each other's good faith, also, they divided the talismans between them, one retaining the scroll and the other the taper; this done, they set off with light hearts and well-lined pockets for Granada.

As they wended their way down the hill, the shrewd Moor whispered a word of counsel in the ear of the simple little water-carrier.

"Friend Peregil," said he, "all this affair must be kept a profound secret, until we have secured the treasure and conveyed it out of harm's way. If a whisper of it gets to the ear of the alcaid, we are undone!"

"Certainly," replied the Gallego, "nothing can be more true."

"Friend Peregil," said the Moor, "you are a discreet man, and I make no doubt can keep a secret: but you have a wife."

"She shall not know a word of it," replied the little water-carrier sturdily.

"Enough," said the Moor; "I depend upon thy discretion and thy promise."

Never was promise more positive and sincere; but, alas! what man can keep a secret from his wife? Certainly not such a one as Peregil the water-carrier, who was one of the most loving and tractable of husbands. On his return home he found his wife moping in a corner. "Mighty well," cried she as he entered, "you've come at last, after rambling about until this hour of the night. I wonder you have not brought home another Moor as a house-mate." Then, bursting into tears, she began to wring her hands and smite her breast: "Unhappy woman that I am!" exclaimed she, "what will become of me? My house stripped and plundered by lawyers and alguazils; my husband a do-no-good, that no longer brings home bread for the family, but goes rambling about day and night with infidel Moors? O my children! what will become of us? we shall all have to beg in the streets!"

Honest Peregil was so moved by the distress of his spouse,

that he could not help whimpering also. His heart was as full as his pocket, and not to be restrained. Thrusting his hand into the latter, he hauled forth three or four broad gold pieces and slipped them into her bosom. The poor woman started with astonishment, and could not understand the meaning of this golden shower. Before she could recover her surprise, the little Gallego drew forth a chain of gold and dangled it before her, capering with exultation, his mouth distended from ear to ear.

"Holy virgin protect us!" exclaimed the wife. "What hast thou been doing, Peregil? Surely thou hast not been committing murder and robbery!"

The idea had scarce entered the brain of the poor woman than it became a certainty with her. She saw a prison and a gallows in the distance, and a little bandy-legged Gallego hanging pendent from it; and, overcome with the horrors conjured up by her imagination, fell into violent hysterics.

What could the poor man do? He had no other means of pacifying his wife, and dispelling the phantoms of her fancy, than by relating the whole story of his good fortune. This, however, he did not do until he had exacted from her the most solemn promise to keep it a profound secret from every living being.

To describe her joy would be impossible. She flung her arms round the neck of her husband, and almost strangled him with her caresses. "Now wife," exclaimed the little man with honest exultation, "what say you now to the Moor's Legacy? Henceforth never abuse me for helping a fellow-creature in distress."

The honest Gallego retired to his sheep-skin mat, and slept as soundly as if on a bed of down. Not so his wife; she emptied the whole contents of his pockets upon the mat, and sat all night counting gold pieces of Arabic coin, trying on necklaces and ear-rings, and fancying the figure she should one day make, when permitted to enjoy her riches.

On the following morning the honest Gallego took a broad golden coin, and repaired with it to a jeweller's shop in the Zacatin, to offer it for sale, pretending to have found it among the ruins of the Alhambra. The jeweller saw that it had an Arabic inscription, and was of the purest gold; he offered, however, but a third of its value, with which the water-carrier was perfectly content. Peregil now bought new clothes for his little flock, and all kinds of toys, together with ample provisions for a hearty meal; and, returning to his dwelling, set all his children dancing around him, while he capered in the midst, the happiest of fathers.

The wife of the water-carrier kept her promise of secrecy with surprising strictness. For a whole day and a half she went about with a look of mystery and a heart swelling almost to bursting; yet she held her peace, though surrounded by her gossips. It is true she could not help giving herself a few airs, apologized for her ragged dress, and talked of ordering a new basquina all trimmed with gold lace and bugles, and a new lace mantilla. She threw out hints of her husband's intention of leaving off his trade of water-carrying, as it did not altogether agree with his health. In fact she thought they should all retire to the country for the summer, that the children might have the benefit of the mountain air, for there was no living in the city in this sultry season.

The neighbours stared at each other, and thought the poor woman had lost her wits; and her airs and graces and elegant pretensions were the theme of universal scoffing and merriment among her friends the moment her back was turned.

If she restrained herself abroad, however, she indemnified herself at home, and, putting a string of rich oriental pearls round her neck, Moorish bracelets on her arms, and an aigrette of diamonds on her head, sailed backwards and forwards in her slattern rags about the room, now and then stopping to admire herself in a piece of broken mirror. Nay, in the impulse of her simple vanity, she could not resist, on one occasion, showing herself at the window, to enjoy the effect of her finery on the psssers by.

As the fates would have it, Pedrillo Pedrugo, the meddlesome barber, was at this moment sitting idly in his shop on the opposite side of the street, when his ever-watchful eye caught the sparkle of a diamond. In an instant he was at his loop-hole, reconnoitring the slattern spouse of the water-carrier decorated with the splendour of an Eastern bride. No sooner had he taken an accurate inventory of her ornaments, than he posted off with all speed to the alcaid. In a little while the hungry alguazil was again on the scent, and before the day was over the unfortunate Peregil was again dragged into the presence of the judge.

"How is this, villian?" cried the alcaid, in a furious voice. "You told me that the infidel who died in your house left nothing behind but an empty coffer, and now I hear of your wife flaunting in her rags, decked out with pearls and diamonds. Wretch that thou art! prepare to render up the spoils of thy miserable victim, and to swing on the gallows that is already tired of waiting for thee."

The terrified water-carrier fell on his knees, and made a full relation of the marvellous manner in which be had gained his wealth. The alcaid, the alguazil, and the inquisitive barber, listened with greedy ears to this Arabian tale of enchanted treasure. The alguazil was dispatched to bring the Moor who had assisted in the incantation. The Moslem entered, half frightened out of his wits at finding himself in the hands of the harpies of the law. When he beheld the water-carrier standing with sheepish looks and downcast countenance, he comprehended the whole matter. "Miserable animal," said he, as he passed near him, "did I not warn thee against babbling to thy wife?"

The story of the Moor coincided exactly with that of his collegue; but the alcaid affected to be slow of belief, and threw out menaces of imprisonment and rigorous investigation.

"Softly, good Senor Alcaid," said the Mussulman, who by this time had recovered his usual shrewdness and self-possession. "Let us not mar fortune's favour in the scramble for them. Nobody knows any thing of this matter but ourselves—let us keep the secret. There is wealth enough in the cave to enrich us all. Promise a fair division, and all shall be produced—refuse, and the cave shall remain for ever closed."

The alcaid consulted apart with the alguazil. The latter

was an old fox in his profession. "Promise any thing," said he, "until you get possession of the treasure. You may then seize upon the whole; and if he and his accomplice dare to murmur, threaten them with the faggot and the stake, as infidels and sorcerers."

The alcaid relished the advice. Smoothing his brow and turning to the Moor, "This is a strange story," said he, "and may be true, but I must have ocular proof of it. This very night you must repeat the incantation in my presence. If there be really such treasure, we will share it amicably among us, and say nothing further of the matter; if ye have deceived me, expect no mercy at my hands. In the mean time you must remain in custody."

The Moor and the water-carrier cheerfully agreed to these conditions, satisfied that the event would prove the truth of their words.

Towards midnight the alcaid sallied forth secretly, attended by the alguazil and the meddlesome barber, all strongly armed. They conducted the Moor and the water-carrier as prisoners, and were provided with the stout donkey of the latter to bear off the expected treasure. They arrived at the tower without being observed, and tying the donkey to a fig-tree, descended into the fourth vault of the tower.

The scroll was produced, the yellow waxen taper lighted, and the Moor read the form of incantation. The earth trembled as before, and the pavement opened with a thundering sound, disclosing the narrow flight of steps. The alcaid, the alguazil, and the barber, were struck aghast and could not summon courage to descend. The Moor and the water-carrier entered the lower vault, and found the two Moors seated as before, silent and motionless. They removed two of the great jars, filled with golden coin and precious stones. The water-carrier bore them up one by one upon his shoulders; but though a strong-backed little man, and accustomed to carry burdens, he staggered beneath their weight, and found, when slung on each side of his donkey, they were as much as the animal could bear.

"Let us be content for the present," said the Moor, "here

is as much treasure as we can carry off without being perceived, and enough to make us all wealthy to our heart's desire."

"Is there more treasure remaining behind?" demanded the alcaid.

"The greatest prize of all," said the Moor, "a huge coffer bound with bands of steel, and filled with pearls and precious stones."

"Let us have up the coffer, by all means," cried the grasping alcaid.

"I will descend for no more," said the Moor doggedly; "enough is enough for a reasonable man—more is superfluous."

"And I," said the water-carrier, "will bring up no further burden to break the back of my poor donkey."

Finding commands, threats, and entreaties equally vain, the alcaid turned to his two adherents. "Aid me," said he, "to bring up the coffer, and its contents shall be divided among us." So saying, he descended the steps, followed with trembling reluctance by the alguazil and the barber.

No sooner did the Moor behold them fairly earthed than he extinguished the yellow taper, the pavement closed with its usual crash, and the three worthies remained buried in its womb.

He then hastened up the different flights of steps, nor stopped until in the open air. The little water-carrier followed him as fast as his legs would permit.

"What hast thou done?" cried Peregil, as soon as he could recover breath. "The alcaid and the other two are shut up in the vault."

"It is the will of Allah!" said the Moor devoutly.

"And will you not release them?" demanded the Gallego.

"Allah forbid!" replied the Moor, smoothing his beard. "It is written in the book of fate that they shall remain enchanted until some future adventurer arrive to break the charm. The will of God be done!" So saying, he hurled the end of the waxen taper far among the gloomy thickets of the glen.

There was now no remedy, so the Moor and the water-carrier proceeded with the richly-laden donkey towards the city; nor could honest Peregil refrain from hugging and kissing his long-eared fellow-labourer, thus restored to him from the clutches of the law; and in fact it is doubtful which gave the simple-hearted little man most joy at the moment—the gaining of the treasure, or the recovery of the donkey.

The two partners in good-luck divided their spoil amicably and fairly, except that the Moor, who had a little taste for trinketry, made out to get into his heap the most of the pearls and precious stones, and other baubles, but then he always gave the water-carrier in lieu magnificent jewels of massy gold, of five times the size, with which the latter was heartily content. They took care not to linger within reach of accidents, but made off to enjoy their wealth undisturbed in other countries. The Moor returned to Africa, to his native city of Tangiers; and the Gallego, with his wife, his children, and his donkey, made the best of his way to Portugal. Here, under the admonition and tuition of his wife, he became a personage of some consequence; for she made the worthy little man array his long body and short legs in doublet and hose, with a feather in his hat and a sword by his side, and laying aside his familiar appellation of Peregil, assumed the more sonorous title of Don Pedro Gil. His progeny grew up a thriving and merry-hearted, though short and bandy-legged generation, while Senora Gil, befringed, belaced, and betasseled from her head to her heels, with glittering rings on every finger, became a model of slattern fashion and finery.

As to the alcaid and his adjuncts, they remained shut up under the great tower of the seven floors, and there they remain spell bound at the present day. Whenever there shall be a lack in Spain of pimping barbers, sharking alguazils, and corrupt alcaids, they may be sought after; but if they have to wait until such time for their deliverance, there is danger of their enchantment enduring until doomsday.—WASHINGTON IRVING.

SCENES FROM "SHE STOOPS TO CONQUER."

Act I.—Scene I.

Hard. Blessings on my pretty innocence! Drest out as usual, my Kate. Goodness! What a quantity of superfluous silk hast thou got about thee, girl! I could never teach the fools of this age, that the indigent world could be clothed out of the trimmings of the vain.

Miss Hard. You know our agreement, sir. You allow me the morning to receive and pay visits, and to dress in my own manner; and in the evening, I put on my housewife's dress to please you.

Hard. Well, remember I insist on the terms of our agreement; and, by the by, I believe I shall have occasion to try your obedience this evening.

Miss Hard. I protest, sir, I don't comprehend your meaning.

Hard. Then, to be plain with you, Kate, I expect the young gentleman I have chosen to be your husband from town this very day. I have his father's letter, in which he informs me his son is set out, and that he intends to follow himself shortly after.

Miss Hard. Indeed! I wish I had known something of this before. Bless me, how shall I behave! It's a thousand to one I shan't like him; our meeting will be so formal, and so like a thing of business, that I shall find no room for friendship or esteem.

Hard. Depend upon it, child, I'll never control your choice; but Mr. Marlow, whom I have pitched upon, is the son of my old friend, Sir Charles Marlow, of whom you have heard me talk so often. The young gentleman has been bred a scholar, and is designed for an employment in the service of his country. I am told he's a man of an excellent understanding.

Miss Hard. Is he?

Hard. Very generous.

Miss Hard. I believe I shall like him.

Hard. Young and brave.

Miss Hard. I'm sure I shall like him.

Hard. And very handsome.

Miss Hard. My dear papa, say no more (*kissing his hand*), he's mine, I'll have him!

Hard. And to crown all, Kate, he's one of the most bashful and reserved young fellows in all the world.

Miss Hard. Eh! you have frozen me to death again. That word *reserved*, has done all the rest of his accomplishments. A reserved lover, it is said, always makes a suspicious husband.

Hard. On the contrary, modesty seldom resides in a breast that is not enriched with nobler virtues. It was the very feature in his character that first struck me.

Miss Hard. He must have more striking features to catch me, I promise you. However, if he be so young, so handsome, and so every thing, as you mention, I believe he'll do still. I think I'll have him.

Hard. Ay, Kate, but there is still an obstacle. It's more than an even wager, he may not have *you*.

Miss Hard. My dear papa, why will you mortify one so!—Well, if he refuses, instead of breaking my heart at his indifference, I'll only break my glass for its flattery, set my cap to some newer fashion, and look out for some less difficult admirer.

Hard. Bravely resolved! In the mean time I'll go prepare the servants for his reception; as we seldom see company, they want as much training as a company of recruits the first day's muster.

Act II.—Scene I.

Hard. Well, I hope you're perfect in the table exercise I have been teaching you these three days. You all know your posts and your places; and can show that you have been used to good company, without stirring from home.

Omnes. Ay, ay.

Hard. When company comes, you are not to pop out and stare, and then run in again, like frighted rabbits in a warren.

Omnes. No, no.

Hard. You, Diggory, whom I have taken from the barn, are to make a show at the side-table; and you, Roger, whom I have advanced from the plough, are to place yourself behind *my* chair. But you're not to stand so, with your hands in your pockets. Take your hands from your pockets, Roger; and from your head, you blockhead you. See how Diggory carries his hands. They're a little too stiff, indeed, but that's no great matter.

Digg. Ay; mind how I hold them. I learned to hold my hands this way, when I was upon drill for the militia. And so being upon drill——

Hard. You must not be so talkative, Diggory, You must be all attention to the guests. You must hear us talk, and not think of talking; you must see us drink, and not think of drinking; you must see us eat, and not think of eating.

Digg. Ecod, I thank your worship, I'll make a shift to stay my stomach with a slice of cold beef in the pantry.

Hard. Diggory, you are too talkative. Then if I happen to say a good thing, or tell a good story at table, you must not all burst out a-laughing, as if you made part of the company.

Digg. Then ecod, you worship must not tell the story of Ould Grouse in the gun-room: I can't help laughing at that —he! he! he!—for the soul of me. We have laughed at that these twenty years—ha! ha! ha!

Hard. Ha! ha! ha! The story is a good one. Well, honest Diggory, you may laugh at that—but still remember to be attentive. Suppose one of the company should call for a glass of wine, how will you behave? A glass of wine, sir, if you please. (*To* Diggory.)—Eh, why don't you move?

Digg. Ecod, your worship, I never have courage till I see the eatables and drinkables brought upon the table, and then I'm as bauld as a lion.

Hard. What, will nobody move?

1 *Serv.* I'm not to leave this place.

2 *Serv.* I'm sure it's no pleace of mine.

3 *Serv.* Nor mine, for sartain.

Digg. Wauns, and I'm sure, it canna be mine.

Hard. You numskulls! and so while, like your betters, you are quarrelling for places, the guests must be starved. O you dunces! I find I must begin all over again.——But don't I hear a coach drive into the yard? To your posts, you blockheads. I'll go in the mean time, and give my old friend's son a hearty welcome at the gate.

Digg. By the elevens, my place is gone quite out of my head.

Roger. I know that my place is to be everywhere.

1 *Serv.* Where the devil is mine.

2 *Serv.* My pleace is to be no where at all; and so Ize go about my business.—OLIVER GOLDSMITH.

MARIA.

THEY were the sweetest notes I ever heard; and I instantly let down the fore glass to hear them more distinctly. "'Tis Maria;" said the postilion, observing I was listening. "Poor Maria," continued he (leaning his body on one side to let me see her, for he was in a line between us), "is sitting upon a bank playing her vespers upon her pipe, with her little goat beside her."

The young fellow uttered this with an accent and a look so perfectly in tune to a feeling heart, that I instantly made a vow I would give him a four and twenty sous piece when I got to Moulins.

"And who is poor Maria?" said I.

"The love and pity of all the villages around us," said the postilion. "It is but three years ago, that the sun did not shine upon so fair, so quick-witted, and amiable a maid; and better fate did Maria deserve, than to have her banns forbid by the intrigues of the curate of the parish who published them."

He was going on, when Maria, who had made a short pause, put the pipe to her mouth and began the air again. They were the same notes, yet were ten times sweeter. "It is the evening service to the Virgin," said the young man; "but who has taught her to play it, or how she came by her pipe, no one knows; we think that heaven had assisted her in both; for ever since she has been unsettled in her mind, it seems her only consolation. She has never once had the pipe out of her hand, but plays that service upon it almost night and day."

The postilion delivered this with so much discretion and natural eloquence, that I could not help deciphering something in his face above his condition, and should have sifted out his history, had not poor Maria taken such full possession of me.

We had got up by this time almost to the bank where Maria was sitting: she was in a thin white jacket, with her hair, all but two tresses, drawn up in a silken net, with a few olive leaves twisted a little fantastically on one side. She was beautiful; and if ever I felt the full force of an honest heart-ache, it was the moment I saw her.

"God help her! poor damsel! Above a hundred masses," said the postilion, "have been said in the several parish churches and convents around for her, but without effect; we have still hopes, as she is sensible for short intervals, that the Virgin at last will restore her to herself; but her parents, who know her best, are hopeless upon that score, and think her senses are lost for ever."

As the postilion spoke this, Maria made a cadence so melancholy, so tender and querulous, that I sprung out of the chaise to help her, and found myself sitting betwixt her and her goat, before I relapsed from my enthusiasm.

Maria looked wistfully for some time at me, and then at her goat—and then at me—and then at her goat again, and so on alternately.

"Well, Maria," said I softly, "what resemblance do you find?"

I do entreat the candid reader to believe me, that it was from the humblest conviction of what a beast man is, that

I asked the question; and that I would not have let fallen an unseasonable pleasantry in the venerable presence of Misery, to be entitled to all the wit that ever Rabelais scattered.

Adieu, Maria! adieu, poor hapless damsel!—some time, but not now, I may hear thy sorrows from thy own lips; but I was deceived; for that moment she took her pipe, and told me such a tale of woe with it, that I rose up, and with broken and irregular steps walked softly to my chaise.

SECOND PART.

When we had got within half a league of Moulins, at a little opening in the road leading to a thicket, I discovered poor Maria sitting under a poplar. She was sitting with her elbows in her lap, and her head leaning on one side within her hand, a small brook ran at the foot of the tree.

I bade the postilion go on with the chaise to Moulins, and La Fleur to bespeak my supper, and that I would walk after him.

She was dressed in white, and much as my friend described her, except that her hair hung loose, which before was twisted in a silken net. She had, superadded likewise to her jacket, a pale green ribbon which fell across her shoulder to the waist; at the end of which hung her pipe. Her goat had been as faithless as her lover; and she had got a little dog in lieu of him, which she had kept tied by a string to her girdle; as I looked at her dog, she drew him towards her with a string—"Thou shalt not leave me, Sylvio," said she. I looked in Maria's eyes, and saw she was thinking more of her father than of her lover or her little goat; for as she uttered them, the tears trickled down her cheeks.

I sat down close by her; and Maria let me wipe them away as they fell, with my handkerchief. I then steeped it in my own—and then in her's—and then in mine—and then I wiped her's again; and as I did it, I felt such undescribable emotions within me, as I am sure could not be accounted for, from any combinations of matter and motion.

I am positive I have a soul; nor can all the books with

which materialists have pestered the world, ever convince me of the contrary.

When Maria had come a little to herself, I asked her if she remembered a pale, thin person of a man, who had sat down betwixt her and her goat about two years before? She said she was unsettled much at that time, but remembered it upon two accounts—that ill as she was, she saw the person pitied her; and next, that her goat had stolen his handkerchief, and she had beat him for the theft; she had washed it, she said, in the brook, and kept it ever since in her pocket, to restore it to him in case she should ever see him again, which, she added, he had half promised her. As she told me this, she took the handkerchief out of her pocket to let me see it: she had folded it up neatly in a couple of vine leaves, tied round with a tendril; on opening it, I saw an S marked in one of the corners.

She had since that, she told me, strayed as far as Rome, and walked round St. Peter's once, and returned back; that she found her way alone across the Apennines, had travelled over all Lombardy without money, and through the flinty roads of Savoy without shoes: how she had borne it, and how she had got supported, she could not tell; but God tempers the wind, said Maria, to the shorn lamb.

"Shorn indeed! and to the quick," said I; "and wast thou in my own land, where I have a cottage, I would take thee to it and shelter thee; thou shouldst eat of my own bread, and drink of my own cup. I would be kind to thy Sylvio. In all thy weaknesses and wanderings I would seek after thee, and bring thee back. When the sun went down I would say my prayers, and when I had done, thou shouldst play thy evening song upon thy pipe; nor would the incense of my sacrifice be worse accepted, for entering heaven along with that of a broken heart."

Nature melted within me, as I uttered this; and Maria observing, as I took out my handkerchief, that it was steeped too much already to be of use, would needs go wash it in the stream. "And where will you dry it, Maria?" said I. "I will dry it in my bosom," said she; "it will do me good."

"And is your heart still so warm, Maria?" said I.

I touched upon the string on which hung all her sorrows; she looked with wistful disorder for some time in my face, and then, without saying anything, took her pipe and played her service to the Virgin. The string I had touched ceased to vibrate; in a moment or two Maria returned to herself, let her pipe fall, and rose up.

"And where are you going, Maria?" said I. She said, "To Moulins." "Let us go," said I, "together." Maria put her arm within mine, and lengthening the string to let the dog follow, in that order we entered Moulins.

Though I hate salutations and greetings in the market place, yet when we got into the middle of this, I stopped to take my last look, and last farewell of Maria.

Maria, though not tall, was nevertheless of the first order of fine forms. Affliction had touched her looks with something that was scarce earthly; still she was feminine: and so much was there about her of all that the heart wishes, or the eye looks for in woman, that could the traces be ever worn out of her brain, and those of Eliza's out of mine, she should not only eat of my bread and drink of my own cup, but Maria should lie in my bosom, and be unto me as a daughter.

Adieu, poor luckless maiden! imbibe the oil and wine which the compassion of a stranger, as he journeyeth on his way, now pours into thy wounds; the Being who has twice bruised thee can only bind them up for ever.—STERNE.

THE BASHFUL MAN.

I LABOUR under a species of distress which, I fear, will at length drive me utterly from that society in which I am most ambitious to appear; but I will give you a short sketch of my origin and present situation, by which you will be enabled to judge of my difficulties.

My father was a farmer of no great property, and with

no other learning than what he had acquired at a charity-school; but my mother being dead, and I an only child, he determined to give me that advantage which, he fancied, would have made him happy, viz., a learned education. I was sent to a country grammar-school, and from thence to the university, with a view of qualifying for holy orders. Hence, having but a small allowance from my father, and being naturally of a timid and bashful disposition, I had no opportunity of rubbing off that native awkwardness, which is the fatal cause of all my unhappiness, and which I now begin to fear can never be amended.

You must know that in my person I am tall and thin, with a fair complexion, and light flaxen hair; but of such extreme susceptibility of shame, that on the smallest subject of confusion, my blood all rushes into my cheeks, and I appear a perfect full-blown rose. The consciousness of this unhappy failing made me avoid society, and I became enamoured of a college life, particularly when I reflected that the uncouth manners of my father's family were little calculated to improve my outward conduct; I therefore had resolved on living at the university and taking pupils, when two unexpected events greatly altered the posture of my affairs, viz., my father's death, and the arrival of an uncle from the Indies.

This uncle I had very rarely heard my father mention, and it was generally believed that he was long since dead, when he arrived in England only a week too late to close his brother's eyes.

I am ashamed to confess what I believe has been often experienced by those whose education has been better than their parents, that my poor father's ignorance and vulgar language had often made me blush to think I was his son, and at his death I was not inconsolable for the loss of *that* which I was not unfrequently ashamed to own. My uncle was but little affected, for he had been separated from his brother more than thirty years, and in that time he had acquired a fortune which he used to boast would make a Nabob happy. In short, he had brought over with him the enormous sum of thirty thousand pounds, and upon this he built his hopes of never-ending happiness. While he was planning schemes of greatness and delight, whether the change of climate might affect him, or what other cause I know not, but he was snatched from all his dreams of joy by a short illness, of which he died, leaving me heir to all his property.

And now, behold me, at the age of twenty-five, well stocked with Latin, Greek, and Mathematics, possessed of an ample fortune, but so awkward and unversed in every gentleman-like accomplishment, that I am pointed at by all who see me as the *wealthy learned clown.*

I have lately purchased an estate in the country, which abounds in what is called a fashionable neighbourhood; and when you reflect upon my parentage and uncouth manner, you will hardly think how much my company is courted by the surrounding families (especially by those who have marriageable daughters): from these gentlemen I have received familiar calls, and the most pressing invitations, and though I wished to accept their offered friendship, I have repeatedly excused myself under the pretence of not being quite settled; for the truth is, that when I have rode or walked, with full intention to return their several visits, my heart has failed me as I approached their gates, and I have frequently returned homeward, resolving to try again to-morrow.

However, I at length determined to conquer my timidity, and three days ago accepted of an invitation to dine this day with one whose open easy manner left me no room to doubt a cordial welcome. Sir Thomas Friendly, who lives about two miles distant, is a baronet, with an estate of about two thousand pounds a year, joining to that I purchased; he has two sons and five daughters, all grown up, and living with their mother and a maiden sister of Sir Thomas's, at Friendly-Hall. Conscious of my unpolished gait, I have for some time past taken private lessons of a Professor who teaches "grown gentlemen to dance;" and though I at first found wondrous difficulty in the art he taught, my knowledge of mathematics was of prodigious use in teaching me the equilibrium of my body, and the use and adjustment of the centre of gravity to the five positions.

Having now acquired the art of walking without tottering, and learned to make a bow, I boldly ventured to obey the Baronet's invitation to a family dinner, not doubting but my new acquirements would enable me to see the ladies with tolerable intrepidity; but alas! how vain are all the hopes of theory, when unsupported by habitual practice. As I approached the house, a dinner-bell alarmed my fears, lest I had spoiled the dinner by want of punctuality; impressed with this idea, I blushed the deepest crimson, as my name was repeatedly announced by the several livery servants, who ushered me into the library, hardly knowing what or whom I saw; at my first entrance, I summoned all my fortitude, and made my new learned bow to Lady Friendly, but unfortunately bringing back my left foot to the third position, I trod upon the gouty toe of poor Sir Thomas, who had followed close at my heels to be the nomenclator of the family.

The confusion this occasioned in me is hardly to be conceived, since none but bashful men can judge of my distress; and of that description, the number I believe is very small. The Baronet's politeness by degrees dissipated my concern, and I was astonished to see how far good breeding could enable him to suppress his feelings, and to appear with perfect ease after so painful an accident.

The cheerfulness of her Ladyship, and the familiar chat of the young ladies, insensibly led me to throw off my reserve and sheepishness, till at length I ventured to join in conversation, and even to start fresh subjects. The library being richly furnished with books in elegant bindings, I conceived Sir Thomas to be a man of literature, and ventured to give my opinion concerning the several editions of the Greek classics, in which the Baronet's opinion exactly coincided with my own.

To this subject I was led by observing an edition of Xenophon in sixteen volumes, which (as I had never before heard of such a thing) greatly excited my curiosity, and I rose up to examine what it could be; Sir Thomas saw what I was about, and (as I suppose) willing to save me trouble, rose to take down the book, which made me more eager to prevent him, and hastily laying my hand on the first volume, I pulled it forcibly; but lo! instead of books, a board, which by leather and gilding had been made to look like sixteen volumes, came tumbling down, and unluckily pitched upon a wedgewood ink-stand on the table under it. In vain did Sir Thomas assure me there was no harm; I saw the ink streaming from an inlaid table on the Turkey carpet, and scarce knowing what I did, attempted to stop its progress with my cambric handkerchief. In the height of this confusion we were informed that dinner was served up, and I with joy perceived that the bell, which at first had so alarmed my fears, was only the half-hour dinner-bell.

In walking through the hall, and suit of apartments to the dining-room, I had time to collect my scattered senses, and was desired to take my seat betwixt Lady Friendly and her eldest daughter at the table. Since the fall of the wooden Xenophon, my face had been continually burning like a fire-brand, and I was just beginning to recover myself, and to feel comfortably cool, when an unlooked for accident rekindled all my heat and blushes. Having set my plate of soup too near the edge of the table, in bowing to Miss Dinah, who politely complimented the pattern of my waistcoat, I tumbled the whole scalding contents into my lap. In spite of an immediate supply of napkins to wipe the surface of my clothes, my black silk breeches were not stout enough to save me from the painful effects of this sudden fomentation, and for some minutes my legs and thighs seemed stewed in a boiling caldron; but recollecting how Sir Thomas had disguised his torture, when I trod upon his toe, I firmly bore my pain in silence, and sat with my lower extremities parboiled, amidst the stifled giggling of the ladies and the servants.

I will not relate the several blunders which I made during the first course, or the distress occasioned by my being desired to carve a fowl, or help to various dishes that stood near me, spilling a sauce-boat and knocking down a salt-seller; rather let me hasten to the second course, where fresh disasters overwhelmed me quite.

I had a piece of rich sweet pudding on my fork, when

Miss Lousia Friendly begged to trouble me for a pigeon that stood near me; in my haste, scarce knowing what I did, I whipped the pudding into my mouth, hot as a burning coal; it was impossible to conceal my agony, my eyes were starting from their sockets. At last, in spite of shame and resolution, I was obliged to drop the cause of torment on my plate.

Sir Thomas and the ladies all compassionated my misfortune, and each advised a different application; one recommended oil, another water, but all agreed that wine was best for drawing out the fire; and a glass of sherry was brought me from the side-board, which I snatch'd up with eagerness; but oh! how shall I tell the sequel; whether the butler by accident mistook, or purposely designed to drive me mad, he gave me the strongest brandy, with which I filled my mouth, already flayed and blistered; totally unused to every kind of ardent spirits, with my tongue, throat, and palate as raw as beef, what could I do? I could not swallow, and clappping my hands upon my mouth, the cursed liquor squirted through my fingers like a fountain, over all the dishes; and I was crushed by bursts of laughter from all quarters.

In vain did Sir Thomas reprimand the servants, and Lady Friendly chide her daughters; for the measure of my shame and their diversion was not yet complete. To relieve me from the intolerable state of perspiration, which this accident had caused, without considering what I did, I wiped my face with that ill-fated handkerchief, which was still wet from the consequences of the fall of Xenophon, and covered all my features with streaks of ink in every direction. The Baronet himself could not support this shock, but joined his Lady in the general laugh; while I sprung from the table in despair, rushed out of the house, and ran home in an agony of confusion and disgrace, which the most poignant sense of guilt could not have excited.

Thus, without having deviated from the path of moral rectitude, I am suffering torments like a "goblin damn'd." The lower half of me has been almost boiled, my tongue and mouth grill'd, and I bear the mark of Cain upon my forehead; yet these are but trifling considerations to the everlasting shame which I must feel whenever this adventure shall be mentioned.—MACKENZIE.

THE PRICE OF PLEASURE.

"I THINK I will take a ride," said the little Lord Linger, after breakfast. "Bring my boots, and let my horse be brought to the door."

The horse was saddled, and his lordship's spurs were putting on.

"No," said he; "I'll have my low chair and the ponies, and take a drive round the park."

The horse was led back, and the ponies were almost harnessed, when his lordship sent his valet to countermand them. He would walk into the corn-field and see how the new pointer hunted.

"After all," says he, "I think I will stay at home, and play a game or two at billiards."

He played half a game, but could not make a stroke to please himself. His tutor, who was present, now thought it a good opportunity to ask his lordship if he would read a little.

"Why—I think—I will—for I am tired of doing nothing. What shall we have?"

"Your lordship left off last time in one of the finest passages in the Æneid. Suppose we finish it."

"Well—ay! But—no—I had rather go on with Hume's history. Or—suppose we do some geography?"

"With all my heart. The globes are upon the study table."

They went to the study; and the little lord, leaning upon his elbows, looked at the globe—then twirled it round two or three times—and then listened patiently while the tutor explained some of its parts and uses. But while he was in the midst of a problem, "Come," said his lordship, "now for a little Virgil."

The book was brought, and the pupil, with a good deal of help, got through twenty lines.

"Well," said he, ringing the bell, "I think we have done a good deal. Tom! bring me my bow and arrows."

The fine London-made bow in its green case, and the quiver with all the appurtenances, were brought, and his lordship went down to the place where the shooting butts were erected. He aimed a few shots at the target, but not coming near it, he shot all the remainder at random, and then ordered out his horse.

He sauntered, with a servant at his heels, for a mile or two through the lanes, and came, just as the clock struck twelve, to a village-green, close by which a school was kept. A door flew open, and out burst a shoal of boys, who, spreading over the green with immoderate vociferation, instantly began a variety of sports. Some fell to marbles—some to trap-ball—some to leap-frog. In short, not one of the whole crew but was eagerly employed. Every thing was noise, motion, and pleasure. Lord Linger, riding slowly up, espied one of his tenant's sons who had been formerly admitted as a playfellow of his, and called from the crowd.

"Jack," said he, "how do you like school?"

"Oh—pretty well, my lord!"

"What—have you a good deal of play?"

"Oh no! We have only from twelve to two for playing and eating our dinners; and then an hour before supper."

"That is very little, indeed!"

"But we play heartily when we do play, and work when we work. Good by, my lord! It is my turn to go in at trap."

So saying, Jack ran off.

"I wish I was a schoolboy!" cried the little lord to himself.—BARBAULD AND AIKIN.

THE MONKEY AND THE MAGIC LANTERN.

"LADIES and gentlemen," said a learned Monkey to a select party of animals he had invited during the absence of his master the showman,—"Ladies and gentlemen, this here wonderful machine is neither more nor less than the magic lantern. Please, Mr. Kangaroo, to pin up that white sheet properly; so, that will do. Now will you just be so kind as hop about and snuff out those candles—sorry for the trouble, Sir. All in the dark?—right. Now, ladies and gentlemen, attention." So saying, the learned expounder of the magic lantern coughed, cleared his throat, hemmed, and began as follows:—"First and foremost, this figure which you behold moving so majestically in his Roman gown, with the ensigns of his office, is that sternest of dictators, Sylla. Look at that polished forehead, those eagle eyes, and the lip, ladies and gentlemen, the curve, the marble composure of that inimitable lip! Next, ladies and gentleman, is the iron frame and gigantic stature of his rival, Marius. Pray, remark the malignant expression of those harsh and vindictive features, the furrowed brow, the shaggy eyebrow, the hollow bloodshot eye. This is he who sat himself down on the ruins of Carthage. What a withering lesson for ambition!" exclaimed the awe-struck Monkey. "But this here," said the exhibitor, resuming the thread of his exposition, "is a figure of a milder aspect, the young, the high-souled Cæsar. History," proceeded our erudite Monkey, "has frequently alluded to his baldness, an accident, ladies and gentlemen, which regards a later period of his life. As he now stands before you easy, elegant, and concealing his grasping ambition under an exterior of indifference, you behold the future conqueror of Gaul, the future emperor of Rome."

Mounted on the hobby-horse of history, Pug would probably have introduced the youthful Pompey to the acquaintance of his interesting audience, had not a slight, though at first scarcely audible murmur, warned him that his hearers were not in the best of possible moods for a continuance of historical figures.

"What is the meaning of this?" grunted the Hog; "I don't see so much as the nose of any one of all the figures he has been chattering about." "Nor I either," growled the Bear, "and if I don't mistake he is making game of us." "The fellow is hoaxing us to a dead certainty," yelped out a pert little Pug-dog; "who ever heard of exhibiting a show without candles? And that Jackass of a Kangaroo to go and snuff them out!" "Jackass yourself, you puppy," brayed the Donkey; "what do you mean by insulting a person of my years and gravity?" "No offence, Sir Donkey," returned the Pug-dog; "positively I meant none; so, pray, don't let an accident like this prevent us from chastising that impudent rascal of a Monkey." "Hiss him out," whistled the Serpent." "Pelt him off," cried the Badger. "Ay, ay, out with him, out with him," roared the enraged audience. "A row by all means," screamed a diminutive but malicious Weasel; let us kick us a row."

Things were fast coming to a fearful crisis with poor Pug, who could not for the life of him comprehend the cause of such outcries, when just at this eventful moment in stept his master. "How now," cried he, "what's this?" "Why," whimpered Pug, "I was just treating my friends to a sight of your magic lantern, and—and"—"Indeed," said the showman, half laughing, half angry—"well, let me see, where's the candle of the lantern? Out! by all that's comical! So your friends have been listening to you all this time in the dark, have they? You must feel vastly obliged to them indeed. But come, gentlemen," said he to the audience, "be pleased to walk out; and do you," added he, addressing Sir Pug, "take care in future how you interfere with things beyond the compass of your capacity. Mere chattering, however pompous it may be, will never clear up any subject."—FLEMING.

THE HYPOCRITICAL RAT.

An old hypocritical Rat, who had just dined with his wife and young ones on a large lump of Dutch cheese, after wiping his whiskers, thought proper to read the younger members of the family a lecture on morality. As the subject was of too comprehensive a nature to admit of but one lecture, he chose to confine himself to honesty. "In the intercourse of life, my little darlings," began our pompous old gentleman, "honesty is of all virtues the most useful as well as the most indispensable. Indeed, my fondlings, without honesty society itself is impracticable. But as these reflections are of too general a nature easily to be understood by your youthful minds, my little dears, we shall choose an example. Suppose, now, that any of our neighbours were to creep in while we are asleep and carry off that fragment of cheese (by the bye, mistress, addressing his wife, just wrap it up and put it carefully by, will you?); and as I was saying, carry off the fragment of cheese, you see to what straits we should be reduced for a breakfast. Of course we could never trust such a neighbour any more, and the bonds of secure neighbourhood once loosened—but I see you are getting sleepy, my little ones, so go to bed; we shall renew the subject to-morrow." "Well, now," said the wife to her husband, "how can you talk so to the children, when you know the very cheese we have dined on was stolen, and stolen too by yourself." "Silence, woman," exclaimed the Rat, staggered by such an unexpected rebuke. "But no," proceeded he, "I am wrong to be angry with you, my good mistress, those are points above your weak understanding; so pray go to bed with the children, and leave me to my meditations."

We should preach what we practice, if we wish others to practice what we preach.—Fleming.

CPSIA information can be obtained
at www.ICGtesting.com
Printed in the USA
LVHW100445110522
718424LV00003B/239

9 783375 001599